Risky Redemption

ALSO BY MARISSA GARNER

Hunted
Wanted
Targeted

Risky Redemption

MARISSA GARNER

**FOREVER
YOURS**

New York   Boston

Copyright © 2017 by Marissa Garner
Excerpt from *Hunted* copyright © 2015 by Marissa Garner
Cover design by Brian Lemus
Hachette Book Group supports the right to free expression and the value of copyright. The purpose of copyright is to encourage writers and artists to produce the creative works that enrich our culture.

Forever Yours
Hachette Book Group
1290 Avenue of the Americas
New York, NY 10104
forever-romance.com
twitter.com/foreverromance

First published as an ebook and print on demand edition: October 2017

Forever Yours is an imprint of Grand Central Publishing. The Forever Yours name and logo are trademarks of Hachette Book Group, Inc.

The publisher is not responsible for websites (or their content) that are not owned by the publisher.

The Hachette Speakers Bureau provides a wide range of authors for speaking events. To find out more, go to www.hachettespeakersbureau.com or call (866) 376-6591.

ISBN 978-1-5387-6068-0 (ebook edition)
ISBN 978-1-5387-6070-3 (print on demand edition)

*This book is dedicated to my wonderful readers.
I'm so excited to tell you this story because it's one
of my favorites. Hang on tight, though, for this is
not your mother's romantic suspense. Trust me,
the happily-ever-after is waiting for you, but
you'll have to survive a helluva roller-coaster
ride first.*

Risky Redemption

Prologue

He slouched on the edge of the bed, his fingers clutching the deadly syringe hidden in his jacket pocket. Despite the timpani drum pounding in his chest and echoing in his ears, he kept his face expressionless.

He stared at the naked, unsuspecting woman asleep on the bed, her slender body seductive even in slumber, her blond hair a halo on the pillow.

The guilt gnawing at his gut did not spring from having been inside her, making love to her earlier in the night, but from what he knew was in her heart and mind and soul. That knowledge made killing her wrong on so many levels. Sadly, he'd known it was wrong for a long time, but he had been powerless to change the course of events set in motion all those weeks ago.

His fingers tightened around the syringe. A heavy sigh escaped his lips, releasing an avalanche of regret, remorse, and resignation, but a mountain of sorrow still crushed his chest.

What kind of monster had he become?

Somewhere along the way, the compass of his conscience had lost the true magnetic north of morality.

The woman stirred and opened her eyes. At first, she smiled, but that quickly faded when their gazes met.

He hated what his eyes told her.

"Why—" she began.

Chapter 1

Fifteen weeks earlier

With long angry strides, Jake Stone paced across his office in Valley Center, California, and growled into his cell phone. "Damn it, you know I'm not in the business anymore. Why the hell are you contacting me?"

"Good to talk to you, too," the mechanically altered voice of the Contractor answered. "The Agency has a delicate situation, and I immediately thought of you."

"I'm not interested."

"But we need your specialty and are willing to make accommodations and compensate well for it."

"Not interested," Jake insisted.

"We're paying three times the normal fee."

He frowned and didn't respond. *Shit, that's a helluva lot of money, even for a high-value target. Must be a serious threat to national security. Definitely a top-level hit.*

When Jake hesitated, the Contractor seized the opportunity. "It's an incredible deal. Want to hear more?"

Even though he'd sworn off the nasty profession, maybe he should at least listen to the critical information. "Not really, but go ahead," he muttered. "Who?"

"A twenty-nine-year-old single woman."

"A woman? Crap." In all his years of killing for the CIA, Jake had eliminated only two women: one, a terrorist, the other, a spy. Both deserved to die. But for a man whose parents had ingrained in him the belief that women were to be respected and protected, killing one was damn hard. "Why?" he demanded.

"Not relevant."

"The hell it isn't. You know I never accept a contract without knowing the target's crime."

After a tense moment, the voice continued, "The woman has connections to the State Department. Apparently, she gained access to some highly classified information and decided to sell it."

"Why not arrest her for treason or whatever, instead of putting her down?"

"I don't question the Agency's decisions, and neither should you."

"Look, jerk, I'm a legitimate security expert and private investigator now. I don't work for you guys anymore, so I can ask all the questions I want."

"You can ask, but I can't answer." The Contractor exhaled impatiently. "Fine. I'll only tell you that the information she sold got one of our operatives murdered. Heard he had a wife and kids."

"Damn, the bitch robbed those poor kids of their father." He shoved his fingers through his hair. "Where?"

"She lives and works near San Diego, across the bay in Coronado."

"A domestic hit? Are you out of your fucking mind?" Jake asked.

"Well, you are within spitting distance of Mexico, and we thought—"

"My specialty is fake suicides. People don't usually run across the border to commit suicide."

"The Agency realizes there are complications, but we need this particular situation handled by the best. And you're the best."

"Kiss my ass."

"I'll pass. The woman looks real hot in her picture, though, so I'm sure you'd prefer to have *her* kiss your ass anyway. Damn, I'd love to screw her."

"You'd screw your own mother to get some action, asshole. What's the timing?"

The Contractor ignored the insult. "Well, that's one of the accommodations. We understand that subtlety is of utmost importance and that your finesse takes time. Delivery would be acceptable any time in the next three months."

"Three months?"

"Yeah, maybe you could get some action out of her yourself." His laugh sounded harsh and crude with the mechanical alteration.

"Isn't the Agency afraid she'll steal and sell more secrets?"

"No. We plugged the leak at the other end." The Contractor snickered. "And we're sure you'll keep a close eye on her until you complete the contract. So, what do you say?"

"I'll think about it. Don't call me. I'll call you. Noon, tomorrow."

Jake slammed the phone on the desk.

Damn, he didn't want to come out of retirement, but someone had to avenge their fallen comrade.

* * *

Fourteen weeks earlier

The tall man scowling at her from the front doorway was intimidating even though he wore only a large bath towel wrapped around his narrow hips. His piercing pewter eyes bored into hers so intently that she had to make a conscious effort not to look away.

"Good morning. I'm Angela Reardon from Heavenly Interiors. I have an appointment with Mr. Jake Stone."

"You're early."

"Excuse me?"

"Fifteen minutes early. The appointment is at nine thirty."

"Yes, it is. I expected worse traffic driving up to Valley Center from Coronado."

"You should've called," he snapped.

She bristled at his rudeness. "I apologize if my timing is inconvenient. I can wait in my car for fifteen minutes, if you prefer."

"Too late. You've already interrupted."

A flurry of activity behind the man caught Angela's eye. A moment later, a nubile young woman materialized beside him. She wore skin-tight denim shorts and a white tank top that exposed a large expanse of cleavage. A straw basket filled with several small, colorful bottles hung from her arm.

"Sorry, sweetie, I didn't take time to clean up the room. Try not to get so stressed out this week. It was hell getting the knots out of your neck and shoulders this morning." She stretched up on her tiptoes, leaned into him, and slid her tongue between his lips. Her hand caressed the curly black hair on his bare chest. The man pulled her body tightly against him and slipped his fingers beneath the waistband of her shorts. When he released her, she flipped her auburn hair back over her shoulders. "See ya Thursday, hunk. And remember, no stress."

"Right, sugar, no stress."

Sugar spun away, flashed a catty smile at Angela, and scampered to a silver Eclipse.

Not bothering to hide her disgust, Angela gaped at the woman until the car sped out of sight down the long winding driveway. When she turned back to the doorway, the gray eyes were studying her.

"My masseuse," he said nonchalantly.

She raised her chin. "Perhaps I should come back at another time," she said, her tone tight with repugnance and reserve.

"No. You're already here." He motioned her to follow him inside.

"Fine." Angela frowned as she bent to pick up the decorator samples. "Would you be kind enough to help me with these?"

When he didn't answer, she looked up to find she was talking to an empty doorway. She sighed and shook her head.

With the unwieldy pinwheel of paint color strips tucked under her arm, she grasped the handles of the two heavy catalogues of wallpaper and fabric samples. After lugging the items inside, she scowled at the man, who was already halfway up a curved staircase.

"I presume you are Mr. Stone," she called to him.

He stopped, turned only his head, and peered down at her. "You *presume* correctly. Close the door."

She pushed the massive, carved-wood door shut with her hip and shoulder. "Where would you like me to wait?"

A sly grin spread across his face. "Bring your stuff up here. The master bedroom is one of the rooms I may have you redecorate." He resumed his climb without waiting for a response.

Angela drew a slow, deep breath and blew it out through pursed lips. She rolled her head to the left and then to the right, trying to loosen the tension squeezing the back of her neck. It had taken only a few minutes to dislike Jake Stone. If he chose to retain Heavenly Interiors, she would pass his design work over to her assistant, who'd set up the appointment a few days ago. A wave of relief accompanied that decision.

She glanced up the stairs. *Bedroom.* Dread quickly replaced relief. A shiver raced across her skin. She swallowed hard and steeled herself. *This is a business meeting. I can do this.*

Finding renewed resolve, she climbed the long staircase. The samples seemed to grow heavier with each step. Finally at the top, she set everything down on the plush, gray carpet. While flexing her fingers, Angela surveyed the portion of the house visible from her vantage point.

A contemporary chandelier was suspended on a long chain from the ceiling of the cavernous, two-story foyer. She noticed the intricate illumination pattern it cast on the pearl ceiling and walls and on the black marble floor far below.

Her gaze moved upstairs. Floor-to-ceiling windows showcased a dramatic view of hills covered with granite boulders, but no houses. Across from the spacious, airy landing where she stood, a small alcove was furnished as a cozy library. To her left stretched a hallway with five closed doors. In the opposite direction, a short hallway ended at the open, double-door entrance to what she guessed was the master bedroom.

A voice emanated from that room. "To your right, Ms. Reardon."

"I'm coming, Mr. Stone. I was just admiring your lovely home."

No answer.

Angela heaved an exasperated sigh and lifted her burdens again. She marched through the doorway but halted abruptly. Her eyes widened.

The master bedroom was enormous, one of the largest she had ever seen. A partially open door revealed a peek into a luxurious bathroom. Across the room, an archway framed the entrance to a walk-in closet. Another arched opening led into an adjoining space containing a massage table and several pieces of weight-lifting and exercise equipment.

A variety of smells invaded her nostrils: spicy, pungent, musky. Her eyes searched for the sources. Two small colorful bottles lay on top of a towel draped across the massage table.

Her gaze traveled the room, stopping at the huge bed. She sniffed. One specific odor assaulted her senses.

Her throat tightened.

A black and tan comforter lay on the floor at the end of the bed. Black silk sheets and four oversized pillows were jumbled in disarray. On the nightstand lay three torn condom wrappers.

Angela's breath caught. She shuddered. Her heart thumped and echoed in her ears.

The scars from her past burned in the present.

Tiny beads of moisture strung themselves across her upper lip. The memories swirled inside her as the room spun around her. The catalogues dropped from her hands.

Black silk sheets. Black creeping into her vision.

Her eyelids and head drooped. That hideous smell. The smell of sex.

Oh God, no!

* * *

Uptight bitch. Jake had seen the disgust on the woman's face as she'd watched his masseuse leave. *Well, to hell with her.* Angela Reardon was a traitor who'd gotten an operative killed, possibly someone he'd known during his time with the Agency. He already resented being pulled out of retirement to kill a woman so maybe he'd complete the contract quicker than originally planned. Perhaps her personality would even make his job easier.

But damn, he was pissed. And it was affecting his work. Acting like a jerk wouldn't lure her into his deadly web of deception. He needed to play nice with the bitch so he could finish the job as soon as possible.

Jake slipped off the towel and hurled it across the dressing area of the walk-in closet. He looked down critically at his tense, naked body. His masseuse was right. He was stressed, coiled. He had really needed the third climax that Ms. Reardon had interrupted. Shaking his head with frustration, he swore silently.

He stepped into a pair of khaki shorts, sans underwear. While flipping through the mass of hangers for a shirt, he paused when he heard an odd one-two *thud* from the bedroom. A louder thump followed a few seconds later.

Puzzled, Jake walked around the closet's center divider and peered out the opening.

"Ms. Reardon?" he called.

No answer.

Despite his instructions, had she refused to come to his bedroom? Was the arrogant snob too prudish to enter a bachelor's personal space?

With a devilish smirk, he strolled across the room toward the door. But when he rounded the foot of the bed, he froze.

Angela Reardon lay sprawled on the carpet.

"Shit."

Two long strides and he knelt beside her. Instinctively, he checked for a pulse. Had nature done the job for him? No. The woman's pulse was fine. A cursory examination revealed no signs of injury so he scooped up her petite body and laid her on the bed.

He returned quickly from the bathroom with a cold, wet washcloth and smelling salts from a first-aid kit. Sitting on the edge of the bed, Jake leaned over the unconscious woman.

While he wiped the sheen of perspiration from her delicate features, he admired her flawless complexion, warmed by a light tan. High cheekbones. Full, tempting lips. He brushed the blond hair off her face and rubbed a few silky strands between his fingertips. The shoulder-length hair encircled her head like an aura on the black pillowcase. He appraised the feminine figure hidden beneath the ivory-colored, linen business suit: ample breasts, thin waist, and slender hips. *Damn, why couldn't she be an ugly traitor?*

He wanted to touch but didn't. She was too vulnerable. He shook his head vigorously to clear it of thoughts that shouldn't have been there.

Finally, he forced himself to wave the smelling salts under her nose. She groaned and turned her head away. Another pass of the acrid substance and Angela's eyes fluttered open. Jake stared into pools of dark chocolate.

For only a second, her eyes reflected confusion. Then her gaze dipped to Jake's naked chest. Terror replaced confusion.

Her scream shattered the silence.

Her palm stung his cheek. He recoiled and blocked the next slap. Changing targets, she pummeled his chest with her fists.

"What the hell, lady!"

Stunned but not hurt, Jake straddled her, caught both her wrists, and pinned them to the bed.

"Don't touch me, you bastard," she shrieked.

"Easy, Ms. Reardon, relax."

Her arms went limp and she shuddered. Tears wet her cheeks. "What did you do to me?"

"Do? I didn't *do* anything. You fainted."

Eyes filled with distrust glared at him. Without warning, her knee came up hard between his legs. He collapsed on top of her and she went still.

"Fuck! What's wrong with you?"

"Please, don't…hurt me," she cried against his chest.

Straining to ignore the blinding pain in his crotch, Jake confined her beneath him. Somewhere in the depths of his mind, the name of her fear registered. *Rape.*

"Easy, now. Easy. Nothing bad is going to happen," he said gently. He raised his body slightly so he could see her face. "Look at me, Ms. Reardon. Please." Her eyes stayed tightly shut. "I'll move once you understand that you're safe." He hesitated. "I won't hurt you."

Her eyes opened. Although brimming with tears, they shone with determination. "Get off me, Mr. Stone."

Jake pushed himself up and swung his feet onto the floor. "Can I get you anything?"

"If you would kindly give me some privacy for a few minutes." She turned her flushed face away. "Then I'll be leaving."

"Okay. I'll be downstairs."

Jake pulled the bedroom doors shut as he left. He stood for a moment with his hands on the doorknobs. What the hell had just happened?

He slammed his fist into his other palm repeatedly as he hurried down the stairs and headed to the kitchen. His plan was at risk. How was he going to salvage this snafu?

He directed his anger inward. Yes, Angela Reardon had betrayed her country, but Jake was furious with himself for letting the Contractor convince him to make the deal to kill her. Earlier, sex had helped relieve what several days of self-loathing had done to his body. But the sources of the tension were still coiled inside him. Resentment at being coerced out of retirement. Anger at having chosen the immoral profession in the first place. And frustration at having to kill a woman.

The last reason was definitely not the least.

Standing in front of the security system console, Jake shook his head at the mess the morning had become. He wasn't sure yet how to clean it up, but he knew the first step was to prevent Angela Reardon from leaving. And damn, he'd have to play nice with the traitor.

* * *

Ten minutes later, Angela set the weighty decorator samples on the foyer floor. Her throat tight and her face still warm, she glanced around but saw no sign of Jake Stone as she reached for the front door handle. *Thank goodness.* When she turned the ornate knob, a chime sounded somewhere in the house. But the door didn't open. She twisted harder and yanked. Nothing happened except another chime. *What's going on?*

"My bad," a voice said from across the foyer behind her. "The security system is on."

A lead weight fell in Angela's stomach. She released the knob and turned warily to face Jake. "The security system locks the doors so you can't get out?"

"It's specially designed."

"Specially designed? It's probably a violation of several fire safety building codes."

"You're right. I confess. I wired it myself."

"Why would anyone want to lock himself in or imprison his guests?" she asked, her voice oddly high-pitched.

Jake chuckled. "My office is down that hall." He pointed across the foyer. "I occasionally do interrogations here, and I must have control. You'd be surprised at the potential scenarios when I might want to prevent someone from leaving."

"Like now?"

"No, Ms. Reardon. You're not my prisoner." He smiled and held up two glasses. "I made us something to drink. I mix a mean Bloody Mary, and I figure we could both use one right about now."

Angela swallowed hard. She wanted to escape and to never see this man again. No amount of decorating fees would compensate for the emotional distress she would suffer at having to face him after what had happened upstairs. The sooner she put the incident behind her and moved on, the better. Just another scar to add to the others she had suffered since the...

"It's really nice outside. Why don't we take our drinks out by the pool?" he coaxed.

"Thank you for the offer, Mr. Stone, but I want to leave. I'll send you some referrals for other excellent interior decorators in San Diego County. Now, if you'll unlock the door—"

"I don't want anyone else." He casually leaned against the wall and crossed his ankles. "You're the best, or so I've read. I was looking forward to learning more about Angela Reardon's design-your-own-heaven philosophy."

A smile came uninvited to her lips. "You did your homework."

"I'm a security expert and PI, Ms. Reardon. Homework is a significant part of what I do for a living. The article about you in *San Diego Woman Magazine* was extremely complimentary."

"Thank you. The editor was quite kind."

"Please," he said, raising the glasses. Serious gray eyes locked onto hers. "We got off to a rocky start this morning. I take full blame for being an ass." A sheepish grin softened his face. "I'd like to start over."

Angela studied the man. How odd—or cunning—for him to take responsibility. His actions had certainly been the trigger, but he'd had no reason to anticipate her violent reaction. No one would. Only a handful of people knew about her past. That was the way she wanted it, needed it.

She averted her eyes. Tension and embarrassment still swirled inside, but no terror. The weight in her stomach lightened. *I can do this.* Clinging to a slender thread of composure, she met his penetrating gaze with courage.

"Fine, Mr. Stone. The Bloody Mary…sounds delicious." She bent to pick up the decorator samples.

"Why don't you leave those things there? Let's just talk." He paused and then added, "Mr. Stone lives in Chicago. I'm Jake."

Chapter 2

The present

"I don't know. I don't know." Jake Stone jerked awake Friday morning as soon as the words burst from his lips. His heart thumped and his breath came in jagged gasps. "Shit. A fucking nightmare."

The black silk sheet beneath his naked body was damp with sweat. Still swearing, he sat up and swung his legs off the side of the bed. He propped his elbows on his knees, burrowed his fingers into his unruly hair, and massaged his throbbing temples. *God, what a night.*

After several minutes, he flexed his shoulders and neck twice before standing. He exhaled heavily and lumbered into the bathroom. While washing his hands, he stared at the strained face in the mirror. A violent urge to slam a fist into his reflection roiled up inside him. He redirected the blow, leaving a noticeable dent in the bathroom wall. The pain throbbing in his knuckles was a welcome, if minor, distraction.

The alarm clock on the nightstand read 8:00 A.M. He had arrived home only three hours earlier, and the nightmare had ruined his few hours of fitful slumber. But Jake knew he'd never get back to sleep.

So time for work. Reclining on a black suede chaise, he pushed aside *all* the nightmarish events of the night and focused on his next move. He could make the first phone call now, the call to notify his CIA handler.

Ten rings and silence answered.

"Contract completed," Jake stated flatly, careful not to reveal any simmering emotions in his tone.

"Problems?" the mechanically altered voice asked.

"No."

"Good. We'll need independent confirmation."

"I know. Get it today," he snapped.

"I will. Should I wire the balance to the same Cayman Islands bank account as the advance?"

"Yes. No later than tomorrow. The account will be closed after that."

"Consider it done. No reason for further communication. Been nice working with you again," the Contractor said.

Jake heard the taunt in the words. "Fuck you. I'm retiring permanently this time. Don't call me again, asshole." A harsh bark of a laugh reached his ears before he ended the call and launched the phone across the room.

Then he returned to bed, but not to sleep.

While he waited for the right time to place his next call, the nightmare crept back into his mind. After an unsuccessful attempt to fight it off, he succumbed to a morbid need to analyze it.

In the dream, he had been alone in a carnival's House of Mirrors.

Encircled by floor-to-ceiling mirrors, he had turned around and around, but the shimmering surfaces were blank, not showing a single reflection of him. Not too surprising, since many times in his life he'd felt invisible.

Suddenly, a multitude of figures had filled the mirrors. But all of them were Angela Reardon, not him. Hundreds of accusing eyes had gazed intently at him.

Then, everywhere, her perfect lips had parted and whispered, "Why?" The images chorused the single word over and over, softly at first, then louder and louder, until the words cracked like thunder.

Finally, Jake had collapsed to his knees, yelling his response. "I don't know. I don't know." Awakening had saved him.

Now, as daylight leaked through the blinds, he stared at the ceiling, the memory of the nightmare crushing his chest like a boulder. *This is crazy. I don't have feelings like this.*

He had trained himself for years to feel nothing so he could successfully practice his repulsive profession. In fact, his feelings were the emotional equivalent of granite.

Angela Reardon had chipped away at that granite. At the appearance of the first fracture, he should have terminated the situation. But that was the past, and now it was too late. Angela had chiseled deep to touch something inside him that hadn't been touched in a long time.

And last night, he had paid the price.

Jake peered at the clock: 9:00 A.M. Time for the second phone call, but he needed caffeine first. With a mug of strong black coffee in one hand, he paced beside the swimming pool as he placed the call.

The phone rang several times before a man answered. "Hello."

"Sorry, wrong number," Jake said and hung up. He grinned. *Good, they're already there.* He waited a few moments before redialing.

"Hello," the same male voice answered.

"Uh, hello. I'm calling for Angela Reardon. Who's this?" Jake asked, trying to sound suspicious.

"Who's calling?"

"A friend. Who the hell are you?"

"Detective Kent Smithson, Coronado Police Department." The detective hesitated. "Stone, is that you?"

"Yeah, Smithson. What the hell are you doing there?"

He heard the man gulp.

"We got a call about seven this morning."

"Angela called the police?"

"No. Her neighbor did."

"God, I can't imagine any trouble in that sleepy little neighborhood."

"Yeah, hard to believe."

Other voices filtered in from the background.

"All right, Smithson, if you're not going to tell me shit, put Angela on."

The cop exhaled loudly.

Jake smiled with relief; he had hoped Kent Smithson would be the detective on the scene. While building his legitimate security and investigation business, he'd put a lot of effort into forging personal and professional relationships with many members of the local law enforcement agencies. Once again, his efforts were going to pay off.

"Can you come down here, Stone? I'd rather talk in person."

"Huh? What's going on? Let me talk to Angela a minute."

"I…can't."

"What do you mean, you *can't*?" Jake's volume rose a notch.

Smithson cursed under his breath. "Angela's gone."

"Gone?"

"Shit, man, I hate to break this to you over the phone. It looks like suicide."

Jake choked. "Suicide? Impossible."

"Just get your butt over here quick. Maybe you can help me sort this shit out. I'm not notifying next of kin until I'm sure."

"On my way."

* * *

Jake barreled down the sidewalk, identifying himself to the Coronado cop standing in the doorway before rushing inside.

Detective Kent Smithson sat on the living room couch with a cell phone to his ear. He motioned for Jake to take a seat. Jake heard voices upstairs, shook his head, and started for the stairs.

"Stone, no. We need to talk first."

He stopped abruptly at Smithson's commanding tone. He turned and shot the detective a don't-fuck-with-me glare but dropped into the nearest chair.

Unfazed, the man continued his phone call. "You said there's also a purse, but no wallet, no ID. Yeah, that is strange. Stolen, maybe, during the night." He listened. "Which side of the bridge? Eastbound, away from Coronado, toward I-5?" His gaze darted to Jake. "Right, bring everything here. I have someone who might be able to help with identification." He ended the call, shoved the phone into his pants pocket, and pulled a small notebook and pencil from his shirt pocket. "Thanks for coming, Stone."

"What the hell's going on?"

"I'll ask the questions first. Then I'll tell you what I can. Okay?"

Jake fastened his steely stare on the detective. "Shoot."

"When did you last see Ms. Reardon?" Smithson scribbled in the notebook.

"Last night."

The detective's eyes came up quickly. "Where and what time?"

"I'll make this easy on you. We had dinner at the Hotel del Coronado about seven. Came back here around nine. I left about midnight."

"Anybody see you leave?"

"Hell if I know. I pulled out of the garage and drove off. Didn't notice anyone."

"Your car was in her garage?"

"Yeah, it's a double. Angela doesn't like me to leave the Corvette parked in the driveway."

Smithson made a note. "How long have you two been dating?"

Jake could have recited the exact number of days, but instead he said, "About three months. The party at Jim Kern's place was one of our first dates."

"I remember that. I couldn't figure out how you got such a classy lady to come to a cop's kegger. But I didn't actually meet Angela until last month at your barbeque. You guys seemed pretty…serious." His eyes held the next question.

"Yeah, we were getting real tight by then. As tight as I ever get. Neither of us has been dating anyone else for a while now."

Smithson lowered his eyes to the notebook. "What was her emotional state last night?"

"She was fine. We had a great time. Are you going to tell me what happened and let me go upstairs now?"

"Just a couple more questions. Had she ever had any psychological problems?"

Jake shuttered his gaze. "How would I know?"

"She ever mention anything—shrink sessions or counseling?"

"Not that I remember."

"Had she suffered any kind of traumatic experience lately? Financial problems? Death of a relative or friend? That sort of thing."

"No, no, and no." Jake's patience ran out. "Can I see her now?" He stood up and took several steps toward the stairs.

Smithson casually stuffed the notebook and pencil into his shirt pocket, stood, and pushed ahead of Jake. "Thanks for answering my questions so cooperatively," he said with a hint of sarcasm.

Neither man spoke again until they entered the bedroom.

"Where is she?" Jake asked, staring at the empty, rumpled bed.

"We don't know."

"Quit screwing with me. What's going on?" He clenched his fists at his sides.

Smithson leaned against the doorjamb and scratched his head. "Okay, Stone, I'm only telling you this because I know you personally. This is how it went down. Mrs. Leona Browning called CPD about seven. She's Angela's neighbor, widow lady—"

"Yeah, I've met Leona. Major busybody, but dotes on Angela like a mother hen."

"That's the one. She called in all upset. Said Angela's dog had been barking since about one this morning. Chelsea was outside in the fenced patio area, which was highly unusual, especially at that hour. By five, Mrs. Browning was phoning Angela and getting no response. She rang the doorbell and knocked. Nothing. Then she peeked into the garage. Angela's car was there." He paused while he ran a hand over his eyes.

"So Leona started freaking out."

"Right. She tried to pacify Chelsea by throwing treats over the adjoining fence, but the damn dog wouldn't quit howling and scratching at the patio door. More phone calls, more howling. The poor old lady was a complete basket case by the time she called us. The dispatcher agreed to have an officer swing by. He made contact with Mrs. Browning. She had a key, but they found Angela's front door unlocked."

"Detective Smithson," called a man from downstairs, "I brought the stuff."

"Bring it up here." The detective straightened away from the doorjamb. "The officer entered the residence with Mrs. Browning. No sign of forced entry. Or Angela. When they got to the bedroom, the officer called in."

"Maybe she had to leave suddenly for some emergency early this morning."

"Without her car?"

"Taxi. Friend," Jake suggested.

"Left the dog outside?"

"Maybe she's going to call Leona later about taking care of Chelsea while she's gone."

"No, Stone. I'm sorry. That tells a different story," he said, pointing at the nightstand.

Two envelopes, a prescription medicine bottle, and several pills cluttered the surface. Jake took a step in that direction, but Smithson grabbed his arm.

"What?" He yanked his arm free.

"Did Angela take prescription sleeping pills frequently?"

"Only occasionally. They weren't a habit. The envelopes?"

"One for you and one for her parents."

A solemn Coronado police officer appeared in the hallway carrying an evidence bag, which he handed to Smithson. Watching Jake's face closely, the detective slipped on gloves before pulling a blue dress from the bag.

Jake's eyes widened as they swept over the silky fabric. Slowly, he met Smithson's gaze.

"Is this what Angela was wearing when you last saw her?"

"No."

"No?" Smithson's eyebrows arched. "What was she wearing?"

"Nothing."

"Damn it, Stone, help me out here. Is this Angela's dress? Did she wear it last night?"

He frowned. "Yes. Where did you get it?"

"On the San Diego-Coronado Bay Bridge."

"Shit."

With three long strides, Jake reached the nightstand, grabbed the envelope bearing his name, and stormed out of the bedroom.

* * *

On the small patio table beside the chaise lounge sat an empty Jack Daniel's bottle. When Jake had opened the bottle after returning from Angela's condo, he'd vowed to drink it all or die trying. Now, eleven hours later, he almost wished for the latter.

He cursed the moon bathing him in a soft glow. The landscaping and pool lights were turned off because he wanted to drink and grieve in complete darkness. Anyone in his right mind would guess he was grieving for Angela Reardon. He wasn't.

Jake Stone was grieving for himself.

He raised his glass, toasted the silence, and tossed back the final swallow of whiskey. Then he hurled the empty bottle over the edge, shattering it against something far below. His harsh laugh reverberated off the boulder-strewn hillsides.

His blurred vision landed on the photograph lying on the table beside him. The identification photo had arrived immediately after he'd accepted the contract fifteen weeks ago. Her blond hair was shorter, and Jake had never seen her wear the red dress that draped the curves of her body so enticingly. But Angela's amazing eyes and inviting lips smiled back at him. His mouth moved with the memory of those warm, soft lips against his.

Pushing his head back into the cushion, he closed his eyes and wished that the liquor could erase his memories. But there was no chance of that. He was too well-trained—and too hardened a drinker—for the alcohol to wipe clean the slate of his mind.

He grimaced. That was only one of his skills. Many others were unspeakable.

As a Navy SEAL, he had been trained to kill efficiently. In fact, he'd done it so well the CIA had recruited him. Under their tutelage, Jake honed the skill of killing stealthily. He carried out political assassinations and sanctions. He taught himself how to murder cunningly. All of his later hits had been successfully disguised as suicides. When he got tired of politics muddling up his missions, he'd resigned.

After months of pleading, the Agency had convinced him to

return as a contract assassin. The independence appealed to Jake. Instead of being ordered to carry out a hit, he could decide which contracts to accept. But even with the greater control, he burned out again after a year. He feared that killing was slowly, irreparably, destroying his soul. Although he'd quit with a welcome sense of relief, he still firmly believed that all his targets had *deserved* their fate.

Until now.

The hours he'd spent researching and investigating Angela hadn't uncovered a single shred of evidence supporting the Contractor's claim that she'd stolen and sold State Department secrets, resulting in an operative's death.

Something was wrong. Someone was lying.

Whoever wanted Angela Reardon dead was the immoral, evil asshole who deserved to die. Not Angela.

Silently, he vowed to ferret out who and why. And then he would execute the bastard.

Jake laughed mirthlessly.

He had killed for patriotism and for money.

This time, he would kill for redemption.

Chapter 3

Fourteen weeks earlier

Sitting in her car and staring at Jake's house, Angela couldn't believe she had returned after the trauma of the previous day. But the stubborn man had steadfastly refused to consider another interior decorator or even to let her assistant do the work. So she had convinced herself last night that this was just another test of her courage to overcome the scars from her past.

"I can do this," she murmured as she left the safety of her car. When Jake's front door opened, she smiled with nervous relief that he was fully dressed. Dramatically, she checked her watch. "Four on the dot. I was careful not to be *early*."

"Very funny. Let me take those," he said, reaching for the heavy decorating sample catalogues. "How are you?"

"Embarrassed to be here. I wish you had agreed to contact one of the other decorators whose names I e-mailed you yesterday afternoon."

"Don't be silly. No need to be embarrassed," Jake said as he led her through the house and outside to the backyard. He gestured toward the patio table where a platter of fruit, crackers, and cheese waited. A bottle of wine sat chilling in a silver ice bucket. "Now that I know about your hypoglycemia problem, I'll be sure to feed you immediately when you visit."

Angela cringed inwardly at the reminder of the lie she'd told him to explain her fainting. *Better than admitting the truth.* Her reservations about returning to his house had nagged at her all day and now threatened to overwhelm her. With resolve, she shoved them aside.

"That's very considerate, Jake. I don't want a repeat of the scene I caused last time," she said in a self-deprecating tone.

"Neither do I. You scared the hell out of me." He avoided her gaze, set the catalogues on a lounge, and pulled out a chair at the table for her. "Chardonnay okay?"

"Lovely."

He poured wine into both glasses and then passed her a china plate. He pushed the platter toward her, and she selected a few items.

"So, you came prepared to start the design process today?" he asked while he filled a plate.

"Yes. First, I'll take a detailed set of pictures of the rooms you want redone. Second, I'll measure everything and sketch a rough draft of the rooms. Third, we'll discuss your ideas and preferences. And finally, we'll look through the paint, wallpaper, and fabric samples so I can get an idea of your tastes."

"Sounds like a lot of work. Are you sure you wouldn't rather stretch it out over a few visits?" His eyes captured hers. "I wouldn't mind."

She squirmed a little in her seat. "It'll take about three hours, and I prefer to do it all at once. But let me know if you need to leave, and I'll come back at a later date. I certainly don't want to interfere with your plans for the evening."

"*You* are my plans for the evening."

Angela's hand hesitated halfway to her mouth. "Well, I'll finish this tasty snack quickly so I don't tie you up too long."

"No need to rush." His gaze caught hers again while he refilled her glass.

She glanced away toward the pool. "I don't believe I've ever seen a more dramatic vanishing-edge pool. It looks like it drops off the edge of a cliff. Who was your landscape architect?"

"The partnership of Me, Myself, and I." He grinned. "I love the view of the hills and the boulders. I wanted the pool to blend in so I designed it to resemble a mountain lake. I also didn't want any visual distractions." Taking a sip of wine, he watched her over the edge of the goblet. "I had some problems with the contractors. They insisted that safety codes required a fence alongside the pool to keep people from falling down the hillside. I said that if someone was stupid enough to topple over the edge, he deserved to tumble fifty feet and crack his head open on a granite boulder. Hell, even with precautions, accidents happen."

"I can't imagine that a reputable contractor would agree with you, but I can see you convinced one not to install a fence," she said, shaking her head.

"Oh, there was a fence. I removed it after the contractors were done and gone."

"And what if you get sued for not having one?"

He scanned the incredible panorama and raised his glass in a salute. "Well, it was worth it."

Angela studied him while he studied the view. She concluded that her impressions from their first meeting had been negatively influenced by the incident in the bedroom so she performed a new appraisal.

Tall, at least six foot one. Deeply tanned, olive complexion. And handsome with a small cleft in the chin of a strong, masculine face. Age: probably mid-thirties. Hair: thick, short, ebony waves that begged female fingers to curl into it. Body: lean, muscular limbs to complement the firm chest and tight abdomen she vaguely remembered.

Suddenly, he turned, hooded eyes connecting with a jolt as if he knew she'd been appraising him.

"I better get started," Angela announced, wiping her mouth with the linen napkin.

Jake escorted her inside to the family room. He lounged in a recliner while she snapped photos, took measurements, and drew a quick sketch.

His presence seemed to fill the room, and she felt his gaze following her every move. Her pulse accelerated under his scrutiny. She dropped the tape measure twice and broke the points on three pencils. If only he would leave her to work alone.

Jake ushered her down the hall to the formal living room, and the process was repeated. Her hand shook so badly she couldn't draw the straight lines of the sketch. Her nerves neared the breaking point. Forcing herself to concentrate on fixing her unsatisfactory drawing, she turned away and tried to ignore him.

"Angela," he said from close behind her.

She jumped, spun around, and dropped her pencil. They both bent to retrieve it. Their heads bumped together, and Angela lost her balance.

Jake caught her arms and pulled her upright against him. His eyes were soft gray, and a spicy, masculine scent emanated from his warm skin.

Instantly, irrational anxiety squeezed Angela's chest.

"Sorry," she mumbled, pulling free and stepping back.

They stood barely a foot apart. Neither moved. Her gaze dropped to the pencil lying on the floor between them.

"No, I'm sorry. I didn't mean to startle you." He stopped as though waiting for her eyes to meet his. When they did, he asked, "Am I making you... nervous?"

She swallowed hard. "Yes. I prefer to work alone. Besides, most clients find this part boring. I'm finished in here anyway." She bent quickly and grabbed the pencil. "Which room next?"

"My bedroom."

Her breath caught, and she felt the blood draining from her face.

Jake's eyes narrowed. "You remember where the master bedroom is. I need to do a few things in the kitchen. I'll see you when you're done." He turned and headed for the hallway.

A half dozen cleansing breaths restored Angela's poise. Thank God the man wasn't coming with her to the bedroom. After the mortifying events of yesterday morning, she wasn't sure she could maintain her composure with him in that room. And this time he had fed her, so the hypoglycemia lie would not work.

She gathered her supplies and climbed the stairs. When she reached the open double doors, she closed her eyes and calmed herself before entering the room.

Her lips parted in a smile. The bed was neatly made, the black silk sheets completely covered. No condom wrappers littered the nightstand. The folded massage table leaned against the wall in the exercise room. The bedroom smelled only of spicy manliness.

Energized by relief, Angela finished the work in the master bedroom quickly. Her watch read 7:00 p.m. when she left the room. She shook her head. Jake's watching her earlier had slowed her process substantially. They still needed to discuss his ideas and to scan the catalogues. Hopefully, she could finish in less than an hour because she desperately didn't want to return to this house again.

As she descended the staircase, she smelled the appetizing aroma of grilling meat. Her mouth watered, but her heart sank. She couldn't blame Jake for wanting his dinner at this hour, but that would mean she'd have to come back to finish phase one. Unless…he came to her office some time later in the week. She smiled at the easy solution and at the thought of going home.

When she hurried into the kitchen, there was no sign of Jake. The patio doors were open, allowing a cool breeze in through the screen. She stepped outside and surveyed the backyard.

Smoke seeped from under the lid of a built-in, stainless steel grill, which stood next to the rock grotto and waterfall end of the pool. The patio table had been neatly set for two. In the center, a crystal globe held a flickering candle. Two uncorked bottles of red wine and two goblets sat nearby.

Oh no, he's expecting a date. The nubile masseuse and the empty condom wrappers flashed from her memory. *I've got to get out of here.*

"I hope you—" a voice behind her began.

Angela whirled around and knocked into Jake.

He raised the glass bowls he was carrying high enough to protect them and laughed. "My bad," he said. "I should stop sneaking up on you. You almost ended up wearing these shrimp cocktails."

"I'm sorry this took so long. I'm finished upstairs. I'll just grab my catalogues and disappear."

"Why? Are you a vegetarian?"

"What?"

He cocked his head and grinned. "Don't you like shrimp and steak?"

"Yes, but..." Realization hit, and with it, a slight sense of panic. Her expression tightened. *Trapped.*

Jake's smile faded. "It's late. We both need to eat. I had some fresh steaks...but if you'd rather not, I won't be offended. I should've asked you first." He headed back toward the kitchen.

Calm down. He's a client. It's just dinner. Just a business dinner. The words repeated in Angela's mind like a mantra. "If you're sure it's not an imposition. I am starving, and the steak smells delicious."

After a slight hesitation, he turned around. "No trouble at all. Here, take these. I'll grab the Caesar salad and the toppings for the baked potatoes. Everything should be done in about five minutes."

His timing was perfect; the sunset provided a breathtaking backdrop for their dinner. Neither spoke as they ate and watched the closing curtain of nightfall descend. For several minutes, the candle provided the only light. Then Jake excused himself to flip on the teal-colored pool lights. A soft, shimmering, romantic glow enveloped the backyard.

"This is my favorite pinot noir, especially with steak," Jake said, refilling her glass. "Do you like it?"

"Yes, I do. It's not too dry. Some pinots are." The wine swirled inside the glass like it swirled inside her head. She blinked, wondering why it was having such a pronounced effect on her. Nerves, maybe. She held up her hand, signaling him to stop, but he continued pouring.

"Don't quit on me now. We still have dessert and work to do." He lifted the second bottle and poured for himself. "Speaking of work, I'm curious how you got into interior decorating."

"Your homework didn't uncover that?" She smiled and slowly pulled a bite of steak off her fork.

Jake's attention locked on her lips. "Huh? Oh, very funny. Seriously, how did you get interested in it?"

"Accidentally."

He grinned. "What does that mean?"

After a sip of wine, Angela leaned back in the chair. "I was doing well in law school at UCLA, but I hated it. I dropped out without telling my parents. My right brain needed a chance to run free. When I visited a friend who was attending the Art Institute of California in LA, I fell in love with the interior design program and enrolled. My parents were livid and refused to support me. I had to work nights as a waitress." She paused, sipped again. Her chin lifted. "I graduated first in my class, but my parents didn't bother coming out from Virginia. I was courted by several designers and ended up working for one in Beverly Hills."

Jake raised his glass. "I'm impressed. Why were your folks so upset? Are they attorneys?"

She sighed. "My father is, but he doesn't practice. He's been with the State Department my whole life. We lived abroad a few times."

"State Department? Sounds exciting. You know, clandestine. You didn't want to follow in your father's footsteps?"

"Clandestine? Hardly." She laughed. "My father was a polished figurehead, groomed to attend Embassy functions. I can't imagine a more boring career."

"And your mother?"

"My mother is…a socialite, loves the high society scene. We aren't close."

"I get the picture. Do they still live in Virginia?"

"McLean, near Washington."

"Whoa. Big bucks."

"They both came from money but always wanted more. I couldn't wait to leave home and get as far away as I could."

"You were a bit of a rebel?"

"I guess."

Jake chuckled. "How did you get down to the San Diego area?"

Angela tensed. She swallowed a long drink of wine. "I didn't…like LA anymore." She changed the subject before he could ask another question. "It's getting late. Let's talk about your ideas, needs, and preferences for the rooms you want redone."

Sipping his wine, Jake studied her for a moment. "Sure. Lead me through it, please."

"Okay. What do you want to change about the family room?"

"Specifically?"

"Specifics would be great, but a general idea is fine, too."

"Um. I'd like…more space."

She arched her eyebrows at him. "More space?"

"Yeah, more space."

"And the living room?" She swirled her wine and took a drink.

"Same thing. More space."

"Nothing more specific than that?"

"No."

"The master bedroom?" she asked.

"More—"

"Space."

He winked. "Right. How'd you guess?"

Angela peered at him through the goblet as she drained the last drop. She carefully set the glass down before addressing him. "Mr. Stone, while I was documenting the rooms, I couldn't imagine what you disliked about them. In my humble opinion, they exhibit excellent design. I assume they were professionally decorated."

He nodded, his expression guarded as if worried about where her comments were headed.

"I thought so. Frankly, I see nothing wrong with the decorating, other than it virtually drips testosterone," she said with a smirk.

"Testosterone? I don't—"

"Puh-leeze. There isn't one thing in those rooms that does not proclaim masculinity. This is none of my business, but my only thought of a reason you would want to redecorate is that a woman is moving in with you."

Jake choked and pinched his nose, probably to prevent himself from snorting wine onto the table. Roars of laughter followed and caused more choking. He grabbed the linen napkin and held it to his face until the coughing subsided. Lowering the cloth to just below his eyes, he stared at her.

"My God, woman. How in the hell did you jump to that conclusion?"

She bristled. "Because, otherwise, I don't see any reason for you to redecorate. 'More space' is a ludicrous motivation. This house is huge, and it's all for one person. I'd be no better than a crook if I encouraged you to redo those rooms."

"You're not going to help me?"

"I didn't say that."

"You're confusing me, Angela. What do you mean?"

"I'll show you."

In the family and living rooms, she identified pieces of furniture to be removed and others to be rearranged. She achieved his goal of "more space" without spending thousands of his dollars, but she felt more relieved than he looked.

Without a word, he led the way to the stairs. She glanced up to the second floor, and her throat tightened.

He reached the fifth stair before stopping and turning. "Angela?"

She still stood at the bottom, clutching the railing, her chest heaving with sharp, rapid breaths. "Huh?"

"Any suggestions for what to do in my bedroom?"

Her gaze rose slowly to the top of the staircase again. In a strained voice, she said, "It's really an enormous room. But, if you want, transfer the chest by the smaller window over to the opposite side. That will allow sunlight to diffuse through the room better and make it seem more spacious. Hanging the flat-screen TV and removing the cabinet would help, too." She glanced around, rubbing the back of her neck. "I really need to go, but I should help you clean up first."

She hurried down the hallway toward the back of the house before he could respond. He caught up with her at the patio table where she was gathering the dishes. Grasping her shoulder, he spun her around. She took a step back and avoided his eyes.

"Is something wrong?" he asked, slight irritation in his voice.

"No, of course not. Thank you for the delicious meal. It was very kind of you to go to all that trouble."

"No trouble. Why are you rushing off?"

"It's after nine. I'm hardly rushing off." She turned back to the table, picked up the stack of plates, and headed for the kitchen.

Jake came after her. In the kitchen, he dumped the silverware on the table.

Before she could move away from the sink, he was behind her. His arms bracketed her body with his hands planted on the countertop. *Trapped.* She could smell his cologne, hear his breathing, feel his warmth. *Too close.* She had to get away.

He leaned forward, speaking softly near her ear. "Did I say or do something to offend you?"

She blinked, trying to clear her head. "Not at all. I enjoyed the dinner and the evening, but I'm done here." She wanted—no, *needed*—him to back off, but he didn't. How ridiculous it felt to talk with her back to him, but she was afraid to turn around. She gripped the edge of the counter. "If you follow my suggestions, I think you'll get the results you want without any additional services from me."

"Then what excuse will I have to see you again?"

Angela didn't answer. Her pulse raced, and her chest tightened. *Escape.* She rotated slowly, careful not to brush against him.

Suddenly, his hands were on her shoulders, and his focus on her lips.

She faked a smile. "We can talk about that some other time. Right now, I'd appreciate your retrieving my catalogues from the patio and carrying them to my car."

He took forever to drop his hands from her shoulders. "Sure. No problem."

As soon as he disappeared, Angela rushed to the foyer. When her hand touched the doorknob, she prayed it wasn't locked by the strange security system.

But it was.

She froze and whimpered at the sound of approaching footsteps.

"Angela?" Jake towered beside her.

Running out of time. I'm not going to make it.

Shuddering, she looked up into his stern face. The soft Koala gray had hardened into cold steel.

"Are you sick?" he demanded.

"No. The door…it's locked," she gasped.

Jake frowned. Keeping his eyes glued to her, he shifted to the side and tapped the commands on the small electronic panel near the door. "Maybe you shouldn't drive, Angela. You're welcome to…spend the night."

The terrifying words were barely out of his mouth before she bolted out the door. *Oh God, help me.*

He raced after her.

As she yanked open the driver's door, Jake grabbed the back door handle and threw the catalogues onto the backseat. He slammed the door and jumped back as the motor roared.

Tires squealed. Her white-knuckled fists squeezed the steering wheel.

At the end of the long, winding, downhill driveway, she braked sharply. Pawing through her purse, she found the small container. She panted as she struggled to extract a pill. With trembling fingers, she tossed it into the back of her mouth and swallowed.

Eyes closed, she dropped her forehead against the steering wheel. A tear slid down her cheek.

Safe.

* * *

Jake lifted the wine bottle to his lips and drank deeply. He had extinguished the outside lights and the candle. He stared into the darkness, not really seeing anything. Sitting alone on the chaise lounge in the cool night air, he was surrounded by quiet solitude.

But inside, Jake was troubled.

Things weren't going well with the Reardon contract. His plan to engage Angela personally to determine the best way to fake the traitor's suicide was failing miserably. And he wasn't sure why.

Without a hint of guilt, he acknowledged that women usually threw themselves at him. Sex was never a problem. He was offered far more than he accepted, and he accepted a hell of a lot.

He grinned, thinking of Angela's encounter with his masseuse. There was an excellent example. He paid her for the massages to relieve his tension, but she volunteered the free sex to benefit them both. The yearlong consensual arrangement had been gratifying. His dick twitched in agreement.

He imagined a firm, pink nipple as his lips closed around the tip of the wine bottle.

Angela Reardon was different. Not only did his charms not attract her, she actually fled from him as if she were afraid. And her dark chocolate eyes unnerved him. One minute, they were warm and welcoming; the next, they were filled with fear and panic.

Chapter 4

"Salami?" Jake asked warily, gripping his cell phone as he paced in his office Saturday afternoon.

Silence answered.

"This is Granite."

"How the hell did you get this number? I've only had it a month, and we haven't talked in three years," a scratchy male voice said.

Jake chuckled. "So you're pissed because I haven't called? You a woman now, Salami?"

The man snorted. "Nah, you got it backwards. It's the women who like the big Salami. And FYI, that's not my code name anymore."

"I know, but I figured you wouldn't believe it was really me if I called you Scarface."

"Fuck. The Agency leaks like a sieve these days. How'd you—"

"Don't ask." Jake paused. "I need your help."

"Shoot."

"This could be…uh…risky for you."

"Hey. Can't be any riskier than you taking that bullet for me in Istanbul. I told you then I could never repay you enough."

"Yeah, but you're getting old, Salami. I thought maybe you forgot."

"Never. What do you need?"

"The identity of the handler on my last few contracts. He uses the code name Contractor."

"Are you serious? Those guys don't officially exist. Of course, neither do you or me."

"I know this is asking for the impossible, but I wouldn't ask if it wasn't important. And if I'm right about this guy, it's damn important to the Agency also."

"Care to share?"

Jake pondered how much to disclose. He trusted Salami, but too much information might put his friend at greater risk. On the other hand, Salami would be safer knowing the kind of corrupt asshole he was looking for. "I think my old handler is arranging private contracts with CIA assassins."

"Holy shit. What made you suspicious?"

"Several things. First, he offered three times the normal fee. Second, it was a goddamn domestic hit. Then, I beat the bushes to confirm the target's crime and came up with nothing."

"But you completed the contract anyway." Salami stated it as a fact, not a question.

Jake sighed with resignation. "I tried to get out of it, even tried to get the contract canceled. The Contractor threatened retaliation for non-compliance. You know how it is…"

"Sucks."

"Yeah. So, you in on this?"

"Absolutely. How do you want me to proceed?"

Jake gave him the specifics of Angela's contract. "See if you can verify its legitimacy and get any kind of lead on the Contractor's identity."

After a long pause, his friend said, "Ya know, you're asking for trouble…and the impossible."

"Ah, Salami, you were always so good with trouble and the impossible."

"No, Granite. That was you."

* * *

Jake broke into Heavenly Interiors shortly after midnight Sunday morning. The locks and security alarm system presented no challenge. He paused a few moments for his eyes to adjust and to get his bearings. Beneath his black sweatshirt and jeans, he was sweating.

Angela had proudly shown him her business shortly after they had started dating, and he'd visited the shop on half a dozen occasions. On Saturday, he had sketched the layout from memory.

The rear door opened into a workroom full of tables covered with drawings and bookshelves overflowing with sample catalogues. Aiming his penlight at the floor, Jake carefully picked his way through the maze to the hallway leading to the front of the shop. On the left was Angela's large office. Her assistant, Stella Jenkins, used the smaller one on the right.

He killed the flashlight halfway down the hall. Sliding along the wall, he approached the compact reception area where the picture windows and entrance faced Orange Avenue, the main drag through Coronado. The stylish window coverings were wide open, allowing the streetlights to illuminate the inside of the shop for security purposes. As he'd expected, the length of sidewalk in view was deserted at that late hour. He peeked around the doorjamb and confirmed there was nothing in the reception area relevant to his search. After another scan of the sidewalk and street beyond, he slowly closed the hallway door.

Once inside Angela's windowless office, Jake shut the door and switched on the desk lamp. He surveyed the room. No files or paperwork cluttered the furniture.

Stella had done a terrific job of closing up after he talked to her late Friday morning. Together, they had decided the business should be shut down immediately, until Angela's parents and attorney figured out the appropriate legal dissolution.

Although completely distraught at the news of Angela's death, Stella had offered to notify all the current clients of the situation and reassure them that appropriate refunds would be forthcoming. At Jake's suggestion, she had also agreed to lock up any company information that was unsecured in Angela's office and to clear out her own office of all her personal belongings. Despite having lost a friend and a job all at once, the woman had efficiently taken care of business.

Jake was reasonably certain Stella would not return to Heavenly Interiors until given permission. Unfortunately, the future actions of Angela's parents were not so easily determinable. He had to find and take whatever he could as fast as possible. There might not be another chance.

He slid into the desk chair, flexed his gloved hands, and flipped on the computer. While it booted up, he rummaged through the desk drawers. Angela's appointment book and Rolodex were the only items of interest, and he set them on the desk.

When the computer was ready, he shook his head at the lack of a required password. Naïve of Angela, but lucky for him. With a few clicks of the mouse, he determined the total gigs of data. He exhaled, relieved the flash drive he yanked from his pocket had sufficient capacity to hold all of it. Now he didn't have to take the time to decide what to copy but could transfer everything and review it at home. He jammed the flash drive into a USB port, clicked a few commands, and left the computer to do its thing.

Next he picked the lock on the first file cabinet. His fingers skipped across the file tabs, stopping occasionally to pull out a colored folder. He grinned. Of course, there were no plain manila folders—not in Angela's world.

By the time the entire computer hard drive had been copied, a stack of four dozen folders rested on the desk. Jake double-checked that he had relocked all the file cabinets. He removed the flash drive and shut down the computer. After retrieving an empty box from the workroom, he piled his booty inside. A careful inspection assured him that the office looked exactly as it had when he'd entered earlier.

Holding the penlight with his teeth, he extinguished the lamp and exited the office. In the hallway he paused, setting the heavy box on the floor and listening for any unusual noise. Nothing. He flicked off the flashlight. Once the reception area door was reopened, he inched down the dark hall, chiding himself for being overly cautious. But his training was so ingrained that he practically performed without conscious thought.

After the security alarm was reset and the rear door locked, Jake dashed to the old, nondescript, black truck that he frequently used to do surveillance. He tossed the box onto the passenger seat and scanned the area before cranking the ignition. He pulled the Glock from his waistband and wedged it beside his thigh.

His watch read 2:15 a.m. He circled the block, finding no other vehicles parked in the alley or on the nearby streets. Pedestrians were nonexistent. Satisfied his little visit had been undetected, he headed for Angela's condo.

He gulped down an entire bottle of water during the ten-minute drive and inspection of the neighborhood. Not a single residence showed signs of activity.

Jake parked five buildings away in the alley behind the condo development. He tried the patio gate, but the padlock was on the inside, and he couldn't reach it. He swore quietly.

Thankful that Angela's was the end unit, he eased around to the front. His vigilant gaze darted from dark shadows to darker shadows. Convinced the neighborhood was dead, he hurried to the front door and let himself in with the key he had stolen from Angela several weeks earlier.

He froze at the familiar barking of a dog—Angela's dog, Chelsea. But the muted sound came from Leona Browning's condo next door. Jake drew a deep breath.

He surveyed the residence, lit only by the moonlight streaming through the transom windows. How strange the place felt without Angela.

Annoyed with himself for feeling so uncomfortable, he moved quickly to the small den on the first floor that Angela used as a home office. He fired up her laptop and pulled a second flash drive from his pocket. After checking its size, he clicked the commands to copy the entire hard drive.

The desk and credenza yielded files of bank statements, brokerage account statements, and paid bills. He located her personal address book. He tossed it all into a paper grocery bag.

Walking into her bedroom, he cringed. He couldn't think about Thursday night. Not now.

Yanking open the drawers of her dresser and nightstands felt like a violation. Framed pictures of the two of them adorned the dresser. A snapshot of him at the beach lay in the nightstand drawer. He lifted it out and stared at it. How empty his eyes looked. Soulless.

He couldn't get out of the condo fast enough.

At sunrise, he sat in his home office, savoring a Bloody Mary. The bounty of the night's expedition was piled on the desk and floor around him. He stared at the stack of Heavenly Interiors files and spotted the one labeled STONE, JAKE.

Setting the drink aside, he pulled out the folder. He wasn't sure why he felt apprehensive about opening it. Finally, he separated the black flaps. *Appropriate color.*

The pages of a log were stapled to the inside of the left flap. The initial entry was dated May 8th. Their first meeting. Jake's tired eyes closed against the painful memory.

Chapter 5

Fourteen weeks earlier

"I wasn't sure I could convince you to have dinner with me," Jake said, peering over the restaurant menu.

I can't believe you did but… Angela raised her eyes to meet his. "An invitation for dinner at the Hotel del Coronado accompanied by three dozen roses is hard to turn down."

She smiled uneasily. He didn't know she had agreed to the date only because it was in a neutral setting, although he looked at her as if he suspected as much. Too bad. This was the best she could do, all she intended to do. And she would make it clear before the evening was over that this was the last time she would see him. She was sure he had plenty of other women at his disposal, so she felt no guilt about pushing him away. Jake Stone meant nothing to her. And other than being another potential conquest, she figured Angela Reardon meant nothing to him.

After a slightly awkward start to the evening, they both relaxed and eased into comfortable repartee. Jake made her laugh and responded appreciatively to her subtle humor.

He was an excellent conversationalist, and they discussed a wide variety of subjects. Nothing personal, but thoughtful, intelligent topics. The few men she had dated since leaving LA had been boring geeks or macho egotists. Those dates had never ended fast enough. But as the three-hour dinner drew to a close, Angela realized she was genuinely disappointed. It had been a very long time since she had enjoyed herself so much. And now she had to say good-bye—permanently—to this intriguing man.

As they exited the restaurant, the brisk ocean breeze greeted them. The crash of waves drew her attention to the white sand beach beyond the manicured lawns of the hotel grounds.

"Would you like to walk on the beach?" Jake asked quietly.

She surprised herself by answering, "That sounds nice."

His hand pressed against the small of her back, guiding her toward the sidewalk that led to the beach. It was the first time he'd touched her all evening. She stiffened slightly. *Please don't...*

Before they reached the sand, Jake bent down to remove his shoes and socks and to roll up his pants.

Angela slipped off her heels and laced her fingers through the straps. She stepped into the wet sand, cool and squishy beneath her bare feet. The wind whipped the hair around her face and the tiered skirt around her legs. Of their own accord, her arms lifted like wings. She closed her eyes and spun around.

How long had it been since she'd sought solace at the beach? The sights, the smells, the sounds were like long-lost friends. Peaceful. Carefree. The demons hiding in her memory were blown away. She was weightless, floating.

Jake Stone ceased to exist until her spinning caused her to stumble. His strong arm caught her around the waist and steadied her.

The physical contact broke the spell, and she plummeted back to earth. She blinked him into focus and saw surprise and something indefinable in his intense eyes. She pushed at his chest, but he pulled her closer.

"Don't," she whispered.

"Don't what?" His lips were too near hers.

"Please...don't." She gulped and turned her face away.

"I just want to kiss you," he said, nuzzling her hair. "One...little...kiss."

"No. Don't." She could hear the hint of panic in her own voice.

After a moment's hesitation, his arms dropped away, and he stepped back. "Why do you treat me like a leper? What's so repulsive about me?" Anger sparked from his flint eyes.

"You're hardly repulsive." She stared out to the black horizon. "Maybe you should just take me home."

"Maybe." He cleared his throat. "But I'd rather take a walk on the beach with you."

For a long moment, she couldn't respond. Then she glanced up at him and locked eyes. "Okay." She started down the beach. When he didn't follow, she stopped and turned. Jake's hands were jammed into his pockets, an unreadable expression on his face. "Coming?" She smiled encouragement.

Not smiling, he trotted to catch up. They strolled for several minutes without speaking.

"I'm sorry," Angela said, breaking the uncomfortable silence. "I've had a lovely evening, and I didn't mean to ruin it."

"Okay." He kicked up the sand with his toes as he walked.

She sighed. "Unless you object, I don't plan to write up the furniture rearrangement suggestions I made since they were so minor. The bill for my services will be minimal, but I'll get it out this week so I can close the file."

He stopped abruptly, snagged her wrist, and swung her around. "I'm just a file to you. Is that it?"

Caught off guard by the resentment in his voice, she stammered, "Y-you're a c-client."

"Right." He shook his head. "What if I want to get to know you on a more personal level?"

She glared at the hand gripping her wrist and tensed. "Why?"

He frowned. "Why? Because you're fascinating, intelligent…and beautiful."

"I don't date much."

He cocked his head. "That can't be because you aren't asked."

"No, it's because I…" Her free hand swept the air between them as if that explained everything. "I'm a very private person."

"Me, too."

A smirk touched her lips. "I highly doubt that."

"It's true. I know a lot of people, but I don't have close friends."

She rolled her eyes. "How many women have you dated in the last month?"

"That's different."

"Is it? Why?"

He looked at her as though she were from another planet. "They aren't…friends. The women I usually date are mostly looking for…something else."

"And that is?"

His grip tightened, and his expression turned cold. Then he

seemed to reconsider. He dropped her wrist. "Forget it. I'm not looking for another fuck buddy. I have plenty of those. I was hoping for a woman with enough brains to carry on a decent conversation. Someone to argue politics. Someone to discuss current events. Someone to commiserate with about the hassles of running your own business." Suggestively, his gaze moved over her, from her polished toenails to the wisps of hair flitting about her eyes. "So, if you're just looking for a good screw, forget it. As I said, I've got plenty of fuck buddies."

Angela's jaw dropped.

Jake snorted and walked quickly back down the beach.

When she caught up with him, she yanked him around hard. "How dare you!"

"What?" he asked, wearing a deadpan expression.

"How dare you accuse me of…of *that*?"

"Isn't *that* what your actions have been silently accusing me of since the moment we met?"

She recoiled at the accusation. The truth hurt. But Jake Stone didn't know her demons. Her past. Her scars.

"You're right. I'm sorry, Jake. I did judge you that way."

They stared at each other, ignoring the cold water swirling around their bare feet.

His fingers lifted her chin as he stepped closer. "May I?"

She nodded just before his lips brushed hers.

* * *

Jake sped north on the freeway toward home. He drove on autopilot because his mind was on Angela Reardon. Specifically, imagining her naked. He had noticed she never wore clothes that attracted attention to her figure, but he was confident that underneath was hidden a gorgeous, sexy body.

His dick hardened when he remembered lifting her onto his bed that first morning. Too bad she'd been unconscious. Too vulnerable. The next night when he'd trapped her against the kitchen counter, she'd aroused him again. And earlier on the beach, when she'd finally let him kiss her, she had tasted so damn good. Being inside her would be even better.

Angela Reardon was, indeed, a fascinating, beautiful, sexy creature.

He frowned.

Hard to believe she was a coldhearted traitor with blood on her hands. What a shame he had to kill her.

Chapter 6

The present

"I don't know. I don't know." Jake slammed a fist into the pillow early the next morning. He rolled over and sat up. Wiping a hand across his sweaty face, he growled with disgust. "Shit. A nightmare rerun. How fucked up is that?"

He had never experienced a nightmare that felt so real. In fact, he rarely dreamed at all. Was his guilt creating the intensity? Whatever the cause, the result was impossible to ignore. Just like in the nightmare, he felt helpless, brought to his knees.

After a quick trip to the bathroom, he returned to bed. For thirty frustrating minutes, he berated himself for letting something as stupid as a nightmare disrupt his rest. Scowling at the 4:30 A.M. glowing on the alarm clock, he conceded defeat and crawled out of bed.

* * *

"Detective Smithson," a gruff male voice came over the intercom. "Jake Stone is here to see you, but he doesn't have an appointment."

"That's okay. Send him back." The Coronado cop pushed his fingers through his hair and closed the file on his desk. He flipped the manila folder over and turned off his computer screen. When Jake knocked, Smithson's feet were propped up on the desk and his hands rested on his stomach. "Come in."

"Looks like you're hard at work as usual," Jake cracked, marching in and grabbing a chair.

"Damn straight. Wouldn't want to waste the taxpayers' money. What brings you all the way down here?"

"The Reardon case."

The detective cocked his head and absently scratched the graying hair at his temple. "Stone, there is no 'Reardon case.' It was a suicide. The file's closed."

"Then you should reopen it."

"What're you talking about?"

Reaching across the back of his chair, Jake pushed the office door shut. He locked eyes with the detective before he continued. "I don't believe Angela committed suicide."

"Shit, I know it's hard to believe. I've read a bunch of shrink stuff about how hard it is for friends and relatives to accept a suicide. It makes people feel guilty—like they failed the victim." He peered hard at Jake. "You must've had it bad for her, buddy."

"Yeah, guess I did. But that's not the point. I knew her frame of mind. Angela was fine. Suicide makes no sense."

"What makes sense is two suicide notes, a bunch of prescription sleeping pills, and her dress and purse found on the bridge."

Jake stood up, clenching his fists at his sides, and paced across the small office. Smithson's eyes followed him back and forth several times and then he glanced at his watch.

"Stone, I'm sorry about Angela, but you gotta let it go. With your SEAL background, I'm surprised—"

"It's exactly because of my background that I don't believe this was a suicide."

"All right, all right. Sit down. Tell me specifically what's bothering you."

Jake sank onto the chair and leaned forward, almost touching the edge of the desk. "First of all, I've read a lot of that 'shrink stuff,' too. I've also had training on the warning signs of suicide. In the SEALs, we were always on the lookout for guys suffering from PTSD."

"Yeah, we get training on that also."

"Good. So when I tell you Angela showed absolutely no signs of being suicidal, you understand what the hell I mean."

"Sure."

"Second. None of the life events that commonly trigger suicide had happened to her recently. In fact, according to Angela, her life was the best it had been in several years."

"And I'm sure you're going to take credit for making her such a happy, *satisfied* woman, right?"

"A little."

Smithson grunted. His gaze fell to the folder on the desk. "Of course, you know there can be subtle reasons apparent to no one. Something from the past that's been building up for a long time."

"True." Jake rested his forearms against the desk and leaned over them. His voice was barely above a whisper. "Third, when was the last time you saw *computer-printed* suicide notes?"

"So what. She didn't want to get writer's cramp. Or she was in a hurry."

"Bullshit. Anyone could've typed them."

"She signed them." Smithson spoke each word slowly and clearly.

"Angela had a signature that was a piece of cake to forge."

"I suppose you're speaking from personal experience." Smithson grinned.

Jake shrugged. "My last point: *still no body*."

"Damn, I shouldn't have told you that when you called earlier."

"But you did, and I could tell it was bugging you, too."

Smithson swung his feet down, pulled his chair closer, and slapped his hands on the desk. "You're right. It was bugging me, so I did some checking. It's not the first time a jumper's body has disappeared. Lots of boats travel through the bay. A body can easily get snagged on the bottom of one and be dragged out to sea. A missing body doesn't mean shit."

Jake shook his head emphatically. "One or two of these things wouldn't bother me. But put all four out there, and I think you've got a whole different ballgame."

"Okay, Stone, you've got all the answers. So, tell me, smartass. What happened to Angela?"

"I see three possible scenarios. In all of them, the suicide clues are only a decoy. One: She was kidnapped. Daddy has money. But there would've been a ransom demand by now. Two: She disappeared on her own. Again, highly unlikely in her stable frame of mind. Three: She was murdered. Bingo."

Smithson and Jake glared at each other. Finally, the detective caved. "If I didn't respect you as a damn good PI, I'd tell you to go screw yourself. But you make some decent points." The detective rubbed his hand across his eyes. "Unfortunately, I don't have any grounds to open an investigation. Angela's parents didn't ask for one. In fact, they took the news pretty damn well. Seems Angela hadn't been very close with them for the past few years.

"They weren't shocked?" Jake asked, frowning.

"More like…surprised. Maybe I'm wrong. They could've been numb. Do you know anything about them?"

"Angela rarely spoke about her family. Randall and Adrienne Reardon live in McLean, Virginia. He's a career State Department guy. Former Ambassador to Spain."

"McLean is a pretty aristocratic neighborhood, as I recall."

"Yeah. Lots of snobs, Congressmen, foreign embassy types. Did the Reardons fly out here?"

Smithson snorted. "Not a chance. Mr. Reardon hardly asked any questions on the phone. Told me to call when we found the body, and he'd arrange to have it *shipped* to Virginia. Told me—not *asked* me—to take the damn dog to the pound. Asshole. Anyway, the old lady neighbor, Mrs. Browning, was happy to adopt the dog."

"Now what do you do?"

Smithson shot him a look of disbelief. "Nothing, Stone. There's nothing I can do. There is *no* evidence of foul play."

"Well, I'm not going to just sit around doing nothing. Promise that I'll have your cooperation. Or at least, you won't get in my way."

Eyeing him warily, the detective asked, "What're you gonna do?"

"Find out what really happened."

"You self-righteous bastard. We know what happened."

Jake lunged from the chair. White-knuckled hands gripped the edge of the desk.

"No, you don't," he seethed through clenched teeth. His gray eyes darkened. He jabbed an index finger at Smithson. "I swear to you: Angela Reardon did *not* commit suicide."

He whirled around, yanked open the door, and stormed out of the office.

For several moments, Detective Kent Smithson stared after him. Absently, he stroked his chin. His gaze dropped to the overturned folder lying on his desk—the file he had been intently studying before Jake's arrival.

Angela Reardon's file.

* * *

Sitting in his black Corvette in a CPD visitor's parking space, Jake wanted to smile at his performance, but the significance of what he had just set in motion kept his expression grave. Was he out of his mind to attempt this? If he wasn't careful—extremely careful—he could get caught in his own trap.

He revved up the engine and barreled into traffic. He grabbed a water bottle and drank deeply, wishing it was J.D. He'd definitely need a stronger drink after his next stop.

Several minutes later, he stood at the front door ringing the doorbell.

"Mrs. Browning, it's Jake Stone. Angela's friend," he called out, knowing she was squinting at him through the peephole. "I need to talk to you about Angela."

The door opened a crack, and a wrinkled face peered at him. "What do you want, young man?"

Jake chuckled. He never felt young anymore. "If you have a minute, could we talk?"

She scowled. "You're not here to take Chelsea away, are you?"

"No, ma'am. I'm sure Chelsea will be very happy with you, and I'm sure Angela would approve."

The old woman huffed. "Well, I should hope so."

Leona Browning ambled away from the door, leaving it ajar. Jake assumed that was an invitation to enter and joined her in the living room. She motioned him to a chair. Chelsea jumped up on the couch and curled up beside her.

"I see Chelsea has already made herself at home," he said, hoping to soften the woman's attitude.

"What do you want?" she asked brusquely.

Jake discarded his planned chitchat and said, "I don't believe Angela committed suicide."

"Heavens, I can't believe it either." She shook her head, and her eyes glistened. "I feel like I failed her as a friend."

"I don't mean it that way. I think Angela was murdered."

She gasped and splayed her hand on her chest. "My word, why would you think such an awful thing?"

"Because the facts don't add up. Angela probably told you that I'm a security expert and private investigator. I gather and analyze facts. Suicide makes no sense to me. I've talked to the police, and they don't plan to pursue an investigation. I'm doing this on my own, and I need your help." Theatrically, he placed his hand over his heart. "Angela was so special. We were very much in—"

"Young man, don't lie to me if you want my help. I'm not a stupid old lady. Angela and I were very close. She told me everything about your relationship."

Jake's eyes widened. "Everything?"

"Enough for me to know that you never said you loved her. But

Angela was very smitten with you. Otherwise, she never would've let you spend the night. She had never allowed another man to do that since she lived here." Leona glowered at him. "You *young* people are too hedonistic these days. Intercourse has lost its sanctity." Her condemning gaze nailed him to the chair. "Did you get Angela pregnant and then refuse to marry her?"

Jake recoiled, unsure how the conversation had taken such an offensive turn. "I would never do that, Mrs. Browning. I was extremely fond of Angela, and I'd never hurt her like that."

The old woman studied him for several moments. She glanced down fondly at Chelsea and scratched behind the dog's ears. Without looking up, she said, "Explain why I should help you, and do it honestly."

Jake cleared his throat. "I apologize for trying to bullshit—sorry—mislead you." He paused and drew a deep breath. "Angela and I liked each other a lot and were in a committed relationship."

She nodded, encouragingly, head still bowed. "Go on."

"And to be brutally honest, I don't say those three little words easily. But I cared for Angela as deeply as I've ever cared for any woman. That's the reason I have to find out the truth about what happened to her."

"I believe you." Her head came up. "How can I help?"

"If Angela was murdered, it wasn't a random act. Too much effort went into making it look like a suicide." He leaned forward, bracing his elbows on his knees. "Murder requires motive. Revenge. Jealousy. Anger. Greed. I knew Angela only three months, and I'm drawing a complete blank on anyone with motive. I was hoping you might remember someone or something that Angela mentioned to you. Even filling me in on her friends and acquaintances would help."

Leona stared into space. "Angela was such a sweet person. It's hard to imagine somebody wanting to kill her. I certainly am not aware of anyone with those motives. She was also a very private person, as you probably know. I often worried that she had so little social life." She pulled a tissue from a pocket and dabbed her eyes. "Let's see. Stella Jenkins was her assistant at Heavenly Interiors. Angela probably considered her a friend."

"Stella's married, right? Two small kids?"

"Yes, and Angela never complained about any problems with Stella."

"Other girlfriends?"

"Hmmm. Debbie Hoover. Single. Lives here in the condo complex. She and Angela liked to go clothes shopping together at the malls occasionally."

"Any problems between them?"

"My goodness, no. Both friendships were very superficial."

"Any other women in her life?"

Forehead furrowed in concentration, Leona shook her head.

"Did Angela ever mention any unreasonable or irate clients?"

"Only an occasional small dispute over a bill or something minor. Her clients seemed to love her."

"Boyfriends?"

"Before you, *young* man, the men never lasted more than a few dates." Her expression became a judgmental scowl. "Angela was not promiscuous, which apparently you men expect these days."

"So, no ugly breakups?"

"There was never anything to break up."

"Then Angela wasn't a heartbreaker."

"Hardly. She also wasn't a conquest. That may have infuriated some."

"I can understand that."

"Is sexual frustration sufficient motive for murder?" she asked in a condescending tone.

"It can be if it's emasculating or sadistic. Was Angela ever like that?"

"Are we speaking of the same person? Of course I never observed her being like that. Did you?"

Jake shot her a frosty stare. *Sly old broad.* "Of course not. Do you remember Angela complaining about any guy being aggressive or abusive?"

"No."

"Any unpleasant incidents? Like a stalker or a persistent anonymous caller?"

"Not really." She sighed. "Do you have any ideas of your own?"

"I've exhausted mine already. As you said, she was very private. Other than you and Stella, I don't believe she ever introduced me to any more friends or acquaintances."

"I wish I had more insight for you."

"Me, too. What do you know about her family?"

"They weren't close, and Angela rarely spoke of them. I don't recall any relatives ever visiting."

"What about her past?"

Leona rubbed Chelsea's head. "Past? I hardly think of Angela as a person with a past. She was a precious girl, and I loved her like a granddaughter. But honestly, she seemed to go out of her way to…to be ordinary, to blend in, to *not* attract attention of any sort. For such a beautiful woman, I never understood that."

His throat tightened. *Unfortunately, I do.*

* * *

The computer screen blurred. Jake ground the heels of his hands against his bloodshot eyeballs. Almost midnight. He'd been working on the computer for six straight hours. His eyes burned, his head pounded, and his back ached. But the worst part was he had nothing to show for his pain.

Not only did Angela have no past, she barely had a present. Leona Browning was right: Angela Reardon worked hard at being invisible.

Even with his investigative skills, three days of research had yielded nothing useful. Neither the legal nor the illegal searches had revealed any secrets. From the CIA angle, he'd confirmed again that there was absolutely no evidence of Angela obtaining or selling classified State Department information. From the personal angle, she had no enemies and few friends. No business, financial, or legal problems. No unscrupulous investments. Nothing. *Nada.*

"Shit," Jake muttered, rolling his head from side to side to work the knots out of his neck.

After shutting down the computer and locking the office door, he lumbered up the stairs to his bedroom. Mechanically, he got ready for bed. When he pulled back the bedcovers, he knocked his cell phone off the nightstand. As he grabbed the phone, his last call to the Contractor echoed in his memory.

One man knew who had put the contract out on Angela.

Jake scowled at the phone cradled in his hand. The fingers of his other hand massaged his forehead.

Each frustrating dead end solidified his conclusion that the CIA handler was arranging private contracts. He trusted that Salami was working in the shadows, trying to identify the corrupt operative, but was there a way for Jake to convince the Contractor to talk? Could greed or fear persuade the bastard to give up the private buyer's name?

Jake would be asking a dangerous question, and the answer might be even more dangerous. It might get him killed.

Anonymity. Everyone in the murderous profession wanted it, needed it, demanded it. The Agency. The Contractor. The assassin. For all the obvious reasons, it was a cardinal rule no one broke.

But could it be bent? For a price? To achieve justice?

Jake grimaced. Many of his peers had long ago lost the ability or desire to know good from bad, right from wrong. He wasn't the only one with a broken moral compass.

He laid the phone on the nightstand and stood to pace and analyze.

If the Contractor cooperated and provided the buyer's name, the operation would be easy. No one else would ever have to know. With nothing more than a name, Jake could track the son of a bitch and put him down. But if someone in the small, dark circle of the profession did find out about the breach of anonymity, then he and the Contractor were as good as dead.

On the other hand, if the Contractor told him to shove it up his ass, he'd be no closer to finding Angela's buyer than he was before. But he'd be in a hell of a lot more danger. The Contractor could do a variety of things, two of which would mean serious trouble. One, he could tell the buyer about Jake's request. In that case, the buyer would most assuredly put a contract out on Jake. Two, the Contractor could be so concerned about Jake's breach that he himself would send someone to put Jake down. Both possibilities were daunting.

In the past, Jake had accepted and obeyed the rules. But suddenly he hated them. He hated the whole damn profession and every bastard involved in it. Including himself.

He slammed a fist into the bedroom wall. By his count, his analysis of possible scenarios ended in more chances of his dying than of his surviving. The odds favored failure far more than success.

Opening the French doors to the balcony, he let the cool, moist night air wash over his naked body in hopes of calming his frustration.

"Shiiiiiit!" he yelled at the boulder-strewn hills.

He gripped the balcony railing and squeezed his eyes shut. Angela's face came to him. Her scent. Her touch. Her voice.

His chin dropped to his chest. Did he really have a choice? He owed it to Angela. Penance for taking the contract. His only chance at redemption was to kill the person who wanted her dead.

"Damn," he sighed into the night as he resolved what he had to do.

He immediately marched back inside, grabbed the phone, and dialed. He paced while listening to the ten rings. Silence answered.

"There's a problem," Jake said.

Nothing.

"Goddamn it, talk to me."

"What's the problem?" asked the mechanically altered voice.

"The Reardon contract wasn't sanctioned by the Agency."

"What the hell are you talking about?" the Contractor growled.

"Angela Reardon committed no crime. There was no motivation for the Agency to want her dead. You're selling private contracts, you greedy bastard. Someone paid you to hire me to kill an *innocent* woman," Jake said, his voice seething with rage.

"For a cold-blooded killer, you have quite an imagination. It's a moot point anyway. You delivered. You've been paid. Good night."

"No! Stop. I don't care that you're screwing the Agency. This isn't about patriotism or national security. This is personal. I need to make this right."

"Right?"

"I want the buyer's name."

The Contractor laughed. "I'm not admitting to any of your crazy allegations, but are you out of your fucking mind?"

"Maybe so, but hear me out. You just give me the buyer's name. I'll take care of everything else. No one will ever know."

The Contractor hesitated. "What if I don't know the name?"

"Don't bullshit me."

"Why in hell would I even consider such an asinine breach of anonymity?"

"Because I'll pay you my entire fee. Remember, three times the normal."

The long silence told Jake he'd hit a soft spot. Greed. Maybe his plan would work.

"No deal. It's too risky. Chances are we'd both end up dead. And if not dead, I'd definitely be out of business."

"You know how good I am. I can pull this off without anyone finding out. Think of all the money you're giving up."

"Yeah, but I'd like to be around to enjoy the money I already have. Forget it. I'm not interested."

A muscle in Jake's jaw twitched, and he spoke through clenched teeth. "We have a long history, asshole. What if I go to the Agency with what I know?"

"I don't think you're that stupid."

"No, I'm not stupid. I'm pissed. I want this buyer brought down."

"Let it go. It's over."

"Well, then, I guess I'll have to go to the Agency."

"Don't screw with me."

"Then give me the fucking name!"

"Don't do this. Don't force my hand."

"Is that a threat?" Jake asked.

"Damn right."

The phone went dead, and Jake hurled it across the room.

"That went well," he muttered as he poured himself a large tumbler of Jack Daniel's at the wet bar in the bedroom. He retrieved the phone and dialed. "I fucked up," he told the silence.

"How bad?" Salami asked.

"Bad. I called the Contractor, confronted him with my theory about his little side business, and tried to get him to give up the buyer's name. He didn't cave."

"Shit, Granite, what the hell were you thinking?"

Jake swallowed a gulp of J.D. "Sorry, Salami, I'm desperate. You better back off. If the bastard hears you're snooping around, he'll come after you as well as me."

"Good advice, but too late. I've already been snooping. Got something, too."

"You're amazing."

"Yes, Grasshopper, I am. Here's the deal. The Agency did *not* put out the contract on Angela Reardon."

"Shit. I knew it. Who is this SOB?"

"Bernard."

"What?"

"That's the only name I found other than 'Contractor,' and it was whispered to me once."

"First, last, or code?"

"Hell, I don't know, you ingrate."

He laughed. "Thanks, Salami. This should square us for Istanbul, right?"

"Never."

Jake exhaled. "I told the prick I didn't care that he was screwing the Agency, but I do. I want to bring this guy down, Salami. I want him bad for taking advantage of me and others like me who have to believe that the unspeakable shit we do is for the good of the American people. But this asshole hired me to kill a beautiful, intelligent, innocent woman for some ball-less buyer with some godforsaken motive that I can't even imagine."

"Damn, Granite. You fell for the target."

"Yeah, hard. But that's not why I want...Bernard. I want his ass for *all* the guiltless targets like Angela Reardon. I want him for all the guys like us who have to do the goddamn killing. But how the hell am I going to get him—"

"Easy, man, easy. You're not in this alone. The information on Bernard and the unsanctioned Reardon hit is going to mysteriously come to the attention of some very important people at Langley, my friend."

"Salami, this isn't your fight."

"The hell it isn't. Look, you take care of Angela's buyer, and I'll take care of Bernard. Deal?"

"Deal." Jake paused. "But..."

"But?"

"But don't put him down until after I find the buyer. Bernard may be the only link to—"

"You know I can't stall. Other unsanctioned targets could be at risk. It may take me a while to find him, though."

Jake sighed. "Bernard knows he's been busted. Watch your back."

"I'm not worried, Granite. Remember, I don't exist and neither do you." Salami disconnected.

Lowering himself onto the edge of the bed, Jake drank deeply. *Now what?* The game had changed. He needed to adjust his strategy.

The whole Agency-contract scenario had been officially eliminated. Sure, he had a corrupt handler breathing down his neck so he would have to be more careful while he continued the search for the real buyer. A search that was going nowhere because the information he'd stolen from Angela's condo and business was yielding no clues.

Exhausted to the core, Jake tossed back the rest of his drink and swore softly. His naked body welcomed the coolness of the silk sheets. With his tired eyes closed, he drew a deep breath and exhaled slowly through pursed lips. God, he wanted to turn his mind off.

Fifteen minutes later, he rolled onto his stomach and stretched the kinks out of his arms and legs. Still, sleep eluded him. His damn mind refused to give up the quest.

Who wanted Angela Reardon dead? And why?

A nagging angst taunted his brain.

Were the answers right in front of him? Was he just too guilty to see them?

Chapter 7

Twelve weeks earlier

Little Italy was alive with celebrating baseball fans. The San Diego Padres had triumphantly trounced the rival Los Angeles Dodgers in a remarkable three-game sweep. The party had moved from Petco Park into the surrounding downtown neighborhoods of The Gaslamp Quarter and Little Italy.

Angela and Jake relaxed at a small table in Filippi's Pizza Grotto. The dimly lit restaurant definitely had the feel of a grotto, with dozens of empty Chianti bottles suspended from its low ceiling. Savory Italian aromas hung heavily in the air.

Despite the high-spirited revelry around them, the mood at Angela and Jake's table was subdued. Even at the ballgame, his behavior had been quieter than usual, and that attitude continued as they perused the menus before ordering.

Angela sighed and closed her menu. Jake didn't seem to notice her studying him.

A hollow sense of disappointment filled her. After two wonderful weeks of dating, her hopes had blossomed that maybe this time would be different. How stupid of her. How naïve. But at least the days since he had first kissed her on the beach had been fantastic.

For reasons that weren't entirely clear, he had ignored the fiasco of their first meeting. And their second. He had asked for no further explanation than she offered and seemed truly relieved she had agreed to see him again.

Reluctant at first, she had soon been overwhelmed by Jake's enthusiastic attention. He arranged for them to be together, to do something enjoyable every day. For a few days there had only been time for him to meet her for lunch in Coronado, but most nights, they dined someplace special. Over the past two weekends, practically every minute had been spent together. His endless list of fun things to do had included the San Diego Zoo and Disneyland. He'd surprised her with horseback riding on the beach, parasailing at Mission Bay, and even a hot air balloon ride in Del Mar. All at sunset. All so romantic.

To Angela's relief, he always behaved like a perfect gentleman. The kiss on the beach had been the first of many gentle, respectful kisses. After uncomfortably watching a sex-filled movie on their second date, she had voiced her disapproval of premarital sex. Jake's struggle to hide his disbelief and dismay was almost comical, but he had heeded the subtle warning in her words.

Never once had he touched her inappropriately or suggestively. Never once had he pushed her for any physical affection beyond polite hugs and kisses. With the masseuse and the three empty condom wrappers still fresh in her memory, Angela was truly astonished by his restraint.

Part of her wanted to tell him the truth. That part wanted to be normal and free again. But another part was still too scarred, too ashamed, too afraid. That part made her panic.

It always won.

She had confided to her dear neighbor, Leona Browning, that she was living a fairy tale, and Jake Stone was her prince. He was definitely charming and ruggedly handsome and devotedly attentive. *But*—Angela hated that there was a *"but"*—Jake's eyes unnerved her. They were pure gray. She had seen them icy cold, smoldering hot, charmingly soft, and flint hard. So many shades of gray. She found it especially unsettling when the message in his eyes didn't match the rest of his demeanor.

Those eyes were usually like windows into the shadowy recesses of the real Jake Stone. But tonight, the gray windows had been shuttered.

She had noticed throughout the evening that his gaze rarely connected with hers, but she tried to ignore the warning signs. God, she had so wanted him to be different from the others.

After they ordered, she attempted to start a conversation with the news of a local political scandal. She soon found herself carrying on a one-sided discussion. Their meals arrived, and she gave up. They ate in complete silence for several minutes.

Occasionally, she glanced up from her plate to watch Jake who seemed fixated on his food. Not once did she find him looking away from his plate.

Finally, no longer hungry, she raised the wine glass to her lips and leaned back in the chair. She sipped the Chianti, wondering how long this mood would continue.

She sighed. She knew what was happening. It had happened before. Many times. Unfortunately, she'd let herself get sucked into believing Jake might be different because it had taken longer this time. She silently chastised herself for feeling disappointed; her disappointment was more her fault than his.

No reason to drag this out any longer. She sighed again. *Time to end this and move on.*

"Earth to Jake." He kept chewing, never missing a beat. "Earth to Jake," Angela said a little louder.

He stopped mid-bite and peeked at her over his fork. "Huh?" Then noticing her barely touched plate, he asked, "Something wrong with your dinner?"

She slowly swallowed a sip of wine while holding his gaze. "No, the food is fine. Something's wrong with the company."

Almost defiantly, he stuck his fork in his mouth and returned to staring at his plate. She waited patiently.

"Sorry I'm not up to your standards tonight," he said without looking up. He stabbed a bite of meatball and jammed it into his mouth.

She shut her eyes and steeled herself for the imminent, unpleasant conversation.

Men are so immature about breaking off relationships, she mused. *They're like children who can't admit they're taking their balls and going home when they don't get their way.* She smiled faintly at the analogy.

Setting down her wineglass, Angela shifted in the chair and rested her elbows on the table.

"You're very distant tonight, Jake. Is something wrong?"

He peered at her through flint eyes. His thoughts and feelings were completely shielded behind an expressionless face. But Angela saw him swallow hard and felt some satisfaction that he was at least uncomfortable about ending their relationship.

He rolled his eyes and shook his head before deliberately dropping his fork on the plate with a loud clatter. "I'm just tired."

"Please don't treat me like a child. Do we need to have *the talk*?"

"What talk? I'm tired and frustrated because I'm…working on a contract that isn't going well," he offered lamely.

"Gee, how romantic. No one's ever called me a 'contract' before."

"What the hell are you talking about?" His jaw was set, his lips a tight line.

"C'mon, Jake. I've been expecting this since our second date. Actually, you lasted longer than most men. They usually disappear after the third or fourth date when there's *no sex*."

He stared at her incredulously, rubbing his forehead. "What does sex have to do with anything tonight?"

"Don't play dumb. You know exactly what I mean. I was being honest when I warned you that I wouldn't sleep with you, but like most men, you thought you could change my mind. You know, seduce me with your manly charms. Now that it's apparent you can't, it's time for you to move on."

"You think I've been dating you just to get laid?" He laughed harshly, attracting curious glances from other patrons.

Fighting back the sting of tears, she looked down at her hands. "I think that was part of it."

"Did you ever consider I might not be interested in sex with you? Shit, Angela, how do you know I haven't been screwing two or three other women in between our dates?"

Heat crept up her cheeks until they burned. "I guess I don't," she answered defensively. "I apologize, Jake, if I'm wrong. But it's been my experience that most men don't want platonic relationships."

"Well, I'll admit it's never my first choice. But sometimes there's another reason for the attraction, something not sexual. How many times are you going to lump me together with 'most men'? Do you ever consider that I might not be like 'most men'?"

Without waiting for an answer, he abruptly stood and yanked out his wallet. Tossing a hundred-dollar bill on the table, he said coldly, "That should pay for dinner and a taxi to get you home. Good-bye, Angela."

* * *

The Corvette peeled out of Filippi's parking lot. Angrier with himself than with Angela, Jake whipped the car onto the crowded freeway. Horns blared. His left hand, middle finger extended, shot out the open window.

Then reality grabbed him by the balls. The contract. *Don't blow the damn contract.*

All day he'd struggled. He didn't like what was happening to him. He wasn't supposed to feel emotions, especially an emotion as foreign as compassion. But he was, and that was dangerous.

As the Corvette flew past the exit to the highway heading home, Jake conceded to himself where he was going. He just didn't know what he was going to do when he got there.

The cool, damp night air blowing on his face calmed him. He ran a hand across his eyes and tried to focus on how to save the night, how to save the contract.

Angela Reardon was the most fascinating woman he'd ever met.

She was incredibly complex. Perhaps that's what he liked most—not being able to figure her out quickly. She'd been right about two things tonight: He didn't like platonic relationships, and he never had to wait more than a couple of dates before the woman was offering him sex. He suffered no pangs of guilt over either fact.

After reaching the Coronado end of the bridge, he drove past Angela's condo and parked half a block away where he would have a clear view of the taxi dropping her off.

Jake knew a relationship with Angela would've been different even if she hadn't been his target. The woman was beautiful, inside and out. Intelligent. Captivating. Sexy. Strong, yet kind.

His eyes narrowed.

But Angela Reardon also had secrets.

Her secrets were her vulnerability. Twice he had unintentionally triggered her fear. Twice he had incredulously witnessed her weakness. After the second incident, he'd analyzed her actions but reached no conclusions. Only after her condemnation of premarital sex did he begin to put the pieces together.

A moral belief didn't cause terror and panic. And that's what he'd seen in her eyes. No, this wasn't a moral issue. She had a deep, dark, painful secret.

Minutes later a taxi turned the far corner and stopped at the curb across the street from Angela's condo. Jake's ruminations ended abruptly as she exited the cab. He cursed when the driver took off while she was still crossing the street. *Neanderthal jerk.*

Jake grimaced as he watched Angela wipe her eyes while hurrying to the front door and letting herself in. For several minutes, he watched the soft glow of lights coming on, downstairs and upstairs. After slamming his hand against the steering wheel, he started the car and pulled into her driveway. He waited, drawing a deep breath and steeling himself, before he approached her front door.

Angela didn't answer the first ring. He pushed the doorbell a second time and called her name. The door opened a crack.

Her wide eyes were red-rimmed and glistening. She didn't speak, just stared at him.

"May I come in?" he asked quietly.

After a few heartbeats, she nodded and walked away. He stepped inside and closed the door behind him. Running fingers through his hair he turned to Angela, who leaned against the wall at the edge of the foyer.

"What do you want, Jake?" She lifted her chin proudly.

His gaze raked over her. She was barefoot. The top two buttons of her shirt were open, the shirttail pulled out of the waistband of her jeans. Her blond hair was tousled as if she'd been lying down.

"I wanted to be sure you got home safely and to apologize for deserting you at the restaurant. My behavior was unforgivable." He smiled repentantly.

She blinked. "Well, you can see I'm safe."

Their eyes locked. Seconds ticked by.

"You're wrong, Angela."

"About what?"

"Several things."

"Such as?"

"First, I wasn't planning to break up with you."

"Really?" She didn't sound convinced.

"Yes, really. Second, all that bullshit about sex and seducing you was wrong."

"I don't believe you."

"Maybe you don't *want* to believe it. Maybe you're a coward," he said, taunting her.

She straightened and pushed away from the wall. "You should leave now." She spun around, and her hair whipped across her shoulders. After two hesitant steps, she rushed toward the stairs.

Jake intercepted her and grabbed her arm, his grip firm but not painful. "No. You don't get to run away this time."

She scowled at his hand. "Let me go," she said in a stern voice.

He tightened his grasp and pulled her closer until their bodies almost touched. He'd felt gentle and apologetic a few moments earlier, but now he was angry and wanted to challenge her.

When Angela tried to turn away, his other arm snaked around her waist and yanked her against him. She gasped and stiffened.

His hand threaded up through the silky hair at the back of her neck. Then he held her head immobile as his lips attacked hers.

His frantic, hungry lips moved over her tightly clenched ones. His mouth was relentless: pressing, massaging, demanding. Her lips softened and parted. His tongue plunged inside, no hesitation. Teasing, tantalizing, thrusting again and again.

Whimpering, she leaned into him.

He ended the kiss as suddenly as it had begun.

Jake's hands dropped away. Angela swayed. He didn't attempt to steady her although his eyes never released hers.

"You were wrong, Angela. That's what I would've done *if* I were trying to seduce you. So, you see, I wasn't."

He marched out and slammed the door.

Chapter 8

The present

"I don't know," Jake mumbled into the pillow Tuesday morning and then opened his eyes. "Shit."

He rolled onto his back and threw his arms out wide across the huge bed. The nightmare was becoming a nightly routine. His chest heaved, but he refused to give in to anger. He coped by believing Angela was motivating him, prodding him to find and punish the person who wanted her dead.

"I'll find him, I promise," he muttered. "Now, please let me sleep."

Three hours later, the alarm clock woke him. He slapped it into silence with his eyes still closed. Finished with several jaw-locking yawns, he swung his legs off the side of the bed and sat up. His gaze rested on Angela's photo on the nightstand. God, she looked great in that red dress.

He lumbered into the bathroom and splashed cold water on his face. His eyes burned from long hours spent reviewing Angela's business and personal files. Every night he'd gone to bed mentally exhausted only to have his sleep disrupted by the damn nightmare. Fatigue. Frustration. Guilt. The mirror reflected his suffering.

The call last night to the Contractor had been a fiasco. Jake had no delusions that the Contractor would feel the burn of guilt and change his mind about disclosing the name of the buyer. It was far more likely the evil man was currently arranging a contract to kill Jake Stone. Looking over his shoulder, watching his back, would slow him down.

His fingers scratched the sandpaper of whiskers on his chin. He desperately needed a break in his investigation. So far, he hadn't turned up a single soul with a hint of a motive. Time was passing quickly, and he feared the trail would soon grow cold. Before falling into bed last night, he had decided how to expand the search.

In the kitchen, Jake poured a mug of strong, black coffee. While he drank the life-preserving caffeine, he flipped through the pages of Angela's personal address book until he found the phone number he sought.

As he dialed, he braced for an unpleasant conversation.

"Reardon residence," a female voice answered.

"Randall Reardon, please."

"May I ask who's calling?"

"Jake Stone."

"Regarding?"

He hesitated. "Angela Reardon."

The voice whispered, "Did you find her?"

Jake frowned. "Who is this?"

The woman drew a deep breath, but her voice still trembled when she spoke. "Please excuse me, Mr. Stone. I am Rosa Sanchez, the Reardon's household manager. I have been praying you would find my baby girl."

"*Your* baby girl?"

A muffled sob. "I practically raised Angela. I can't believe my angel baby is gone."

"I'm very sorry for your loss, Ms. Sanchez."

"Are you working with Detective Smithson?"

Jake paused. "Collaborating with him."

"I see. Please bring Angela home, Mr. Stone. I'll connect you with Mr. Reardon now."

"Thanks."

A minute passed before a man's voice came on the line. "Randall Reardon."

"Good morning, Mr. Reardon. My name is Jake Stone."

"Yes, Rosa told me."

"Right. First, I'd like to offer my sincere condolences."

"Thank you. What do you want?"

Jake tensed. "If you have a few minutes, I'd like to ask you some questions about Angela."

"Rosa said you were 'collaborating' with Detective Smithson."

"Yes. Closely."

"Really?" Randall Reardon paused. "What are your questions, Mr. Stone?"

Jake forced himself to tamp down his rising anger. "Let me explain that I don't believe Angela committed suicide."

"What are you suggesting?" Reardon asked warily.

"I think she was murdered."

"Murdered? What about the suicide notes? The sleeping pills?"

"I think someone went to a lot of trouble to make it look like a suicide."

"Why would someone murder Angela?" Reardon said with apparent disbelief.

"I don't know, but I swear to God I'm going to find out." Jake made sure his tone left no doubt of his intensity or intentions.

Reardon cleared his throat. "Your questions, Mr. Stone?"

"The obvious one: Did Angela have any enemies?"

"Of course not. My daughter was a kind, loving, compassionate woman. She was also exceptionally talented and smart, although her strong-willed independence made her difficult at times."

"Her independence caused problems at home?"

"Angela's mother and I were disappointed in some of her choices."

"Like dropping out of law school and becoming an interior decorator?"

"One of many," Reardon said curtly.

"Many?"

"Angela made no secret of her disdain for our lifestyle, our respect for proper society. After high school, she wasted no time getting as far away from our societal universe as possible. She practically destroyed me—I mean, us—when she fled to Los Angeles, of all places." He snorted. "But in the end that didn't work out so well. Excuse me a moment."

Jake heard a muffled female voice in the background and guessed the man had covered the phone mouthpiece. He listened to the two voices grow louder, angrier.

Then Reardon was back. "I apologize. Where were we?"

"LA."

"Oh, yes. We tried to warn Angela about the perils of California, but she wouldn't listen. Her move was disastrous for the whole family. When she was…when the incident occurred four years ago, we thought she'd have the good sense to come home. But some offspring never learn."

Incident? What Angela had endured was no goddamn *incident.* Listening to her father's judgmental attitude, Jake could better understand why she hadn't returned to Virginia afterward. She'd gone through hell just telling him about it years later.

A click alerted him that someone had picked up another phone extension. He waited, listening, curious.

"Adrienne, you weren't invited to join us," Reardon spoke sharply to his wife.

"I have a right to know what's going on." She turned her anger on Jake. "Why can't you respect our privacy as we deal with the death of our daughter? Just what are you up to, Mr. Stone?"

"I'm trying to learn the truth about Angela's death, Mrs. Reardon."

"Detective Smithson told us the truth. Angela committed suicide."

"Well, ma'am, I don't believe she did."

"Please let us grieve in private and don't make trouble for us."

"Trouble?"

"By drawing even more attention to this...this disaster. Like Angela would want." Her tone changed. "I wouldn't be surprised if the timing was intentional." The venom in her mother's voice shocked Jake.

"Adrienne, watch what you say," Reardon snapped.

Jake's fist clenched, but his tone was smooth, conciliatory. "You might be onto something, Mrs. Reardon. What do you mean about the timing being intentional?"

"Adrienne—" Her husband tried to stop her.

"Shut up, Randall. Mr. Stone won't let this go until he knows the truth about our darling daughter, who obviously didn't care how much she hurt us. So I'm going to tell him."

"I appreciate your honesty, ma'am."

"We'll see if you do. Now, where do I start? I overheard Randall telling you Angela was difficult. That's an understatement. She lived to undermine our place in society, destroy the respect we worked so hard to earn. Randall spent a lifetime making a successful career in the State Department. He was Ambassador to Spain while Angela was in high school. He and I were in Greece most of the time she was in college. But we moved back to McLean four years ago to wait for his appointment as Ambassador to the UK."

"Adrienne, please stop."

"No." She exhaled impatiently. "The UK was to be his crowning accomplishment, the pinnacle he would retire from. But Angela decided to destroy our dream. She managed to be involved in that…that awful incident just in time to trigger an avalanche of bad press. We hoped it might generate a sympathetic reaction, but instead the powers-that-be decided Angela needed her parents in the US instead of in the UK. She never even came home. Stayed in goddamn California." Adrienne's voice cracked, but with anger, not grief. "We've waited four years for another ambassadorship. A week ago, Randall was the favorite for the opening in Panama. My God, it's humiliating. *Panama.*" She paused. "Then this whole mess with Angela happened. Yesterday, Randall got a call informing him Thornton Spiegel had been chosen instead." She laughed bitterly. "Can you imagine? Thornton has a handshake like a dishrag, and he can't even dance." She choked back tears. "Angela ruined everything again. We gave our daughter a wonderful life. How could she be so heartless?"

Rage squeezed Jake's throat and left him speechless. Was this woman for real? A heavy silence hung on the phone line. There was a *click* and then more silence.

Finally, Randall Reardon cleared his throat. "You'll have to forgive Adrienne. She's so distraught over Angela's death she's not herself."

"Do you share your wife's opinions?" Jake asked tightly.

"Heavens no. Angela had a wonderful heart. She was never hateful or vengeful. I don't believe there was any intention to hurt us with her actions in either incident. But she changed after what happened in LA, became even more distant from her family. I don't think she was ever truly happy again."

"Are you saying her unhappiness led to suicide?"

"Yes, I believe it did."

"And you can't think of any enemies or anyone else who would have wanted her dead?"

"If you're intimating that about my wife, I strongly resent it, Mr. Stone."

"I'm not."

"Then—as I just told Detective Smithson—I can think of no one with a motive to kill Angela."

Jake did a double take. "Smithson asked you the same question?"

"Yes, and several other distasteful ones."

"When?"

"About an hour ago. If you're 'collaborating closely' with the detective, I would think you would know that," Reardon said snidely. "I'm sure I should've inquired earlier, but what *exactly* is your role in this matter, Mr. Stone?"

"I'm a PI," Jake said, his anger about to boil over. "Detective Kent Smithson and I have had a professional relationship for several years. We've officially discussed Angela's case. He knows I don't think she committed suicide."

"And what was your relationship with my daughter?"

Jake wanted to curse and tell the asshole it was none of his damn business, but he had to keep this resource open. "Angela and I had been dating for about three months. We were in an exclusive, committed relationship."

A long silence followed.

"Pardon my skepticism, but my understanding was that—after LA—Angela wasn't interested in relationships with men. We didn't know she was seriously dating anyone."

"Pardon my bluntness, but I can't say I'm surprised she didn't share the news with you."

The insult must have hit a vulnerable spot because Reardon's tone suddenly changed to one of sorrow and remorse. "It's a shame, but you're absolutely right." He cleared his throat again. "Do you think Angela was happy?"

"Yes. Definitely. She told me she hadn't been so happy in a long time."

"I'm glad." He paused. "She was my daughter, and I loved her—whether you believe me or not."

"Then help me find out the truth about her death."

"I don't know anything that would help."

"I understand, but if something comes to you, call me anytime, day or night."

Jake recited his contact numbers and ended the call as quickly as possible. He swore vehemently. Poor Angela. It was amazing she had grown up to be the terrific person she was, considering her horrible parents. Her life must have been hell when she lived with them.

After pouring a second mug of coffee, Jake paced while he sorted through the minimal information gleaned from the call. For a fleeting moment, he entertained the thought that Adrienne Reardon had put a contract out on her own daughter. But that didn't make sense. True, she seemed to wish Angela didn't exist, but her death in any manner would have produced attention. And attention on Angela was *not* what her mother wished for.

Jake wandered outside to stand at the edge of the patio. Staring down at the fifty-foot drop, his mind switched gears.

Smithson had called the Reardons and asked "distasteful" questions. Jake grinned. Kent could be a real son of a bitch when he wanted to and, hopefully, he'd been at his worst. But had the detective learned anything? Probably nothing more than what Jake had learned. The bigger question was why Smithson had called in the first place. Yesterday, the man had said there was no Reardon case, and today, he was calling the parents and asking questions.

Jake pulled his cell from his pocket and slid onto a chaise lounge. He smiled as he dialed.

"Smithson."

"You lying sack of shit."

"Morning, Stone."

"Did you have a nice chat with the Reardons?"

"Damn. News travels fast." He chuckled incredulously. "Probably as nice as yours. Wonderful folks, aren't they?"

"I have a new level of respect for Angela. That's for sure."

"Agreed."

The banter ended, and Jake turned no-nonsense. "Why did you call them?"

During a long pause, he heard a door shutting.

Smithson's voice was firm and low. "Look, Stone, I don't have any grounds to officially pursue this. And I have too many cases to go chasing after anything unofficial. Besides, I could get my balls in a bind if I did, and I happen to like my balls. But something doesn't smell right about this."

"Damn straight. My gut says the same thing."

"Yeah, well, if it's ever your gut against my balls, I'm sticking with my boys."

"No argument there. What changed your mind?"

Kent snorted. "I was already having trouble with it when you came to see me. Plus, all your points were valid. I can even add two more."

"Two more?"

"Yeah. Number one: If you can simply take an overdose of sleeping pills, why bother with the scarier, messier method of jumping off a damn bridge? Overkill. You can't die twice. Number two: Since when does a jumper take off her dress and shoes? It's not like she's going to need them again. No woman I know would want to stand out on that bridge half-naked in the middle of the night, even if they were committing suicide."

"What're you saying?"

"The clothes on the bridge were a cover-up. No pun intended."

Jake stroked his chin. "To explain the disappearance of the body?"

"Right."

"So you're thinking murder?"

"First degree. The bastard put a lot of planning into this. He killed her in the condo. The sleeping pills were only a prop—probably didn't even use any. Then he removed the body to God knows where, but left the clothes on the bridge as a decoy."

"Devious."

"Yeah. Also, there was no sign of forced entry or struggle. The perp knew her signature well enough to forge it. Knew she took prescription sleeping pills. Knew the neighbor lady would be concerned about the dog barking. Which means Angela definitely knew her killer."

"It all makes sense. What about motive?"

"Beats me. What do you think, Stone? You're my prime suspect."

* * *

After his double-edged conversation with Detective Smithson, Jake left his beautiful backyard and secluded himself inside his office. He also switched from coffee to a Bloody Mary.

Smithson's message was a mixed blessing. He was no longer convinced Angela had committed suicide. That was good. He was thinking murder. Even better. He considered Jake a suspect.

Bad, very bad.

Jake had known the risks when he went to Smithson's office yesterday and set the chain of events in motion. At least the detective wasn't opening an official homicide investigation. *Yet.* Their friendship—if it could be called that—probably made the man uncomfortable with his suspicions. Jake would have to keep it that way. He needed to be careful how he manipulated the cop to garner whatever information he could. He had to avoid getting caught in the net at all costs.

His cell phone rang, and he glanced at the screen. The caller's phone number was "unavailable," so he didn't answer. His attention returned to his computer monitor, which was displaying information from Angela's personal laptop. The phone rang again: unavailable. He pushed it aside and clicked the mouse through several commands.

When his cell rang the third time, Jake frowned and answered but remained silent.

"Hello?" A woman's voice.

She didn't continue so he disconnected.

Thirty seconds later, the phone rang. "Shit," he muttered. After ten rings, he answered.

"What the hell—"

The female voice sounded familiar, but Jake still ended the call. The process started again. He hesitated. His finger hovered over the talk button before finally touching it.

"Jake Stone? Don't hang up. I need to talk to you, damn it."

He froze. "Angela?"

"What? Are you crazy?"

He pushed end and exhaled the breath he'd been holding. He shook his head to clear it. The damn phone rang again.

This time, he stabbed the talk button immediately. "Who the hell is this?"

"Well, it's about time, Mr. Stone." The woman laughed, but it wasn't Angela's charming laughter.

"Who are you?"

"Maleena Reardon." When Jake didn't respond, she continued in a mocking tone. "You have no idea who I am, do you?"

"No."

She laughed again, an annoying, grating sound. "I'm Angela's sister."

"Sister?" No wonder the voice sounded familiar. "Angela never told me she had a sister."

"Not surprising. We weren't close."

"Your father didn't mention you, either."

"What's that supposed to mean?"

"Nothing. Are there any more siblings?"

"Thank God, no."

Jake shook his head to clear the shock waves. "What do you want?"

"I want you to back off."

"Back off?"

"You really upset my parents this morning. They don't need some pompous PI putting outrageous theories in their heads. Can't you appreciate what a difficult time this is for them?"

"Yeah, I could tell they're really broken up over Angela's death."

His sarcasm was apparently not lost on Maleena because she struggled with a response. "As…as diplomats, my parents have learned to…to keep their emotions under control, Mr. Stone. My sister's death was devastating, but they're coping in their own way."

"Your mother's way is a little unorthodox."

"Her reaction was a byproduct of wanting to protect me."

"I don't understand."

"I'm getting married in a few months. She has been totally immersed in the wedding planning. This is a big deal for her. First child getting married and all that."

"Congratulations, Miss Reardon. I wouldn't want to overshadow the happy event by trying to find out the truth about her other daughter's death."

Maleena's voice tightened. "Don't be cruel, Mr. Stone. My wedding is a very public, high society event. I'm marrying Senator Jim Blackwell."

Jake whistled. "I can understand your concern. I'm sure you wouldn't want to see the headline: One Reardon daughter gets murdered, and the other gets married."

"Fuck you!"

"*Tsk, tsk*, Miss Reardon. That's no way for a young society maiden to talk. What would your mother say?"

"I don't really give a damn. But I'm beginning to think I need to talk to Detective Smithson myself."

"Go ahead. Be my guest."

"I don't need your permission to ask him why he's not investigating *you*. If you're right and Angela was murdered, you should be the prime suspect. As I recall, women are murdered most often by a significant man in their lives. And my father said you were sniffing around Angela."

Jake bristled. "For your information, I don't sniff. Maybe you let men sniff around you, Miss Reardon, but Angela was too much of a lady to ever allow that sort of male behavior."

"So, if you weren't after sex, were you after her money?"

"If I was after her money, why would I kill her? I'm sure I'm not a beneficiary in her will. You can't have it both ways. Maybe *you* were after money. A bigger inheritance is a great motive for murder."

"I'm warning you, Mr. Stone. Back off. You're hurting my parents and me, not helping us. If you make trouble, my fiancé has the power to deal with you."

"Don't screw with me."

"Then disappear. Let Angela go peacefully. And don't ruin our lives with your goddamn inability to cope."

"Now you listen to me. If you or your parents get in my way, I'll contact every media outlet on the East Coast to tell them the Reardon family is impeding the Angela Reardon murder investigation. Will my news play very well with your wedding announcement in *The Washington Post*?"

"Is that a threat, Mr. Stone?"

"No, Miss Reardon. It's a promise."

Chapter 9

Twelve weeks earlier

Saturday morning was hell.

Angela peered at her reflection in the bathroom mirror. Puffy, bloodshot eyes revealed pain and disappointment. The relationship with Jake was over, and she cared that it was.

Would she never learn? Men were after only one thing. Why had she thought Jake would be different? For Christ's sake, she'd interrupted him having sex the first time they'd met. If she'd held on to her first impression that he was a jerk, she wouldn't be in pain now. Jake was charming, but she should have been strong enough to withstand those charms. Jake was complex, but she should have known that beneath all those intriguing layers was still the same hideous male core.

She needed to escape. Fresh air. Fresh start.

Chelsea barked insistently as Angela clipped the leash to the dog's collar before strolling to Tidelands Park. San Diego Bay stretched out toward downtown and the Coronado Bay Bridge rose like a graceful ribbon of concrete, but she was oblivious to the beautiful setting. She hardly noticed Chelsea tugging at the leash, trying to run to the solitary man sitting several benches away. The entire time, she could only think about how much she missed Jake.

Despite the walk with her dog, she still couldn't stop the downward spiral of her emotions. Desperate for a distraction, she tried to finish some work at her shop and thoroughly cleaned the condo. But by evening, the walls were closing in on her. Without looking for the movie schedule, she drove across the bridge into downtown to the Horton Plaza mall.

Once ensconced in the sparsely occupied theater, she wondered what in the world she was doing. Did she have a subconscious need not to be alone? When the lights dimmed, her agony swelled. Would the pain ever stop? It had been four years, but there were moments when she suffered as if it were yesterday. Moments like the morning she'd fainted in Jake's bedroom. Moments like the night she'd suffered a panic attack at his house. Moments like last night when he broke up with her.

No one understood—not the police, the shrinks, or the support groups. How could she ever have an intimate relationship with a normal man, a real boyfriend, or a faithful husband, if she wasn't a complete woman? Didn't want to be a woman? Was afraid to be a woman?

She hadn't allowed herself to cry all day, and she'd worn sunglasses so no one could see her pain. Now she stuffed them in her purse. Staring straight ahead at a movie screen she didn't see, she let the tears come. First a single teardrop, then another. Soon, salty wetness glazed her cheeks, but she didn't care. Her sobs were stifled, caught in her throat and trapped in her ears.

"Is this seat taken?" a man whispered.

Cocooned in misery, she almost didn't hear him speak to her. She ignored him and stared blindly toward the screen.

"May I—"

"No. I'm saving it for my boyfriend," she snapped without looking at him. *Go away. Don't even think about bothering me.*

Even in the dark theater, Angela sensed the man sitting down next to her. Despite the tears on her cheeks, she turned to confront him for his rudeness.

"Hello, Angela," he said.

"Jake?" She blinked rapidly as if seeing a ghost.

"Do I still qualify as your boyfriend?"

The lump in her throat refused to budge. "I don't know. Do you?"

"I'd like to." He lifted her hand from the armrest, raised it to his lips, and kissed it gently. "We need to talk."

"How did you find me?" Reason was returning.

"PI, remember?"

"You've been spying on me?"

"Let's call it surveillance."

"Ssshhh," a voice in the darkness scolded.

He kissed her hand again and grasped it firmly. "Let's grab a drink or cup of coffee and talk."

He stood and pulled her up with him. She allowed him to lead her down the row of seats and into the aisle. As she exited the theater with Jake's hand on the small of her back, Angela struggled to regain her composure. She swiped the remaining wetness from her cheeks and brushed her hair back from her face. She avoided looking directly at him until they were in the parking garage.

He turned her toward him and bracketed her shoulders with his hands. "Where do you want to go?"

"Home."

Jake frowned. "Hmmm. I thought…Never mind. Am I invited?"

Angela pressed trembling fingers against her mouth and closed her eyes. She wanted him to come home with her so badly, but why prolong the inevitable breakup? She was almost through Day One of rehabilitation. Why put it off and have to start over again later?

Why? Because she wanted this man more than she'd wanted anyone in a long time.

* * *

Angela's white BMW pulled out of the Horton Plaza parking garage just ahead of him. He hung back in his black Corvette, shaking his head at the ironic symbolism: her in white, him in black. *Crap.*

The irony wasn't the only thing bothering him.

Last night's passionate kiss had backfired.

To Angela, the kiss had apparently signaled the end of the relationship, and frankly, her reaction stunned him. Their dates had been very enjoyable, but the lack of sex or even sexual attraction on her part had convinced him Angela didn't consider the relationship serious. There was always a certain distance, a slight aloofness in her manner that kept him at arm's length. But today, not knowing he was watching, she'd let down her guard. Without her shield of detachment, Angela had exposed the depth of her emotional attachment.

So why didn't Jake feel smug about his discovery? He grimaced. Because the damn kiss had backfired by having an unintentional effect on him.

Shit. His fingers threaded through his hair as he watched the

BMW's turn signal blinking rapidly. Last night, his heart had raced just as fast during the kiss. It had taken all his willpower to pull his lips away from her warm, sweet mouth. Her whimper of surrender had sparked a sudden hot desire inside him. Simple lust. Lust for the unattainable, for the prize he couldn't have.

He shook his head miserably. What was he trying to prove? He should never have gone without sex this long. At Filippi's, he'd lied when he suggested he'd been screwing other women. In fact, he had canceled his masseuse appointments and hadn't been with another woman since meeting Angela.

He didn't believe in celibacy. Why the hell was he practicing it?

As he drove across the bridge, the scene distracted him for a moment. Hundreds of reflections from downtown lights danced on the black velvet bay while thousands of stars twinkled in the black satin sky. Peaceful. Beautiful.

Wrong. Jake's expression hardened. Peaceful and beautiful didn't exist for him. He was a killer with a job to do. But he was also a human being. And he knew in his soul that killing Angela Reardon was wrong.

Despite his best efforts to uncover anything about the government secrets she'd stolen and sold, he had failed. Her only connection to the State Department was her father, who appeared to be nothing more than a lackluster diplomat. The countries where Randall Reardon had served were not hotbeds of terrorism or even old Cold War enemies. Jake struggled to imagine what possible national security-compromising information had tempted Angela and led to her downfall.

She wasn't an angel, but she was damn close. She certainly didn't deserve to die.

What had she done to piss off someone at the CIA enough to want her murdered? Jake couldn't fathom a single possibility. God, it would help if he knew.

* * *

Angela busied herself with switching on the lamps in the cozy family room of her condo while she waited apprehensively for Jake to arrive. She'd left the garage door open, and when she heard it close, she straightened and drew a deep, cleansing breath. *I can do this.*

Jake appeared in the doorway, his expression serious.

"Coffee?" she asked.

"No. I'll fix drinks." He headed for the wet bar in the living room.

Angela's gaze followed him, his rugged attractiveness registering for the millionth time. *If only—* She pushed the wistful thought away and focused on choosing a seat. Not the couch where they usually sat together. Instead, she chose the chair farthest from the couch. She settled into it, slipped off her shoes, and pulled her feet up under her. Casual. Relaxed.

A façade.

Jake returned with two glasses filled with Jack Daniel's on the rocks. His eyes shifted between the couch and Angela's chair.

"Have you already forgotten I don't drink whiskey?"

He ignored the jab. Handing her a glass, he smiled. "I think this talk will go better if you have a *real* drink."

"That bad, huh?" She sipped, choked, and coughed. "Can't be any worse than this stuff." But she drank again, carefully.

She peered at him defiantly while he swallowed a long drag and kept his eyes locked on her.

"I apologize again for my behavior at Filippi's. I don't like being accused of something I'm not guilty of. You blindsided me. I have no idea where the whole idea of breaking up came from. It certainly wasn't on my mind."

She sipped the whiskey and grimaced. "Then I should apologize for jumping the gun. But thinking about it today, it's probably better to get it over with sooner than later."

"You want to break up?"

Angela stared at the amber liquid before raising it to her mouth and then said, "It's probably the right thing to do."

He studied her with darkening eyes. "Well, speaking for myself, I was enjoying our relationship. I guess I was the only one."

"You know that's not true."

"Do I? I like you, Angela. I'm attracted to you. But I don't get a similar vibe in return."

She rested her head back against the chair and raised her gaze to the ceiling. "It's not your fault."

"Look at me, damn it. Look me in the eye and tell me you don't feel anything for me."

His harsh tone slapped away her protective façade. Suddenly, she felt naked. A familiar tightness in her chest warned her to be careful. "You don't understand, Jake."

"Try me."

"If you insist. But I spelled it out last night. I know how things go with men. No sex—no relationship. Been there, done that. You want to sleep with me. That's the truth, isn't it?" She squirmed under the increasing intensity of his gaze.

Jake's eyes never left hers as he downed the remainder of his drink. He slammed the glass on the coffee table, causing her to jump.

"Yeah, that's the truth. Damn right, I want to sleep with you. You're a beautiful, sexy woman, although you work very hard not to be. And I'm a normal, horny guy. You turn me on big time." He shrugged. "Maybe this wouldn't be so hard if I hadn't gone without sex since I met you and—"

Angela started. "But you said—"

"I lied. I was mad. I wanted to hurt you." He paused. "I'm sorry."

"Your masseuse?"

He shook his head. "No, not even her. Now help me out here. Why are you so down on sex?"

She drained her glass. Jake grabbed his tumbler and reached for hers. She hesitated before allowing him to take it.

He returned a few minutes later with both refilled. Angela deliberately set hers on the end table as she watched Jake drink deeply before dropping back onto the couch.

His gaze caught hers and held. "Have you come up with an answer yet?"

"I don't think I need to repeat what I told you about my moral objection to premarital sex."

"I agree. Please don't repeat that bullshit. Tell me the truth."

"You think I'm lying?"

"That or you've told the lie so often you've started believing it yourself. But I don't think that's the case."

The tightness in her chest morphed into a burning ball in her stomach. She pulled her gaze away from his, snatched her drink from the end table, and downed two large swallows. She coughed and licked a drip off her lower lip. Her gaze rose to find Jake's eyes glued on her mouth. Her pulse accelerated, panic bubbling just below the surface. Carefully, she set down the glass and stood up. *Escape.*

"This isn't going to work, Jake. You should leave," she said.

The thin line of his lips, the firm set of his jaw, and the smoldering anger in his eyes were his answer.

Angela swallowed hard and stood her ground. "Please go." She coughed on a ragged breath. *I can't last much longer.*

His expression softened slightly, and he looked down at his hands before rising. With three long strides, he towered in front of her. His face revealed a hint of uncertainty, but he wasn't surrendering or leaving.

She took an involuntary step backward when he reached for her shoulders, but his strong hands caught her anyway.

"I'm not leaving until you tell me the truth."

She looked past him. Her words came in staccato bursts. "I-told-you. I'm-morally-opposed—"

"Cut the crap! Moral opposition doesn't make you pass out or trigger a panic attack."

"You knew?" Her voice trembled.

"Not at first. Your hypoglycemia excuse was a crock, although I bought it that morning. But when you fled in panic the next night, it didn't take a rocket scientist to realize something more serious was going on."

Suddenly, her knees buckled. Jake's arms slipped around her and pulled her to him. She went rigid, her heart thundering.

"Talk to me, Angela. Did you date an abusive bastard?"

She buried her face in his shoulder but didn't respond. Volcanic pressure was building inside.

"I haven't hurt you. Don't punish me for another guy's sins."

"Stop, Jake."

His lips touched her ear as he whispered, "Don't sacrifice our relationship because of some asshole's bad behavior. Tell me—"

"No. Stop. Leave me alone." Her fists shoved at his chest.

"Damn it. Tell me."

"No!"

The volcano erupted. Her hands flew into his face, clawing, scratching. He handcuffed both her wrists in one strong hand. Her knee launched toward his groin, but he blocked it with his thigh.

"Easy, babe, easy," he said firmly.

"No!"

She jerked her body around violently, elbows flailing. He released her wrists and held her against him in a bear hug.

"Stop, Angela. Talk to me."

"I can't!"

Her entire body was lava. *Don't make me say the word. I can't say it. God, help me.* She twisted. Bucked. Kicked.

"Tell me what happened!" he yelled.

An anguished scream burst from her soul. She threw her head back with such force she almost ripped herself from his arms. "Raped! I was…raped," she gasped before collapsing in his arms.

Jake stiffened. "Raped," he breathed, and then growled, "Son of a bitch."

Limp, motionless, she clung to him for a long minute, fighting the panic. Her secret. She had revealed her vile secret. If their relationship wasn't already over, it surely was now.

She cringed when Jake's arm reached under her knees and lifted her. He carried her to the couch, sitting down with her on his lap. Still they didn't speak. He leaned back and cradled her against him. His heat radiated to warm her, comfort her.

"God, I'm sorry. I shouldn't have pushed you. Forgive me?"

She nodded and closed her eyes against the sting of tears. *Be strong.*

"How many years did the bastard get?" he asked with obvious bitterness.

Angela burrowed closer, shaking her head.

"What? Hasn't it gone to trial yet?"

She shuddered.

"No? Why the hell not?" Anger vibrated in his voice.

"I can't...remember. Event...amnesia."

"Amnesia? Shit."

She could almost hear his brain piecing the puzzle together. She didn't have to explain there had been no trial because she—the victim—couldn't identify the rapist or describe what had happened.

Jake could understand that. But he would never understand how not remembering made it even harder to heal. That she might never heal.

Chapter 10

Wearing only boxer briefs, Jake leaned back in the leather chair Wednesday morning and stared at the computer screen. He'd been working since 4:00 a.m., thanks to the nightmare. Again.

His succinct summary of Angela's life stared back at him.

Affluent, sophisticated, fiercely independent, well-educated.

Alienated from family. Not a positive fact, but definitely not unusual.

No enemies, few friends.

Twenty-nine years old, physically healthy.

Successful businesswoman.

Raped at age twenty-five.

The only significant black spot in her life was the rape. His analysis kept returning to that critical point.

Rape was horrendous in all cases, but something in Angela's experience had been especially devastating. She'd fought valiantly to recover in every other aspect of her life, but the sexual consequences of the rape had still plagued her.

As the victim, she'd lived with an ongoing, unrealistic fear of men, but someone else might also have continued to live with fear. Not fear of assault, but fear of discovery. Angela's rapist had never been identified. Would the bastard risk murder to silence his victim forever? Especially after four years of successful anonymity. Were his chances of being discovered now, after all this time, worth the risk of another heinous crime? A "yes" answer didn't seem reasonable.

But the possibility had been needling Jake for days. Unfortunately, he knew little about the crime. Angela's inability to discuss the rape had limited his knowledge of the facts, so his whole theory was a stretch. But it was the only theory he had to work with.

He was on his second pot of coffee when he phoned Detective Kent Smithson. It was a calculated gamble he chose to take. Getting arrested would put a serious kink in his plans.

"Morning, Smithson. It's your prime suspect." Hopefully, that was still only a joke. "Seriously, Kent, you got a minute?"

Smithson hesitated. "Yeah. You're not leaving town, are you?" He chuckled under his breath.

"Not unless you're after my ass."

"Not yet, Stone. Still working on it. What do you want?"

"I need to get some information from LAPD about an incident involving Angela four years ago. Can you help me?"

Long pause. A door clicked shut. "You talking about the rape?"

Jake's head jerked back in surprise. "Yeah. How'd you know—"

"I'm not stupid, Stone. I've been working this."

"I thought there was no Reardon case," he said mockingly.

"Shut up, asshole, and listen. The rape's a cold case. No leads. Nothing. How much do you know about it?"

"Angela shared a few things the cops and doctors had told her, but not much. She could hardly talk about it." He swallowed hard. "The rape left some damn serious psychological scars. I understand it's a horrible thing for any woman to recover from, so this may sound cruel. But as strong as Angela was in so many other ways, it puzzled me that she had such a terrible time recovering sexually. After four years, she still couldn't…She wasn't…okay."

Smithson cleared his throat. "When you hear the details, Stone, believe me, you'll understand."

"What do you mean?"

"Forget it. The guy you need to talk to is LAPD Detective Tim Olsen. He was the lead detective on the case. He'll remember it like it was yesterday."

"And you know all this how?"

"Because I talked to him yesterday."

"Shit. Why didn't you call me?"

"Because you're a suspect."

"Yeah, in a case that doesn't exist."

"That's right." Smithson read him Olsen's phone number and then paused. "Tell him I sent you and…good luck, Stone."

Jake stared at his suddenly silent cell. "Well, I'll be damned."

He tapped in the LAPD phone number. Within minutes, he was connected to the detective.

"Good morning, Detective Olsen. My name is Jake Stone. Coronado PD Detective Kent Smithson gave me your number and suggested I talk to you about the Angela Reardon rape case. Is this a good time?"

"No, actually, it's not. I'm heading into an interrogation. What's your connection to this?"

"What did Smithson tell you?"

"He told me about Ms. Reardon's suicide. Nothing about you. Care to enlighten me, Mr. Stone?" Olsen replied testily.

"Sure. I'm a security expert and private investigator. I've worked cases with Smithson a few times. Angela and I were dating. I don't think she committed suicide."

"You're thinking what? Murder?"

"Yeah. But I'm having a helluva time finding anyone with a motive."

"An unidentified rapist would work."

"Damn right. Can you help me?"

"Probably. I'm free this afternoon."

"What time should I call?"

Olsen hesitated. "You need to *see* this file, Mr. Stone, to really understand what happened to your girlfriend. It won't be easy, but—"

"I can be there by two."

"Fine." Olsen provided his address, got Jake's cell phone number, and then disconnected.

Jake was already frantically devising a plan. Before shutting down his laptop, he booked a hotel room for two nights. Logically, he knew not to get his hopes up, but his gut told him this was the break he'd been waiting for.

While throwing a few clothes into a duffel bag, he spotted Angela's picture lying on the nightstand. He'd placed it there as a reminder on Friday night when he vowed he would find the person who wanted her dead. Gingerly, he lifted the small photo.

"God, you're beautiful. I wish you'd worn that red dress for me," he murmured and then cleared his throat. "I may be on to something. Could be a twofer: a rapist and a murderer. Wish me luck."

He carefully slid the picture into his wallet and finished packing.

In the garage, he checked his box of "trade tools" before locking it in a hidden compartment in the Corvette's trunk. From his earliest days as a SEAL, he had learned to always be well-prepared, since his life often depended on it. He carried all the standard security and PI equipment: high-tech audio and video recorders, digital cameras, binoculars, latex gloves, disguises, handcuffs, various guns, and plentiful ammo. The combination-locked steel box also stored *special* tools—some legal, some not—for his darker occupation: silencers, chloroform, Kevlar vest, syringes, and vials of various substances.

Two hours after talking to Smithson, Jake headed north to meet with Detective Olsen. The ominous warnings from both detectives about the details of the rape tamped down his enthusiasm, but he refused to let his mind conjure up possibilities. He would wait for the facts.

LA traffic and smog enveloped him, further dampening his mood. When he finally jetted down the exit ramp, he breathed a sigh of relief.

Hoping to avoid unwanted attention in a building full of cops, Jake locked his Glock and shoulder holster in the car's custom-made, under-seat compartment. Before entering the LAPD offices, he assessed the area, activated the car alarm, and silently hoped the Corvette would still be there when he returned.

Inside, he surveyed the cluster of armed officers manning the security area. His throat tightened with a touch of uneasiness. During his years as a CIA assassin, he had served the citizens of America, too. His lethal services had filled his bank accounts but emptied his soul. Transformed him into an unlovable monster. His retirement from that heinous profession and the time spent reincarnating himself as a law-abiding security expert and private investigator had been tainted when he'd accepted the fraudulent Reardon contract.

Jake jammed his hands into the pockets of his sport coat and approached the security area. He breathed more easily when the process was completed without incident.

"Mr. Stone?" called a bear of a man standing off to one side as Jake stashed his wallet back into his pocket.

He glanced up. "Yes."

"Detective Tim Olsen."

The two men shook hands.

"Thanks for seeing me on such short notice, Detective."

"Sure. Follow me."

They wound their way through the maze of hallways until they reached a small office.

"Grab a seat," Olsen said, gesturing into the dreary room. "Coffee?"

"Thanks. Black."

A few minutes later, the man returned with Styrofoam cups in both hands. After handing one to Jake, he set the other cup on the desk and dropped heavily into his chair. Detective Tim Olsen looked forty-something with graying temples and a beer belly. He pulled a small ring of keys from his shirt pocket, unlocked a drawer, and retrieved a folder. Sighing, he laid the file on the desk.

Jake waited patiently while Olsen drank a long swig of coffee and grimaced.

"Tastes like shit by this time of day," he complained, placing the cup farther away. He eyed the folder as though dreading opening it.

"If Detective Smithson hadn't referred you, I wouldn't be wasting my time with you, Mr. Stone."

Jake swallowed a sarcastic response. "I know you're busy, Detective. I appreciate any information you can give me. I understand Angela Reardon's rape is an old case for you, but her disappearance occurred less than a week ago."

"Disappearance? Smithson said suicide, and I thought you suspected homicide."

"Well, that's the rub. I'm convinced she didn't commit suicide, but there's no evidence of murder. Since there's no body, who knows anything for sure."

"Now you're telling me you don't think she's dead?"

"I wish, but I'm a realist, Detective. And I intend to find the truth."

Olsen grunted in disbelief—or amusement. He opened and leafed through the file. "And why do you think you know so much more than the Coronado PD?"

"Well, I definitely know more about Angela than they do. We were very close."

The detective glanced up from the paperwork and smiled coldly. "Maybe you should be a suspect."

He glared back. "I'd gladly offer myself up as one if it would convince CPD to investigate the case as a homicide. But they're not interested. No, that's not fair. Smithson is a good man, a good cop. If he had any evidence to start an official investigation, he would. At least he pointed me in your direction. What can you tell me, Detective?"

Olsen stared, seeming to size him up. His gaze dropped to the file before he asked, "Did your girlfriend ever tell you about the rape?"

Jake wondered if the question arose from a professional or a prurient interest, but he kept his distaste hidden. "After we'd been dating a while, she told me it had happened. It was difficult for her to talk about, and I had no interest in hearing the details. Why?"

"Well, even immediately after the rape, the victim was unable to provide the investigating officers with details. And I mean *any* details. All the physical evidence pointed to rape, but the vic didn't have any memory of what had happened."

"Aren't rape victims often in shock?"

"Absolutely, and shock was considered. But a psychiatrist met with the vic several times and concluded she had event amnesia. I'm sure you know what that is."

Jake nodded. "A person's subconscious blocks the memory of a specific traumatic or unpleasant event. The few times Angela talked about the rape she sounded like it had happened to someone else, even though she got upset. It was objective, third-person, you know, not a first-person account."

"So the vic's memory never came back."

"The vic's name is Angela Reardon," Jake reminded him roughly.

"Right. Sorry." Stroking his chin, Olsen glanced back at the file. "Obviously, Ms. Reardon's amnesia made the case extremely difficult for us to pursue, but we did try. We interrogated her boyfriend, neighbors, family, friends, clients, fellow employees, and the owner of an…" Olsen frowned and peered more closely at the paper.

"What?" he asked, leaning forward.

The phone on the desk rang.

"Olsen." He listened. "Yeah, he's with me. I heard you got tied up in court, but I knew you wanted to talk to him. I was going to arrest him for murder and hold him here until you got back." He laughed at his joke and narrowed his eyes at Jake. "Okay, I'll tell him." Olsen hung up thoughtfully. "That was Detective Sean Burke. He was a patrol officer at the time and was one of the first at the crime scene. Shortly afterward, he was promoted to detective. I was the lead on the Reardon case, and he came to me and practically begged me to assign him to the investigation. Burke worked it longer, harder, deeper than anyone. He was a damn pit bull. Just wouldn't let it go. I got worried he was too personally invested. Thought he might have a crush on Ms. Reardon, you know. Anyway, he's *the man* on this one. He's been in court testifying today, but I left him a message about you." He jiggled the file. "You know how it is. The paperwork only tells you so much."

"True. And thanks."

Jake's surprise that Olsen had bothered to contact the other detective must have shown on his face because the detective suddenly grinned. "You didn't really think I was that much of an asshole, did you? Well, maybe you did."

A knock on the door saved Jake from answering.

A red-haired cop poked his head into the office. "Hey, Olsen."

"Come in. Burke, this is Jake Stone, the PI from San Diego." The two men shook hands and exchanged nods. Olsen closed the folder, stood, and handed it to Burke. "Why don't you go someplace private? Give Mr. Stone all the help you can."

"Yes sir."

Jake extended his hand across the desk. "Thanks for your help, Detective Olsen. If I come across any info that would help close this cold case for you, I'll be in touch."

"We'd appreciate it. Good luck, Mr. Stone. I hope you find what you're looking for."

Jake followed Detective Burke down a narrow hallway to a conference room, which wasn't much bigger than Olsen's office. The
metal folding chairs and table looked decades old. A huge white-
board hung on the front wall. The room smelled like stale coffee and
sweat.

The cop laid the file on the table and disappeared without a word.
A few minutes later, he returned with two Styrofoam cups and a
backpack.

"Special LAPD coffee. If you can swallow this shit, it's guaran-
teed to keep you awake until you pass out from exhaustion," Burke
said.

Jake cringed when the detective set a cup of the black sludge in
front of him. He'd carefully avoided drinking any of the coffee offered by Olsen and hoped he was as lucky this time.

Burke's expression turned grim as he opened the folder. "This was
my first rape case and also my first case as a detective. Maybe that's
why I can't forget it." He sighed heavily. "What exactly are you looking for, Mr. Stone?"

"Can you drop the 'mister'? Makes me feel real old." The crack
brought a faint smile to the man's face, a face Jake judged to be only
a few years younger than his. "I'm looking for a motive for murder.
I'm sure Olsen told you the Coronado PD has ruled Angela's death
a suicide, but I'm not buying it. Angela wouldn't commit suicide."

"I agree." Burke's gaze fixed on the paperwork. "At least not the
Angela I remember. She was a fighter. Before she...died, did she remember anything about the rape that might help us?"

"Not that she told me. But it was hell for her to talk about, so I
barely know anything."

When the detective's eyes slid up to Jake's, they reflected a myriad of emotions: sorrow, frustration, regret, helplessness. But anger was what resounded when he spoke. "I'd give my right nut to catch the bastard who did this to Angela." He paused. "You don't mind if I call her by her first name, do you? While I was working the case, she insisted on using first names."

"I'm sure she would still prefer that."

"Thanks." He shook his head. "I can't believe she's dead. Suicide or murder, either one is unbelievable. It just doesn't seem right for such bad shit to happen to such a nice lady." He paused as if debating internally. "I never gave up on her case," he said, pulling the backpack onto his lap. He extracted a large manila envelope and laid it on the table. "I'm not supposed to have this stuff, but I wanted my own copies so I could work it whenever I had some time. Never solved it, though, and now it doesn't matter." He ran a hand across his eyes.

Jake's instincts registered sincerity and integrity as he listened to Burke's lament. He could understand the man's frustration. This cop had gone above and beyond the call of duty hoping to get justice for Angela. He would be a good ally.

"Detective—"

"Sean or Burke works better."

"Okay, Burke. It may still matter. A rapist wanting to guarantee eternal anonymity is the only lead I have as a murder motive. I've got to work it, until I prove or eliminate it. How much can you help me?"

"I'll do everything I can. I don't mind bending a few rules, but nothing illegal. I hope to have a career here."

"Understood. Now, can you start from the beginning? Angela told me so little, and she may have sugarcoated it."

"All right, but brace yourself. I hope you have a strong stomach because it's some pretty sick shit."

Jake's stomach knotted. "Just give it to me straight."

Burke glanced briefly at the reports but then leaned back in the chair. "About ten thirty Sunday morning, LAPD got a call from Becky Smelter, one of the spinster ladies who lived in the other unit of the duplex. She and her sister, Mary Smelter, were worried for several reasons. Angela's dog, Chelsea, had been barking all night. Also, the three ladies had a standing date for Sunday breakfast at nine thirty. When Angela didn't come over for breakfast, Becky called but got no answer. They also tried her cell phone. No answer either."

He spoke as if he had every word from the file memorized. Maybe he did.

"They thought they'd heard faint noises from Angela's unit earlier in the morning so they put their ears against the adjoining walls in several places." He smiled. "Can't you just picture two old ladies with their ears glued to the walls? Anyway, thank God they did. Eventually, they heard moaning and crying through the bedroom wall. After knocking on Angela's front door and getting no answer, they got spooked. They had a key but didn't go in. They were convinced something was terribly wrong."

Absently, he sipped his coffee and stared off into space as if he was seeing that distant morning unfold. Jake considered asking a question but decided to let Burke's recollection flow naturally.

"My partner and I rolled in at about eleven. Still no answer at the door, so they let us in with their key. God, it was awful. We found Angela on the bed, totally naked, gagged, blindfolded, ears plugged, arms and legs tied down. Mary Smelter followed us in. She screamed and fainted. We called for two ambulances. Angela was out of her mind. When I removed the gag, she tried to bite me. After my partner and I untied her, we had to restrain her. She was fighting us like she thought *we* had raped her."

Lost in thought, he raised his cup but set it down without taking a drink. Still staring into space, he spoke quietly. "Angela was a mess. Bruises already darkening all over her body. Big red welts that looked like whip burns. And her eyes…God, I'll always remember her eyes. I've never seen eyes as wild as hers. I thought the ambulance would never get there."

Burke took a swig of coffee and shook his head, perhaps trying to erase the images that seemed too horrible even after four years.

Jake waited patiently for him to continue. Detective Olsen had been right. The young cop was obviously too emotionally involved in the case. Not good from a law enforcement point of view, but exactly what Jake needed to get the whole story.

"She was babbling nonsense. Couldn't even tell us her name. The paramedics shot her up with a sedative. They don't like to do that, but they were afraid she was going to hurt herself. Or one of them. When they were wrapping her in a sheet before lifting her onto the gurney, I noticed the cuts on her butt."

"Cuts on her butt?" Jake asked, frowning. He leaned forward in his chair.

Burke exhaled loudly. "Shit yeah. It was sick, just sick. The perp had carved two checkmarks—each about an inch long—in her right butt cheek. I'll tell you more about the cuts later."

The cop set his cup on the table and stood. He cracked his knuckles and started pacing.

"They kept Angela in the hospital for a week, mostly on the psychiatrist's orders. The medical report made me puke. The perp had worked her over bad. Even bruised her ribs. Blood and semen…everywhere…if ya know what I mean. He obviously wasn't worried about a DNA match. He was right—we never got one. He lucked out in another way, too. Angela had event amnesia. The shrinks told her details about the nature of her injuries trying to trigger her memory." Burke turned tortured eyes to meet Jake's. "Can you imagine living through hell and then having someone tell you what you went through? She had to survive it twice."

"No, I can't imagine living through any of it. It's amazing Angela recovered as much as she did. I knew she was brave, but this…this…" Jake cleared his throat and then looked away. "Didn't the Smelter sisters hear anything during the night?"

Burke grabbed the nearest chair, swung it around, and straddled it. He gripped the back with one hand and ran the other through his short, wavy red hair. His hazel eyes focused hard on Jake. "Yeah, they did. This is where it started getting freaky. Remember I said Mary Smelter fainted?"

Jake nodded, straining to catch every word.

"We followed the ambulances to the hospital. After they checked Mary over, the ER doctor let my partner go in and question her. Meanwhile, I questioned Becky in the waiting area. Their stories were identical, practically used the same vocabulary. A little spooky, actually."

He jumped up from the chair and paced rapidly, his hands gesturing constantly.

"They both reported hearing a lot of noise from Angela's place until about three that morning. Said it kept them awake. And it was totally out of character for Angela, who was usually very quiet and considerate. When her front door slammed, they peeked out the upstairs windows. Angela was leaving with a tall, blond, medium-built white man wearing a suit and carrying a department store-type shopping bag. They claimed Angela was dressed in a tight, black mini-skirt, skimpy red halter-top, and high-heeled red boots. Becky Smelter said she distinctly remembered the outfit because Angela never dressed 'like a slut.' Her words, not mine. The couple walked down the block and drove off in a large black sedan. Mary thought it was a Benz; Becky wasn't sure."

"What happened when you interrogated the guy?" Jake asked.

The cop slammed his fist into the wall and then spun around, his eyes burning with pain and anger.

"Fucking nothing happened," he snapped harshly. "Angela said she hadn't been on a date. Said there was no guy. She denied having company, going out at all, or making a lot of noise. Even worse, she claimed she didn't own those clothes. A search of her place didn't turn up the outfit either."

"Damn. Were the old ladies hallucinating?"

The detective stomped over to stand directly in front of him. "Hell if I know. They seemed to be very credible witnesses. They repeated the exact story several times."

"I'm confused about the timeline," Jake said, rubbing his temples. "The noise lasted until three o'clock. *After that*, the Smelters saw Angela leave with a man. I take it she didn't look beat up then. So the rape occurred later when Angela returned, with or without the same guy. Right?"

"Right."

"What time did she come home?"

"The Smelters went to bed. Never heard Angela return."

"Did they hear any noise later during the rape?"

"Nope. Nothing until they heard the faint noises after they got up in the morning."

Scowling, Jake threaded his fingers through his hair. "Strange. Forced entry?"

"No. No scratches on the locks, no damage to the doorjamb. When we got there, the front door was locked. Patio door was locked. No broken windows, all closed and latched. Weird, huh? Angela opened the door to someone, and he was polite enough to lock up when he left after raping her. Bastard."

"Prints?"

"Must've worn gloves. Funny thing. Didn't give a damn about leaving his DNA everywhere but wore gloves the whole night."

"His prints must be on file somewhere, and he knew it."

"Good guess. All kinds of organizations, schools, and businesses require a fingerprint check, though. Who knows where his prints could be recorded. Anyway, we don't have a single print from the perp to run against any database."

"What about the cuts on her butt?"

Burke dropped back into his chair and scooted it nearer to Jake. "Those were freaky, too. A Vice detective heard about them and offered an explanation. They weren't checkmarks. They were J's. There's this pimp—goes by J.J.—who runs a high-priced escort service for a very select clientele. Supposedly, the johns—er, the clients—are an elite bunch: politicians, corporate execs, Hollywood big shots, religious muckety-mucks. You get the idea. There's so much pressure from city hall because of the political connections of these assholes that LAPD is forced to keep its distance from J.J.'s escort service. Pisses us all off big time." He shook his head with disgust. "Anyway, the story goes that, before this pimp signs up a new girl, he has to fuck her. Then he cuts two J's into her ass to show she's been approved. Kinda like J.J.'s Good Fucking Seal of Approval."

"Holy shit. Did you question the pimp?"

"Of course. He had an ironclad alibi. At least two dozen witnesses confirmed he was at a private party on Sunset until three. Then he went home with two bimbos and his girlfriend, who all vouched for him. Besides, he's a short, fat, black dude. Doesn't fit the Smelters' description."

"But their tall, white mystery man might not be the perp if he didn't come back with Angela later."

"True. But J.J. wasn't a DNA match to the fluids left at the scene. And neither Angela nor the sisters recognized him from mug shots." Burke paused. "You knew Angela. Do you think she was auditioning to be a hooker?"

"Good God, no."

"Well, neither do I."

"What else do you have?"

"Nothing, really. The shrink worked with Angela until she couldn't take it anymore. I think she moved to San Diego to get away from us. We kept trying to make her remember something so painful her brain had blocked it out." Burke pressed both hands against his temples. "Sometimes I felt like we were torturing her. I hated it."

"I'm sure she understood and appreciated what you were trying to do."

"God, I hope so. It tore me up when she left. Part of me wanted to, you know, help her heal. Protect her. Take care of her. Maybe *I* scared her away."

"Hey, don't beat yourself up over it. Even after all this time, it was hard for me to get close to her."

"Hard? But you did get close." Burke's eyes narrowed slightly, as if seeing Jake in a new light. "How long were you two together?"

"We dated for only three months. But we were serious."

"As 'serious' as you wanted, or did you want more than Angela was willing to give?" the detective asked with more than a hint of suspicion.

"Shit. Not you, too." Jake's eyes turned to flint, ready to spark a full-blown blaze in a heartbeat. "I'm sick and tired of you cops looking at me like I'm a suspect."

Burke returned a red-hot glare. "Has anyone checked *your* alibi?"

"I don't need a goddamn alibi. Coronado PD already took my statement. But for your fucking information, I was with Angela earlier that night. She was perfectly fine when I left her condo about midnight. Ask yourself this: Would I be stirring up all this shit if I'd killed her?"

Tension crackled between them as Burke considered Jake's argument. Finally, he eased back. "Sorry, man. The closest male is often the guilty male. I just can't believe…" He sighed.

Jake inhaled deeply and blew some tension out along with the air. "I understand. I'm barely holding it together myself."

"So, what do you think?"

"Possible motive. The rapist could've been afraid all this time that Angela would eventually identify him. Chances are he wouldn't have known about her amnesia," Jake speculated.

"Workable theory, although rapists who murder their vics tend to kill them at the time of the rape, not years later."

"Agreed. Maybe something happened recently that triggered a renewed threat of identification."

"True. If he tracked her all the way to Coronado, he must've known who she was," Burke said.

"Not necessarily. I'm sure the rape made the news."

"Yeah, the rape did, but not the vic's name."

"Really?" Jake's tone was skeptical.

"Yeah. No leaks. I think everyone connected with the case felt like she'd been through such hell they were especially careful to protect her identity."

"Okay. That means the guy knew who Angela was when he raped her and has kept tabs on her for the last four years."

"Without her knowing, obviously," Burke said.

"Right. You know, I'm still confused about the Smelters seeing Angela leaving with the guy. And the missing clothes."

"I lost a lot of sleep over it, too."

"Remember anything else that might help me?"

"Wish I did. Damn, I'd love to solve this one." Burke paused. "Even though she's gone."

"Well, I'm focused on what just happened, and this rape is the only potential lead I have. Maybe we can get a twofer. I really appreciate your help." His gaze shifted to the official LAPD file. "I sure hope I can remember everything you told me."

"Oh, I don't think that'll be a problem." Burke stared at the large manila envelope he'd taken out of his backpack earlier. He pushed it over to Jake. "Put it to good use. I need it all back if you don't solve this. But honestly, I hope I never have to look at it again. Now that Angela's at peace, I'd kinda like some myself."

* * *

Jake's brain was firing on all cylinders during the drive from the LAPD building to the Doubletree Hotel where he'd made a reservation. He glanced repeatedly at the envelope lying on the passenger seat. Burke's information was a gold mine, and he couldn't wait to start digging. Finally, something concrete to work with.

Out of habit, Jake patted his Glock in the shoulder holster under his sport coat as he climbed from the Corvette. Comforting familiarity. He scanned the area, taking inventory of vehicles, people, and landmarks before retrieving the computer case and duffel bag from the trunk. While checking in, he added five nights to his reservation. He had a lot of work to do and people to find.

Antsy with anticipation, he settled into the two-room suite quickly. With his gun and bottle of Jack Daniel's on the table, he sat down to work.

Jake switched on his laptop and dumped the contents of Burke's envelope on the table. Since his first action item was to find the Smelter sisters, he snagged the contact information sheet. Older people didn't generally move often so he hoped they would still be living in the duplex.

He spotted their phone number on the list and called.

"Hello," answered a woman with a raspy voice.

"Hello. I'm trying to reach Mary and Becky Smelter."

"I'm not buying anything," she said loudly and hung up.

Jake pulled the phone away from his ear. "Damn." He redialed. This time, he said, "Hi, my name is Jake Sto—"

The phone went dead. He laughed, sipped his J.D., and thought a few moments before a third try.

"I'm a friend of Angela Reardon," he said quickly when she answered. He held his breath, waiting to see if she was going to hang up. Again.

After a long pause, the woman said, "Angela doesn't live here anymore."

Jake released his breath. "I know. I'm actually trying to reach former neighbors of hers, Mary and Becky Smelter."

Another long pause. "What do you want?"

"Is this Becky or Mary Smelter?"

"Yes."

Jake arched his eyebrows. "Ma'am, which Smelter sister are you?"

She cleared her throat. An avalanche of words followed. "I'm Becky. My dear sister passed away two years ago. I wrote Angela all about it. How Mary had a heart attack and lingered for weeks until the big one hit her and took her home. Angela called, very upset. She sent flowers to the funeral home for Mary *and* flowers here for me. So sweet. Just the way she always was. We missed her terribly when she moved, but we understood why she had to leave. I haven't heard from her in a long time. If you're a friend of Angela's, how come you don't know Mary's gone?"

It took Jake a second to realize Becky had come up for air and asked him a question.

"Huh? Well, you see Angela doesn't like to talk about living in LA because of what happened to her."

Becky's breath caught. "You know about that?"

"Yes. And it's why I need to talk to you. I'm working with Detective Burke, trying to finally solve the case."

"Oh my. Sean is such a sweet boy. He was so kind when he interviewed Mary and me all those times. Not like the other detective who treated us like we'd lost our minds. Mary's mind was sharp as a tack until the day she died, I'll have you know. And my mind is better than many young people's minds today. So many of them have fried their brains with drugs. It's a wonder they can even think at all. Sean was so broken-hearted when he couldn't find the...the jerk who hurt Angela. It was all so mysterious. But Sean kept working and working. He had a crush on her, you know. Even after Angela moved, he'd call us to see if we'd remembered anything—"

"Yes, Sean told me you and Mary were terrific witnesses. May I come talk to you tomorrow?"

"I suppose so. You know it's been four years, but I remember it like it was yesterday. And to think that awful, awful crime occurred right next door. It was the most horrible thing that ever happened to anyone we knew. Other than dying, of course. And at our age, many of our friends have been dying lately. Just last week, Shelly—"

"Would nine tomorrow morning be okay with you, Ms. Smelter?"

"It's *Miss* Smelter, but I may let you call me Becky after I meet you. I'll have to wait and see if I like you. I can't stand the way perfect strangers get too familiar these days."

"May I come see you tomorrow morning at nine?" Jake asked again.

"Fine. Bring donuts." She hung up.

Chuckling, Jake drained his glass and closed his eyes. His stomach growled, reminding him it was after 6:00 p.m. He grabbed the room service menu and ordered a full steak dinner and a bottle of pinot noir. It was going to be a long night.

While waiting for dinner to arrive, he began to organize the pile of documents from Burke's envelope. He forced himself into objective work mode, keeping himself detached from the subject.

Scanning the contact sheet, he found addresses and phone numbers for everyone he could think of, including the infamous J.J. and his girlfriend. He leafed through the stack of reports, thinking how the officers and detectives had probably hated doing the paperwork. He arranged the reports in chronological order for more understandable reading. Next came dozens of pages of interrogations—old, but required, reading. Several sheets were lab reports. Jake already knew there hadn't been a DNA match and no prints belonging to the perp had been found at the scene. But Burke had never given up. The last DNA test had been run only six months ago. No match with any database. Again. The perp still wasn't in the system.

The last item was an envelope labeled "Photographs." Jake was holding it, staring at it, when a loud knock announced the arrival of his dinner.

He switched on the television and tried to watch the news while he ate, but none of the stories held any interest for him. The only thing in the world that mattered to Jake Stone at that moment was finding who had paid to have Angela Reardon killed.

After moving his dinner to the table, he grabbed the pile of reports. The first one was written by Burke's partner. Despite the poor writing and sketchy details, the crime scene materialized inside Jake's head. He finished reading, drained his wine, and poured another glass.

Burke's report of that morning was next. Jake's stomach clenched as he laid it next to his plate and stabbed another bite of steak. He ate slowly, distractedly. Burke's words painted a heartbreaking, gut-wrenching picture of a brutal, sadistic rape. Jake stopped chewing and pushed the plate away. The words on the paper came alive with the agony of the victim, the sympathy of the young cop, and the unimaginable evil of the rape.

Suddenly, Jake lunged from the chair and raced to the bathroom.

After puking his dinner into the toilet, he sat on the bathroom floor for a long time. His arms were draped over his bent knees, and his head rested back against the cool, ceramic tile wall. He squeezed his eyes shut and gritted his teeth against the pain. But the burning was not the need to vomit again.

It was guilt. Pure, unadulterated guilt. Guilt like he'd never experienced.

The pain swelled inside his chest until he thought he would explode. Still it didn't stop. The pressure swept up his neck into his head, a pounding crescendo climbing to a climax.

He ripped a towel from the rack and buried his face in it.

The thick terrycloth muffled his anguished cry.

Chapter 11

Twelve weeks earlier

The next morning Jake maintained a silent vigil. Watching. Pondering. Grieving.

Even in sleep, agony plowed furrows in Angela's forehead.

Pain and guilt gripped Jake. Feelings born from forcing her to tell him the truth about her problem with sex. He'd never felt this way after any of his kills. In fact, he had watched brave comrades die in battle and not grieved this deeply. Was he suffering because he had pushed her so hard to reveal something she wanted to keep secret?

He gulped as terrible memories of last night drifted in. Angela's anguish had enveloped them both as she'd struggled to give a brief description of the trauma from four years ago. He'd listened, asked no questions.

After she fell asleep in his lap, he'd sat for an hour lost in thought.

A devil on his left shoulder had coaxed him to finish the job, to complete the contract. To use the sleeping pills in her medicine cabinet. Now. Tonight. Get it over with. Put Angela out of her misery. And him out of his.

But an angel on his right shoulder had pleaded for compassion. Jake's insistence on knowing the root of Angela's opposition to sex had brought her suffering to the surface. His lack of empathy had probably destroyed the progress she had fought so hard to achieve. He must bear the responsibility for reopening her excruciating wounds. Feeling he owed Angela for his horrid behavior, Jake had sided with the angel and shoved thoughts of the contract aside.

Eventually, he'd carried Angela to bed and tucked her under the covers. After taking care of Chelsea and securing the condo, he stood at the door with his hand on the knob. He closed his eyes and leaned his forehead against the wood. A sense of protectiveness like he'd never experienced washed over him. Finally, he'd surrendered, returned to her bedroom, and lay down beside her. Beside the traitor he was supposed to kill.

What the hell was he going to do now?

Absently, he lifted a strand of hair off her face, rubbed the silkiness, and draped it onto the pillow. He savored her high cheekbones, her long lashes, her full, luscious lips. His dick responded, but he shook off the lust guiltily. Maybe Angela was right about men—about him.

She stirred.

Instantly, he shut his eyes.

* * *

Angela's scream died in her throat. A man was in her bed, but he was fully clothed and on top of the covers. Still, she gasped sharply at the sight of Jake's head on the pillow next to hers. With a sigh of relief, she realized that, under the covers, she too was dressed.

She closed her eyes. The sheer effort to keep them open seemed too much.

And her emotions were as leaden as her body. Revealing her vile secret had not lightened her burden. Disappointment that their relationship was now definitely over actually added more weight. Of course, she'd known from the beginning it would end—just like all the others.

But, in fact, it hadn't ended like the others. This was the worst yet. Jake knew. Oh God, he knew the horrible truth about the rape, about the reason for her frigidity. About the amnesia that held her prisoner.

Tears welled up in her eyes, and she rolled over. *Dear God, let me be normal again. Please. Isn't four years of suffering enough?*

Drawing on strength she hadn't known she possessed, she silently climbed out of bed and tiptoed into the bathroom. She avoided her reflection in the mirror as she washed her face and brushed her teeth. While running a brush through her hair, she finally glanced at the mirror and practiced a smile. She might as well look nice when they said their last good-bye. Inhaling deeply, she opened the bathroom door and froze.

Jake was gone.

Angela stumbled forward and collapsed on the bed. She gritted her teeth and willed the tears not to come.

It's better this way. No drama. No pity. No excuses. No lies.

She rolled onto her back, pressed her palms against her eyes, and then raked her fingers through her hair. *Today is the first day of the rest . . .*

A noise from downstairs intruded on the inspirational thought.

She bolted upright. Her wobbly legs carried her to the bedroom doorway. Cabinets closing, cups clanging, coffeemaker sputtering.

Jake.

Gripping the railing, Angela steadied herself as she hurried down the stairs. A minute later, she leaned against the kitchen doorjamb and watched Jake pour two cups of coffee.

"I thought you left," she said.

"Why would I leave?" he asked, turning toward her.

Her eyebrows arched in disbelief. "Oh, I don't know. Maybe because you found out I'm damaged goods."

Jake frowned. "Damaged goods? I can't believe you said that. What kind of jerk do you think I am?"

"A normal male jerk."

"Stop it, Angela. Give it a break." His expression grim, he set both cups on the kitchen table and sat down.

She hesitated, drew a deep breath, and joined him.

For several minutes, neither of them spoke as they sipped the steaming coffee. Finally, she broke the uncomfortable silence.

"Thank you for spending the night, but you don't need to stay any longer. I'm fine."

"If you believe that, then you're doing a damn good job of lying to yourself. But I'm not buying it."

She sighed emphatically. "I don't care if you believe me or not. I've done the best I could since it happened. If you don't like the results, too bad. It's my life."

Jake slurped his coffee while he stared out the kitchen window. His face failed to mask the debate inside his head. He turned back to Angela, his steel gray gaze nailing her to the chair. "Did you have a good sex life *before* the rape?"

Her lips pressed into a tight line. That he could say the word so easily meant he didn't fully comprehend the totality of the violation. "Yes. But it's none of your business."

"It is if I want to help you get it back."

"What are you talking about?"

"I agree you've done a tremendous job of moving on with the rest of your life. You're an incredible woman, Angela. But without sex, will you ever feel normal? Will you marry? Will you adopt children?" he asked, his tone challenging, as if he knew his words touched sensitive chords.

"None of your business."

"Look, damn it, I'm trying to be a nice guy. I can help you."

"Why would you want to?" She eyed him suspiciously. "Oh, I get it. It's a trick so you can sleep with me."

"Been there, done that."

"What?" Her voice rose a notch.

"Last night. Actually, I didn't sleep much, but I sure as hell spent the whole night in bed with you." He jiggled his eyebrows mischievously.

"You jerk."

"Sometimes. But last night, I was a perfect gentleman."

Folding her hands in her lap, she nodded. "Yes, you were. Thank you."

"Angela, look at me." Slowly, she met his gaze. "You don't want to cringe every time a man touches you. You don't want to panic every time a man kisses you. And if you're not dying to get your libido back, I'd bet your previous sex life wasn't really all that great."

"It was fine."

"Let's see if I can describe 'fine.' At twenty-five, you'd had maybe four or five sexual partners. They were all normal young men, no perverts or anything, but they never did much for you. Your pleasure wasn't their first priority." Jake stroked his chin, looking thoughtful. "Sex probably two or three times a week after you finally got to that point in the relationship. You'd only climax occasionally, maybe twice a month. But you'd always fake it the other times so the guy wouldn't feel bad. Never once did a man totally, completely satisfy you or make you lose control. Or make you scream in ecstasy without caring who heard." His eyes searched hers, but they weren't mocking, they were imploring. "Am I right?"

Angela swallowed her pride. "Close. Very close."

"I can fix all that," he said, his voice husky. "Sex with me would be a whole different experience. Believe me."

She huffed. "See. You do want to sleep with me." She jumped up and started for the door.

Jake swung off the chair and caught her by the shoulders. He gently pushed her back against the counter. "Yes, you're right. I already confessed last night, remember? I've wanted you since the day we met. But I haven't done anything to force myself on you, have I?" When she didn't answer, he shook her once. "Have I?"

"No."

"Honest to God, Angela, I won't hur—" He stopped abruptly, blinked, and gulped. "I won't…hurry this any faster than you want to go. And if you don't like it, you can tell me to go to hell."

She studied him for a long moment. "I don't know, Jake." She shook her head, cringing with indecision. "I'm…afraid," she whispered.

"Of me?"

"No. Of failing."

"Failure is not an option. What do you say?" He grinned seductively. "May I begin my twelve-step, sexual recovery program?"

She gulped. "I'm not sure. How would we start?"

He smiled. "Slow and easy. Actually, the kiss Friday night was step one. You didn't panic, which was good. While we continue practicing step one, we'll add step two."

"Which is?"

"This." He slid one arm around her back and pulled her closer. Instinctively, she crossed her arms in front of her. Jake eyed them and shook his head. "Wrap both arms around my waist." She didn't move. "Angela." She smiled faintly and obeyed. "Now I'm going to embrace you by holding you against my chest. Of course, that means those beautiful tits are going to be pressed against me. You'll know I can feel them, and I like it. Don't freak out. It's normal. Try to enjoy the sensation."

She angled her face up toward his as he embraced her. Tension traveled down the length of her body.

"It helps if you're not as stiff as a board," he joked, lowering his head and placing his lips near her ear. "Easy, babe. Relax."

She inhaled deeply, shuddered, and released some of her tension.

"Better," he whispered, nuzzling her ear. "Now, we're going to practice step one at the same time. Ready?"

She nodded. *I can do this. I need to do this. I want to be normal.*

His lips brushed lightly across her cheek to her lips. Her eyes widened when he softly caught her lower lip with his teeth. His warm breath mingled with hers. He released her lip to capture her entire mouth.

She stiffened when his tongue traced her lips teasingly. With gentle probing, they parted. Without hesitation, he thrust inside. She felt, as much as heard, his groan.

His arms tightened around her as his exploration deepened.

She fought the urge to pull away, tried to enjoy the frightening sensations his tongue provoked. She trembled and suppressed a whimper.

Jake stopped. His tongue retreated, but his heart still thundered against her. He finished with a simple, firm kiss before resting his chin on top of her head. His hands tenderly stroked her back.

"You okay?" he asked. She nodded against his neck. "You did good, but we're going to need lots of practice. And then we'll tackle step three."

Chapter 12

The present

Jake parked the Corvette at the curb in front of the duplex at nine sharp Thursday morning. An uncomfortable tightness squeezed his chest as he studied the front of the unit where Angela had lived. White stucco walls, red tile roof, brilliant purple bougainvillea climbing trellises to the roofline. Nice. Normal. He wondered if the current residents had any idea of the atrocity committed within those walls.

He shook the thought from his mind and pulled a credit card-sized recorder from his shirt pocket. He turned it on and then slid it back into its hiding place. His gun and holster were already locked in the secret compartment. Sighing heavily, he grabbed a folder and a bag of donuts from the passenger seat and exited the car. Behind his sunglasses, his eyes darted around the neighborhood, inspecting the surroundings and cataloguing images as he sauntered along the sidewalk.

He rang the doorbell and waited, smiling at the peephole where he suspected Becky Smelter's eye was glued.

After a few minutes, he rang the bell again and called, "*Miss* Smelter, it's Jake Stone. I brought donuts." He raised the bag so she could see it.

The door opened only as far as the security chain allowed, and a wrinkled face peered through the crack.

"I want to see your identification," the elderly woman demanded. Jake moved to set the donut bag on the ground. "Don't do that. I'll take those," she snapped.

He squeezed the bag through the opening. As he reached into his pants pocket for his wallet, the door closed.

"Shit," he muttered and took a deep breath.

He flipped open his wallet to show his PI and driver's licenses and then knocked. As seconds ticked by, he frowned at the thought that old *Miss* Becky Smelter might have outsmarted him.

The rattle of the chain being unlatched eased his tension, and by the time the door opened, Jake wore his most charming smile.

"Good morning, Miss Smelter. Here's my identification." He thrust his arm through the opening so she would have to cut it off to close the door again.

She squinted at the pictures on the licenses and then at his face three times before she stepped aside for him to enter.

"Come in, Mr. Stone. I don't have all day." She ambled away, leaving him to close the door.

He followed her into the dining room where the donut bag sat on the table. She motioned for him to sit, and he did.

"How do you take your coffee?" she asked, already walking toward the kitchen doorway.

"Black, thank you. May I help?"

"No. Stay put. I don't let strangers wander around my house."

She reappeared shortly with a tray, which she lowered unsteadily onto the table. After handing Jake a plate and a cup of coffee, she lifted her items from the tray and set it aside. With childlike eagerness, she selected a donut from the bag before passing it to him. He took one just to be sociable.

"Delicious," he said. "I can't remember the last time I ate a donut."

She gauged his sincerity with sugar glaze stuck to her lips. "No wonder you have an unpleasant edge to you, young man. Donuts should be eaten regularly to sweeten your disposition."

He stifled a laugh when he realized she was serious. "I'll remember that. Thank you. Do you mind if we talk while we eat?"

"Of course not. I don't want you here any longer than necessary. I have a busy schedule on Thursday. Lunch at the Senior Center at noon. Bingo at church at two. What time is it?"

Jake glanced at his watch. "Nine twenty. I'll make this as quick as possible. And I do appreciate you agreeing to talk to me." She nodded with her mouth full so he continued. "I'm sorry to have to tell you the sad news, but I should let you know up front that…that Angela…passed away about a week ago."

Becky Smelter's face blanched, and she blinked rapidly as if she couldn't comprehend what her ears had heard. Her chest rose and fell with each deliberate breath. Then her eyes filled and overflowed. She stared at him, seemingly unaware of the tears sliding down her cheeks.

He watched her closely with alarm. Was she about to suffer a heart attack? "Are you all right?"

"No, of course not. How?" she whispered.

"The police are calling it suicide, but I disagree. I think Angela was murdered, and it's why I'm here. I'm trying to figure out if her death is connected to the rape. Will you help me, Miss Smelter? For Angela's sake."

She nodded slowly.

"I understand this is a terrible shock, and it's going to be hard for you to talk about what happened four years ago. If I could wait, I would. But I'm afraid the trail will only get colder. Are you up for this?"

Hand trembling, she raised her coffee to her lips and drank deeply. Her gaze traveled toward Angela's former home, and she stared at the adjoining wall for several moments. Her thoughts seemed far away.

Jake waited patiently. Would the old lady be strong enough to do this?

Finally, her attention came back to him. She took another long drink of coffee and set the cup down. After dabbing her eyes and mouth with a napkin, she squeezed it into a tight ball.

"Well, what are you waiting for, Mr. Stone?" She smiled bravely. "If we're going to catch the bastard, we should get busy. What can I do?"

Jake's brows arched, and he grinned. "Great." He opened the folder and removed several sheets of paper. "I have copies of all your interrogations. I know it happened a long time ago, but I'd rather you talk from memory without using these to refresh first. Sometimes, perceptions change over time. Sometimes, a fact will surface from your subconscious, and you don't even know it. And I don't want you to be influenced by these." He tapped the pages. "Okay?"

"Mr.—"

"Please call me Jake."

"Of course. You're the professional, Jake. I'll follow your lead."

"Thanks. Now walk me through that night, from beginning to end. If you forget a detail as you go along, just throw it in when it comes to you. Understand?"

"Certainly." She sighed deeply and focused on the hands folded in her lap. "It was a Saturday night, so Mary and I had gone to bed about ten. We slept in separate bedrooms, but we were both awakened about midnight by noise coming from Angela's place." She paused, narrowing her eyes as if taking herself into the past. "Mary came into my room to see if I was awake. We talked for a while, trying not to listen. You understand, we weren't snoops."

"Understood."

She nodded and continued. "We heard a man's voice, but it didn't sound like David, Angela's boyfriend. The voice was older, deeper. We heard Angela, too. But they weren't talking loud enough for us to understand what they were saying. Didn't even try, mind you. There was some laughing and other loud noises. We thought they might be drunk, which was highly unusual for Angela. Mary and I were getting peeved when it went on for hours. Angela was always so considerate. And David, too. We knew he spent the night occasionally—so improper, you young people—but they never made noise like that night. We were both still awake when Angela's front door slammed at three in the morning. We watched her leave with a man whom we'd never seen before. He was tall, white, blond, nicely dressed. Angela looked like she was going to a costume party dressed as a…a prostitute. My God, it was such a shock. The man had his arm around her waist, and she was kind of clinging to him. They staggered a little walking down the street to a big black car and drove away. Mary and I were puzzled but relieved to be able to go to sleep. So we did." Her watery eyes looked up at him. "That's it."

"Very good. Now I'm going to ask you some questions before we move on to the next morning. Okay?"

"Okay."

"Did you hear Angela and the man arrive before midnight?"

"No. We thought Angela was home alone earlier because we could hear her television just a little. But the television had been turned off before we went to bed at ten."

"Did you hear any more noise after Angela and the man left?"

"No."

"Did you hear her come home later?"

"No."

"Did she look like she was hurt when you saw her leaving at three?"

"No, absolutely not."

Jake stroked his chin. "So Angela was fine when she left at three with the mystery man. Which means the rape happened later. And we don't know if she returned with the same guy, another guy, or alone." He shuffled the papers and then looked up. "I'm sure you know Angela denied having a man at the house or going out with one that night."

"Oh, yes, I know. Poor thing. Her memory was so messed up. But there's no question Mary and I saw her leaving with a man."

"You're absolutely sure it was Angela? You did say she looked like a hooker."

"Hooker?"

He grinned. "Prostitute."

"Ah. Yes. Her outfit was appalling. Even stranger was that the clothes disappeared." She leaned closer. "I think the pervert gave them to her to wear just for their date and then took them when he left." She nodded sharply. "Shouldn't you be writing this down?"

Smiling, he tapped his head. "Good memory, but I'll take some notes." He scribbled "pervert provided clothes" in the margin of the paper and then glanced at another page. "The police said there was no sign of forced entry, so I doubt the rapist was waiting for her inside when she got home. Perhaps he assaulted her while she was opening the front door."

"At first, I thought her boyfriend might've gone crazy if he found out she was cheating on him. David did have a key. But when I learned how badly Angela was injured, I knew he couldn't have done it. They were in love."

"Really?"

"Oh, yes." Becky smiled and sighed.

"How serious were they?" Odd fingers of jealousy plucked Jake's heartstrings.

"Very. We thought David was going to propose soon, and Angela most assuredly would've said yes." Her smile faded, and she dabbed her eyes. "But after the… Well, things were never the same."

He cleared his throat. "Let's see. The police report says David had flown out Saturday morning to Seattle to visit his parents but came back immediately on Sunday after Angela called him."

"Angela didn't call him. I did."

"Oh?"

"Angela wasn't right in the mind that day. She didn't want to call anyone, not David, not her parents, not her sister. Mary and I thought she needed someone to stay with her at the hospital so we called Maleena first."

"Maleena?"

"Her sister," she explained.

"Yes, I know, but wouldn't it take longer for her to come from Virginia than David from Seattle?"

The old woman grinned. "I like you, Jake. You can call me Becky."

He returned the smile. "Thank you, Becky. I like you, too. About Maleena?"

"Oh, Maleena lived in LA then."

He frowned. "She did? I didn't see that in the file."

"Well, it got very confusing."

"Enlighten me."

"Maleena had moved out to California after Angela finished interior decorating school. Against her better judgment, Angela let her sister move in with her. It was a disaster. The sisters were nothing alike. Maleena was always partying, causing trouble. Angela confided to Mary and me that she thought Maleena had fallen in with a bad crowd and was using drugs. The really hard kind, like cocaine or heroin. I've read about the awful stuff, you know." Her gaze drifting to the window, Becky took a bite of donut and a sip of coffee and seemed to forget she was in the middle of an explanation.

Jake faked a cough to recapture her attention.

"What? Oh, yes," she continued. "Anyway. After tolerating Maleena for as long as she could, Angela finally kicked her out about a year before the…the rape, I think. We didn't know where Maleena was living, but I did have her cell phone number. I called several times that morning, but Maleena didn't answer so I left messages." Becky sighed. "Finally, I called David's cell phone, and he flew back on the next flight from Seattle."

"Did you ever talk to Maleena?"

"Yes, when she landed."

"Landed? I don't understand. Did she admit she'd been high?"

"High?" Becky's nose wrinkled. "Heavens no. She'd never tell me that, even if she was high when she landed in Dulles."

Confused, Jake wondered if they were speaking the same language. He shook his head to clear it. "Dallas…Texas?"

"No. Dulles. What's wrong with your ears, young man?"

"Dulles? The airport in Virginia?"

"Yes. She'd flown home that morning. Back to Mommy and Daddy," she said snidely. "She was a no-account if I ever met one. Mary and I disliked her from the day we met her. Angela tried her best to straighten her sister out, but Maleena never appreciated it. There was no love lost between those two."

"I agree."

"You know about Maleena?" Becky asked with surprise.

"I called the Reardons to discuss my theory. Maleena chewed out my ass—sorry—yelled at me on the phone."

Becky laughed but quickly turned grim. "What do you think of the family?"

He snorted. "Sophisticated jerks. I couldn't stand the parents either."

"I'm glad to hear that. I mean, we thought Angela was the only good one of the bunch. So sad for her to have such an awful family. They were no help to her at all during her crisis. Actually, we decided she was better off without them here upsetting her."

"They didn't fly out to be with her?"

"The parents came two days later and stayed for three days. Maleena never came back to LA as far as we knew. She showed no concern whatsoever about what had happened to her own sister."

Becky dabbed at her eyes. "We could never understand how the two girls could be so different, especially being…being—"

"I know."

"You do?"

"Well, I can imagine how hard it was to understand their relationship with as close as you and Mary were."

"That's true, too. This sounds awful, but I've never met anyone more evil than Maleena Reardon."

He studied the intense expression on Becky's face. "Angela never even told me she had a sister."

"Ha. I'm not surprised. Angela would never admit it, but I think they hated each other. At least, they did after Maleena lived with her. And the parents. What a waste. They were so wrapped up in their high-society world, they hardly seemed to remember they had a wonderful daughter living out here."

Her voice cracked, and Jake changed the subject for fear of losing her. "How did David handle the situation?"

Becky covered her eyes for several moments, and he wondered if she would be able to continue.

When she answered, she spoke very softly. "David was a prince. And it wasn't easy. Angela pushed everyone away. Even Mary and me. David stayed with her at the hospital for the first few days. When she was discharged, he tried to move into her place temporarily, but she threw him out. He was heartbroken. Every day, he came to see her. We could hear her yelling 'Don't touch me.' It got worse and worse until David quit coming. Angela would never talk about what happened between them, but Mary and I thought she probably couldn't stand to even be touched by…by a man, any man. Poor David. None of it was his fault, but Angela did what she had to in order to survive."

Becky sniffled, her grief palpable.

He waited respectfully. "I'm sorry to put you through this." He stood with his cup and reached for hers. "May I get you another cup of coffee, Becky?"

"Thanks. Just sugar, please."

When he returned with the coffee, she sat with her elbows on the table and her head cradled in her hands. He set the cups down and knelt beside her.

"If this is too hard on you, I'll understand. But you have to tell me."

She cocked her head to study him. He stilled as her bleary hazel eyes searched the depths of his gray ones.

"You loved Angela, didn't you?" she said.

Jake started at the impact of her question. He straightened and moved to his chair. He avoided her gaze while he contemplated an answer. When he finally spoke, his voice cracked. "I *think* I loved Angela, but I'm probably the worst person in the world to judge whether I did or not."

Becky's mouth opened but shut without speaking. She seemed to ponder his answer. "How many of us can ever say if we're truly in love? But this I know: You cared deeply for her. And I bet she felt the same for you."

He swallowed hard. "I think…she did."

Becky leaned back in the chair. "I'm tired, Jake. Old and tired. I'm sure you have more questions, but I need some time now to grieve for Angela. Call me tomorrow."

He left Becky Smelter with her head resting on the table, eyes closed. He clicked the lock on the doorknob and quietly pulled the front door shut behind him. Glancing at Angela's former residence, his mind flooded with Burke's description of that horrible morning. His stomach lurched, and he swore under his breath. When he got back to the hotel, he'd go through the rape case with a fine-tooth comb and look at the crime scene pictures he hadn't been able to handle last night. And then what?

Jake unlocked the door of the Corvette with an impatient flick of his key fob. He slid behind the wheel and scanned all three car mirrors. His foot was already on the accelerator when he did a double take at the reflection in the driver's side mirror. Casually, he slipped the transmission out of gear and fiddled with the sun visor while his gaze remained glued to the outside mirror. Another angled glance confirmed the crumpled front bumper of the black Land Rover parked three vehicles behind him. Jake adjusted his sunglasses in front of the vanity mirror before picking up the folder and pretending to peruse its contents. Surreptitiously, his gaze darted between the vanity, side, and rearview mirrors.

Patience.

Then he saw it: movement inside the Land Rover. He tossed the folder aside. Bending as though accessing the glove compartment, Jake unlocked the hidden space containing his Glock. He stashed the gun between his thighs. After several slow breaths, his eyes narrowed in a last glimpse of the Land Rover and a final check for approaching traffic.

He jammed the transmission into gear, stomped on the gas, and spun the car around in a tight U-turn. In seconds, he was abreast of the Land Rover. He flipped his middle finger at the tinted driver's window and sped off.

He barreled down surface streets until he flew onto the freeway entrance. Since he recognized the Land Rover from the Doubletree

Hotel parking lot, the unidentified occupant or occupants knew where he was staying. Jake wanted only to reach the lobby first so he could observe the vehicle's arrival. With any luck, he'd have the opportunity to get a good look at who was following him.

Squealing into a parking space near the hotel entrance, he killed the engine as his head swiveled for a full view of the parking lot. If the Land Rover had an accomplice waiting for him here, getting inside could be dicey. He leaned back, yanked his shirttail free of his jeans, and stuffed the Glock into his front waistband.

Spotting a group of about fifty Asian tourists loitering ten yards from the Corvette, he plotted his next move. He grabbed the file, jumped from the car, and set the alarm system with the fob as he hustled toward the entrance. Hunching down, he was soon lost to view in the midst of the crowd. He spun around and scrutinized the area.

No sign of the Land Rover. No goons racing toward the hotel. No vehicles careening into the parking lot. He stayed immersed in the group until the strangers became uncomfortable with his presence and began drifting away.

Without turning his back to the parking lot, he moved inside the lobby. Staking out a position with an unobstructed view, he waited. Five minutes passed before the Land Rover drove into sight. It crept along the street. Jake regretted that the Corvette was so conspicuous, but his first objective had been to get his butt safely inside. The black SUV disappeared around the corner but reappeared a few minutes later. It stalked by a second time and then sped away.

A quick scan of the parking lot revealed no sign of any unusual or suspicious activity. After waiting ten more minutes, Jake turned his attention to the lobby. Still nothing seemed out of the ordinary, so he strolled to the elevator.

The DO NOT DISTURB sign hung from the door handle of his room just as he'd left it. He wished he knew if it had been respected—by everyone. What was wrong with him? He always marked a hotel room door when he went out. Forgetting little things like that could get a man killed. He glanced cautiously up and down the long hallway and then put his ear to the door. Nothing.

Holding the Glock steady in one hand, he opened the door and squeezed inside as quietly as possible. Skillfully, he flowed through the two rooms, checking everywhere: under the bed, behind the doors and drapes, inside the closet, and in the bathroom. Then he performed a more thorough inspection, examining the furniture, his duffel bag, the computer, the clothes in the dresser and closet, and his toiletry bag. He searched the phones for bugs. Climbing up on a chair, he removed the vent cover to inspect the space behind it. No sign of a video camera. After a second meticulous sweep of the room, he breathed easier and concluded no one—not even the maid—had been in his room.

His gun resting within easy reach on the table, he poured a large drink of Jack Daniel's and dropped onto the small couch. From now on, he'd have to be more careful. His computer and files might have to travel with him, which was risky in its own way.

He frowned and swallowed a gulp of his drink, focusing on the heat it ignited. He didn't need this additional hassle.

And who the hell was following him?

He didn't like the answer that flashed immediately in his mind.

When the hotel phone on the end table next to him rang, Jake jumped. He stared at it but made no move to answer it. He hadn't told anyone where he was staying. No one—correction, no one except whoever was in the Land Rover—knew he was there.

After several rings, it stopped. He relaxed and took another drink. It was probably simply an employee calling to confirm his extended reservation or to ask if he wanted maid service yet today. He decided to call the front desk to deal with both issues and avoid any more calls, but as he reached for the phone, it rang again.

His first impulse was to ignore it, but after three rings he wavered and answered.

"What the hell do you think you're doing?" the obnoxious mechanical voice growled.

Jake tensed instantly. "What the hell do you think *you're* doing? Call off the Land Rover before I put some ventilation holes in it."

"You're playing with fire, Stone."

Hearing the Contractor say his real name paralyzed Jake for several heartbeats. "Get your goons off my ass," he said after he recovered.

"I told you not to force my hand. And talking to the police is yanking my hand hard. What I don't get is why LAPD. The confirmation I received said the hit went down in Coronado. So I repeat: What the hell are you doing?"

Jake's mind raced. He forced a laugh. "Damn, you're a paranoid bastard. My chat with the LAPD had nothing to do with the Reardon deal. I'm looking for a deadbeat dad."

"What's his name?"

"John Smith."

"Nice generic name."

"Yeah. That's why he's been so damn hard to find."

"Who'd you visit at the duplex? And don't lie to me. You know I can find out myself in a less pleasant way," the Contractor warned.

"I shared donuts with a little old lady. She's a connection in a long-lost relative case I'm working for a friend in Virginia. She was too senile to be much help, unfortunately."

"Think your little ole lady would confirm your story to my Land Rover boys?"

Jake's hand clenched into a fist at his side. His bluff better be damn good—for Becky's sake. "I'm sure she'd be delighted to."

"Remember, Stone, I know where she lives."

"I know. Warn your boys she'll talk their ears off. And bring donuts. It's her weakness." His eyes narrowed as he waited for the next volley.

"I can feel your smug-ass grin from here. You think you're so damn smart."

"Hey, what can I say? I've got a PI and security business to run."

"Okay, smart ass. I'll tell you what I'm gonna do."

"I'm all ears."

"I'm getting out of the middle of this. I don't trust you, and I don't trust the buyer. I'm going to let the buyer know the hitman is on the warpath, but I won't give up your name. That way you're on an even playing field. And for all I care, you can take each other to Hell."

"What if the buyer wants a contract on *me*? You gonna turn him down?"

"Good question. I'll have to think about it."

"Well, just so you know, I've already planted the seed with the Coronado PD that Angela's suicide was actually murder. To ensure the seed doesn't die with me, I've left all of the information about the contract, you, and my theories on the buyer in a very safe place so that, if something happens to me, the police and the Agency will have the leads they need to track you down."

"Track me down?" the Contractor said with mocking disbelief.

"Yeah. You're so full of shit you forgot I still have a lot of friends at Langley, and I'm a damn good PI. You're not as safe as you've always thought, *Bernard*."

"Fuck you, Stone. You've just signed your own death warrant."

* * *

"Hello, Becky. It's Detective Sean Burke. How are you?"

"Oh, Sean, I feel miserable, but it's good to hear from you."

He frowned at how old and frail she sounded on the phone. "I just wanted to let you know a man named Jake Stone may be contacting you to discuss Angela's case."

"He just left."

"Really?"

"Is there a problem, Sean?"

"No, but he sure didn't waste any time. I just met with him yesterday afternoon." Burke cleared his throat. "What'd you think of him?"

"I like him. Jake brought me donuts."

Burke chuckled. "Smooth, isn't he?"

"You don't like him?"

"I didn't say that. Other than the donuts, why do you like him?"

"He loved Angela, and he's trying to make things right. You know about Angela passing away, don't you, Sean?"

"Yeah, it sucks. I mean, it's awful. Poor lady. So, you think he's telling the truth about his relationship with Angela?"

Becky hesitated. "Are you jealous, Sean?"

"Wh-what?" he sputtered.

"Mary and I knew you had a crush on Angela and were so disappointed when she moved to San Diego."

"I didn't have a...Never mind. My point is: Did you sense anything unusual about Jake Stone?"

"Not really. The donuts were yummy. He spoke highly of you. Why don't you trust him?"

"He's...Wait a minute. I'm not saying I don't—"

"What are you saying then?"

"I don't think this guy is what we see on the surface. There's something lurking underneath. I don't want to call it sinister, but it's dark...edgy."

"Sean Burke, quit beating around the bush. Get to the point."

He rubbed his hand across his face. She had him. "All right, but hear me out before you lay into me. Statistically, a woman is most likely to be killed by a man she knows. Especially one close to her. Awful? Yes. But it sure helps focus an investigation. I spoke to a Coronado PD detective this morning about Jake Stone. Apparently, Stone and Angela had been dating for about three months. But I gathered from the conversation that this was highly unusual for Stone. He has a reputation as a real player."

"Player?" Becky asked.

"Uh, let's see. You'd call him a...a womanizer, I guess."

"You're saying Jake has lots of meaningless sex with promiscuous women."

Burke snorted. "Yeah. You get the idea. So, anyway, you and I both know Angela had problems with sex and any physical male contact after the rape. Stone admits to being with her that night. What if Angela didn't put out? I mean, what if she refused to have sex with him? What if he got royally pissed, lost control, and killed her? No premeditation, just a simple crime of passion. But then he covered it up as a suicide. If Angela's death were my case, Jake Stone would be my *prime* suspect."

A long silence followed Burke's rant.

"Wouldn't Jake be taking a huge risk by trying to prove she didn't commit suicide?" the old woman asked.

"Absolutely."

"So why in the world would he do that?"

"Damned if I know, but I sure as hell plan to find out."

* * *

As soon as Jake recovered from the unnerving conversation with the Contractor, he dialed Becky Smelter's number. He didn't know what he was going to say, but he needed to know she was all right. She'd been cautious with him at her door, but she'd be no match for a couple of goons wanting to make a point. How could he warn her without scaring her?

After ten rings, Jake disconnected and redialed. Another ten rings, and still nothing. No answering machine either, which didn't surprise him. His palms were sweaty as he paced the room and dialed a third time. He glanced at his watch: 11:45 a.m.

"Crap," he muttered.

What had she said about her plans? Lunch at the Senior Center and then something else at two. He slammed the cell phone on the table. It might be better if she was away from her house for a while. Unless she came home to find it occupied by the Land Rover guys. He debated driving to her house, but if she were there, she would have answered his calls.

Unless she couldn't. He didn't want to think about that possibility.

He pressed his palms against his temples and groaned. Had he convinced the Contractor that his activities today had been unrelated to finding the buyer? He scrunched his eyes tightly closed and replayed the conversation. Maybe by the end of it, the Contractor hadn't cared what the hitman was up to. The Contractor just wanted out of the middle. He cringed. Or to make more money on a new contract with Jake Stone as the target. Bingo.

Aha. Bingo. Becky was playing bingo at two. How long did old people play bingo on a Thursday afternoon? He had no clue. He resolved to call her again at three and to not give up until he talked to her.

Until then, he'd listen to the recording of his visit and transfer it to his computer. Then he'd review Burke's papers again. His interrogation of Becky had been cut short. If he had some new questions for her, they might mask the real reason for his call.

After ordering lunch, he got to work. He was so engrossed he almost missed the room service knock. With the Glock tucked in the back waistband of his pants, he peered through the peephole at the uniformed delivery boy. He quickly handed the guy a tip and took the tray instead of letting him inside.

Jake ate without tasting and pushed away the plate still half full of food. Reading about the rape killed his appetite.

He leaned low over the list of DNA tests, studying each entry. Burke had been right. The rapist had left semen everywhere, and none of it ever got a DNA match. Angela's DNA had been matched from several samples, which wasn't surprising. Jake frowned at one of the entries.

The sample had been taken from a red lace thong. Red lace thong? Why did that ring a bell?

The date of the test triggered his memory. That sample had been submitted two months after the rape. Jake thumbed through the papers until he found one dated the day of the submission.

According to the report, Angela had called Burke to inform him she had discovered a red lace thong underneath her nightstand. She swore it wasn't her underwear. Burke had bagged the evidence at her house and submitted it immediately. The DNA test showed the thong contained Angela's vaginal fluid and the rapist's semen. According to Burke, the results had devastated Angela. Burke hadn't speculated on the source of the thong, apparently dismissing the ownership issue as simply a result of the victim's amnesia. However, the detective had noted with concern Angela's diminishing mental stability. The young cop's escalating affection for the victim bordered on unprofessional, as his descriptions grew more sympathetically subjective rather than analytically objective.

Jake rocked onto the rear legs of the chair and chewed on the end of a pen. Burke had definitely become emotionally involved with Angela. Becky even mentioned it on the phone yesterday. Had Burke tried to force his affections on Angela only to have her reject him even in her vulnerable state? That would piss a guy off.

He scowled, trying to remember exactly what Burke himself had said about the relationship. His eyes narrowed when he remembered. *Protect... take care of... I scared her away.*

The front legs of the chair dropped back to the floor with a loud thud. His fingers flipped through the pages until he found the report on the last face-to-face meeting between Burke and Angela. Reading between the lines, he could easily imagine the detective pleading with her not to move away. God, the cop was pathetic.

Shuffling through more paper, he grabbed the notes from Burke's phone calls to Angela in Coronado. He scanned the contents and then leaned back, frowning. From the lack of meaningful information, the phone conversations must have been short and sweet, or maybe not so sweet. Angela was trying to move on with her life, leaving the rape behind her. Which meant leaving Burke behind also.

When Angela had confided in Jake about the rape, she'd briefly mentioned Sean Burke, but only in his capacity as a detective on her case. Jake reasoned he would've detected in her words or body language the existence of a personal relationship. Undoubtedly, in her considerate way, she'd been nice and attentive to the man, but there was no indication she had returned his affections.

Had Burke unsuccessfully pursued Angela for the last four years? Frustrated. Resentful. Vengeful. Had he snapped?

Unrequited love. A well-known motive for murder.

Well, shit, that puts a whole new spin on things.

Yesterday, Burke had seemed like his best ally; now Jake wasn't so sure. He'd come to LA looking for connections, but he hadn't expected the detective on the case to become one of the suspects.

He mentally slapped himself. His investigation into the possible connection between the rape and the hit contract was barely two days old. Way too early to be jumping to any conclusions. His first impressions of people were usually correct, and his original take on Burke had been that he was a straight shooter committed to getting justice for Angela. The theory that the young cop took out a contract on her because she broke his heart was a stretch, and frankly, he didn't want to believe it.

Was he so desperate that he was grasping at straws? He answered with a strong shake of his head. At this point in the game, though, it was wise to keep all options on the table, regardless of how weak or improbable.

He shoved the chair back and sauntered over for a J.D. refill. Closing his eyes, he tilted his head and savored two long swallows.

He stepped to the window. LA smog lay like a dingy blanket across the landscape. Millions of people lived and worked under the dirty sky. Was Angela's rapist one of them? Was the person who wanted Angela dead one of them? Was it one person or two different people? *Damn.*

Jake glanced at his watch: 3:15 p.m. He set the drink down and pulled his phone from his pocket. Her phone rang four times before she answered.

"Hi Becky. It's Jake."

"Who?"

"Jake. Jake Stone."

"What do *you* want?"

The icicles in her voice sent a chill through him. He hesitated, puzzled.

"I'm just calling to check on you."

"Why?"

"Uh, gee, I don't know. Maybe because I knew you were upset when I left, and I wanted to be sure you were okay." She didn't respond. "Becky, are you all right?" Jake's nerves, already taut, tightened a notch.

"No."

"Are you upset about our talk or…did something happen after I left?"

"After."

His throat constricted. "What happened?"

"I can't say."

"Becky, tell me what's wrong. Did someone scare you?"

"Yes," she said after a lengthy pause.

"Damn it, talk to me, Becky!" Jake exploded. "Do I need to come back over there?"

"Don't you dare, young man. And don't call me Becky anymore. How could you pull the wool over my eyes about Angela? Was it fun playing with an old woman's emotions? Shame. Shame on you."

Jake pulled the phone away from his ear, frowned, and shook his head vigorously. "What the hell—"

"Watch your language, Mr. Stone."

A long, slow breath whistled through his lips. "Give me a break, Miss Smelter. Tell...*please* tell me what's got you so upset." Through the silence, he heard her labored breathing. Again, he shuddered at the possibility of a heart attack. "Miss Smelter?"

"Sean...Sean said—" Her voice cracked. "You killed Angela."

* * *

Casually tucking the receiver between his ear and shoulder so he could continue typing on the keyboard, the detective answered. "Sean Burke."

"You son of a bitch."

He straightened in his chair. "Who is this?"

"I should rip your goddamn head off."

"Stone?"

"Yes, you asshole. How dare you turn Becky Smelter against me. I have more questions for her, but now she's afraid to talk to me. Where the hell do you get off telling her I killed Angela? I thought you wanted to help me catch Angela's murderer, not string me up by my nuts. I should come over there and kick your—"

"Careful, Stone," Burke said sternly, running a hand across his forehead. He wanted to kick his own ass for sounding off to the old lady. "I didn't tell Becky that."

"Bullshit!"

"I didn't," Burke insisted. "What I said was, statistically speaking, you'd be a prime suspect based on your personal relationship with Angela."

"Yeah, the personal relationship you wanted with her but never got. Getting denied is tough on the old ego, isn't it cop-boy? Wanted to fuck the pretty lady, but she said no. Rejection is a bitch, but it's a great motive for murder."

"Fuck you, Stone. I admitted how involved I got with trying to solve the rape. I thought someone owed it to Angela after what she'd been through. Her vulnerability triggered the whole macho-protectiveness thing we guys do."

"Becky thought your interest in Angela went way beyond that. After reading your reports, I agree with her."

Burke's first reaction to the accusation was hostile silence. "Becky Smelter has a big mouth," he finally offered, trying to tamp down his anger.

"Yeah, she does. So, what's it going to be, Burke? Allies or enemies? Trust or distrust?"

His fist tightened on the receiver. His eyes narrowed and stared, unseeing, at the computer monitor. "How about a temporary truce to our mutual distrust?"

Jake hesitated. "Okay. Does that mean you'll still help me?"

"Yeah. What do you need?"

"Couple of things, for now. Was there ever any resolution to the mystery about the clothes the Smelters saw Angela wearing?"

"No. Angela always denied owning the clothing, and it was never found."

"What about the red thong?"

"Oh, yeah. I'd almost forgotten about that. She didn't find it for quite a while. Again, she said it wasn't hers, but her DNA was on it."

"Becky suggested the perp supplied the clothes. What do you think of her theory?" Jake asked.

"It's possible. He'd need to know her sizes, which also suggests familiarity."

"Right. But why take the clothes? Could there have been something incriminating about them?"

"With nothing more to go on than the Smelters' description of the outfit, we didn't try any kind of trace. We had an artist work with them on sketches of Angela and the mystery man. A copy of the sketch is in the envelope."

"Yeah, I saw it. It didn't trigger any response from Angela?"

"Nothing. It was dark, and the angle was from the side and back so we didn't have any luck with matching the guy to a mug shot either," Burke said.

"And the thong?"

"Standard Victoria's Secret item. No identifying marks."

"Shit. You ever hear of a rapist dressing up the victim and then taking the clothes home with him?"

"Hell no. It's damn frustrating we can't gain anything from it. I've got a meeting in ten minutes. What else do you need?"

"Do you have current pictures and addresses for J.J. and his girlfriend? And any info on the vehicles they drive?"

"I don't, but I can check with Vice. Probably not the same girlfriend now."

"Whoever he's screwing these days is fine. I just want to track him for a while."

"Track him, huh?"

"Maybe have a chat."

"Yeah, well, he's short, but lethal. Watch your back," Burke warned.

"Thanks for the tip. Can you e-mail me the pictures and addresses?"

"I'll do what I can."

Jake gave him an e-mail address to use.

"I've got to go if I'm going to call my buddy in Vice before I split. Anything else?" he asked impatiently.

"Yeah, call Becky and tell her you were wrong about me."

"Sure. Later."

Burke dropped the receiver onto the phone cradle, swearing under his breath. He leaned back in his chair and scowled at the information on the computer screen—the scarce data he'd found on Jake Stone. A muscle in his jaw twitched. Stone was good at covering his own tracks. How good was he at uncovering other people's?

He scrubbed his hand across his hair. Becky Smelter's mouth was becoming a liability. How was he going to shut her up?

* * *

The black Corvette prowled along the asphalt like a hungry panther. No sign of the Land Rover. Jake breathed easier. The exclusive West Hollywood address of J.J.'s condo was in the next block.

Beneath his calm exterior, Jake's anger simmered. A pimp living like a king was just wrong. And if the pimp had carved his initials in Angela's sweet ass, that wrong was about to be righted. Permanently.

The luxurious condominium complex covered an entire block. Jake circled it twice, mentally noting the guard at the main entrance, the perimeter cameras, and the eight-foot wrought iron fence. In addition to the main entry, each side of the block had a locked entrance. In his experience, normal security procedures would also include additional video cameras monitoring the interior courtyards and elevators. The parking garage was underground with access through a keycard-only electronic gate. The complex should have sported a sign reading Visitors *Un*welcome.

He swung the car into a parking spot at the curb as a formally dressed, elderly couple alighted from a limousine and approached the west side entrance. He jumped out and trotted up the walk as the man opened the door. After the woman entered, Jake caught the edge of the door as the man stepped across the threshold. The older man turned, startled.

Jake smiled, nodded politely. "Good evening. Opera or philharmonic?" he asked, following them inside and closing the door.

The woman stepped around the old man to stand directly in front of the young stranger. "*La Bohème*. It was wonderful," she cooed.

"Ah, very nice, although my favorite has always been Verdi's *Othello*."

"Oh, yes, but it's so dark."

Jake's eyes raked over her before gazing seductively into the older woman's face. "Yes, but filled with so much testosterone that masculine passion seems to fill the theater."

She blushed, swallowed nervously, and batted her eyelashes. A chime sounded, and her companion grasped her elbow to turn her toward the elevator.

"Evelyn, the elevator's here. Good evening," he said with a curt nod to Jake.

After the elevator doors closed, Jake said a silent prayer of thanks for the many boring embassy functions he'd been forced to attend as a CIA operative, for opera was definitely not his thing. Then he hustled through the glass doors at the opposite end of the foyer and into a lush garden courtyard. He strolled nonchalantly to the desired building. A young couple returning from the Jacuzzi unwittingly provided him admission into the building.

The elevator took him to the eighth floor. The hallway was deserted, and Jake quickly located J.J.'s place. He sauntered by, glancing sideways at the lock. He turned the corner at the end of the hall, waited a minute, and then retraced his steps. Another critical glance told him all he needed to know about how to break into the condo.

A few minutes later, Jake drove to the address of the current girlfriend's apartment located approximately five miles farther west toward Beverly Hills. J.J.'s bright yellow Hummer shone like a neon sign where it was parked at the curb near the entrance to the posh complex. The second recon stop lasted only fifteen minutes. With his years of experience, it didn't take long to glean the necessary information.

As he returned to the Doubletree, Jake's steely eyes glinted back at him in the rearview mirror. The predator loved stalking his prey.

Chapter 13

Twelve weeks earlier

"Congrats, Angela, on giving up your lumber imitation in only four days," Jake said, loosening his embrace and brushing a wisp of hair from her face.

"Lumber imitation?"

"Yeah, you no longer stiffen up like a board when I hold you."

"Ha. Very funny." Warmth filled her in a comforting sensation. In the past few days, she had genuinely enjoyed Jake's kisses and embraces. Only she knew how significant that was.

"Seriously, you've made a helluva lot of progress. I think you're ready for step three. Don't you?"

She wiggled out of his arms and turned away. "Depends on what it is."

"Touching."

Several awkward seconds ticked by.

"Where?"

He bent around so he could see her face. "Here. There. Everywhere."

Her eyes widened. "Jesus, Jake, I don't know."

"Hell, we won't know until we try."

She slipped beyond his reach and stood up. Wringing her hands, she paced from the couch to the kitchen and back. Her gaze avoided his. "Let's practice steps one and two for a few more days."

When her path brought her closest to the couch, Jake sprang up and caught her by the shoulders. She tensed and pulled back.

"Hey, hey, what's that about?" he asked. He brought her up close, lifted her chin, and kissed her lips lightly. "No backsliding, Angela. Talk to me."

Her lips curled inward while she organized her thoughts. "Touching is so…so personal."

He chuckled. "Of course it is. That's the whole point."

"I like what we're doing. Why risk ruining it?"

He hugged her tighter. "I'm relieved to hear you like it, and we can't 'ruin' it. If you don't like the touching, we stop. Wait a while longer. No harm done." Unconvinced, she rolled her eyes. "Hey, did I mention we stay fully clothed, and you can touch me first?"

"Fully clothed?" she said, skeptically.

"Yeah, but if you insist on taking something off, I won't object."

Finally, she smiled. "What if I strip *you* naked?"

His eyebrows bounced. "I definitely won't object. Come on. Let's try it."

Her smile faded slightly, and she sighed. "Okay. How do we do this?"

"Would you rather I lie on the couch or on your bed?"

"Couch," she said instantly. Inviting a man into her bedroom? Not a chance.

Jake grasped her hand and led her back to the couch. Anxiety building, she watched him toss the decorative pillows onto a chair and stretch out on his stomach. He patted the carpet next to the couch, and she knelt on the spot. He faced her and smiled encouragingly.

"Now, you can start anywhere you want, but I'd suggest my head. The idea is to give *and* get pleasure from the experience," he explained. She frowned doubtfully. "Shit, Angela, keep an open mind, would you?"

"Okay, okay. Close your eyes. I don't want you watching."

"Can I trust you not to take advantage of me?" he quipped.

"Shut your mouth and eyes before I change my mind."

He complied.

Angela's hands hovered above his hair for several moments. She'd touched his hair before, but the simple action suddenly seemed very intimate. Her fingers trembled, and her chest tightened.

One gray eye peeked at her. "It's okay, babe. It's only hair, and I washed it this morning."

The joke dispelled her tentativeness, and she laughed with relief.

Her slender fingers dove into the ebony waves near his ear, hesitated, and then glided to the top of his head. She paused, withdrew them, and repeated the motion, applying slightly more pressure. She splayed her fingers and massaged his scalp with her fingertips. With nails scratching lightly, she wove through his thick hair, captivated by the heavy strands parting and then enveloping her hands.

He moaned his approval.

While her hands continued losing themselves in his hair, she studied his face. Like the rest of his body, it was lean and chiseled. His nose bore subtle signs of two breaks. A strong jaw tapered to a rugged chin, all covered with the dark whisper of five o'clock shadow.

Absently, her fingers left his tousled hair and slowly traced his eyebrows. Thick, but not bushy. Her gaze settled on his long black eyelashes, lashes some women would die for. She marveled that they didn't appear at all feminine on this masculine face. They evoked another impression. Sensual. A strange sensation tugged below her belly.

Her fingertips moved to the small creases in his forehead and between his brows. His worry lines seemed the only evidence of internal stress. Gently massaging the etched spaces, she wondered what a man like Jake Stone worried about. From all appearances, his life was full, orderly, successful. Happy? Probably. But appearances could be deceiving. *Look at my own life.*

Her palm drew circles on his cheek, alternating between smooth at his cheekbone and sandpapery at his jaw. Her index finger traced his earlobe and the sensitive area behind it. She ran a hand down his nape onto his back. Even in repose, his muscles felt strong and defined beneath his T-shirt.

Angela's progress stopped at the waistband of his shorts. Her gaze lingered on his tantalizing ass while her mind coped with the idea of touching it. *Not today*, her brain decided, and her hands skipped to the outsides of his thighs.

Although she was sure he had noticed the omission, she appreciated that he didn't comment. In fact, he lay perfectly still, eyes closed, breathing evenly. No signs of arousal.

She reached his ankles, massaged them briefly, and stopped.

Laying her hands in her lap, she announced with satisfaction, "Done."

Jake's eyes opened and met hers. "Great job. Now the other side." As he rolled onto his back, Angela tensed. "You did my face already, so why don't you start with my chest?"

"Chest?"

"Yeah."

Her right hand landed in the middle of his chest and began to move. It must have operated on autopilot because her mind was on the first time she had seen his chest naked above a bath towel wrapped around his hips. As her palm circled one side and then the other, she remembered taut muscles, curly hair, and dark nipples, which now felt hard beneath the soft jersey shirt.

Hard.

Her eyes darted to the fly of his shorts. The rigid bulge was unmistakable.

Breathing grew harder.

"Angela?"

Her brown eyes flew back to meet his gray ones. "Huh?"

"What's wrong?"

"Nothing."

She gulped. His gaze refused to release hers. Panic tiptoed up her spine.

"Skip my dick, would ya, please." He smiled sheepishly. "I might embarrass myself."

She blinked rapidly with relief. "If you insist, Jake."

She scooted sideways and finished with a strong rub of his long legs. "There. Done."

Opening his eyes again, he arched his arms over his head and stretched his entire body. "God, that felt great. Now it's your turn." He rolled onto his side. "You're up for it, right?"

Tamping down the jitters, she nodded.

They changed places, and before she was really ready, he knelt beside the couch and tunneled his hands into her hair.

"Wait," she said, rising up onto her elbow.

"What?" His fingers froze.

"I...I'm not comfortable."

He studied her face. "Physically or psychologically?"

She swallowed hard and ignored his question. "Why do we need to do this?"

He sighed, withdrew his hands, and rocked back onto his heels. "The goal is for you to enjoy sex again. Right?"

"Right," she said after a slight hesitation.

"To reach your goal you have to be comfortable with a man touching your body and you touching a man's body. Touching. Get it?"

"Don't talk down to me."

"Then toughen up. You didn't get raped yesterday," he said curtly.

She gasped.

"Don't look at me like that, Angela. You're stronger than you give yourself credit for. Now lie down and shut up."

She glared at him until she realized that he had successfully replaced her anxiety with anger. "You're good, Jake Stone."

"So they tell me."

After his skillful massage of her scalp, she sighed when his fingers began their gentle exploration of her face. As if he were blind, his fingertips seemed to be reading every inch, rounding every curve, relishing every texture, and recording the entire image in his memory.

Although more often passionate and possessive, Jake's kisses and embraces had also frequently been tender, so the tenderness in his touch was not a total shock. But the time and attention he put into each caress was.

When his fingers seemed reluctant to leave her slightly parted lips, she peeked at him from under her thick lashes. His expression caused her breath to catch. He must have felt it because his fingers stopped abruptly, and his gaze flicked to hers. His eyes bore the guilt of a young boy caught doing something forbidden. As their gazes melded, Angela's tongue snuck between her lips to touch his fingers. The jolt registered in his eyes, but his fingers didn't move.

"Angela?"

The lump in her throat prevented her from answering. Instead, she closed her lips and eyes.

The emotionally charged moment passed.

The touching exercise progressed down her back. His large hands softly squeezed her slender waist. With a moment's hesitation, but without a word, he skipped over her butt and thighs and resumed at her calves. After slipping off her sandals, he massaged each foot for a few minutes.

His lips brushed her ear. "Roll over."

Angela raised her eyelids, which had turned strangely heavy. "Okay."

She rolled onto her back and squirmed into a comfortable position. Jake turned her face and firmly kissed her lips. His eyes, warm and soft, searched hers.

"Ready?" he asked, moving closer on his knees.

"Uh huh." Her eyelids drifted shut.

All ten fingers brushed the hair away from her face. They caressed her cheeks, stroked her jaw, and dipped into the hollow of her neck.

When his hands splayed across her breasts and gently kneaded, she stiffened.

"Easy now, it's okay," he whispered.

She nodded jerkily.

His palms revolved around her nipples in ever-larger circles until he'd touched every inch of her breasts. She held her breath. His fingers lightly pinched her firm, erect nipples, which pressed urgently against the soft, stretchy material of her bra. Then he cupped both breasts and molded them under his strong hands. A groan of frustration escaped his lips.

Angela's eyes popped open. "Stop!"

"Huh?" he said, trancelike, still holding her breasts.

Frantically, she pushed at his hands and scrambled to sit up. Her eyes widened, and her breathing turned ragged. "No, no."

He blinked, shook his head, and then grabbed for her shoulders, but she batted his hands away. "It's okay. Relax, babe."

"No, it's not. Damn you, don't touch me."

A spark ignited in his warm, gray eyes. They turned hot, smoldering. "Fine," he snapped and raised his arms over his head in surrender. "I give up."

Angela buried her face in her hands, inhaling and exhaling slowly through her mouth.

Wordlessly, Jake moved to the chair.

Once composed, she lowered her hands and glared at him defiantly. "I can't do this. I'm not a chameleon that can change in the blink of an eye. You don't understand what a torturous process this is for me. Do you want *out* now?"

He scowled, eyes flashing. "Why do you think I want out?"

"Because…because you want to…to screw me, and I won't let you."

"Where the hell did that come from?"

"Then deny it. Tell me that wasn't what you were thinking about while you were playing with my breasts."

"Guilty as charged, but damn it, I didn't act on it. But I guess that doesn't count for anything. To you, all guys are black-hearted, horny bastards."

"Pretty much."

His jaw clenched, and a muscle twitched in his cheek. "I'm not the son of a bitch who raped you, Angela. I'm not a monster who would hurt an innocent wom—"

He seemed to choke on his words and grimaced. Angela tensed as she read the rare emotions on his face. Shock morphed into guilt and then regret.

"Are you all right?" she asked.

His face contorted as if he was in pain. He pinched the bridge of his nose for several seconds. When his hand dropped away, his self-control had been restored. No warmth, no fire, just silver ice staring at her.

"Yeah, fine," he mumbled. "I have to go." He stood up.

She jumped to her feet and grabbed his arm. "Jake, I'm sorry. I don't think you're a black-hearted whatever-you-said."

"Sure you don't."

"I'm afraid I'm not as ready for step three as you thought."

"You've got more guts than any woman I've ever met, Angela, so don't tell me you're afraid. I think you're confused about what you want. Or maybe you *are* frightened of what you're feeling. Cut me some slack if I occasionally get frustrated." He peeled her hand off his arm.

"Please don't be angry."

She stared into eyes that had changed from warm to hot to cold in the span of a few minutes. Her breath caught at the realization: Jake was a chameleon. And now he looked down at her with unreadable steel eyes, his face as expressionless as an iron mask.

"I'm not angry, Angela. You're doing great. Sometimes I push too hard, and you should tell me so." He planted a quick kiss on her forehead.

"You *are* angry. I can tell."

His lips pressed into a thin line, and he didn't respond immediately. "All right. If I'm angry, it's with myself, not you." He grasped her shoulders, held her slightly away, and kissed her lips. "See you tomorrow."

Angela stared after him until she heard the front door close. Then she dropped onto the couch and cradled her face in both hands.

"Oh God," she muttered.

One of these days, Jake was going to walk out the door and never come back. She knew it. Knew it with the same certainty that told her the sun came up in the east, the sky was blue, and men were not to be trusted. She didn't want to care that he would never come back, but she did.

What made Jake different from the other men who had flitted through her life in the past four years? She had known they would leave, and they had. And she hadn't cared—at all. This time she cared, and that scared her to death.

She rubbed her hands across her forehead and then combed them through her hair. With her eyes closed, she raised her face toward the ceiling and breathed deeply.

Why is this so hard? If someone asked her if she wanted to be "normal" again, she would answer with a resounding yes. She didn't want to be frigid. The road back was just so rough and full of potholes. No, not potholes, sinkholes. Sinkholes capable of burying her.

What's different this time? The answer frightened her. She wanted to be "normal" as much for Jake as for herself. She didn't want him to disappear from her life, but she knew that without sex, he would. He also ignited sensations inside her that she hadn't felt in years. A spark here, a tingle there. A prickle. A tickle.

An ache.

She groaned. Was it desire or dread?

* * *

Jake stopped on her doorstep. He bent at the waist, braced his hands on his knees, and let his head droop. He drew several slow, fortifying breaths into his lungs. *What the hell is happening to me?*

Jake Stone didn't suffer from feelings like this. Years ago, his emotions had petrified. But this woman was chiseling through the rock, fracturing it. Compassion and so many other unwanted emotions were bubbling up through the fissures like lava, burning reason and incinerating caution.

He was in trouble, big trouble. If he wasn't careful, his world was going to come crashing down on his head. This contract wasn't worth the risk. He wanted out. He *had* to get out.

After the epiphany hit him, he couldn't get home fast enough. The Corvette flew across the Coronado Bay Bridge. He didn't care if he got a hundred speeding tickets. He was blinded by the overwhelming need to void the contract.

He arrived home in record time. Within minutes, he stood in his bedroom, dialed, waited. The ringing stopped, and he spoke to the silence.

"The contract is off. I should never have come out of retirement for this. I'll return the deposit the same way it was sent."

Silence.

"Tell the Agency there's a problem with their intel. No way has this woman stolen or sold State Department secrets." His chest heaved with simmering anger. "Talk to me, damn it. I'm serious. No deal."

The mechanically altered voice finally spoke. "You've been in the business long enough to know it doesn't work that way. Is the price not high enough?"

"The price is not the issue."

"Then what's the problem?"

"I don't want to kill her," Jake spat into the phone.

The Contractor's laugh was chilling. "If you don't, someone else will."

"Shit, I know that. It's why I want you to put the Agency in touch with me so I can talk them out of this. The contract should be canceled completely. It doesn't make any sense."

"It doesn't have to make sense to you. Just do your job. And you know I can't connect you directly to the Agency. Anonymity is mandatory. I'm simply the facilitator."

"A perfect, upstanding CIA operative hiding in the shadows. What if I yanked your ass out of the darkness and into the light?"

Silence. Then, "You wouldn't want to do that."

"Then get the contract canceled. Completely."

"You're out of your fucking mind. It's not going to happen. And if you back out, you know what that means."

"Yeah, I've heard stories."

"They aren't fiction."

Jake scrubbed a hand across his face. "Look, we've done business for a long time. I've never asked a favor before, and I know this is a big one. Convince the Agency to cancel the contract. I don't know how to get through to you, but this woman shouldn't be a target."

The Contractor laughed. "Have you suddenly grown a conscience?"

"Possibly. Are you going to talk to them or not?"

"No, I'm not. Think this through, asshole. You decide not to consummate the contract because suddenly you have a big hard-on. The Agency isn't going to just walk away. I have other Agency assassins willing to make the hit. So it goes down anyway, and you have no control over how or when. Could be a lot messier than how you would handle it. Then there's the issue of what to do with you for backing out. Rogues are bad for business. The best approach is to eliminate them."

"Shit."

"Yeah. I'd say you're in a no-win situation here."

Jake squeezed the bridge of his nose. He didn't want to admit defeat, but everything the Contractor said was true.

"Would you at least insist the Agency verify the intel? This target is so clean, it squeaks."

"I told you before that the Agency's motivation is irrelevant."

"It's relevant to me, asshole."

"Why?"

"I like to believe I'm making the world a better place by offing someone. It helps me sleep at night."

"My, aren't we moral these days. Have you gone soft on me?"

"Maybe so. Remember, I wanted to stay retired. This is your fault."

The Contractor snorted. "So sue me."

Jake was left listening to the dial tone. He yelled obscenities and hurled the phone across the room.

It *was* a no-win situation. He had known that before the call, but he'd also known he had to try.

Someone was going to kill Angela Reardon. If he stayed on the contract, at least he could control it. He could make it as painless as possible.

What else could he do? He had no other options.

* * *

Angela negotiated the last curve and slowed to turn into Jake's driveway. As the BMW climbed the winding concrete, she glanced at her watch. It was not quite 9:00 a.m. Jake would be up; she hoped he was home.

After last night's disaster, she wanted to surprise him so she hadn't called this morning. Showing up at his door, unannounced, with fresh bagels would certainly be a huge surprise since she hadn't been to his house since the night she'd fled in panic more than three weeks ago. Her throat tightened at the thought.

Several times during the drive, she'd almost changed her mind. She was saved by the epiphany she'd had last night after Jake left. She wanted to be with Jake Stone, emotionally, physically, sexually. For the first time since the rape, she cared about a man. Cared? Liked? Whatever the label, she didn't want it to end. And that meant finding the courage to continue with the twelve-step program.

After rounding the last bend at the top of the hill, the car cruised into the circular drive. She slammed on the brakes. A silver Eclipse was parked near the front of the house.

Reflexively, she slapped a hand across her mouth to stifle her cry. Tears stung so sharply she whimpered and closed her eyes. Panic attacked.

Her hand dropped away, and her chest heaved rapidly as she gasped for breath. She pressed her palms against her eyelids until the stinging stopped.

Don't panic. Breathe slowly. Be strong. Relax. Relax. Relax.

She coaxed herself away from the edge. Then she opened her eyes and fled.

As the BMW raced down the hillside, she struggled for self-control. What had she expected of Jake? He wasn't a saint. A week ago, he'd told her he hadn't had sex since they'd started dating. That was probably a record for him. And now she'd halted the twelve-step program in its tracks. Could she blame him for being frustrated, especially sexually frustrated?

She stopped the car at the bottom of the hill and gripped the steering wheel like a lifeline. The objective argument sounded fine, but it didn't feel fine. She felt betrayed. Disappointed. Why did everything have to be so painful? Squeezing her eyes shut, she pushed her head back against the headrest. What should she do?

Minutes passed. She didn't want to leave. If she did, she would have already escaped.

Angela pulled onto the road in the opposite direction from the route to town and the freeway. Fifty yards down the road, she pulled a U-turn and parked on the shoulder in the shade of a eucalyptus tree. After lowering the window, she killed the engine and slouched in the seat to wait.

The wait was only fifteen minutes. The Eclipse appeared at the end of the driveway and turned down the road away from Angela's hiding place. She inhaled slowly and started the car.

Before she could reconsider, she sped up the hill to the house. She grabbed her purse and the bag of bagels and jumped out. Heart pounding in her ears, she rang the bell. No answer. She pushed the button a second time. Her upper teeth clamped down on her lower lip to keep it from trembling.

"Angela?"

She jumped before squinting at the peephole. "Jake?"

"Look up," the disembodied voice from the intercom speaker instructed.

She did and spotted a shiny circle the size of a nickel above the doorframe. "Oh."

"Uh, this is a surprise. I just got out of the shower so I'll let you in from up here. Make yourself at home. I'll be down in a minute."

A loud click sounded in the door handle. Angela opened the front door and exhaled loudly, steeling herself for what she feared would be a hostile confrontation.

Suddenly, an idea struck her. She dropped her purse and the bagels on the foyer table and raced up the stairs. She reached the master bedroom just as Jake emerged, bare-chested, through the closet archway.

But her eyes weren't on him. They focused on the bed. The neatly made, un-rumpled bed. Even the accent pillows were perfectly arranged. No condom wrappers adorned the nightstand. Her gaze swept around the room to the massage table in the exercise area. A towel was draped haphazardly across it. Two small, colorful bottles lay on the carpet beneath it. Angela sniffed. Spicy. Woodsy.

"Are you going to faint?"

She blinked and faced him. His expression grim, Jake stomped around the room toward her.

"I didn't fuck her," he growled.

"I didn't say you did."

"You didn't have to. Your eyes made the accusation."

"I...I thought—"

"Forget it. I know what you thought. Maybe I should have. She was pissed that I only wanted the massage. At least if I'd screwed her brains out, I'd deserve your distrust."

He marched past Angela into the hallway.

"Jake."

He stopped, hung his head, and sighed. "What?" She didn't answer. "What?" he repeated irritably, peering back over his shoulder.

She swallowed hard. "Can we finish what we started yesterday?"

He frowned, suspicious. "You mean—"

"Yes."

"In there?"

She glanced down at the bed and nodded.

"You're sure?"

"No, but I'm willing to try."

Chapter 14

The present

"Detective Smithson, this is Maleena Reardon."

The Coronado PD detective leaned back in his chair and rubbed a rough hand across his face. This was not the way he wanted to start a Friday.

"Good morning, Ms. Reardon. What can I do for you?"

"Has there been any progress toward recovering my sister's body?" she asked.

"Unfortunately not. And I'm afraid the odds of recovery are minimal after this amount of time. I'm sorry."

"Me, too, but I understand. You don't think the disappearance of Angela's body is indicative of another problem, do you?"

Smithson scowled. "Such as?"

"Murder."

The detective straightened and rested one forearm on the desk. "No, I don't, but what makes you ask?"

"Not 'what.' Who. I understand Mr. Stone is working with you on investigating my sister's death."

"I wouldn't put it that way."

"Then how would you put it, Detective?"

He bristled. Maleena's ingratiating tone was beginning to chafe.

"Stone was a good friend of your sister's. He has his own theory about her death."

"And his damn theory has emotionally devastated me and my parents at an important time in our lives. We're overwhelmed with preparations for my wedding. I'm marrying Senator Jim Blackwell in a few months, and we don't need this distraction or the bad publicity."

"Congratulations and best wishes, Ms. Reardon. What do you mean by 'bad publicity'?"

"Just like the media frenzy over my sister's rape ruined my father's ambassadorship appointment, her death is going to ruin my wedding. As if a shocking suicide weren't bad enough, a murder investigation is intolerable. My wedding is a very public event, Detective. If you were familiar with Washington society, you'd understand. It's cutthroat. Gossip in this goddamn town can kill a marriage before it begins. Angela's death is a black cloud hanging over my joyous occasion."

"I see," he said, disrespect changing to dislike. "I didn't realize this was making news back East."

"We'd like to keep it that way. I…we have an image to maintain. Mr. Stone yammering about a murder in the Reardon family would spoil everything. I understand he's a personal friend of yours."

"More like an acquaintance."

"I don't care if you're screwing each other, Detective. I want him stopped."

Smithson's eyes narrowed. He paused and stroked his chin. "Stone's theory has some valid points, but not enough for me to open an official investigation. I don't really see any harm in his pursuing it. I'm sure your family wants to know the truth about Angela's death."

"We know the truth. My sister was emotionally dysfunctional as evidenced by her estrangement from us. She never recovered from the damn incident in LA. I'm sure her explicit memories of the attack finally pushed her over the edge. Case closed."

Frowning, Smithson pondered her response. "You think that's the only connection between the rape and her death?"

"What do you mean?" Maleena snapped.

"Part of Stone's theory is that the rape and murder are connected. In fact, he's investigating the possibility in LA right now."

"What?" she exclaimed. "What the hell is he doing?"

"Talking to people."

"Who?"

"LAPD Detective Tim Olsen, the lead detective on the rape case."

"That's all?"

"I'm not sure, Ms. Reardon, but you're welcome to ask Stone yourself."

"I don't want to talk to him again. I find him…despicable. Apparently, he was screwing Angela, so I have to wonder why—if you place any credibility in his theory—you don't consider Mr. Stone a suspect."

"That's a very good question."

"Then do something about him, damn it. Either arrest him or stop him. Today, for Christ's sake. I'm warning you. I…we want him stopped."

"'Warning'?"

"My fiancé and my parents have a lot of influential connections. We can make your life miserable, Detective Smithson."

"You already have, Ms. Reardon. Good-bye."

* * *

Claustrophobia gnawed at the edges of Jake's mind. His limbs were cramped. He needed to take a leak. It was only 9:00 Friday morning, and the rental car was already getting hot. God, he hated stakeouts.

At least the Land Rover guys seemed to have lost interest. An encouraging sign. But Jake never underestimated his enemies. They could have simply changed vehicles to avoid detection as he had. A sobering thought.

For the past two hours, he'd watched the parking garage exit from J.J.'s condo building in West Hollywood. His rented, white Buick sedan blended in well with the line of cars parked at the curb. On the other hand, J.J.'s bright yellow Hummer would be obvious pulling out of the garage, and Burke had provided the license plate number for confirmation.

Jake drained a third large Styrofoam cup of black coffee and immediately wished he hadn't because his bladder objected painfully. Soon he'd be forced to leave the car and find a place to relieve himself. This wasn't the kind of neighborhood where he could simply piss in an alley. He shook his head at the irony of getting arrested for exposing himself while staking out a pimp.

So far this morning, he'd allowed his mind to wonder, hypothesize, and theorize. A successful investigation often needed creativity. Instead of earth-shattering insights, though, incriminations had clouded his mind. His guilt sprang from the nightmare that had awakened him twice during the night.

Now he peered at the large envelope lying on the seat. To ward off boredom, he'd brought Burke's file to study. He planned to read every single word again. And again and again. Until that one minute detail hit him in the face and said, "This is it, stupid. This is the clue that explains it all."

As he reached for the envelope, his cell rang. Recognizing the number, he answered, joking, "Morning, Smithson. Got an arrest warrant for me yet?"

"Look, Stone, I figure you killed plenty of people when you were a Navy SEAL. And you're definitely a scary motherfucker. But I can't see you killing a classy lady like Angela Reardon."

"Thanks, buddy. I appreciate your seal of approval on my character."

"Don't mention it."

"So, if you're not coming after me, what's up?"

"Got a call from Maleena Reardon."

"Ah shit. Sorry to hear that."

"You should be. You were the subject."

"Me?"

"Yeah, she's a lot more worried about you stirring up a hornet's nest over this murder thing than she is about recovering her sister's body."

"I'm not surprised. Nice family, the Reardons. What did she want?"

"You stopped."

"And you said?"

"Fuck off. But I'm not sure she's going away. The witch warned me that she could make my life miserable. I'm sure she wouldn't hesitate to put a hex on you, too."

Jake chuckled. "Thanks for the warning, but she's not going to stop me."

"Didn't think so. Hey, there was one thing Maleena said that hit me kind of funny."

"What?"

"She said something about her sister's 'explicit memories' of the rape. I thought Angela never recovered from the amnesia."

"She didn't."

"Well, Maleena was very pointed about those memories causing her sister's suicide."

"Interesting. From what I've learned, there wasn't a lot of contact between the family and Angela after the rape. Maybe they just assumed she eventually regained her memory. Or Maleena could've been referring to memories created by the cops' and doctors' descriptions of things."

"Yeah, makes sense. How's it going, by the way?"

"Slow."

"Hang in there."

After disconnecting, Jake laid the phone on his lap, leaned against the headrest, and closed his eyes. Maleena Reardon. He didn't need that thorn in his side. Was there a chance she had information useful to his investigation? He doubted she would cooperate if asked. But she had lived with Angela in LA—she might know something important and not even realize it. Could Maleena be aware of some crucial fact about her sister's personal life that no one else knew? Had Maleena's drug use created the wedge between the sisters or only widened it? Had she ever come back to LA after the rape?

He thought of a hundred questions he'd like to ask Maleena Reardon, but he wasn't sure even one had any real relevance.

He was still contemplating when his cell rang again. The screen displayed an LA phone number he didn't recognize so he answered without identifying himself. "Hello."

"Stone?"

"Who's this?"

"Burke. Where are you?"

"Waiting for J.J. to invite me in for breakfast."

The detective laughed. "Good luck with that. Have you seen him?"

"No, but I figure his Hummer will be hard to miss."

"And he's a flashy little perv, too. You'll have no trouble recognizing him from the photos I sent you."

"Good. What's up?"

"I just got off the phone with Maleena Reardon. Olsen owes me one for siccing that bitch on me."

"Shit." Jake shook his head. "She called Detective Smithson this morning also. Bet she had some choice things to say about me."

"Damn straight. The woman has a potty mouth, and she was flushing you something fierce."

"Does she want you to arrest me?"

"That or shoot you. I don't think she'd care which."

He chuckled. "Thanks for the warning."

"Yeah, well, take her seriously. I get the impression she'd do just about anything to keep from having her wedding screwed up."

"How much do you know about her?"

Burke hesitated. "Very little. Why?"

"I don't remember much on her in your file."

"That's because there's hardly anything there. She wasn't involved in the rape investigation."

"Becky told me a few things. If you'd give me your version, that'd be great."

"Uh, there's not a lot to tell. What do you want to know?"

"Everything. Start with that morning."

"Okay." Burke cleared his throat. "After we got Mary Smelter and Angela to the hospital, Becky told us about the sister living in LA. She tried to contact Maleena but couldn't, so she gave us Maleena's cell phone number. We had no better luck so we called the parents at a Virginia number Becky found for us. She finally caught up with Maleena at the Dulles airport. But by then, Angela's boyfriend, who was in Seattle, was planning to fly back as soon as possible. Besides, I remember Becky saying she didn't think Angela would really want her sister around anyway."

"When did Maleena leave LA?"

"Early that morning. Out of LAX, around seven, I think. A few days later, I tried to call her just in case she might know something relevant to that night. A real long shot since Becky said she didn't think the sisters had spoken in a year. No one ever answered, and then the cell phone service stopped completely. The parents told me Maleena had checked herself into a discreet rehabilitation clinic for a two-month detox program the day after she arrived. The Reardons wouldn't disclose the location. That was it."

"You never met or talked to her?"

"Nope. Because Becky had told me the girls had a shitty relationship, I decided Maleena probably didn't know anything useful. I couldn't get to her without a bunch of red tape so I stopped trying and followed up on more promising leads."

"Did Maleena know about the amnesia?"

"I guess."

"Meaning?"

"Meaning, we told the parents, so I guess they told her. Although…" Burke's voice trailed off.

"Although what?"

Frustration filled his exasperated sigh. "The assholes didn't believe it."

"Come again."

"Mommy and Daddy Reardon didn't believe the amnesia diagnosis. They thought Angela was hiding something, protecting someone."

* * *

At 5:00 p.m., after ten hours of waiting, Jake's patience was finally rewarded. The Hummer passed through the security gate as it exited the parking garage. Before the bright yellow monster turned left, the Buick was in gear. Three cars back, Jake's gaze was riveted to the Hummer's rear end. At the first traffic light, he pulled up even. No one was riding in the front passenger seat. The darkly tinted back windows hid any sign of occupants in the rear seats.

The Hummer laid rubber on takeoff. His Buick eased in behind and tailed it for five blocks. Before the next light, Jake pulled around to the driver's side. Idling at the line, he leaned across to open the glove box. While prone, he sneaked a peek at the driver.

Definitely J.J.

Smiling, Jake straightened. Adrenaline pumped into his veins.

The Buick backed off, let the Hummer pull ahead, and switched to the same lane. Slowing even more, Jake allowed two cars to crowd in between. Like a ghost, the white car hovered around the yellow vehicle as it wound through the freeways and streets of Los Angeles to the Bonaventure Hotel.

After J.J. parked at the curb, Jake passed and slid into a space half a block away. He patted the Glock in the shoulder holster under his sport coat and jumped from the car.

Although meticulously groomed and dressed in a well-tailored royal blue suit, J.J. walked with the stereotypical swagger of a punk from the hood. When the pimp sauntered through the hotel entrance, Jake broke into a trot but slowed to ease through the doors.

From behind his sunglasses, he scanned the huge lobby and spied the short, fat black man advancing on a pretty, young white woman wearing an elegant evening gown and sitting in an upholstered chair near the fountains. Spotting J.J., the woman stood and spun away as if trying to escape, but he clamped a hand on her shoulder and stopped her.

Pulling out his cell, Jake pantomimed a conversation while he strolled into the adjacent seating area. He watched as J.J. gripped the woman so hard her shoulder drooped with the pain. Her eyes were wide and tear-filled. J.J.'s face and body were rigid while he spoke to her forcefully but quietly. With his fingers still pressing into her flesh, the woman fumbled with her purse and withdrew a white envelope. The pimp snatched it from her hand, held it for a moment as though he might slap her face with it, and finally stuffed it into his suit coat pocket. He leaned forward and kissed her cheek before releasing her shoulder. When he walked away, the woman slumped down into the chair and wiped a tear from her cheek.

Poised to follow, Jake discreetly observed J.J. take up a position near the elevators. He put away his phone, glanced at his watch, and moved to a spot near the exit from which he could monitor the pimp and the woman. The calm demeanor he projected to the hotel patrons belied the controlled aggression burning inside him.

Fifteen minutes later, a tuxedo-clad gentleman hesitantly approached the woman. He spoke to her, and she nodded. The man glanced around and then offered his arm. Without talking, the couple strolled across the lobby and joined several other formally attired couples waiting for the elevators. J.J. stood barely ten feet from them. His beady eyes were fixed on the woman, but she never looked in his direction. Once the elevator doors closed behind the pair, J.J. headed for the exit.

Jake was halfway to the Buick when the pimp came out the hotel doors. He watched in the rearview mirror as the black man climbed laboriously into the massive vehicle. When the Hummer's turn signal blinked, the Buick pulled away from the curb and crept ahead until the yellow SUV joined the flow of traffic. A few moments later, J.J. passed, and Jake slid the white sedan in behind him. The two vehicles caravanned onto the freeway and sped up.

The ride ended at the Crystal Chandelier in Beverly Hills. J.J. relinquished the Hummer to the parking valet and swaggered through the shimmering doors. Jake cursed and circled the block twice before finding a parking space suitable for a quick get-away.

Inside the dimly lit restaurant, he reluctantly removed his sunglasses to see into the shadowy recesses of the bar and dining room. J.J. had disappeared. Jake's gaze touched again on every patron. His hands clenched into fists at his sides. No J.J. *Shit.*

The restroom sign caught his eye, and he hurried into the small hallway. The men's room was at the end just before the hall turned to the left. An exit sign was barely visible on the opposite wall just past the corner. As Jake's hand smacked the wooden restroom door, his ears caught the low growl of a man's voice.

"You think you're fuckin' smarter than me? Huh, bitch? Huh?"

"No, J.J. It's not what you think," a woman's strained voice said.

"Looks to me like you're turnin' tricks on the side."

Skin slapped skin with a sharp crack. The woman gasped loudly but didn't scream.

Jake let the restroom door slam shut before he glanced back down the hall. No one was in sight. With his back pressed against the hall-way wall, the predator stalked his prey.

"I'm not," the woman exclaimed. "Mike's my boyfriend. He's not a john."

"You're lyin'. No guy wants a *ho* for a girlfriend."

"Mike doesn't know what I do. I only told him my real name: Sara. He doesn't even know my trade name."

"Sara," J.J. said venomously, "what *I know* is Mike's gettin' free pussy from my ho, Cayenne. That's bad for b'ness, bitch."

"I never let Mike interfere with work, J.J."

Jake inched toward the corner.

The woman groaned in pain. "Stop, you're hurting me."

"This ain't nothin'. If you don't get rid of this fuckin' Mike, I'm gonna hurt you and him a lot worse."

A stifled scream filled the small space.

Jake spun around the corner.

J.J.'s bulk smashed a petite white woman against the dark wood paneling. Over the man's shoulder, her terrified eyes connected with Jake's.

"Sara? What the hell? You two-timing slut. Who the fuck are

you?" Jake said, wrenching J.J. around by the shoulder and slamming him against the wall.

Clearly shocked, Sara froze.

J.J.'s head bounced off the paneling, and his eyes blinked wildly. "Get your…fuckin' hands…off me," he gasped.

Jake's hand gripped the man's windpipe, and his thigh wedged powerfully into J.J.'s groin. "If you want to breathe again, don't move, asshole." The pimp obeyed. With a sideways glance, Jake sneered at the woman. "So, Sara, this is how you treat my best friend behind his back. Letting some black dude feel you up in a bar. When Mike hears about this, you're done. Hear me? Done."

Dumbfounded, she covered her face and sobbed.

Pressing his face within an inch of the pimp's, Jake snarled, "You can have the bitch. She's not good enough for Mike. Get the hell out of here. I'm not finished with her." He released the man's throat and shoved him toward the corner. J.J.'s hand slipped into his pants pocket as Jake yanked the Glock from inside his jacket. "You touch that knife and you're a dead man."

J.J.'s hand flew out of the pocket, and he held both arms over his head as he ran down the hallway toward the bar. Jake waited several moments before sliding the gun back into hiding. Turning to Sara, he asked quietly, "Are you all right?"

Pale and trembling, she stared at him. "Yeah. Who are you?"

"Doesn't matter. Mike doesn't know me either."

"I don't understand." Her lips quivered.

"I made all that up to make it sound like Mike would be out of the picture. But J.J. may figure out I was lying. If I were you and Mike, I'd get as far away as possible."

"You know J.J.?"

"Know *of* him, sweetheart. And his little pep talk to you fits exactly with what I've heard. Make the break while you have the chance."

Her gaze dropped to the floor. "I'm screwed whatever I do, but thanks anyway, mister."

He sighed with resignation. "You're welcome. Good luck, Sara."

He peered around the corner at the empty hallway. With his hand resting on the Glock inside his jacket, he trotted back to the bar. No sign of J.J.

He hustled to the front of the restaurant and spotted the pimp waiting outside at the valet station. After ducking out the door behind a large group of customers, he darted to the Buick.

Stuck at the traffic light, he watched the Hummer pull away. He squeezed around a Mercedes and whipped an illegal turn, earning a middle finger from the driver he'd cut off.

Craning his neck, he spotted the target a few blocks ahead as J.J. turned at a major intersection. He launched the Buick onto a parallel street, stomped on the accelerator, and caught up with the Hummer at a cross street several blocks later. Horns blaring, drivers braked hard to avoid colliding with the white sedan diving into the heavy traffic on the main street.

Following at a safe distance, Jake barreled onto the freeway. When the Hummer swerved into the exit lane, he laughed and loosened his grip on the steering wheel. Stress dissolved with the recognition of their destination: the girlfriend's apartment.

The Hummer parked in the passenger-loading zone at the front of the upscale apartment complex, and the pimp climbed out. With much less swagger than he'd displayed earlier, J.J. sauntered to the swank entrance and disappeared inside.

When his watch finally read 10:00 p.m., Jake surmised his prey might not reappear until morning. Besides, he was exhausted. With a sigh of relief, he headed to the freeway. He berated himself for intervening in the dispute between Sara and her boss. Sure, it had been the right thing to do, but it wasn't part of his plans for tracking J.J.'s activities. It could come back to haunt him when the time and place were right to confront the bastard about Angela. He resolved to take the necessary precautions so J.J. wouldn't recognize him.

Forty-five minutes later, Jake lumbered into his hotel room. He stashed the Glock beneath his pillow. Before laying his wallet on the nightstand, he extracted Angela's picture. He stared for several moments at the beautiful woman in the red dress, sighed, and then carefully placed it beside the alarm clock.

With a large glass of J.D., he stretched out naked on the bed. Burke's envelope with the rape investigation photos lay beside him. Slowly, he picked up the envelope and slid out the pictures.

His breath caught at the sight of Angela's eyes staring up at him. He knew that wild, panicked expression. He studied the photos with morbid fascination. The evidence of her physical injuries jarred his conscience. Burke hadn't exaggerated the extent of the vicious rape and brutal beating she had survived.

He ran a hand over his forehead and down his face. Helplessness. Guilt. Regret. He didn't feel like a tough guy as the brutality of what Angela had endured sank in. No wonder she had been emotionally scarred.

He shoved the pictures back into the envelope. Leaning against the pillows, he scrunched his eyes tightly shut and clenched his teeth, but the sting behind his eyelids didn't stop. He tried repeatedly to swallow the lump in his throat but to no avail. His throat constricted until breathing hurt. His face contorted with pain. His fists pressed into his temples.

His lips parted. An anguished groan burst from deep inside him. A tear squeezed out from beneath his eyelashes.

Then Jake Stone—ex-Navy SEAL, former CIA assassin, cunning security expert, and hard-ass PI—hung his head and cried.

Chapter 15

Eleven weeks earlier

Passion flared in their kisses.

Despite his brain's command to stop, Jake's body responded naturally, lustfully. He shifted his hips in hopes Angela would not detect his swelling problem.

When she pulled away, he figured they had once again reached the end of the night. But her hand slid suggestively down the front of his shirt.

"Touch me like you wanted to the other night," she whispered.

"Are you sure?"

"Yes. I *promise* not to slap you this time," she said, her face reddening.

He gently lowered her to a reclining position on the couch and lay down beside her. She gazed at him with anxious eyes as he snuggled against her rigid body. When his hand trailed down her neck

and smoothed over her breasts, she shuddered and turned her gaze
to the ceiling.

Keeping an eye on her hands in case she reneged on her promise,
Jake gingerly caressed one breast. His thumb stroked the nipple
through the silk of her blouse and bra. Angela gasped. He nuzzled
her hair and slipped his leg across hers, no longer caring if she felt his
erection pressing against her hip.

After several minutes, her body relaxed, and she once again
turned her face to him. He kissed her lips, his tongue begging for admittance. Her lips parted, and he instantly thrust into the sweetness.
He groaned with satisfaction at the symbolic action.

His hand fondled more aggressively, kneading her nipple between his thumb and index finger. She trembled under his touch.
He rolled over so he lay partly on top of her. His hand left her breast
and crept gently past the waistband of her shorts. Heat singed his
fingers when they pressed against the fabric at her crotch.

Angela whimpered, jerked back to rigidness, and turned her face
away.

He yanked his hand up and held it momentarily in mid-air, not
knowing where it was safe to put it. Eventually, he grasped the back
of the couch, pulled himself upright. He saw the pain and tears
on Angela's face. He tenderly brushed aside her hair and kissed her
forehead before climbing off the couch. Dark eyes, blurred with disappointment, followed him.

After several deep breaths, he was able to speak. "We're headed
for a place where *you're* unable to go. Before we get to a place where
I'm unable to stop, I'm going to leave."

"I'm sorry, Jake. I'm not—"

"I know."

"I'm trying. I mean I want to—"

"I know that also. Good night, babe."

Impatiently, he tugged at his pants to ease the pressure on the bulge beneath his fly. He felt her gaze as he trudged stiffly across the family room. Before he closed the front door, he glanced back and watched Angela bury her face in the couch cushions, hot tears of frustration bathing her cheeks.

* * *

Five days later, Angela flipped through the racks of clothes in the Nordstrom store at the Fashion Valley mall in San Diego. "I really don't understand why you feel it's necessary to buy me a new outfit for this *thing* in Malibu next week. I already own several beautiful cocktail dresses."

"Cut me some slack. I'm trying to be generous, and I have something specific in mind," Jake said, holding up a hot, strapless number covered with red sequins.

She rolled her eyes and shook her head in disgust. "'Something specific' like the last ten dresses you've shown me?"

"Yeah, like the last ten you've turned your nose up at." He stopped his search, scowling with frustration. "What's the problem? Tell me the truth. Were they too…too sexy?"

She braced her hands on her hips. "No, the styles were fine. The color was wrong."

"They were all red."

Angela splayed her fingers in the air and shrugged. "Red is wrong."

"Come again."

She eased around the rack and sidled up to him. Brushing a stray strand of hair from his forehead, she pecked a kiss on his cheek. "I never wear red, silly. Haven't you noticed?"

He frowned. "Really?"

"Really."

"Since when?"

"For-ev-er."

When she started to move away, he grasped her arm and pulled her back against him. "Why?"

She looked up into his puzzled face. "I don't like red, that's all." Seeing the simple answer didn't satisfy him, she continued. "Red looks garish…gaudy on me. I blame it on my extremely light blond hair. I don't know. Red makes me feel…slutty, I guess."

"I'm sure I've seen you in red," he insisted stubbornly.

Smiling, she wagged her index finger in his face. "Jake, that's a terrible *faux pas*. You have me confused with another woman."

"Sorry." He grimaced. "Would you try it once—for me?"

Her smile faded, and she glanced away.

"I guess that's a no," he said.

"It's a matter of principle."

"I make a mistake, and you make a *principle* out of it. Give me a break."

"I'm sorry, Jake. Ma—" She bit her lower lip. Her dark chocolate eyes were liquid when she turned them on him. "My mother loves red. She forced me to wear it as a child. When I became a teenager, I refused to wear red anymore. Only one of my many independent acts that thoroughly annoyed her."

"Jesus. Tears over a damn color. Women." He planted a firm kiss on her lips, paused, and then deepened it. When he came up for air, he grasped her shoulders and set her away from him. He gulped. "Okay. Sounds like you've already got something at home you want to wear next Saturday. Let's forget this shopping crap and head to my place to work on step six."

She fluttered her lashes at him. "What is step six, Mr. Stone?"

He winked suggestively. "It's a surprise."

* * *

The hot, bubbling water swirled around Angela, relaxing her muscles and her mind. Closing her eyes, she leaned back on the plastic pillow of the Jacuzzi seat and stretched her legs out in front of her. God, she loved Jake's spa. When they used the Jacuzzi at night, he always turned off the security and landscape lighting and lit a dozen candles. Conversation during these interludes was sparse and quiet. Tonight her favorite Celine Dion CD played on the outdoor stereo.

Jake's romantic streak was only one of his traits that had surprised her. She smiled. He'd surely cringe if he knew she considered him amazingly tender. For someone who had originally portrayed the stereotypical slam-bam-thank-you-ma'am player, Jake Stone was far more sensitive and considerate than she would have ever imagined. The patience he showed, although occasionally stretched, in her slow journey through sexual re-discovery was exemplary.

Tightness gripped her chest; her eyes stung. Her feelings for Jake after five weeks of dating were too strong. When he did leave—and he would—it was going to hurt. Badly. She swallowed hard. *Enjoy this while it lasts, stupid.*

Movement on the opposite side of the spa roused her, and she lazily opened her eyes to see what Jake was doing. Something floated on the churning water beside him. At first, she couldn't distinguish what it was. Squinting, she gradually identified his swim trunks. Her gaze shot to his face. His expression, lit only by the candlelight and moonlight, made her breath catch.

She stiffened and straightened in her seat. "What're you doing?" she asked, unable to stop peering into the dark water directly in front of him.

"Step six: getting naked. You should try it." He chuckled. "If you like, I'll turn on the underwater light so you can see the part of my body you're searching for."

"Good God, no." She couldn't control the note of panic in her voice.

"Easy, now, easy."

He started to come to her, but she held up both hands, palms out. "Don't, Jake."

He eased back onto the seat, concern written on his face. "Listen to me, Angela. You're doing great. You're ready for this next step. It's time to get comfortable with being naked." He paused. "Trust me, please."

"I…I trust you."

"Do you, really? Do you know how long I agonized over how to make this step as easy as possible for you? I'm not asking you to *stand* naked face to face with me. I'm not asking you to *lie* naked in bed beside me. The water and the darkness should be physical and psychological buffers to help you."

Their eyes locked. Long, tense moments passed.

"Okay," she whispered, "but don't touch me. Understand?"

He nodded. "Take your time. Don't focus on me. Focus on how wonderful the water feels. How liberating—"

"Close your eyes."

"Huh?"

"Close your eyes. I'm not putting on a show."

"All right."

Once his eyes were shut, Angela drew a deep breath. Her fingers fumbled with the straps tied at her nape. She slid farther down into the water. Reaching behind her back, she unfastened the clasp. The bikini top bobbed among the bubbles. She shivered despite the one-hundred-degree water jetting around her.

"Need my help?"

"Jake!"

"Just kidding. Relax."

"I'm trying."

"Can I open my eyes?"

"No."

"Are you done?"

"No."

"Hurry up. I need to get out and take a leak."

"Jake."

"God, Angela, I'm joking."

"Just shut up."

When she was sure his eyes were still closed, she slipped the bikini bottom down and off. Slowly, the swimsuit drifted away, floating between them teasingly.

"Okay," she said.

Jake's gaze settled immediately on the two pieces of colorful fabric swirling in the turbulent water. Then his eyes rose to meet hers in the candlelight. Lust flared dangerously in the darkening gray depths. His expression was strained, controlled.

"You okay?" he asked.

"Yeah, I guess. You?"

"Yeah. Sure."

"Can you see—"

"No," he said roughly. "But my imagination's going wild."

She giggled, and then musical laughter flowed freely.

Jake's jaw dropped at her reaction. A moment later, his head fell back, and he roared with laughter, too.

Tension evaporated with the steam from the spa.

* * *

The tiny bell above the front door jingled frantically when Jake barged into the Heavenly Interiors reception area four days later.

"I'll be right there," a voice called from the workroom at the rear of the shop. Stella Jenkins appeared a few moments later. "Oh, hello, Jake. How are you?"

"Good. Where's Angela?" he asked. "I've been trying to reach her all day."

"Uh, it's been a hectic one. First, we had an urgent problem with the Clarksons' carpet that was supposed to be installed this morning. Then the award luncheon ran late. Angela didn't even have time to swing by the office to check on the Clarkson situation before she rushed off to her doctor's appointment."

He frowned. "Award luncheon? Doctor's appointment?"

"Uh oh. I thought you knew." Stella's eyes widened, and she bit her lower lip. "Angela should be back any minute. Make yourself comfortable." She turned on her heels and escaped down the hallway.

Jake lowered himself into a chair. After a couple of minutes, he stood and paced, his hands jammed in his pockets. Why was he so anxious? He'd simply been unable to contact Angela for a day. For Christ's sake, he wasn't the woman's keeper. Or was he?

Since his last conversation with the Contractor, he'd felt the need to be constantly aware of Angela's schedule and whereabouts, subtly keeping tabs on her. Was he subconsciously afraid the Contractor had hired another assassin to complete the contract? Wouldn't the Contractor have notified him that the contract was no longer his?

He rubbed a hand across his furrowed forehead. *Shit.* If there was no honor among thieves, there definitely was none among killers. Who the hell could predict anything about the Contractor's actions?

He heard the rear door of the shop slam shut. Then Angela's voice drifted down the hall.

He was leaning against her office doorjamb before she walked out of the workroom. His apprehension mushroomed when he spied the tense, strained expression on her pale face.

"Damn, you look like you've had a helluva day," he said and embraced her.

"It's been a roller coaster, that's for sure. I'm sorry I haven't returned your calls."

"I was getting worried."

She pulled out of his arms and headed into her office. "Good grief, you're such a mother hen lately." Picking up a stack of phone messages, she said without looking at him, "I wasn't expecting you, Jake. I'm awfully busy and tired."

"Yeah, I imagine an award luncheon and doctor's appointment in the same day would be tiring."

She raised a questioning gaze to his. He closed the office door before responding.

"Stella. Obviously, she thought you'd told me. How silly of her." His sarcasm crackled like static. "So, now, would you like to tell me about your day?"

Angela slapped the messages on the desk and dropped into her leather chair. She tunneled her fingers through her hair and blew out a long breath. "Why are you making me feel like a truant child?"

"Sorry. Didn't realize I was. How was the luncheon?"

She smiled wearily. "It was the high point of the roller coaster. I was honored, but embarrassed, to receive such praise and recognition."

"You were the award recipient?"

"Yes." She sighed. "I thought about inviting you as my guest, but I figured you'd be bored."

"Thanks for considering my social limitations."

"Please. I'm too tired for your taunting barbs."

He bit back a sharp retort and smiled instead. "Truce. What was the award for?"

"A few months ago, a local charitable organization purchased a run-down house in Coronado to use as a shelter for rape and domestic violence victims. I redecorated it *pro bono*. They were thrilled with my designs. What supplies my generous vendors didn't donate, I bought myself. I must say, it's one of the most satisfying projects I've ever done. Meeting some of the women who are now living in the shelter was the best part of the luncheon." Her eyes glistened.

Jake studied her. "Congratulations. That's a wonderful accomplishment. I would've been proud to be there with you, Angela, not bored."

"Thanks. Now I need to wrap up some loose ends around here," she said, reaching for the phone messages.

His hand landed firmly on the slips of paper. "Not so fast. Why did you go to the doctor?"

"It's none of your business."

"Ouch. Who's launching barbs now?"

She exhaled. "This is not the right time or place to discuss it."

He tamped down his irritation. "All right. I'll make you a deal. You look beat, but I know you wouldn't appreciate me forcibly removing you from the shop. While you take care of those loose ends, I'll grab Chinese takeout and meet you at your place in thirty minutes. If you're not there on time, I'm coming back to get you. And I promise, you won't like the way I haul you out of here."

"Wait a—"

He held up a hand to silence her. "Thirty minutes. Starting now."

* * *

"Don't think I've forgotten about your doctor's appointment," Jake said as he scraped the remaining cashew chicken from the small, white container. "I just wanted to get some food and wine into you before I brought it up again. You look better than you did at the shop."

"I feel a little better. Thanks for dinner and for forcing me to come home."

Angela refilled both wine goblets with chardonnay and slouched down in the chair with hers. She closed her eyes and wished Jake wasn't there. *Damn. Why did Stella have to blab about my day?*

"Do I have to pry it out of you one question at a time or will you just enlighten me?"

Reluctantly, she opened her eyes. "You're making a bigger deal out of this than it deserves. It was a simple visit to the doctor. I do have a right to some privacy, you know."

He glared at her. "Okay. Question one: what kind of doctor?"

Without answering, she stood up and marched into the family room.

Before she could sit down, Jake caught her arm. "What the hell's wrong with you? Why are you acting like this? I'm concerned, and you're treating me like shit," he said. His grim expression softened, hurt reflected in his eyes. "Damn, babe, don't shut me out. I'm worried about you."

"All right. I'm sorry for being bitchy." She feathered a kiss across his lips and then drew him to the couch with her. While gathering her thoughts, she rested against him, partly for his strength but mostly so he couldn't see her face.

"I went to see my shrink, the one who treated me for two years after the rape." She waited for him to interrupt with a question, but he didn't. "I've been having nightmares about four times a week since we began the twelve-step recovery program. Until recently, I couldn't remember anything when I woke up. Now I know it's the same nightmare each time."

"Is the nightmare about what we've been doing? You know, the sexual recovery stuff?"

"No, although the doctor thinks that might've been the spark that started it."

"I'm sorry, Angela. So then, what's it about?" When she hesitated, he angled his head to look into her face. He frowned. "Oh, hell. It's about the rape, isn't it?"

"Yes," she whispered and shuddered.

His arms tightened around her. "Talk to me."

She gulped. "I'm tied down on my bed. There's a man on top of me...raping me. He's only a shadowy figure—no details, no face. I can feel him hurting me. I can smell the sweat, the semen. There's someone else in the room. I can't actually see him, just a vague shape, but he's getting closer and closer. He climbs on me...does disgusting things. And something happens. It's like an explosion or fireworks. Then everything goes black, and I wake up."

"Jesus Christ. You think there were two men?"

"I don't know. My nightmare suggests that. But as far as I remember, the cops never found more than one man's DNA and no one's fingerprints except mine and my boyfriend's."

"Maybe the 'vague shape' represents something intangible—like death. You could've been afraid the guy was going to kill you."

"My shrink speculated on a similar theory. She's convinced there was some especially traumatic factor that triggered the amnesia, and now, this nightmare."

"Then it's amazing you've been able to recover at all."

"Thanks, Jake. There have been so many times over the past four years when I thought I'd go crazy. Why can't I move on, heal, be normal again? It's eroded my confidence, caused unbearable frustration. A million times, I've asked why. I don't know how much more I can stand."

Lifting her chin, he searched her eyes. "Do you want to stop the recovery program?"

"Oh God, no. This might be my last—very last—chance."

Chapter 16

J.J.'s routine had been disrupted, and not by choice. While Jake watched from the Corvette, J.J.'s girlfriend had confronted the pimp as soon as he arrived on the concourse in front of her apartment complex in West Hollywood. With his tiny surveillance camera, Jake snapped several pictures of the battling couple. After much yelling, the two climbed into the Hummer and sped off. Maybe the woman was tired of J.J. showing up only to screw her brains out and never take her anywhere.

Although it was 10:00 p.m. Saturday night and he was tired from a full day of spying, Jake dutifully followed them to a popular steakhouse in Beverly Hills. The pair parked and stomped inside, still sniping at each other. Jake lowered the vanity mirror and applied the minimal disguise he had retrieved earlier from the "toolbox" in the trunk. He smiled at the significant change the simple baseball cap and black-rimmed reading glasses made to his appearance. He scratched the thick layer of whiskers that had grown since his last shave about forty hours ago on Friday morning. The black sandpaper on his face augmented his new look.

"Scruffy" was the adjective that came to mind as he sauntered toward the entrance. He decided, if the restaurant refused to admit him, he would simply call it a night and return to the hotel.

A short time later, while enjoying a prime rib dinner as his reward for another frustrating day of surveillance, he studied the couple from the back of the dining room. Their raised voices, rigid body language, and angry gestures conveyed trouble in paradise.

A spark of hope flickered. Could the spat create an opportunity?

With that thought, Jake finished dinner quickly, left the restaurant, and made a beeline back to the girlfriend's apartment complex. After leaving the Corvette a block to the east, he reconnoitered the area immediately in front of the main entrance.

Scrutinizing. Strategizing. Stalking.

Now midnight, the street was quiet by LA standards: no pedestrians, few vehicles. The passenger-loading zone where J.J. preferred to park was empty. With the Glock tucked in his front waistband, Jake crouched between two large vehicles located a short distance away.

The predator waited patiently for his prey.

He didn't have to wait long before the Hummer screeched to a stop at the curb. The girlfriend jumped out and hurried toward the building entrance. J.J. stormed after her. The filth spewing from the pimp's mouth earned him a hard slap across the face when he grabbed the woman's arm and spun her around. J.J. returned the favor with a vicious swipe.

The loud, hissing voices and wild gestures lasted several minutes. Finally, the pimp shoved her toward the entrance. The girlfriend stumbled and fell against the glass door. She yelled an obscenity, flipped him the finger, and ran inside.

J.J. shook his fist and fired hair-curling insults at her. After an apparent moment of indecision on whether to follow, he turned abruptly and stomped back to the Hummer. He yanked open the door and climbed in, cursing to himself.

Jake landed in the front passenger seat, his Glock pressed against J.J.'s temple before the pimp could turn the key in the ignition.

"What the fuck?" J.J. yelled.

"Hands on the wheel, eyes forward, and don't move. You do, I shoot." Jake tapped the business end of the gun against the man's head. "Understand?"

"Yeah, yeah. You Vice?" the pimp snapped, placing his hands as instructed.

"Nope." Still aiming at J.J.'s head, Jake lowered the gun to his lap.

"Narc?"

"Nope."

"Fed?"

"No, prick. I'm your worst nightmare."

"Fuckin' funny guy, huh. I got a grand on me. Take it and get the hell outta my car." He leaned forward to expose the wallet in his back pants pocket.

"Relax, asshole. I don't want your filthy money."

Cautiously, J.J. sat back. His breathing came faster, and he was shaking slightly. "Ya want pussy? I got any kinda cunt ya want."

"No thanks."

The pimp turned beady, black eyes on his captor. "I got it. You're with that dickhead, Lionel. He's been after my b'ness for a long time. Ya can tell him to go to hell."

"Never heard of Dickhead Lionel."

J.J. gulped loudly.

With cold, unwavering eyes, Jake studied the fat black man. Not such a tough guy after all. Tough on women but not another man. A bulge near his right ankle suggested a small piece. Probably also still had a knife in his pocket. Both would be difficult for him to reach from behind the steering wheel.

Jake let the pimp squirm while he watched a dark Suburban and a tan sedan pass slowly on the opposite side of the street. Fear loosened a man's tongue, and Jake was an expert at instilling fear.

J.J.'s gaze darted from Jake to the street to the apartment building. A tic twitched in his right cheek.

Tension built inside the Hummer like inside a pressure cooker.

"What the fuck do ya want?" the pimp asked, his chubby hands trembling on the steering wheel.

"Information. The truth. You do remember what the *truth* is?"

"Yeah, yeah. Just my memory ain't so reliable sometimes." He gulped repeatedly.

Using the gun, Jake pulled J.J.'s face toward him. Icy gray eyes pierced the rapidly blinking black ones. "Bullshit. You better hope it's damn reliable this time. Your fucking, worthless life depends on it."

"What do ya wanna know?" Despite the cool night air, a bead of sweat rolled down J.J.'s cheek.

"Tell me about the rape of Angela Reardon," Jake said through clenched teeth.

"Who?"

"Angela Reardon."

"She ain't one of mine."

"I know that, you bastard. Let me refresh your memory. Four

years ago, a beautiful, blond, twenty-five-year-old white woman was viciously raped and beaten in her LA home. The perp left your seal of approval carved in her butt cheek. The cops hauled you in for questioning. Ring any bells?"

"Yeah, yeah, I 'member that. Like I told the pigs back then, I didn't do it. I had a tight alibi."

"Maybe you didn't do it, but I think you know who did."

"I don't know nothin.'"

"Don't lie to me," Jake yelled.

The Glock slammed into J.J.'s right temple, and the left side of his head bounced off the car window.

"Fuck!" he hollered. One hand jerked up to blot the dribble of blood.

"Hands on the wheel," Jake growled. "Now, think…real hard, J.J. Like I said, your life depends on it." He squinted at a black Suburban cruising past. The car had no license plates. He frowned. "Time's up. Talk to me."

"Look, man, I got no facts. All I got is guesses."

"I'll take guesses, as long as they're honest ones."

"You can understand I didn't really wanna know the facts."

"Quit stalling."

"Yeah, yeah. One of my girls had a regular who roughed her up a lot. This john was into kinky shit and liked threesomes. Really special threesomes." J.J. snickered. "The bastard done crap before like what happened to that woman who got raped. He knew 'bout my seal of approval. He had an appointment that night. When my ho disappeared, I started putting the pieces together."

"Did you tell the cops?"

"Are ya crazy, asshole?"

"What was your girl's name?"

J.J. cackled. "The hos don't use their real names."

Jake smacked the back of the man's head so hard his forehead hit the steering wheel.

"Shit!"

"Quit jerking me around, J.J. What name did she use?"

"Bad Angel."

The Suburban drove toward them on the opposite side of the street again. The sun visors were flipped down, and the other windows were darkly tinted. Two large, shadowy figures occupied the front seats, but the back seats were a mystery.

Jake tensed. "Those your friends?" he asked, motioning with the gun.

J.J.'s head jerked up. "In the black SUV?"

"Yeah."

The man hesitated too long to be telling the truth. "Better than that. They's my homeys, my bodyguards."

"You don't have bodyguards, you prick. Maybe Dickhead Lionel is coming to visit after all. Should I turn you over to him when I'm done?"

J.J.'s eyes widened and followed the vehicle. His mouth opened but snapped shut as if reconsidering a smart retort.

"Then tell me about Bad Angel. Now."

The pimp's face turned ugly with a sneering grin. "You don't fuckin' know, do ya, Mr. Smartass?"

Out of the corner of his eye, Jake spotted the Suburban pulling a sharp U-turn at the end of the block. "Forget it. Who was the john?"

"I don't 'member."

The Glock was instantly pinned against J.J.'s temple.

"You better remember. I'm getting pissed."

"I can't tell ya. He's still a customer," J.J. said in a shrill voice.

"If you don't tell me, you won't be around to need customers."

Through the Hummer's rear window, Jake watched the Suburban crawl closer. Its dark front passenger window slid down.

Jake shoved the Hummer door wide open and flung himself flat on the sidewalk. "Get down!"

The first shot rang out. The pimp shrieked.

Bullets sprayed through the car.

The Suburban rocketed away in a squeal of tires.

Heart pounding, Jake waited a second to be sure the shooter wasn't coming back. Then he scrambled onto his knees and leaned into the Hummer.

J.J. was sprawled across the front seats. Blood was everywhere.

Jake's lips hovered next to the dying man's ear. "The john! Who was he?" he screamed. "Time to try and save your sorry-ass soul, J.J."

The pimp's voice gurgled. "Lion...water...fuck...you."

He went still.

Sirens blared in the distance. In this upscale neighborhood, someone had already called 911.

Jake extracted himself from the car and bolted around the corner. He sprinted for five blocks and then slowed to a brisk walk. He tossed the baseball cap and glasses into a dumpster in a deserted parking lot. By the time he doubled back from several blocks away, two patrol cars with lights flashing were on the scene.

J.J. was dead. He'd never give up any more information.

Rot in Hell, bastard.

Lion water?

Damn, damn, damn.

Jake watched the crime scene develop for five minutes before pulling out from the curb. Then the predator disappeared into the night.

* * *

Detective Sean Burke's cell phone roused him from a deep sleep. "H'lo," he mumbled.

"Burke, it's Stone. Wake up."

"Huh? I'm awake." He glanced at the alarm clock, yawned. "Do you know what time it is?"

"Shut up and listen. Someone just took down J.J."

Sean shook the fog from his head. "Shit. You killed J.J.?"

"No, damn it. Not me."

He dragged himself to his feet. "Talk to me, Stone."

"I was having a friendly chat with J.J. We were sitting in his Hummer parked in front of his girlfriend's apartment building. A black Suburban, no plates, kept cruising by. Last pass, they sprayed us."

"You hit?"

"No, but thanks for your concern." Jake chuckled. "Or are you disappointed?"

"Cut the crap, Stone. Did you get a look at anyone?"

"No, they were careful."

"Any ideas?" Sean dropped back onto the bed.

"J.J. mentioned Lionel somebody was after his business. Could be a turf war."

"Or not."

"Yeah. That's what worries me."

"Did you give the cops your statement already?" Sean paused. "Stone?" He sighed heavily. "Where the hell are you?"

"On the freeway."

"Damn. You left the scene?"

"No shit, Sherlock. I don't need any more problems."

Sean rubbed his eyes and then threaded his fingers through his tousled hair. "Did you get any info from J.J. before—"

"Yeah. I just hope the bastard was telling the truth. He was scared shitless of my Glock, so I think he was."

"You said it was a friendly chat."

"I lied. Look, I'll tell you what I got after I've had some sleep."

"What's your plan?"

A long silence followed.

"Maybe you don't want to know, Burke. I'm not sure I know. I gotta figure out some things first."

"You don't trust me?"

"Yeah, that's it." Jake laughed. "No, man, I really don't have a plan. Honest. I'll get back to you when I do. Just thought you'd want to know about J.J."

"Thanks. Couldn't have happened to a more deserving guy. I'll work this on my end, Stone. As quietly as possible, of course."

"Understood. Let me know ASAP if you learn anything. I don't know where I'm going to be, but you can always reach my cell."

"You expect me to share?"

"Hell, yes. You want the asshole who raped Angela as much as I do."

"Damn straight. At least we agree on something."

After disconnecting, Sean slowly slid the cell phone onto the nightstand. Lying back, he stared at the ceiling.

His attempts to covertly investigate Jake Stone had yielded little. The man was a shadow. And Sean's gut instincts warned that *that* shadow was deadly dangerous.

His experience also told him the guy was a maverick who thumbed his nose at rules—and laws. Teaming up with him could be either the answer to Sean's prayers or the end of his career.

*　*　*

The Corvette turned into the parking lot of a cheap, run-down motel still flashing a vacancy sign. Jake didn't dare go back to the Doubletree Hotel until daylight. Although sure he hadn't been followed, he sat in the car watching intently for any signs of trouble. When no traffic passed by for several minutes, he trudged into the motel office. After paying cash for the night, he parked directly in front of the window of his room. He prayed the Corvette—all of it—would still be there in the morning.

A hot shower pounded some of the tension out of his neck and shoulders. He stumbled naked out of the bathroom and collapsed on the bed. Exhaustion and frustration overwhelmed him.

Who had killed J.J. and why?

Lion water? What the hell was lion water?

Had J.J. managed to win, taking the secrets of Angela's rape to his grave?

Jake grabbed his wallet and pulled out the picture of Angela in the red dress. He stared at it for a long time.

"This isn't over, babe, but I'm one step closer. I'll get the bastard yet," he muttered.

After a deep sigh, he replaced the photo and flopped back on the bed, covering his eyes with his forearm. God, he needed some J.D.

His head was spinning with possibilities.

None of them good.

Chapter 17

Nine weeks earlier

Jake whipped the Corvette into the driveway of Sergio Zurlini's Malibu beachfront mansion shortly after 6:00 p.m. Saturday night. The sleek black car idled in front of the security gate while he lowered his window. The distinct smell of salt air filled the interior. A burly black man with a shaved head bore down on the driver's side of the vehicle.

"Yo, Stone, thought those were your bad wheels." The huge man's voice rumbled.

"Hey, Curly. What did you do to piss Chuck off and pull gate duty?"

"Shit, I don't fuckin' know. Oh, sorry, ma'am," Curly said, spotting Angela in the passenger seat. "Didn't expect Stone to have a classy chick with him."

"Thanks, man. Way to help my image." Jake quickly handled the introductions.

"Yeah, here she is," the guard said, checking her name off the list on his clipboard. "I'll let Chuck know you're here. He'll catch ya at the front door. Nice to meet ya, ma'am."

"You, too, Curly." Angela smiled.

"Behave yourself, and I'll send some chow out to you later," Jake said.

"Deal."

Curly pushed aside his suit coat, revealing a large gun hanging in a shoulder holster. Angela's gaze swept from the weapon to Jake's face, but he showed no reaction. The guard poked a button on a remote clipped to his waistband, and the wrought-iron gate swung open.

Jake drove around the circular driveway twice before reversing into a spot quite a distance from the house and aimed toward the gate.

"I never like to take a chance of getting boxed in. Hope you don't mind the walk," he added while retrieving the garment bag containing her dress and his suit, as well as an overnight case, from the backseat. He patted the small Glock in his pants pocket. The larger version and his shoulder holster were packed at the bottom of the garment bag.

The short walk wasn't the hassle that concerned Angela. She hoped the movie producer's party warranted the convoluted plans Jake had explained. Since Chuck Thompson, his former Navy SEAL commander, had hired Jake to help with security, he was required to arrive at six even though the affair didn't officially begin until eight.

With Angela as his date, he would be acting in an undercover capacity, blending in as a guest unless needed. Neither had wanted to wear their fancy clothes on the long drive so arrangements had been made for them to change in one of the mansion's bedrooms. Chuck had insisted they spend the night at his home in LA afterward so he and Jake would have an opportunity to visit. Jake's enthusiasm had been almost boyish when he invited her, so she could hardly say no simply because the arrangements were inconvenient.

The massive front door opened before they reached it. There was no mistaking the former military man who embraced Jake in a bone-crushing bear hug. Although probably in his early fifties, Thompson still looked fit for battle.

"What the hell is wrong with your hair?" the older man grumbled.

"Sorry, Chuck, didn't have time for a haircut."

"You're getting soft, too," he said, punching Jake's six-pack abs.

"Yeah, I miss the fun little workouts you used to put us through."

Laughter roared from both men. Angela smiled politely.

Wrapping his arm around her shoulders, Jake pulled her closer. His chest seemed to swell with pride as he performed the introductions. As she'd suspected, Chuck was obviously a respected father figure to his former subordinate.

Chuck ushered them through to the back of the mansion, which was bustling with activity. The catering staff was busy setting up bars and food stations. They laughed and joked as they worked.

In contrast, Chuck's security team wore deadly serious expressions as they checked the large room that opened out onto an incredible deck overlooking the beach and the Pacific Ocean. Noticing Chuck and Jake in the doorway, the three men issued their greetings with a simple jerk of their heads. In unison, their gazes brazenly appraised Angela from head to toe and then flicked to Jake. A quick, group nod and they returned to work.

Cheeks burning, Angela spun toward Jake.

He turned a Cheshire cat grin on her. "You pass muster."

"Show Angela upstairs, then we can reconnoiter," Chuck said, hiding a smile and marching off to his team.

She chuckled. "I guess I've been dismissed."

"You heard the commander."

Still hauling the bags, Jake led the way back to the foyer and up the sweeping staircase. They headed toward the bedroom designated for their use. Two men, arguing heatedly in Italian, barreled out of the hallway and nearly plowed into them.

Angela guessed the shorter, older man with salt-and-pepper hair and full beard was the B-list movie producer Sergio Zurlini. The younger man, who could be described succinctly as tall, dark, and handsome, had to be the guest of honor, actor Marco Romano. Jake had explained the party was a celebration of Zurlini's first highly acclaimed production. The movie critics had lauded Romano's performance and credited him with the film's success.

"Who are you?" Zurlini barked rudely.

Jake bristled, set down one bag, and extended his hand. "Jake Stone. I'm with the Thompson security team, Mr. Zurlini."

The producer ignored the proffered handshake. "And the woman?"

In a possessive gesture, Jake touched the small of her back. "This is Angela Reardon. She's assisting the team tonight."

"Well, then, you should be working instead of wandering around up here." Without waiting for a response, Zurlini brushed around them and tromped down the stairs. "Come, Marco," he hollered.

But Marco stayed, smiling at Angela. "*Buona sera, Signorina* Reardon." He grasped her hand and raised it to his lips, causing her to blush.

"*Buona sera, Signore Romano,*" she answered smoothly.

The actor's smile widened, and he clutched her hand to his chest. "No, no, you must say Marco. To me, you can be Angela. *Sì?*"

"Certainly." Her eyes cut to Jake, whose eyes were firing bullets at *Signore Marco Romano*.

"Marco, down here, now," yelled Zurlini from the foyer.

"Coming, Sergio." Marco squeezed Angela's hand and then released it. His obsidian eyes peered from under long, dark lashes directly into hers. "*Amo donne molto belle.* You will drink and dance with Marco later. *Sì*?"

"Yes. I'll look forward to it."

"*Ciao*, Angela." He nodded curtly at Jake before hurrying down the stairs.

She avoided looking at Jake while they walked to the bedroom. He waved her inside. After closing the door and setting the bags on the bed, he caught her arm and spun her around.

"I sure hope the dress you brought isn't too hot. That bastard is already having wet dreams about you."

"Jake."

"Don't '*Jake*' me. The asshole was imagining you naked."

"How dare you talk to me like that?" She stopped abruptly, her mouth gaping. "Oh my God. You're jealous."

"Damn straight, I'm jealous. And I don't trust him."

"He was just being polite to compensate for Zurlini's rudeness. When the actresses arrive, he won't even remember me."

"Don't count on it, Angela." She pulled away, but he yanked her back. "Seriously, be careful tonight," he warned.

She sighed and hung her head against his chest. "I'm not a child."

"No, but you're damn naïve."

"Thanks a lot."

"Listen to me. I've done these parties with Chuck before. They aren't tea parties. They get wild. Drugs, sex, fights. I won't be able to stay with you all the time." His arms wrapped around her protectively, and he kissed the top of her head. "Promise me you'll be careful."

"I promise," she said, offering him her lips.

* * *

An hour and a half later, Jake pounded on the locked bedroom door. Angela was supposed to rest, shower, and dress while he worked. She was smiling happily when she opened the door.

Adoration brightened Jake's expression. Inch by inch, his eyes admired the beautiful woman in the chic, black silk cocktail dress. The lustrous fabric subtly emphasized her slender curves. A silver scarf wrapped her breasts in soft folds, revealing a small amount of cleavage. The shimmering cloth draped under her arms and continued around to the back. Sparkling crystals lined the tiny straps and the slit that ended high on her right thigh.

Suddenly, his mood turned sullen. "Oh shit," he muttered.

Her smile faded. She turned on her heels toward the mirror where she'd been finishing her makeup.

He watched the floating ends of the scarf tease the curve of her firm tush. The low-cut back of the dress accentuated her small waist.

"Oh hell," he said, shutting the door.

Angela glared at him, indignation and hurt on her face. "Well, gee, Mr. Stone, you sure know how to flatter a girl. I'm sorry you don't like my dress."

"Don't like? I want to eat you alive, and so will every other guy here. All the straight ones, at least."

"You're ridiculous. This is a simple, classy dress. It's certainly not racy or risqué."

"I agree, but who knew classy could be so sexy? Those vultures will be circling you all night."

"Good Lord, Jake. With you working, I'm afraid of being lonely."

A harsh laugh sliced through the tension. "Lonely? I guarantee you won't be alone. And that's what *I'm* afraid of."

"For a playboy, you sound awfully possessive and protective," she snapped.

His mood darkened dangerously before he grabbed his suit from the closet, stomped into the bathroom, and slammed the door.

Jake emerged from the bathroom twenty minutes later. He fastened the shoulder holster with the larger Glock in place. The small gun was transferred to an ankle holster. He pushed an earphone deep into his right ear, listened to the team already communicating. He clipped the mic under his shirt collar. After buttoning his suit coat, he appraised himself in the mirror.

Angela sat primly and silently in a chair by the window, watching people arrive at the gate. She didn't turn or speak. He walked up behind her and gingerly placed his hands on her almost bare shoulders.

"I'm sorry," he whispered, "for so many things."

Her shoulders rose and fell beneath his hands. "I wish I hadn't come."

"I wish I hadn't asked you. It was selfish of me. I wanted to show you off, but now I don't want those bastards leering at my woman."

She tilted her head back and peered up at him. He curled a wisp of blond hair loosely around his finger.

"Am I your woman, Jake?" Her eyes searched his.

He blinked slowly—twice. "Sure, I guess. If you want to be." He shrugged as though he didn't care.

Angela caught her lower lip with her teeth. Her eyes glistened.

"How silly. We sound like teenagers. Forget it." She lowered her head. "If you want, I'll stay here in the room tonight."

My woman. He blinked again.

"Jake?"

"Huh? Oh. Uh, locking you in and boarding up the door is tempting, I admit, but I'm not quite that paranoid. The guys and I will keep a close eye on you."

"Does the contract require you to do this?"

His heart skipped a beat, but his training kept his face expressionless. "Contract?"

"Chuck's contract. Is the undercover guy required to have a date?"

"I don't know or care. Let's go. I have to get down there."

At the top of the stairs, he took her arm, but he moved in a trance. Keywords from their disturbing conversation exploded like landmines in his brain, destroying his focus. *My woman.* The scene below melted into a swirling pot of indistinguishable shapes and colors. *Your woman.* When they reached the foyer, Jake parted the crowd like an icebreaker. *Eat you alive.* He nodded discreetly to Chuck as they passed him en route to the main room. *Possessive.*

Through the long expanse of several sliding glass doors, he noticed the band warming up on the deck. *Protective.* He made eye contact with the security team member stationed out there. *Afraid.* Eyes sweeping the mass of people, he spotted the man in charge of the main room and nodded slightly. *Playboy.* His hand at the small of her back, he guided Angela to the line leading into the formal dining room where the catered dinner buffet was being served.

Contract. Contract. Contract.

As they filled their plates, Jake spoke to one of the catering staff.

"I need someone to take a plate—make that two plates—and a large, non-alcoholic drink out to the guard at the gate. His name is Curly." He slipped the young girl a twenty.

"Sure, mister."

Angela glanced at him sideways. "Curly will be very grateful." It was the first she'd spoken since they'd left the bedroom.

"Yeah, he's not keen on missing meals."

They fell silent again, finished the buffet line, and wedged their way to a loveseat in the living room. They ate without talking, each observing the mass of diversity milling about them.

"*Ciao*, Angela," called a familiar voice from across the noisy room.

"Shit," Jake murmured.

"Is good? *Sì*?" Marco asked, approaching with a scantily clad woman hanging on each arm.

"*Ciao*, Marco. The food's delicious," Angela said, averting her eyes from the women.

He cocked his head to catch her gaze and smiled. "The party. You like?"

"Yes, very interesting."

"I see you later, *Signorina*." He led the women like a pair of terriers toward the deck.

Angela watched them leave. "I told you so," she said quietly.

"He came over specifically to speak to you," Jake countered.

She flashed angry eyes at him. "Did you see those two women? Do you see the dozens of glamorous women at this party?"

"Yeah. Do you see the 'get' look in the eyes of all the guys?"

"The what?"

"The 'get' look."

"All right. Tell me."

"*Get* down. *Get* dirty. *Get* some. *Get* lucky. *Get* laid."

She rolled her eyes and sighed. "Is that all you think about?"

His finger darted to his ear, saving him from answering.

"I got a situation out here," Curly was explaining to Chuck. "Car-load of guys say they were invited, but their names aren't on my list."

"Give me the names. I'll check with Zurlini," said Chuck. "Watch your back."

While he waited for the conversation to resume, Jake peeked at Angela. She picked at her food while studying the guests, seeming more interested in the eccentric people than the gourmet fare. She laid her plate on an end table and stood.

"I'm going to get another drink. Want something?" she asked without looking at him.

"Can't. On duty," he said curtly, as Chuck spoke again in his ear. He was vaguely aware of Angela being swallowed up by the crowd.

"No good, Curly. Get rid of them," Chuck ordered.

"Right. I could use some backup. I'd bet money they're packin'," Curly said.

"I'm available," Jake interjected. "On my way."

* * *

Angela returned with her Cosmopolitan to a loveseat now occupied by two men totally absorbed in each other. Jake and her plate had dis-appeared. Sipping the drink, she glanced around the packed room. When a hand squeezed her shoulder from behind, she jumped.

"You are wanting to dance with me. *Sí*?" Marco's teasing voice greeted her. "Come."

He eased her through a doorway into an adjoining room, which opened onto the deck where the band was playing. A temporary dance floor had been installed, and it was alive with swaying, gyrating bodies. Marco set both of their drinks on a table as they neared the dancers.

"*Per favore scusarci,*" Marco chanted, creating room for him and Angela.

A little dazed, she joined Marco in a fast dance. His brilliant smile and excellent dance moves soon put her at ease. She was annoyed with Jake, but why let him completely ruin the party? He had deserted her without a word. Why shouldn't she drink a little, dance a little?

After the fourth dance, Marco's hand clenched her waist and led her out the doors to the bar set up on the deck. They leaned on the railing, sipping fresh cocktails, watching the surf crash on the beach, and talking. Marco was attentive, beguiling. He edged closer until their hips touched.

"Rome is much warmer at night," he said, his arm snaking around her shoulders and pulling her against him.

She stiffened, the familiar flutter of panic in her stomach. "I'm ready to dance some more. Coming?" She wiggled out of his grasp and hurried back to the dance floor.

With each dance, Marco's dancing grew more suggestive. He touched her continuously despite her attempts to stay out of reach. Growing increasingly uncomfortable, Angela tried to bolt when the band started a slow song, but Marco refused to be denied. He grabbed her arm, dragged her flat against him, and guided her across the floor. His embrace was so tight she could barely breathe.

"I want you all night," he whispered in her ear, one hand sliding down to caress her ass.

"Stop, Marco. I...I need a break," she stammered, her pulse accelerating.

"Later, we rest." He smiled seductively. "Together."

Marco's head jerked around at a tap on his shoulder.

"May I cut in?" Jake asked.

"No," Marco snapped.

"Yes," Angela said, reaching for Jake's arms.

Forced to step aside, Marco scowled at Jake and then stomped off the dance floor and out of the room.

"Sore loser," Jake said flatly. "Having fun?"

"Yes, thank you. I don't want to dance anymore." She stopped moving her feet.

"You didn't mind dancing with the Italian stallion. I've been watching. Move, or we're going to get crushed."

Her feet followed his again. "I'm thirsty."

"I'll get you a drink after this dance." He rested his head against hers and closed his eyes, a faint smile on his lips.

A short time later on the deck, sipping a strong Cosmo, she kept a wide space between them.

"I had to give Curly a hand. Party crashers," he explained.

She glanced at her watch. "Two hours. Must've been a horde."

"At first, I couldn't find you when I came back in. Then I remembered the gigolo. You two seemed so happy together, I didn't want to intrude."

"Give it a break, Jake," she said, tossing her hair with the ocean breeze. "Why shouldn't I have a good time? You made it clear we don't have any strings attached. A little flirtation might help my ego."

His eyes darkened. "Be careful what you wish for, Angela." He cocked his head, listening to the voice in his ear. "On my way. Stay cool, man." He met her eyes. "Trouble on the sand. I gotta go."

He aimed for her lips, but she offered only her cheek. He hesitated and then planted a quick peck. Before she could speak, he was gone.

She ordered another Cosmo before returning to the main room. Marco was instantly by her side. She wasn't sure she wanted company.

"Angela is not happy? Marco fix," he said, clutching her free hand and pulling her into the dance room. He motioned the universal sign for drinking. "How you say? Chug, chug."

She laughed and gulped the rest of her drink. Bending to set down the glass, she swayed, but Marco caught her arm. He peered down at her with a lascivious grin.

After five fast dances, Angela began to watch for Jake, but he didn't reappear. A clock on the wall showed 1:00 a.m. She was tired and anxious.

The mood on the dance floor had changed. The dances now resembled mating rituals. Men and women wandered off in groups of two or three. The proximity of so much sexual tension clawed at her composure. Escape beckoned.

"Marco, I'm exhausted. I need to stop," she said, breathing hard.

"One more, then break." Marco leered at her through hooded eyes.

He gyrated suggestively and circled her. From behind, he grabbed her hips, pulled her against his pelvis, and pumped his hard erection into the cleft of her butt.

Angela gasped. "What— No. Stop!"

He spun her around. One hand kept her pressed to him as he

ground his swollen dick against her. The other hand pulled her face to his. His lips and tongue attacked hers. She pounded his chest and tried to break out of his grasp.

"You want to fuck Marco now? *Sí*?" he purred before nipping at her ear.

"No. God, no. Let me go!"

Other dancers stopped to watch, but no one interfered.

He recoiled from her hammering fists and frowned. "What's wrong, Angela?"

She twisted out of his arms and stumbled backward a few steps. "I'm not going to—" She gulped air into heaving lungs. Her skin prickled with gathering sweat. She rubbed trembling fingers across her forehead.

Marco stepped closer but didn't touch her. His aggressiveness vanished. He bent his head low to speak quietly. "I scared you, Angela?"

Staring at the floor, she said, "Yes, you did. No sex. Understand? No sex."

He scowled, puzzled. "I thought you liked Marco."

"To party with. To talk to. Not to sleep with."

"How you know if you not try me?"

"Believe me, I know." She shuddered violently.

"Come, you sit. Too much to drink." Hugging her shoulders, he gallantly led her to a chair along the wall. After settling her, he lifted her chin and lowered his face to within inches of hers. His smile didn't reach his eyes. The piercing, dark orbs held a completely different message. "I think Angela plays hard to *get*."

The last word echoed inside her head. Men. Anger simmered just beneath the surface as she clung desperately to her poise.

"I get you a drink," Marco said, straightening.

"No. I'm done. I'm going upstairs."

A seductive smile curled his lips. "Drink *water*. Then I help you upstairs."

Too dazed and tired to argue, she nodded. After Marco hurried away, she covered her face with her hands, trying to calm the turbulent emotions churning inside. Anger. Panic. Disappointment.

In a few minutes, Marco returned with a small tumbler. He swirled the water vigorously and then handed it to her. "Drink fast."

"Thank you, Marco."

She tipped the glass to her mouth and sipped. Her eyes widened. She choked, coughed, and then lowered the glass deliberately.

"There's something—" She peered into the water again. Her eyes rose accusingly to meet his lewd gaze. "What's in here?"

"Water," he snapped, impatiently. "Drink it all. Then we go."

"Jesus." Angela drew a deep breath, let it out slowly.

Tamping down rage, she rose carefully from the chair. Dipping her fingers into the glass, she pinched something at the bottom. She extracted it, shook off the water, and stared at the pill before shoving it in front of Marco's face.

"What…is…this?" she asked shrilly.

Dancers stopped. Heads turned.

Marco's eyes narrowed. "Nothing."

"How dare you? You couldn't seduce me so you decided to drug me," she shouted for everyone to hear.

The room stood still. The band stopped mid-song. All eyes were riveted on the arguing couple.

Angela blinked in disbelief at the pill clamped between the fingers of her left hand. Not knowing the chemical or street name for it didn't matter. She knew its purpose. Her outrage burned in her defiant glare that assaulted Marco's smug expression.

Suddenly, the water exploded in his face.

He sputtered and swore lavishly. His hand sliced hard against her right arm, launching the glass across the room. A woman squealed.

Angela's right hand ricocheted with surprising force, catching Marco solidly on the cheek. "You bastard!" she screamed.

He growled and raised his fist.

"Don't touch her," Jake snarled, jumping in between the Italian and Angela.

With Jake's steel-dagger eyes promising great bodily harm, Marco hesitated, his fist hanging in the air.

Jake reached for Angela, but she shrugged him off. "Stop. This is my fight."

He glanced at her swiftly, meeting her eyes for only a moment. He grinned, raised both hands in surrender, and stepped aside. "He's all yours, babe."

Marco recovered his courage. With one wary eye on Jake, he strutted forward like a peacock, positioning himself only a few inches in front of Angela.

With arrogant machismo, his belittling gaze undressed her. His tongue licked his lips lustfully. The actor snickered. "You would *not* be a good fuck, Angela. You are stupid American woman. You do not know what you want."

She glared into his mocking eyes. Shaking her head, she lowered her gaze and smiled wickedly. "But I do know what I *don't* want: Italian sausage and meatballs."

Then her knee blasted into his genitals.

* * *

The trip to Chuck's house in LA was long and silent. Jake drove mechanically, as though his thoughts were miles away. Was he annoyed about their conversation in the bedroom before the party? Was he gloating about being right regarding Marco Romano? Was he angry Sergio Zurlini had ordered them to leave?

Angela didn't care. She peered out the side window without really seeing, her mind flying free.

What an awful night. What a fantastic night.

My God, what had happened to her? Her pulse still raced. Her insides tingled. She felt electrified. Reborn. Strong. Empowered.

She closed her eyes against the sting of tears. Joyful tears. A new Angela, capable of dealing with sexual aggression, had risen from the ashes. What a glorious night.

"This is it," Jake said.

He was out of the Corvette before his announcement registered in her mind. She sighed, exhausted but happy.

After opening the door with Chuck's extra key and disarming the security system, Jake hauled their garment and overnight bags inside. He motioned Angela upstairs before he reset the alarm.

She was standing in the hallway when he arrived at the top of the stairs. He strode past, opened the first door, and closed it. Opened the second and third doors, closed them. Sauntered to the end of the hall, peeked in, turned around.

"Shit, there's only one," he muttered.

"Yeah, shit," she echoed.

Annoyed, he glanced down the hall at her. "Honestly, I didn't know. Chuck just assumed we…I'll sleep downstairs on the couch."

He lumbered into the guest room with its one bed and dropped the bags on the floor. He turned to leave, but Angela blocked his exit.

"You need something?" he asked irritably.

"Yes. You."

Her arms went around his neck and pulled him down to her. Her mouth found his.

Whatever had been tormenting Jake seemed to drift away as he enveloped her in his arms. His lips massaged hers into parting. His tongue caressed hers, and they groaned simultaneously.

The duet caused them to separate, chuckling. She laid her head against his shoulder.

"Are you angry?" she asked.

"Angry?" He kissed the top of her head and threaded his fingers through the hair at her nape. "No, not angry. Proud as hell."

She laughed and looked up. Their gazes locked.

"Jake, do you realize the significance of what happened?"

"I think so."

"I didn't faint. I didn't panic. I fought back."

"I know. Damn amazing."

"Yeah…damn amazing." She framed his face with her hands. "Forget about the stupid stuff we said before the party. I was being adolescent." She kissed him quickly and then pulled back. "You can sleep with me. Sleep—literally. If you don't behave yourself, I'll honor you with the same knee. Understand?"

"Yeah. You don't have to warn me twice. They may not be Italian, but I want to keep my sausage and meatballs intact."

Chapter 18

The present

"I don't know, I don't know," Jake mumbled, thrashing about on top of the cheap, stained bedspread where he'd fallen asleep only a few hours earlier.

He rolled over and crashed to the floor.

"Shit."

Rubbing his tired, burning eyes, he peeled his naked body off the grungy carpet. He glared at the bed as if it had intentionally ejected him.

"Damn midget bed," he grumbled, stumbling to the bathroom.

He returned fifteen minutes later, trying to dry off with a towel only slightly larger than a hand towel. Finally giving up, he flung the inadequate piece of terrycloth at the bathroom door.

Sunlight streamed through the threadbare drapes. The loud rumble from the freeway invaded the room. Offensive odors hung in the air.

Jake closed his eyes and recalled fondly the peace and quiet of his secluded Valley Center home. Had he been away only four nights? It seemed an eternity.

While he dressed, he planned his next moves. Increasing urgency tightened his chest. Working without his computer would be a major inconvenience, but with Internet access through his cell phone, he'd survive.

Within an hour, Jake had reservations for the next three nights at a Holiday Inn Express. The hotel had reluctantly agreed to let him check in at 10:30 a.m. A rental car was being delivered there at eleven. No phone messages had been left for him at the Doubletree, and the front desk staff was unaware of anyone asking for him or his room number.

By nine, the Corvette was creeping down the freeway with the rest of the Sunday morning traffic. Jake was acutely aware of every dark Suburban, and there were dozens of them. Since his call with the Contractor on Thursday, he'd exercised every precaution to avoid being followed, but LA just had too many damn cars.

As a black Suburban cut in behind him, he visualized the vehicle bearing down on J.J.'s Hummer. Had he seen it before last night? Tinted windows. No plates. Damn it, he couldn't be sure.

Jake crisscrossed the streets around the Doubletree Hotel before pulling into the parking lot. He canvassed every line, stopping behind two dark Suburbans. One had Texas plates, the other California. Finally, he parked in one of the registration spaces nearest the entrance.

Outside his room, he listened at the door. Nothing. The DO NOT DISTURB sign and the marker he'd left were still in place. He waited until the hallway was clear. With Glock in hand, he flung open the door.

He pivoted, scanning quickly. No sign of intrusion. He kicked the door shut behind him. Primed for action, he moved through the suite like a SEAL. His heart pounding, his gaze darted from corner to corner, ceiling to floor.

Finally, a loud sigh of relief escaped his lips. He lowered the Glock and rolled his head from side to side. But he stopped for only a minute. Time to leave. No one, not even Burke, would know he was switching hotels.

* * *

"Hey, Williams, this is Sean Burke. I heard about J.J."

LAPD Vice cop Mike Williams hesitated. "Good news travels fast even on a Sunday. How'd you hear?"

"A little bird told me. Shit, since when was Sunday different from any other day around here?" Burke tapped a pencil on his desk. "Does the LA Sheriff's Homicide Bureau have any leads?"

"I don't think so. Clean getaway from what I hear. What's your interest in it?"

"I have an unsolved rape from four years ago. We questioned J.J. The asshole had an alibi, but I'd swear he knew something. Any chance I could have a peek at the information you have on him? With J.J. being dead and all, no one should mind."

"That's tough, Burke. You know how touchy City Hall is about J.J.'s escort service. I won't be surprised if the whole murder investigation gets swept under the rug."

"Yeah, I've thought about that, too. Not that I really give a damn about prosecuting J.J.'s murderer."

"Agreed. Whoever it was did us all a favor. Except maybe the regular johns. They may be in for a *hard* time."

Both men snickered.

"Let me get the pulse of the thing today," Williams said. "If there aren't too many eyes watching, I might be able to do something for you."

"Thanks, buddy. I'd sure love to solve that old rape case."

* * *

"Lion water." Jake repeated J.J.'s last words as he stretched out on the king-sized bed in the Holiday Inn Express room.

It sure didn't sound like a name. A product? A place? Maybe.

The pimp had barely whispered the words with his last breath. What had Jake expected—a miracle?

He'd already searched the Internet. There were lots of lion water fountain websites. Ebay offered everything from lion water pistols to lion water bottle tops. Nothing helped.

Jake's head ached. His fast-food breakfast churned in his stomach. He closed his eyes. No time for sleep, but God, he was so tired. He'd just rest his eyes for a few minutes.

The cell phone woke him an hour later. He grabbed it from the nightstand and squinted at the phone number. Virginia. The Reardons. The parents or Maleena? *Screw them.* The call went to voice mail as Jake's head dropped back on the pillow. But curiosity got the better of him, and five minutes later, he listened to the message.

"Hello, Mr. Stone, this is Maleena Reardon. Where are you? Uh, I thought you'd always be available on your cell. Uh, I hope you…hope everything's all right. Call me back." There was a long pause before the call disconnected.

"In your dreams, bitch, but it's nice to know you're worried about me," he muttered.

The phone rang again in his hand. An LA number.

"What's happening, Burke?" Jake answered.

"You were supposed to call."

"You sound like a woman. Are you my mother or my girlfriend?" He chuckled. "I was kind of busy this morning."

"I'm not laughing, Stone. They opened a homicide investigation. I know an eyewitness, but I'm withholding that information. I could get royally screwed."

"You're right. Sorry."

"Start at the beginning and stick to the truth."

While he paced the hotel room, Jake recounted the entire episode, beginning with the girlfriend scene before dinner. When he finished, the detective was silent.

"Just five more minutes, Burke, and I would've scared it out of him. I can't believe the rotten luck."

"Yeah. Strange, the 'lion water' thing. Got any ideas?"

"I ain't got shit. I've already checked the Internet. No help. I wish I'd gone straight to J.J.'s place last night and tossed it until I found his Rolodex or something. Now it's too late. I'm sure the cops are all over it." He slumped onto a chair.

"Afraid so. The good news is J.J. essentially admitted this Bad Angel and her john were involved in the rape. Now you just need to find them."

"You make it sound so easy. He said the hooker disappeared, so I'm probably out of luck there. But the john is still a customer. If he's as kinky and violent as J.J. said, then some of his hookers must know who the asshole is. I thought I'd pay his girlfriend a visit tonight."

"For a friendly chat?"

"You got a problem with that?"

"Not unless she ends up dead."

"I had nothing to do with J.J.'s murder," Jake said without any inflection.

"Well, you would've needed an accomplice, and my guess is you work alone. So, what do you do now?"

"This is where you come in. Get your hands on a list of the escort service's customers. *Suspected* customers, even. I don't give a shit. I'm looking for a murderer, not passing judgment on their sex lives. Vice must have something."

"If they do, it's locked up tighter than a chastity belt. I told you, it's hands-off, per orders from City Hall," Burke said.

"Get creative. Just don't get caught."

"Thanks. I would've never thought of that. So, Stone, you're convinced this shooting is related to the rape?"

"Yeah."

"Because?"

"It fits. If the rapist was worried enough to kill Angela, then he would've also been worried about J.J.," Jake said.

"And anyone else who could finger him." Burke sounded deep in thought.

"Like Bad Angel. He probably offed her right away. It explains why she disappeared."

"Makes sense."

"If the victim, hooker, and pimp are all dead, the guy must be feeling home free," he speculated.

"They make mistakes when they get cocky or comfortable."

"Agreed. Are you drawing a blank on lion water?"

"Hell, yes. Never heard of it or him."

"You know, there's a chance J.J. wasn't even answering my question about the john. He could've been identifying the shooter as the Lionel guy he said was after his business. Lion…Lionel. You ever heard of this Lionel guy?"

"That would be Vice's area if he runs a prostitution ring," Burke reminded him.

"Check it out."

"Yes sir."

"Sorry. *Please* check it out."

"Better."

"What am I missing, Burke?"

"Besides the answers, the rapist, and the murderer?" The detective laughed and then was silent for a long moment. "Who knows about your investigation?"

"Huh?"

"Who knows you're digging into this rape case in connection with Angela's murder?"

Jake straightened in the chair. "Let's see. You and Olsen at LAPD. Detective Smithson at CPD. Becky Smelter, of course. I told the Reardons I suspected murder but didn't mention a connection to the rape." He frowned with concentration. "I think that's it."

"Can't see why anyone on that list would mind you poking around." Burke paused. "But what if…" He stopped and cleared his throat.

"What?" Jake said impatiently, his lack of sleep catching up with him.

"Well, what if the shooter wasn't after J.J.?"

Jake's eyes narrowed, and he scowled. "You're dreaming, Burke."

"Yeah, I guess. But what are the odds that, after four years, the john decides to off the pimp—while you're in the car?"

"Nice try, detective. You really need to curb your wishful thinking. Call me when you get something from Vice."

Without waiting for a reply, Jake disconnected. He carefully set the phone on the nightstand. At the small table, he tossed two ice cubes into a glass and filled it with J.D.

Stretching out on the bed, he leaned on the pillows against the headboard. He swallowed a long drink of the amber liquid and closed his eyes.

He couldn't tell Burke. He couldn't tell anyone.

It sure didn't help to hear the detective—who knew nothing about the precarious situation with the Contractor—voice the question that had been gnawing at Jake since last night.

The very real possibility had flashed through Jake's mind the second the Suburban window slid open and the muzzle of a gun emerged.

Was *he* the target?

Chapter 19

Nine weeks earlier

So this is how it ends. No explanations, no excuses. No good-byes. Nothing. Angela stared at the computer monitor on her desk, no longer seeing the floor plan displayed on the screen. She hadn't heard from Jake since he'd dropped her off in front of her condo Sunday afternoon when they arrived home from Chuck's house in LA. That was two days ago.

Glancing at the clock for the thousandth time, she sighed heavily at the thought of spending the evening alone. Again. She checked her cell phone for missed calls. None, of course. Briefly, she considered leaving another message for Jake, but since he hadn't bothered to respond to her three previous messages, calling him again seemed useless.

Stella Jenkins poked her head into the office. "If you don't need anything else, Angela, I'm heading home."

"Huh? Oh, fine. I should leave also," she said halfheartedly.

The assistant cocked her head sympathetically. "Guy troubles?"

"How'd you guess?"

"I can tell."

"It's obvious?"

"Afraid so. Is it Jake?"

Angela nodded. "He's disappeared." She forced a laugh. "Oh, well, at least he lasted longer than the others."

"Crap, I'm disappointed in him. He seemed different, you know, stronger or something. Anyway, I'm sorry it didn't work out. You gonna be okay?"

"Sure. Hey, he was just another guy. Besides, I'm a survivor. See you tomorrow."

Stella gave her a thumbs-up and left.

Angela released another sigh and shut down her computer. She stood and began locking the file cabinets. When her cell phone rang she froze momentarily, then spun around and grabbed it. *Jake.* Her throat tightened.

"Hello," she answered tentatively.

"Hey, babe, how are ya?"

Keeping all emotion from her voice, she lied, "I'm fine. In a bit of a hurry, though."

A strained moment passed before he continued. "Well, I won't keep you. I know this is short notice, but I was hoping you could come over."

"Come over? Why?"

Another silence. "Because I'd like to see you."

She pulled her lower lip between her teeth.

"What's wrong, Angela?"

"You honestly don't know?" she snapped.

"Of course I know," he said defensively. "I haven't called and—"

"Right. *You* are 'what's wrong.'"

Jake hesitated. "It was a tough weekend."

"Really? I was there. Remember?"

"Yeah, and you were spectacular." He cleared his throat. "I want you to spend the night, here, with me."

Her jaw dropped. "What?"

"You handled it so well at Chuck's house, I think we should try it here. Alone. As the next step, you know."

Her heart skipped a beat. "Jake, I thought—"

"I know what you thought, but it's not that. Crap, I just needed time to come to grips with…with everything. We can talk about it tonight." He paused. "Will you come…and stay?"

Eyes burning with unshed tears, she pressed her fist over her mouth and struggled to compose herself before answering. "Yes, Jake, I will."

* * *

Moonlight reflected off the boulders like white chocolate chips sprinkled atop mounds of crumbled brownies.

Admiring the view, Angela stood at the end of the flagstone patio next to the vanishing edge of the swimming pool. A step in front of her, the steep hillside fell away into nothingness. She smiled at the memory of Jake's impudent explanation of circumventing the fence requirement to preserve the pristine panorama.

A persistent west wind tugged at her hair and the pool towel wrapped around her naked body. Relaxing in the spa after dinner, Jake had coaxed her into shedding her swimsuit again. It had been easier this time, almost comfortable sitting in the darkness, knowing they were both naked but unable to see the evidence of it.

Angela shivered as the breeze brushed across her wet skin. Something about the night made her shudder inside as well. Her hopes of discussing what Jake had "come to grips with" had been dashed against his granite façade. Despite his earlier offer to discuss it, the topic had been carefully avoided at dinner and afterward in the spa. And in contrast to his invitation for her to spend the night, his attitude toward her all evening had been restrained and distant. Now she stared into space, wondering if the night would end well or not.

Running footsteps from behind startled her. Suddenly, a large hand landed roughly on her back. She stumbled forward. Her left foot slipped off the patio onto the ground; her right foot slid close to the edge. The loose dirt beneath her gave way. Arms flailing, she teetered precariously toward the boulder-covered hillside below.

She screamed.

"Angela!" Jake yelled, grabbing her arm with both hands. He yanked her back onto the patio and enveloped her in his arms. "What the hell are you doing?"

Gasping for air and trembling, she gazed up at him in disbelief. "Y-you p-pushed me," she stammered.

"Pushed you? Shit. Are you crazy? I was pulling you back."

She shut her eyes and went limp against his bare chest. His arms tightened around her, his heart pounding against her ear. They stood, motionless, speechless, for several minutes.

"Come sit down on this lounge while I get you a drink," he finally said, leading her away from the edge. "Are you okay?"

"I think so."

He lowered her onto the lounge and stroked her hair tenderly before leaving her.

Her perplexed gaze followed him into the house. Jake had pushed her. She was almost sure of it. Almost. But why? Why would he do such a dangerous thing? Did he want to play the hero by saving her? How childish and reckless if that were his motivation.

A violent shudder shook her. She forced her breathing to slow, forced her thoughts away from the incomprehensible.

She had to be wrong. In the terror of the moment, she had misinterpreted his protective gesture. His face had shown shock and fear when he held her. The incident had unnerved him as well.

Angela drew a deep breath and rubbed the back of her neck. The fright had left her shaken, jittery. Her eyes were drawn to the tranquil water of the swimming pool where the full moon plated the surface with shimmering silver.

On impulse, she stripped off the towel and dove in. The warm water caressed her body as she swam, the liberating sensation calming her nerves.

Several minutes later, Jake emerged from the house carrying two tumblers of Jack Daniel's. He walked to the patio table, set the glasses down, and glanced around.

"Angela?"

She quietly treaded water in the deep end, thankful the pool and landscaping lights were off.

"Over here, Jake," she called.

With the pool towel still wrapped around his waist, he turned and strolled toward the pool. "Are you feeling bet—" Stopping abruptly near the edge, he stared, transfixed, into the water. A groan escaped as his darkening eyes rose to hers.

Her breath caught at the heat in his expression. She followed his gaze back down. *Oh God*. From that angle, the moonlight pierced the water, illuminating her nudity like a spotlight. Instinctively she began to swim away, to the shallow end of the pool.

She heard and felt him dive in. Frantically, her arms and legs thrashed through the water, but she sensed him gaining on her. As soon as her toes could touch the bottom, she stopped swimming and tried to cover herself with her hands and arms.

But it was too late.

He was on her. Strong arms clutched her to his naked body, his rigid erection pressing into her belly. His mouth attacked hers, a moan vibrating against her lips.

Her fists wedged between them and shoved into his gut. He grunted.

"Stop, Jake. Stop it!" she shouted.

His forehead dropped forward to rest on hers. One hand traced her spine from nape to tush.

"Please let me touch you. God, you feel so good."

She struggled to twist out of his grasp, but he was too strong. "No, Jake, stop!"

His kiss silenced her. His hands cradled her head as his tongue sought hers.

Slowly, uncertainly, she relaxed and responded. This was a step toward her goal, wasn't it? She should enjoy being touched like this. Her eyes closed, and she savored the taste of him. Her tongue followed each symbolic thrust of his. When his lips nibbled down her neck, she clasped her hands at his nape and hung her head back, allowing him better access. Yes, this was good.

Reacting to her surrender, Jake splayed both hands across her butt, lifting her up. His breathing turned ragged, and his kisses frenzied. Warm lips trailed the slope of her breasts, but hesitated, and then avoided her nipples.

Angela's pulse raced, heat sweeping through her, flaring in her groin. Her insides burned, clenched, liquefied, in sensual anticipation. The sensations were so foreign—nearly forgotten—they shocked her.

With her thighs balanced on his, Jake strode to the pool steps. Bending carefully, he set her on the third step so the water reached just below her shoulders. She leaned back when he pushed her legs apart and knelt between them. Frantically, strong hands explored: breasts, belly, thighs. Everywhere, except her most intimate spot.

He stretched out over her, supporting himself on one arm, resting his body lightly on top of her. His skin. Her skin. She trembled beneath him. Her hands clutched his waist. With his lips locked to hers, he pumped his swollen dick against her crotch, probing but not penetrating.

The insistent pressure triggered a spasm of arousal and a spark of panic inside her. *Not there. Don't touch me there.* In an instant, reality resurfaced. Familiar fear flooded through her. *Too much. Too fast. Stop. I can't. Can't.*

When she sobbed, his frenzy fizzled. He released her mouth and pressed her face against his heaving chest.

"Shit. I can't take much more of this. Can you feel how much I want you?" He slid his rigid dick across her thighs.

"Don't," she gasped. "Please, don't force me."

"Damn it, I'm not the bastard who raped you. I'd never force you. But this is killing me. I want you. I need you. Don't you…feel anything?" He choked on the words.

She said nothing, her feelings imprisoned by her panic.

He studied her face for a long time. "Jesus Christ," he whispered. He lowered her gently, supported himself above her with his hands bracketing her shoulders on the step. "I'm sorry, Angela. I lost control. It won't happen again."

Her eyes were drawn to his lean torso rising out of the water. Twisting around, she watched his taut ass and muscular thighs splashing up the stairs.

"Jake," she called softly.

He didn't stop, didn't respond.

"I feel—" she began, but the breeze blew away the rest of her words.

* * *

Jake fought the impulse to run, instead placing one foot deliberately in front of the other until he reached the privacy of the kitchen. Dripping wet and naked, he braced his hands on his knees and hung his head. His head throbbed with each heartbeat. *What have I done?*

Grappling with a myriad of alien emotions, he climbed the staircase to his bedroom. In the bathroom, he dried off before lumbering into the dressing area of the walk-in closet. Despite his attempt to clear away all thoughts of the evening, the devastating events kept replaying like a bad video in his mind. *How could I let this happen?*

After pulling on a pair of boxer briefs, he checked the security system panel. He confirmed all the exterior doors were unlocked. Since the episode at the front door during Angela's second visit, he'd been careful not to utilize the lock-in option. He sighed with resignation. He was sure she'd leave immediately, if she hadn't already. *How could I be so stupid?*

Jake swept the comforter toward the foot of the bed, exposing clean black silk sheets. He dropped heavily onto the coolness and scrunched his eyes shut. His fingers burrowed into his hair and gripped handfuls in desperation. He lay rigid, tempted to scream his frustration. *What kind of monster am I?*

The scene with Angela standing at the edge of the patio flashed under his closed eyelids. Something had snapped when he saw the potential danger. Shocked, he'd run up behind her. He remembered hesitating to grab the towel wrapped around her for fear of pulling it off. Instead, he'd reached for her shoulder. But his open hand had landed firmly on her bare back. *Dear God, did I push her? Did I? Did…I?*

His hands rubbed up and down his face, and the memory changed to the scene in the pool. Angela naked in the moonlit water. God, she was so sexy. Who could blame him for responding like a normal male? She would, that's who. He had violated her trust—if there had been any. And it was clear she didn't feel anything. *No heat. No desire. No lust. No…nothing. Shit.*

"Jake?"

His eyes popped open, and he lurched upright.

Angela stood in the bedroom doorway. A long, pink, silky nightgown draped her figure. His gaze swept over her, pausing at all the strategic spots. Her face was as pink as the gown when his eyes rose to meet hers.

"Angela?"

They studied each other.

She squared her shoulders. Her chest rose and fell. Her chin lifted. "Am I still invited to sleep over?"

Jake blinked. "Of course." He patted the sheet beside him.

She stared at the black silk, trepidation shining in her eyes. Her feet moved and then stopped.

He extended a hand. "It's okay," he whispered and gulped.

She nodded jerkily, inched toward the bed, and reached for his outstretched hand.

Feeling as unsure as she looked, he tried to radiate reassurance but failed miserably. Perhaps his own uncertainty gave her the confidence to climb into bed with him. He didn't try to pull her close; he allowed her to find her own comfort zone. When she was settled, he fluffed the top sheet over both of them. He stayed on his back, letting her roll onto her side to face him.

"Are you angry?" she asked.

"No."

"Disappointed?"

He shot her a sideways glance. "I'm a guy, Angela. What do you think?"

"I'm sorry."

"Don't apologize."

"Then what am I supposed to say?"

"How about nothing?"

She sighed tremulously, and he guessed she was close to tears. He inhaled deeply and expelled frustration through pursed lips. How much more celibacy could he take?

"I'm trying, Jake, really I am."

"I know."

"Maybe this isn't going to work. I'm not naïve, you know. You must be incredibly horny by now." She looked away. "If you're still not sleeping with someone else, that is."

His fingertips gently turned her face to his. "I'm not screwing anyone. Honest. But you're right, I'm about to explode." His thumb traced her lips. They parted, and warm breath bathed his fingers. He moaned and pulled his hand away.

"I'm sorry."

"Stop apologizing." His gaze dipped to her cleavage hidden modestly behind delicate lace, and to her nipples pressing against pink silk.

Angela yanked the sheet up to her neck. "I...I think you should call your masseuse tomorrow and have her come...come...take care of you."

Jake's eyebrows shot upward. "What?"

"I'm a pragmatist. I don't want to lose you."

"Lose me?" He cocked his head. "Does that mean you have me?"

A disconcerted expression replaced the concern on her face. "Uh. I...I didn't mean—"

He scooted closer and chuckled as his hand stroked her cheek. "Relax. You're damn right. You've got me good." He planted a chaste kiss on her forehead.

"But I can't satisfy you. You need sex. Your masseuse can relieve your frustration. And if I rationalize it as purely physical, I can accept that you need a woman other than me—"

"Bullshit. You're the most amazing woman I've ever met. I'd rather be sleeping beside you than screwing my masseuse or any other woman."

"Don't bullshit me, Jake. I don't believe that for a minute."

"Well, maybe it's an exaggeration," he admitted, grinning sheepishly, "but it sounded noble, didn't it?"

"Very noble."

"So reward me and drop this nonsense about another woman.

I've got my eye on the grand prize." But he shook his head to clear it of visions of claiming that prize. In desperation, he changed the subject. "By the way, I've been meaning to ask if you'd like to come with me to Rosarito Beach."

"Mexico?"

"Yeah, it's only a short drive south of Tijuana. Have you ever been there?"

"No."

"Great. I own a little place near the beach. It's quiet, secluded. Interested?"

"Sounds wonderful. When?"

"How about this weekend?"

"Perfect."

"Okay, now let's go to sleep."

After another chaste kiss, he stretched out a respectful distance away and closed his eyes. He suspected Angela was also wide awake, but he was still surprised when she spoke.

"Jake?"

"Hmmm?"

"I'm sorry I accused you of pushing me."

Pangs of guilt prevented him from responding.

"It was a stupid thought. I was just so frightened I didn't understand at first what had happened."

"Okay," he managed to say.

When her hand caressed his cheek, he opened his eyes to find her peering at him intently.

"I heard you running, and I started to spin around to see what was going on. You must have been reaching for my arm or shoulder, but when I turned so quickly, your hand landed on my back instead.

My motion sent me backward as your hand came forward. That's why it felt like a push."

"So I wasn't trying to kill you?" he said, joking to hide his relief.

"Of course not. I'm so sorry for what I said." She rolled over and snuggled her backside against him. "Do you forgive me?"

"Sure."

He carefully draped his arm across her waist. His teeth clenched as her silk-covered ass brushed provocatively against his frustrated dick. *God help me.*

Chapter 20

The present

Jake thought he was going blind. He pressed the balls of his hands against his eyes and rubbed. No help. The computer screen was still blurry. He'd lost track of how many hours he'd worked at the computer trying to decipher "lion water." Every directory, every database, every website with any potential had been researched. Nothing. Not a damn thing to show for his aching back, bloodshot eyes, and splitting headache.

He hadn't left the Holiday Inn room since he'd checked in over twenty-four hours earlier. Even when the maid arrived to clean the room and politely suggested he leave, he had steadfastly kept his butt glued to the increasingly uncomfortable chair. Despite the long hours and his investigative expertise, the meaning or identity of "lion water" eluded him.

The knowledge that he was racing against time percolated in his gut. Frustration coiled inside his chest and tightened minute by minute, hour by hour. He was so tightly strung that his head snapped around at the sound of his cell phone.

"Morning, Stone," Burke said in a voice that needed sleep.

"Damn, I hope you've got good news. I'm climbing the walls here."

"Where's 'here,' by the way?"

He frowned. "LA."

"I mean what hotel…? Hell, you're not going to tell me."

"Sorry, buddy. I'm keeping a real low profile. Jake Stone isn't even registered. Don't you just love fake IDs?"

"I don't wanna hear it. I got enough trouble at this end." Burke swore under his breath.

"That doesn't sound good."

"It's not. The shit's hitting the fan. Even those of us not in Vice are ducking turds."

Jake laughed. "What's happening?"

"Word leaked out about J.J.'s murder. Some asshole in the media made the connection to the escort service. Now every reporter in town is calling City Hall, the police commissioners, and the chief of police demanding to know if the information obtained in connection with the murder investigation will be used to prosecute the escort service's customers. A lot of scared johns are out there pissing in their pants. And some of them are bigwigs. I'd guarantee it."

"Look, I don't give a shit about the politics. I just want to know if 'lion water' was one of J.J.'s customers."

"Back off, Stone. I'm doing the best I can. Vice is battening down the hatches before they get ripped to shreds from all sides."

"Sorry." Jake pinched the bridge of his nose. "So you called to tell me you don't have anything."

"I've got a crumb, but you're not going to like it."

"Toss it to me anyway."

"The Lionel that J.J. mentioned is actually another pimp. His full name is Lionel James Brown. No 'water' in his name. He talks a big game, but he's really a small-time operator. He's already been interrogated. Has a verified alibi."

"Any homeys?"

"No."

"Contract kill?" Jake cringed.

"Not likely. Vice doesn't think Lionel was even after J.J.'s business. He just talked the talk to blow himself up in the hood. The cash for that sort of thing would probably have put a squeeze on him, too. He's all mouth and no balls."

"Well, shit, thanks for nothin'."

"I warned ya."

"Yeah. Any hope of getting my hands on the customer list?"

The detective laughed so loud Jake had to hold the phone away from his ear. "Not unless Santa Claus or the Easter Bunny gives it to you."

"Damn."

"Listen, Stone." Burke's voice lowered to a whisper. "My guy doesn't give a horse's ass about finding J.J.'s murderer, but he's royally pissed the whole prostitution ring may get swept under the rug because of some whoring muckety-mucks."

"So?"

"So he's willing to put his ass on the line. Right now, he's talking to the LA Sheriff's Homicide Bureau about access to the evidence gathered at J.J.'s place. He's afraid it's going to disappear, and soon."

"Smart guy."

"Maybe. But not if he gets caught making a copy of the damn list."

"Ballsy."

"Or crazy. He wants to turn it over to the media."

"Ouch."

"Yeah, he's liable to end up dead in a ditch if he's not careful. Anyway, he said he'd check the list for anything like 'lion water.' If his plan works, he may let us see it."

"What? So I can end up dead in a ditch with him?" Jake chuckled nervously. "You wouldn't be setting me up, would you, buddy?"

"Who, me? Never. You just better hope the guy owns a red velvet suit or a bunny costume. Gotta go."

Jake tapped his fingers on the table for several minutes, digesting Burke's call. His stomach growled. He glanced at his watch. Noon. He ordered a pizza and Coke to be delivered.

Taking a break from his search, he reclined on the bed while he ate. He chewed with his eyes closed. He desperately needed eyedrops or sleep.

As he finished the last slice of pizza, his cell phone rang again. He scowled at the Virginia number and let the call transfer to voicemail. Another message from Maleena. Another joy to brighten his day.

"Mr. Stone, this is Maleena Reardon," the recording began. "I left a message yesterday. Is everything all right? We need to talk about your investigation. Call me." She mumbled something vulgar under her breath before ending the call.

He grinned. "The feeling's mutual, lady, but it's nice to know you're worried about me."

His stomach full, his eyes burning, he flopped onto his stomach and punched the pillow into comfortable fullness. Before five minutes passed, he was asleep.

He dreamed of Angela. The image was not the woman in the red dress or the multitude in the mirrors, but his gorgeous girlfriend strolling across his bedroom wearing a pink silk nightgown. When she reached the bed where he lay, she seductively slid the straps of the gown down her arms until he was staring at her inviting tits. With a wiggle of her hips, the silk slithered to the floor, revealing a voluptuous body. He crawled across the bed and pulled her onto the sheets. She stroked his hardened dick until he spread her legs and moved between them. Smiling, she opened herself to him. Poised to thrust, his body suddenly, inexplicably, froze.

Why? the dream Angela asked.

I don't know, the dream Jake replied.

The real Jake woke up, grimacing with a hard-on from Hell.

Cursing fluently, he rolled off the bed and walked stiffly to the bathroom. *This is worse than the nightmare.*

A few minutes later, he tugged at his zipper as he burst out of the bathroom to grab his ringing cell phone.

"Where have you been?" Burke snapped. "I called an hour ago."

"Shit, I fell asleep. I can't believe I didn't hear the phone. What's up?"

"We got the fucking bastard, Stone!"

"Who is it?"

"Leonard Waterton. Name sound close enough to 'lion water' to you?"

"Damn straight. He was on the list?"

"With two stars after his name. Must be a valued customer."

"Do you know anything about him?"

Burke snorted. "He's an LA city councilman."

* * *

Jake dialed the number for Councilman Leonard Waterton's LA City Hall office on the untraceable, disposable cell phone he'd bought with cash at a convenience store a short time earlier.

"Good afternoon. Councilman Waterton's office. This is Ms. Jacobs. How may I help you?"

"Good afternoon. My name is Bob Smith, and I'm an old high school buddy of Leonard's. I'm in LA for a sales meeting, but I'm flying out at six. I decided to call on the spur of the moment to find out if I could pop in and see him for a few minutes if he's in the office and available this afternoon."

"I'm so sorry, Mr. Smith, but Councilman Waterton is booked with meetings in his office until six thirty. I'll tell him you called, and I'm sure he'll be sorry he missed you. Would you like to leave a number where he can reach you?"

"No, I'll try him the next time I'm in town. Thanks, ma'am."

Jake ended the call and tossed the phone onto the passenger seat of the rented white Ford Explorer. Good, the bastard was in the office. Now all he had to do was wait for the councilman to pull out of the City Hall parking lot in his dark blue Lincoln Navigator.

Using the zoom on his surveillance camera, he scrutinized the area for anything of concern, especially familiar SUVs. No Land Rovers. But he spotted two black Suburbans. The license plate of the one parked on the street wasn't visible. The one in the parking lot had California tags and a parking permit. Of course, removing or switching license plates was easy. Physical damage on a vehicle was a much better method of identification.

His eyes narrowed, and he rubbed the prickly heat on the back of his neck. The Suburban parked at the curb two blocks behind him warranted watching even though the constant flow of patrol cars to and from City Hall provided a cushion of security.

With another glance at the Suburban, he grabbed a manila folder off the floor and opened it. After Burke had called with the astonishing news, they'd worked together to compile a dossier on Leonard Waterton. They had gathered a wealth of information in a couple of hours. The file wasn't complete by any measure, but it was enough for Jake to start stalking.

He flipped through the pages. Recent photographs. Information on two vehicles. Driver's license. Principal residence address and property description. Bank accounts. Credit cards. College degrees. Marriage and divorce records. News headlines. Biographical articles. Tabloid gossip.

He peered at the photographs. Tall, blond, medium-build white man. Waterton definitely fit the Smelter sisters' description of the man leaving with Angela on the night of the rape. The pictures also revealed a sophisticated, reserved appearance and a strong but not handsome face. He appeared slightly older than the forty years documented on his driver's license. The close-up portrait exposed signs of heavy drinking and/or drug use. The man's financial information confirmed abundant money to enjoy vices lavishly. And according to the tabloid articles, Waterton was no stranger to vices. Gambling. Drinking. Womanizing.

Jake sneered. If he and Burke were right, the esteemed councilman had another vice: a darker, nastier, illegal one.

He surveyed the landscape again. No change in the Suburban. Vehicle and pedestrian traffic increased as 5:00 p.m. passed.

After finishing another water, he returned to studying the file, but it was difficult to focus. Pumping adrenaline made him tense, edgy. His body didn't want paperwork; it craved action, violence. The predator was poised to rip apart its prey.

His gaze darted to the side-view mirror. A nicely dressed, middle-aged woman climbed into the Suburban. He observed until the vehicle drove past and disappeared into the busy intersection ahead. Relief registered.

Thirty minutes later, he gave up trying to memorize Waterton's information. Instead, he trained his gaze on the stream of vehicles leaving City Hall. The blue Navigator didn't appear until shortly after 6:30 p.m. Jake lifted the camera to his eye, confirmed the license plate and driver, and snapped a picture.

He pulled the Explorer away from the curb and followed the Navigator, eventually merging onto the freeway. Jake had already mapped out the most likely routes Waterton would take from City Hall to his house in Brentwood. This knowledge would allow Jake to anticipate moves and decrease the likelihood of losing his target in the horrendous LA traffic.

As expected, Waterton exited onto a second freeway. Jake followed at a discreet distance. When a black Suburban suddenly appeared in the rearview mirror, Jake tensed. At the first opportunity, the Suburban pulled into the next lane and crept past. Fully tinted windows, bent rear California license plate. He memorized the number as he watched it slide in behind the blue Navigator like a panther stalking dinner.

Only briefly unlocking his gaze from the two SUVs, Jake shifted to the right when the next freeway exit appeared on the overhead signs. He waited patiently for Waterton to make a move toward the off-ramp, but the Navigator with its black tail continued straight ahead.

"Damn."

He racked his brain for anything in the dossier that would give a clue to another destination. Nothing surfaced. He could either follow blindly or circle back and lie in wait at Waterton's home. Since at this point he was primarily in surveillance mode, getting a sense of the target's behavior, he decided to tag along and to consider staking out the councilman's house as a backup plan. Jake accelerated and jumped into the lane to the right of his target.

He swung the sun visor around to partially cover the side window before pulling even with Waterton and sneaking a backward look in the side mirror at the occupants of the Suburban. Two men, one black, one white, both wearing baseball caps and large sunglasses. Grim expressions. No conversation.

Jake frowned as he eased off the gas and let both vehicles pull ahead. God, he wished he knew if those were the goons who'd shot at him and J.J. If so, they didn't seem to recognize him in the rented Explorer. Their attention was clearly focused on Waterton.

Was that attention friendly or unfriendly?

Enveloped by hundreds of vehicles, the three SUVs sped onward while Jake wrestled with his analysis. His theory was based on the buyer of Angela's contract being the rapist. That person would also have been motivated to arrange for J.J.'s murder. If Waterton was the buyer/rapist/murderer, why were the goons following him? Were the same guys now operating as his bodyguards? If the Contractor had tipped off the buyer as threatened, Waterton might have hired them to stay around as protection.

The scenario seemed logical. The Contractor must not have identified Jake by name or sold a contract on him. Therefore, Waterton knew simply that the hitman who had been hired to do his dirty work was on the warpath. Did the councilman understand that Jake's warpath would only end when he was dead? Definitely not. If he did, he would have known bodyguards were useless, and he would have bought a contract to kill the anonymous assassin.

Sucks for you, bastard. Your goons are a waste of money. I'm still going to kill you.

Jake felt primed to explode and knew that was a dangerous condition. Adrenaline overload. Following several deep, cleansing breaths, he guzzled a bottle of water as he drove. Still, his heart pounded like a ticking time bomb.

Waterton signaled and swung into the far right lane. Jake followed immediately, ending up sandwiched between the Navigator and the Suburban as the caravan exited onto yet another freeway. He recalled that this one ran through Southeast LA and Watts. Before Jake could get his bearings, though, Waterton swerved onto a surface street off-ramp. Jake cut off a small pickup in order to follow.

Feeling trapped, he changed lanes and braked abruptly as though preparing to turn. The other two SUVs continued without hesitation. He sighed with relief, slowed until three more vehicles passed, and then swung in behind them.

A few blocks later, Waterton turned into a residential neighborhood of older homes. The houses were generally small and rundown with yards in dire need of care.

More exposed now with the lack of traffic, Jake stayed farther back even though he risked losing his target. Two blocks ahead, the Navigator hung a right. The Suburban followed.

"Shit," he muttered, speeding to catch up before they disappeared.

He whipped around the corner so fast he almost passed Waterton before noticing him parked at the curb. Resisting the urge to slam on the brakes, he drove to the next cross street. The bodyguards were pulling a U-turn, and Jake lowered his head as he swerved around them.

Putting some space and time between him, Waterton, and the goons after the nerve-racking trip from City Hall seemed a good idea. Praying Leonard wouldn't be leaving too soon, Jake zigzagged through the neighborhood until he reappeared on the original street five minutes later. He squeezed the Explorer into an opening between two trucks, facing the Navigator on the opposite side of the street. No sign of the Suburban. Probably hanging out on a side street.

After killing the engine, he peered through the camera, expecting to see an empty Navigator. To his surprise, someone was climbing out of the car.

"What the hell?"

He squinted at the transformed figure and snapped a picture.

During Jake's brief absence, Leonard had shed his suit coat, tie, and dress shirt. The man now wore a baggy, red and white football jersey, a worn Dodgers baseball cap pulled down low, and oversized sunglasses as he hurried toward the nearest little house. Most miraculous was the full beard he'd grown in the past few minutes. Waterton unlocked the front door and rushed inside.

Jake jotted the address on the folder. Scooting down in the seat, he panned the neighborhood. Poorly maintained, nondescript houses and yards. Shabby, but not trashy. Older vehicles in the driveways. Quiet. No one outside.

Odd place for the councilman to visit. Alone. At night.

Why the disguise? And where were his bodyguards? They sure weren't sticking close enough to do any good.

Jake grinned, thinking how easy it would be to take down Leonard if his sniper rifle were handy. But he didn't want to kill the bastard that way. He wanted to grip the man's neck, look into his eyes, and tell him *why* he was dying. He needed to hear Leonard confess and apologize for what he had done to Angela.

The door of the house opened, and Jake jerked upright. Barely ten minutes had passed. After yanking the door shut, Leonard trotted across the yard, clutching the handles of two department store shopping bags.

When the Navigator executed a U-turn and headed back the way they'd come, the Suburban shot out of a side street. Jake would have preferred to wait, but he jumped in line for fear of losing them if he missed the light.

Once the caravan was on the main avenue, he dropped back, hiding behind a van and a small pickup. After several turns, he was uncertain whether they were still in Southeast LA or whether they had crossed into Watts. The surroundings supported the latter.

Small shops with boarded up or barred windows lined the streets of the commercial district around him. Dozens of homeless people camped in abandoned doorways. Rap music blared from groups loitering on street corners. Graffiti scrawled everywhere was the dominant advertisement.

At a stoplight, Jake leaned over, pulled his Glock from the glove compartment, and stuck it in the front of his waistband.

Approximately ten miles from the little house, the Navigator stopped suddenly at the entrance to an alley. The Suburban passed by and turned at the next corner. His Explorer cut in behind a delivery truck and parked in a yellow loading zone half a block away.

Waterton popped out of the car with both shopping bags and

glanced around nervously. He locked the door and hurried toward the alley.

While he quickly surveyed the scene, Jake slipped the camera into his shirt pocket and patted the gun at his waist. What the hell was this guy doing? God, he hated not understanding what was happening.

He jumped out of the car and skirted the row of vacant shops. His gaze darted to the alley, to the street, to the sidewalks. Disaster could come from anywhere.

He reached the entrance safely. No sign of the bodyguards or Leonard. The odors emanating from the alley made him gag. He scanned again before peeking around the corner.

Fifty feet away, Waterton stood in the shadows next to a large, overflowing dumpster. His head swiveled constantly; he seemed to be searching for something or someone. When Leonard bent to set the shopping bags on the ground, Jake identified a small gun in the man's free hand. *Shit.*

Waterton shattered the silence of the smelly alley with a shrill whistle. Then a second whistle. He cupped a hand to his ear. A full minute passed before a pair of whistles answered. Immediately, the man spun around and ran back toward the street.

Jake had only seconds to hide.

He sprinted to the recessed doorway of the first closed shop, dropped to the ground, and curled up in a ball with his head against the boarded-up door and his feet sticking out onto the sidewalk. With his face and head hidden by his arms, he heard footsteps, a car door slam, and an engine growl before driving away.

He waited, his chest heaving against the concrete.

Damn. He'd never catch up with Waterton now. And where the hell were the man's bodyguards?

Jake rolled over and peeked between his arms at three passing vehicles. Then tires squealed nearby. Leaping to his feet, he spotted the Suburban barreling down the street in the opposite direction.

He patted the Glock and exhaled. *Too close.*

Voices drifted out of the alley.

Curious, he followed the sound and cautiously peered around the corner.

Two women stood over the shopping bags, rummaging through the contents.

"What's this shit?" one said, lifting a blond wig from the bag.

The other woman pulled a blond wig from her bag, too. She picked up a white top and red skirt and showed them to her companion. "Hey, don't complain. Looks like nice stuff to me." Then she bent over again to examine the remaining items.

"Nice, but weird," the first woman said, plucking a red skirt and a piece of paper from her bag. "Check this out."

They leaned together to read something on the paper.

"I'll be damned."

The pair laughed and stuffed everything into the bags.

When they glanced toward the street, Jake yanked his head back. Then he heard footsteps jogging away.

He shook his head in disbelief. Waterton had a charitable streak? Hard to believe.

Something didn't smell right, and it wasn't the noxious fumes from the alley. The disguise. The location. The entire scenario.

Back behind the wheel of the Explorer, Jake considered his next move. One option was to stake out the councilman's Brentwood house. He sighed.

It was almost 9:00 p.m. He was tired and starving. The little house in Southeast LA had to be researched. Burke deserved an update and needed to run the plate number from the goon's Suburban. What would be gained from sitting outside Waterton's home for hours anyway?

Speeding back to the hotel, Jake pondered a strategy.

He knew his prey. He knew his goal. He knew what he had to do.

Now he had to plan *how* to do it.

And how to keep Detective Sean Burke from getting in the way.

Chapter 21

Eight weeks earlier

In the moonlight, the froth on the gently breaking waves shone like delicate, white lace on black velvet. The rhythmic rush of water across sand was hypnotic. Damp salt air clung to their skin and invaded their noses.

Jake stoked the fire in the *chimenea* on the patio of his Rosarito Beach house. Sparks, like brief-lived fireflies, spiraled upward, and warmth spread through the night air.

"This is terrific," Angela said, reclining contentedly on a chaise lounge.

"Glad you like it."

"What's not to like? But this is hardly a secluded little place near the beach as you described it."

"Are you saying that was a lie?" Jake asked, chuckling and settling back on his lounge.

"Not a lie, but definitely an understatement."

"How would you describe it?"

"Hmmm. A spacious bungalow with no prying eyes in sight, nestled on the sand with not a blade of grass between it and the ocean."

"You sound like a real estate agent. I just didn't want you to expect too much. It's far from fancy."

"Unpretentious. One of the many things I love about you."

The "L word" rolled easily off her tongue, but when her ears heard it, she gasped softly. Jake flinched. She watched a pained expression skim across his face. He glanced away toward the waves and swallowed hard. She wordlessly begged him to say something to break the awkward silence because her own mind seemed paralyzed.

An interminable time passed, filled only with the sounds of the sea. He refused to look at her, but she couldn't tear her eyes away from him. Swinging his legs off the lounge, he grabbed a Corona bottle from the small table between them and stood.

"I'm empty. Do you want a fresh one?" he asked, heading inside.

"No thanks. I'm fine."

She heard the patio door slide open and then close behind him. Her chin drooped to her chest, and she sighed heavily.

With one word, she had ruined a fantastic weekend. It was a cliché, but undoubtedly, there was some truth to it. And the possibility of that truth had spooked Jake. He wasn't the kind of man who fell in love or wanted women falling in love with him.

Although it had never been her plan either, she could no longer deny or defy it. She was in love with Jake Stone. Which meant, of course, the pain would only be worse when he disappeared from her life. And she was well aware of when that would happen: as soon as he tired of screwing her. Jake's patience, protectiveness, and possessiveness weren't borne of love but of lust.

Tears stung her eyes. She was sure his twelve-step recovery program would eventually achieve its goal. She wanted it to succeed; she needed it to succeed. For four years, she had agonized over her failure to heal her libido. Why was it so hard? What was so devastating about the rape that had forced her mind into amnesia and her sexuality into oblivion?

Every day now, she felt stronger, more confident. Soon, she and Jake would have sex. Finally, she would not just survive; she would conquer her demons. Unfortunately, in the process, she was losing her heart to a man who didn't want that part of a woman's body.

At least this man would leave behind a wonderful gift: her restored sexuality.

Thirty minutes passed, and Jake hadn't returned. Angela drained her Corona and languidly dragged herself from the lounge. It was late, and they wanted to get an early start Monday morning for the drive back to Coronado.

Inside, the bungalow was dark and quiet. She locked the patio door and dropped her beer bottle into the kitchen trash.

"Jake?" she called softly into the darkness.

"In here."

She squinted to see him sitting in the recliner in the living room with his back to her.

"I'm tired. I'm going to bed. Good night," she said.

"Fine. I'll be in later. Good night."

She stopped in the hallway.

"It's just a cliché, Jake. It didn't mean anything," she said without turning.

"Of course not."

* * *

"No, no, no." Angela jolted awake. "Bad dream, bad dream," she repeated like a mantra.

"Easy, babe, easy," Jake whispered, reaching across her back to hook his arm around her. She resisted his attempt to pull her against him so his hand rested on her hip instead. "Relax, it's me." He kissed her cheek. "The nightmare?"

"Yes."

"Want to talk about it?"

She shook her head, distracted by something with more substance than a dream.

The warmth of his hand penetrated the gossamer gown until her bottom bore a fiery handprint brand. It drew her focus away from the imaginary fright and toward his very real touch. Involuntarily, her muscles tightened beneath his hand. She watched his gaze wander down her body to the curve within his palm.

"I know what'll help," he said hoarsely. "A simple massage. There's nothing sexual about it. I want you to relax."

But there was nothing *simple* about it.

With incredible tenderness, Jake rubbed her from head to toes. The pressure varied from featherlight to probing. The texture changed with fingernails, fingertips, or palm. And the warmth—the delicious heat—was ubiquitous.

True to his word, he never touched any explicitly sexual points, but during the massage—which indisputably became a caress—her entire body transformed into one, all-encompassing, erogenous zone. Even as her external muscles relaxed, a deeper, more carnal part of her coiled tighter and hotter.

The contrast evoked shudders of pleasure.

"Angela?" he whispered huskily.

"Hmmm?"

He cleared his throat. "Touch me."

She kept her eyes closed, but her hand crept from beneath the pillow and stroked his cheek. He caught her pinkie with his lips and sucked it into his mouth. He pushed and pulled her finger back and forth between his lips suggestively and then circled it with his tongue. Angling his head back, he let her finger slide out of his mouth.

"I don't mean touch my face."

His fingers left her back and rearranged something under the sheet. Then he caught her hand, kissed the palm, and placed it on his bare chest.

Her eyes opened to his Cheshire cat grin. "What're you doing?"

"Helping you touch me."

Her gaze lowered to the fingers grasping her wrist. He began to slide her hand slowly down his torso. She jerked. He stopped but tightened his grip.

"Stop it, Jake. Let go."

"Easy, now. This is the next step: you getting comfortable with my dick. Then we'll work on getting comfortable with me touching your…uh…intimate spot."

He moved her hand a few inches downward, but she yanked it free and clutched it under her chin.

"I don't want to."

"C'mon. You can do it. It's not going to bite you. A dick is only flesh and blood. Touch it. Stroke it. Squeeze it, but not too hard. Okay?"

"No."

"Angela, you're in control. It's not going to hurt you."

"I know you'd enjoy it, but I can't do it."

"This isn't for me."

She arched her eyebrows. "It's not?"

He grinned. "All right, a little. Didn't the massage put you in the mood?"

She hesitated. "Yes, it was wonderful." She gulped. "I'm sorry, Jake. I hate to admit it, but I guess I'm afraid."

"Of me?"

"No, just that part of you."

"Liar." He rolled her onto her back. "You're not afraid of my dick. You're not afraid of me physically at all. What you're scared of is psychological. You're afraid I'm going to leave after I fuck you."

She winced. "Stop it. Don't be crude." She pushed his hand away.

"Admit it. You don't believe I care for you, so obviously I'm only in this to get laid. Am I right?"

She cringed. "Can you blame me? Tonight, I used the 'L word' in a silly cliché, and you freaked out and froze up. What am I supposed to think?"

"Damn." He jumped off the bed and spread his arms in exasperation. "I've never been this emotionally involved with a woman before, but that's not good enough for you. Lady, I wouldn't hang around this long just for sex. And I'd never force you to do anything against your will. I thought you knew me better than that."

"Liar. You're a shadow. Sometimes I feel like you hide the real you. But I know all I need to know: You're a man."

Jake's mouth fell open. His voice dropped to an incredulous whisper. "I see. All men are the same. Modern-day cavemen. Grab the bitch by the hair, drag her into the cave, and fuck her until we get bored. Is that what we do?"

"Close enough."

* * *

Jake stood at the edge of the flagstone patio, overlooking the rocky hillsides and drinking his second large tumbler of J.D. He and Angela had driven back from Mexico that morning. It had been a miserable ride. They'd spent an hour waiting in line with hundreds of other cars at the San Ysidro border crossing. Smiles and conversation had been strained. When he had pulled up in front of her Coronado condo, she'd pecked him on the cheek and fled from the car.

Although they had both apologized for the argument, her wary animosity swirled just beneath the surface. Angela had revealed a deep-seated philosophy much darker than the classic *Men Are from Mars, Women Are from Venus*. Her fundamental belief was that men are predators, women are prey. Jake feared they had taken two steps backward over the weekend.

As he absently lifted the glass to his mouth, the cell phone rang in his pocket. Extracting it quickly in hopes it might be Angela, he swore at the information on the screen.

"What the hell do you want?" he growled in greeting.

"Good afternoon to you, too." Jake didn't reply so the Contractor continued. "When are you going to finish the job?"

"You said I had three months."

"It's been two. You never take this long."

"I am this time. What's the problem?"

"The Agency is getting antsy."

"I don't give a damn."

"You're not having any more stupid thoughts about reneging on the contract, are you?"

"Fuck off, asshole. I do this my way."

The mechanical voice laughed. "You always do. But the Agency has an interesting offer."

Jake's jaw clenched, but he remained stoic.

"How does an extra ten grand sound?" the Contractor asked.

"For what?"

"For delivery by the end of this week."

* * *

Angela unlocked the front door of her condo and waited. For the third date in a row, Jake kissed her chastely, whispered good night, and walked away.

"I wish you'd quit pouting like a little boy," she called.

He stopped, sighed, and slowly looked back over his shoulder. "Pouting?"

With her hands planted on her hips, she marched around to stand in front of him. She should have read in his steely eyes that he was itching for a fight.

"Definitely pouting," she said tightly.

"About what?"

"The other night."

"Which night?" he snapped.

"Okay, smart-ass, play dumb. But you know damn well 'which night' and 'about what.'"

"Go on."

"You're pissed because I wouldn't do what you wanted me to."

"And that was?"

She smirked. "Fondle you."

"Fondle me?" He arched a brow.

"Cut the crap, Jake, and quit answering me with questions. You wanted me to fondle your…your penis, but I wouldn't. Now you're pouting to punish me."

A growl of frustration rumbled in his throat. "Shows how little you fucking know me. Yeah, I was disappointed you couldn't touch me—or fondle me, as you so aptly put it—but not for my sake as much as yours. I thought you were ready to confront the awful violence done to you, but you weren't. Since that night, I've been trying to avoid putting you in the position again since you're obviously not ready for that step. So, that's what I'm fucking *pouting* about. May I go now?"

Her smugness faded. "That's a pretty deep answer."

"Well, I'm a deep kinda guy." He cringed as if he regretted the unintentional double entendre.

Angela's repentant gaze searched his eyes. "I'm trying, Jake, really I am. I want to be a complete woman again. More than ever since—"

"I know, and I don't want to spook you. The right time will come. I should go now."

He turned away and strolled toward the Corvette. He hadn't gone but a few steps when she caught his arm and pulled him around to face her.

"I'd like to try again. Tonight."

"Are you sure? There's no pressure."

"Yes, I'm sure. I'd like to see…and touch…you. Who knows? It might grow on me." She smiled coyly at her own wordplay.

He chuckled and reached for her. "Ya never know."

Chapter 22

The present

Despite his exhaustion, Jake was so wired he'd hardly slept. He was close. He could taste it. And revenge served cold would taste very sweet.

Last night, Burke had been a royal pain in the ass when Jake called to update him on the results of the Waterton surveillance. Sounding like a kid on Christmas morning, the detective wanted to know every detail. For someone not used to sharing, Jake struggled to hide his annoyance.

When Burke offered to take a day of sick leave to work with him from the hotel, he blew a gasket. Not only was the secret of his location at risk, he didn't want a damn cop looking over his shoulder while he planned to murder someone—an LA city councilman, to be exact. Was Burke naïve, or too excited to understand? Jake had scrambled to convince the man that he was far more useful in his office where he had access to the LAPD computer system.

He rubbed the sleep from his eyes before downing the remainder of his fourth cup of coffee. It was only 8:30 a.m., but he already had a plan. Keeping Burke out of it was the biggest problem.

"I don't understand why we can't move on him tonight, Stone," Burke said on the phone, his voice rough with exasperation.

"*We* aren't doing anything, Detective. You don't have an arrest warrant or a search warrant. And no judge in his right mind is going to give you one based on our evidence. In fact, as you've pointed out repeatedly, you can't even divulge where you got the suspect's name. If you participate in this little interrogation, you're going to get your ass in a legal crack and probably blow the whole case. Now back off and let me handle this solo."

"Yeah, well, the last time you handled an interrogation, the suspect ended up dead."

"Are you mourning for J.J.?"

"Shit, no. But I want my chance to *spit* in this asshole's face."

"Understood. Let me think about it. Tonight I'm just doing additional surveillance," Jake lied. "I need more info about Waterton's schedules and patterns."

"Yeah, he might not return to the house in Southeast LA for a while. He and his brother certainly didn't try very hard to hide their ownership of it under their partnership, Waterton Enterprises. I'm beginning to think the place isn't used in his illicit activities."

"Good point. But you couldn't find any information about someone actually living there, like utility bills in another name. What do the Waterton brothers use it for? To store giveaway clothes? Doesn't smell right to me."

"No shit, Sherlock. Give me a little more time to do some digging."

"Good idea. I don't want any surprises when I decide to beat a confession out of him."

"Just don't beat him to death, Stone."

"I'll try to remember that."

* * *

Jake ate a cheeseburger and fries inside the black Chevy Trailblazer the rental company had delivered earlier in the day. His gaze swept between the City Hall driveway and the black Suburban parked discreetly two blocks away. It was nearly 6:00 p.m. and Waterton was still in meetings, according to his secretary.

After a two-hour wait, Jake was stiff and impatient. He wadded the fast-food trash into a ball and slammed it into the backseat. It felt good but did nothing to lessen his edginess. He realized he was wound too tight, but he couldn't fix it. Maybe he didn't really want to.

Finally, thirty minutes later, Waterton pulled out of the driveway. A young woman rode in the front passenger seat. Jake swore vehemently.

The Trailblazer idled until the Suburban took up its position. Joining the parade, Jake shook his head in frustration. The woman was a problem. Tonight might be a bust after all.

Waterton led the caravan to a prestigious Italian restaurant in Hollywood. A valet accepted the car keys, and the couple strolled leisurely inside. Jake circled the block, searching for a parking space. He was tempted to leave. Based on the councilman's womanizing reputation, he anticipated the date could be an all-nighter, which meant access to his target would be denied.

Marissa Garner

His hand thumped rapidly against the steering wheel while he waited for a sedan to vacate a space at the curb. He swerved into the spot and killed the engine. God, he missed his Corvette.

He exhaled frustration. Even if he didn't get a shot at Leonard tonight, additional surveillance could be beneficial. But the idea of spending two or three more hours shut inside the Trailblazer was more than he could stomach. He deserved a respite.

Pulling down the visor, he checked his new reflection in the vanity mirror. He smiled and wiggled his eyebrows. Waterton wasn't the only one who could don a disguise. In anticipation of a face-to-face confrontation with the rapist, Jake had changed his appearance. He had learned well from his years as a Navy SEAL and CIA assassin that even the best laid plans could go awry, and an unexpected witness could prove disastrous.

He smoothed down the black mustache, goatee, and bushy eyebrows. Satisfied with his new façade, he glanced around for the Suburban. Unable to find it, he used the zoom on the camera to search again. Still out of sight. He would've preferred to know its location, but as he hurried toward the restaurant, he concluded it didn't matter.

Once inside, he scoped out the situation. Mingling unobtrusively with the other patrons, he kept a close eye on Leonard and his date, who stood chatting with the maitre d'. Even in public, the councilman couldn't resist stroking the woman's extreme lower back. She angrily brushed his hand away.

After the couple had been seated in the dining room, Jake selected a stool at the bar from which he had a slice of a view of them and a clear view of the exit. He ordered the fried calamari appetizer and a Corona. But not even a long, cold swig of beer could put a smile on his grim face. Angry and focused, he bided his time and reviewed his options. His glare flung daggers at Waterton's back until dinner was finished two hours later.

When the woman left for the restroom, Jake paid his bill and returned to his car. He scanned the area for the Suburban, but once again to no avail. By the time the valet delivered the Navigator to the waiting couple, the Trailblazer was poised to follow.

With no idea of where they were headed, he hung tight. Before long, though, City Hall became the obvious destination. He snapped photos as Leonard said good-bye to his date in the parking lot. Glancing at his watch, Waterton wasted no time getting back on the road. Jake was in close pursuit. Still no sign of the Suburban.

When the Navigator sped past the freeway exit toward home, Jake's pulse jumped. He straightened in the seat and gripped the steering wheel tighter. Maybe tonight wouldn't be a bust after all.

Shortly before ten, Waterton parked at the curb in front of the Southeast LA house. He was already stripping off his dress shirt when the Trailblazer drove by. A block away, Jake pulled a U-turn and crawled along the curb with the lights off until he found a good vantage point.

His alteration complete, the bearded Leonard Waterton unlocked the front door of the house and disappeared inside. The front porch light flicked on, and a few windows began glowing with interior light.

Scanning the area, Jake waited. Five, ten, fifteen minutes. No sign of Leonard. No sign of the Suburban.

Jake stroked his fake goatee. Patience. *Pa-tience.*

Twenty minutes crept by. Jake started the car, pulled away from the curb, and circled the block twice. The entire neighborhood seemed asleep. The absence of the bodyguards gnawed at his gut. Instinct and experience warned him to watch his back.

He chose a spot on the opposite side of the street, half a block closer to and heading toward the main avenue. Torn between planning for a quick getaway and risking the car being stolen, he jammed the key back into the ignition. The car was replaceable. His life wasn't.

After checking his disguise in the mirror, he slid the Glock and silencer into his pants pocket. Then he retrieved a small, white plastic case and latex gloves from the center console and stuffed them into the other pocket. One last scan of the surrounding area and he stepped from the car.

He sauntered across the road. His calm demeanor belied the hatred raging beneath the surface. His eyes explored the street, houses, and yards. No sign of any movement.

Strolling along the sidewalk, he was within thirty feet of the house when a red Ford Mustang shot past. The driver slammed on the brakes and yanked the car into a space immediately in front of the Navigator. Jake paused, and his hand slid around the Glock inside his pocket.

Two women, carrying department store shopping bags, jumped from the Mustang. One was swearing at the other and ranting about being late. Distracted by their argument, they barreled down the sidewalk oblivious to the man in their path.

Jake stared, his mouth gaping. The two young women were dressed identically: white, low-cut tank tops; red, skin-tight miniskirts; and black, knee-high boots. Bulging boobs threatened to bounce right out of their tops as the women raced toward him.

To avoid a collision, he called, "Hello, ladies."

Startled, the women bumped against each other in an abrupt, ungraceful stop. The shopping bags fell to the ground, revealing a change of clothing, shoes, and a purse packed inside each.

"Shit!" they exclaimed in unison and then laughed.

When their shocked faces turned up to his, Jake got a shock of his own. Their blond hair and make-up were also identical. They even had the same dark brown eyes, gold hoop earrings, and tiny fake moles near the right corner of their mouths. If not for different facial bone structure and a slight difference in size, the two could have been mistaken for identical twins.

Their eyes appraised him brazenly, lingering on his fly. He squirmed under their inspection but smiled amiably.

"Hey, big boy, what's your name?" one asked, reaching up and tracing his mustache and lips with a bright red fingernail. She smiled at him seductively.

Jake caught her wrist and held it against his chest. "John. What's yours?"

"I'm Cayenne, and she's Chili. Hot and spicy. You like?"

Cayenne…Sara. Shit. Thank God for his disguise. "I'm sure the indigestion would be worth it." He ran a finger across the slope of her boob. "It's a little early in the year for trick or treat, isn't it?" His gaze raked over her voluptuous curves.

"It's always time for tricks with us, stud. Want our number?" Chili asked.

"Sure." He released Cayenne's wrist, pulled out his cell phone, and recorded the number she gave him. "Who are you gonna trick tonight?"

"Wouldn't you like to know?" Cayenne teased.

"Yeah, that's why I asked."

They giggled.

"We never fuck and tell," Chili said. "It's bad for business. Call us, baby. We'll spice up your life." She rubbed her hand roughly across his package, gave it a quick squeeze, and blew him a kiss before turning toward the house. "C'mon, Cayenne. We're late."

Without another word or glance, the women scampered to the front door with their bags. Keeping his face averted, Jake hurried down the sidewalk. When he heard the door slam shut, he stopped, swore, and jogged back to the house.

Why was everyone intent on ruining his plans for the night?

From the sidewalk, he studied the three people silhouetted against the thin, white curtains in the large picture window. He heard raised, angry voices, which faded when the figures disappeared.

He checked quickly for prying eyes in neighboring windows before slipping into the shadows next to the house. Listening intently, he traced the trio to the back of the residence. Through a broken window blind, he spied the party in progress in the kitchen.

Bottles of vodka, Scotch, soda water, orange juice, and cranberry juice sat on the counter. Each person sitting at the kitchen table was already enjoying a drink. In front of Waterton lay a mirror with a small pile of white powder. He was focused on separating it with a razor blade into three lines. One of the women fanned herself and then spoke to Leonard. He nodded. She sashayed around him and opened the sliding glass door to the backyard.

After all three had snorted a line of powder, Leonard handed each woman an envelope. They both thumbed through the contents before dropping the envelopes into the shopping bags. Then the three refilled their glasses and left the kitchen. A new light emanated through the partially open blinds on a window at the other back corner of the house. Jake crawled under the kitchen window and pressed up against the wall near the open door. Crouching in the shadows, he was barely more than a shadow himself.

For several minutes, he listened to the voices and sounds coming from the other room. It didn't take a rocket scientist to figure out what was happening. J.J.'s words, "really special threesomes," echoed in Jake's head. It made sense now. Leonard liked seeing double, fucking double. The man even provided the outfits ahead of time so he didn't have to witness the transformation.

Other words surfaced from his memory: "…roughed her up a lot…kinky shit." He wondered if Chili and Cayenne knew about Leonard Waterton's deviant behavior.

Jake reviewed his options. He could still kill Waterton. The hookers wouldn't be able to identify the murderer because of his disguise. He doubted they would be motivated to anyway.

His eyes narrowed. The predator could smell his prey. So close. So damn close. He wanted to finish this. Now.

He stood up and, with seven silent steps, crossed the space to the bedroom window. Turning his head slightly, he peered through the blinds.

Damn.

Hanging from hooks on the wall was a diversified collection of whips, collars, leashes, and scarves. An open dresser drawer exposed a variety of disgusting dildos. A small handgun—probably the same one Waterton had carried in the alley—and a pocketknife rested on top of the dresser. On one nightstand lay several handcuffs and blindfolds, and on the other, boxes of condoms.

Holy shit.

The councilman lay stark naked on a king-size bed. Cayenne and Chili were topless. One of the hookers was working hard on a blow job, while the other was feeding Leonard her tits and riding the hand probing under her skirt. The one with his dick down her throat wore a dog collar and leash, which Waterton yanked rhythmically to control her up-and-down motion.

Disgust and bile burned inside Jake. He cursed, turned away, and inched back to the kitchen's screen door.

Leaning against the wall in the shadows, he patted the artificial facial hair to be sure it was secure. Then he pulled on his latex gloves. He slid the Glock out of his pocket, checked the magazine, and attached the silencer.

An all-too-familiar change swept over his body, external and internal. As adrenaline pumped into his system, his pulse accelerated. He breathed slow and deep to control it. Tightness squeezed his gut and chest. Vision and hearing intensified. All brain function focused on the mission. Every nerve, every muscle, was primed for action.

The metamorphosis was complete: Jake Stone, assassin.

The screen door slid open with a slight scraping noise. He paused, but no reaction came from the other room. As silent as a snake, he slithered through the kitchen and down the hallway. His back pressed against the wall, he stopped just short of the open bedroom door.

This was the beginning of the end. He always took a nanosecond to acknowledge the enormity of ending a human life and to reassure himself that the person deserved to die. The simple rite had failed him only once. He hoped that counted for something on Judgment Day.

One final cleansing breath…

Jake spun around the doorjamb.

Feet braced wide. Arms extended. Glock aimed steadily. "Sorry folks, the party's over," he announced.

Three shocked faces jerked his way and then froze at the sight of the gun.

"Who…who the hell…are you?" Waterton sputtered.

"The Grim Reaper. Start saying your prayers, Leonard, if you know any." The councilman's eyes widened upon hearing his name spoken by the armed assailant.

Cayenne and Chili began to sob. "D-don't kill us. P-please," one of them stammered.

"I'm not going to hurt you. Grab your shit and get out of here." Too dazed to comprehend, they didn't move. "Leave," he shouted.

Without taking time to put on their tank tops, they jumped off the bed. Fearfully, they approached the doorway. Jake's gaze stayed locked on Waterton as he stepped aside for them to pass.

"Good night, ladies. Don't forget your money."

They scooted past him. He heard them grab the shopping bags from the kitchen, dash through the living room, and slam the front door.

"Well, now, isn't this cozy, Leonard? Just you and me."

"Wh-what do you want? M-money? I can p-pay," Waterton said, his voice faltering.

"I don't want your stinking money, asshole. You and I are gonna take a walk down memory lane, and you're going to apologize." His unwavering steel eyes pierced the trembling man like a spear. "And then I'm going to kill you."

Leonard sobbed. "I'm s-s-sorry for whatever I-I did to you. Don't…kill me. Please."

"Shut up." Jake's gaze flicked to the knife on the dresser, and he grinned wickedly. Never lessening his attention on his target, he stepped to the dresser and pocketed the knife. He removed the magazine from Waterton's handgun, slipped it into his pants pocket, and tossed the weapon into the open drawer. "Get up. This room gives me the creeps. Move."

Leonard attempted to stand. "I-I can't," he cried, falling back on the bed.

"I don't care if you have to crawl. Get your ass into the living room, or I'll give you some encouragement," Jake warned, gesturing toward the dildos.

Using the headboard for support, Leonard stood up precariously. Jake motioned to the door with the Glock, and the naked councilman teetered out of the bedroom.

In the living room, Jake shoved him onto the couch in front of the thinly draped picture window. The man's teeth chattered, and his body shook convulsively. Fear shone in his eyes.

In contrast, Jake was calm, cool, and deadly.

Settling on an ottoman two feet away, he faced his victim and made his gaze cold and unyielding. "You can make this easy on yourself, Councilman Waterton, or you can make it hard. Your choice. Understand?"

He nodded his already shaking head.

"Good. Four years ago, you assaulted and raped a beautiful young woman named Angela Reardon in her LA home. Your favorite hooker, Bad Angel, from J.J.'s escort service, was involved. She disappeared right away. Last Saturday, J.J. was shot and killed. Twelve days ago, Angela committed suicide. Only it wasn't really suicide. Someone paid to have her murdered. That *someone* was you."

"I don't know…what you're talking about. You have the wrong man." Waterton brightened as if seeing a ray of hope.

Jake leaped to his feet before the man could blink. He slammed the Glock into the side of Leonard's head. The councilman hollered in pain.

"Don't bullshit me," Jake hissed. "This will get real hard, real fast. Last warning." He stepped back, holding his rage in check. "Think again, Leonard."

Waterton gulped and blinked. "I don't—"

The bullet struck the couch between his legs, inches from his genitals. He shrieked. Pee squirted from his shriveled dick, darkening the cushion beneath him. His chest heaved as he gasped for air. "I k-kinda remember the thing with B-Bad Angel. Sh-she set it up. She needed the m-money. Told m-me it was consensual."

"Bullshit. When you got there, you would've figured out it wasn't consensual."

"Yes, b-but it was t-too late."

"Too late? You went ahead and raped an innocent woman. You goddamn bastard!" He aimed the gun at the man's penis.

Helplessly, Waterton howled and covered the target with his hands. "Y-you're right. I am a b-bastard. I'm sorry. I'm sorry…I did it."

"And the contract on Angela. Why? After four fucking years, why did you need her dead?"

The blood vessels on Waterton's neck bulged, ready to burst. His eyes threatened to pop out of his head. His voice was a whisper. "I-I don't know anything—" He stopped, gulped. "Not me. I swear…to God…I-I didn't—"

Jake grabbed Leonard by the hair and yanked him off the couch. Jamming the muzzle of the Glock into Waterton's bare gut, the predator stood nose-to-nose, eyeball-to-eyeball with his prey. "Last chance. Confess, asshole!"

The living room window exploded.

Shards of glass and bullets rained down on the room.

Waterton slumped forward onto Jake. A flood of warm liquid surged from the councilman's back.

White-hot fire branded Jake's upper left arm. He and Leonard's limp body collapsed to the floor simultaneously. Pushing aside the bloody mess, Jake scrambled for cover behind an armchair.

On the street, tires squealed.

It was over in less than a minute.

Jake stuffed the Glock into his waistband while his other hand withdrew the small plastic case from his pocket. He crawled to the bleeding body in the center of the room. His gloved fingers frantically searched for a pulse, found a fading one.

"Don't you dare die. You have to apologize first. And no one is robbing me of the pleasure of killing you either."

He yanked Angela's picture from his back pants pocket and shoved it in front of the dying man's face.

"Apologize to Angela," he shouted.

Waterton's glazed eyes shifted slightly. "Help me."

Jake's right hand snapped open the plastic case and clutched the syringe. He pulled the cap off the needle with his teeth.

Waterton's eyes rolled upward. Jake shook him and pressed the photo closer.

"Apologize to Angela."

"Sor…ry An…gel."

"Not Angel! Angela. Angela Reardon, the woman you and Bad Angel raped." Jake slapped him. "Apologize!"

"Sor…ry An…gels. H-help," Leonard sputtered, his lips barely moving as blood oozed from the corners.

Jake stuffed the photograph into his back pocket. He pushed Leonard's chin up and jammed the needle into the man's neck. He rammed the plunger down. "Fuck you," he snarled as a sob clenched his throat.

Footsteps pounded on concrete seconds before the front door burst open.

Jake's Glock greeted Detective Sean Burke when he bolted through the doorway, gun drawn.

"Police! Hands up!" Burke yelled and froze. "Shit."

Air rushed out of Jake's lungs. He lowered his Glock.

"Fuck, Stone, is that you?"

"Damn, Burke, I almost killed you." His head drooped, and his eyes closed. He sucked in much-needed oxygen. When his eyes opened, they were suspicious. "What the hell are you doing here?"

Burke didn't answer. He stared at the syringe protruding from the neck of the bloody, naked body of *former* City Councilman Leonard Waterton. "Jesus Christ, what the fuck is that?"

"Insurance."

Automatic pilot kicked in. Jake seized the syringe, capped it, inserted it into the case, and shoved it into his pocket. He removed the silencer from the Glock and hid both in the other pants pocket.

Then he stood and gave Waterton's limp body a small kick. "I think he's dead."

"Ya think? What was in the needle?"

"Don't ask." Jake moved menacingly close. "You didn't answer my question, Detective. What the hell are you doing here?"

Burke glared at him. "I came for the same reason you did." He looked down guiltily at his gun before holstering it. "Maybe it's a good thing you beat me to him. You're hit, by the way."

Jake glanced at his bloodied left arm. "Just a scratch. Did you see—"

"Yeah. Black Suburban. Tinted windows. No plates. Cruised by twice with its lights off before he unloaded."

The two men stared at each other. Sirens screamed in the distance.

"I gotta go," Jake said.

"Yeah, you do. I'll stick around and clean up your mess."

"Thanks."

He lumbered toward the kitchen and his escape route. He stopped, turned to tell Burke about the crap in the bedroom. But the cop was focused on the motionless body. Jake watched as he crouched beside it.

Burke tilted his face toward the ceiling. His lips moved silently.

Then he leaned over and spat in Leonard Waterton's face.

Chapter 23

Six weeks earlier

"You were a spook?" Angela asked, glancing up from her plate.

Jake's eyes seemed to look right through her. "Sort of. I worked for the CIA in a related line of work."

"Sounds mysterious."

"Not the adjective I'd choose. It was all covert ops, and definitely not as romantic as Hollywood makes it seem." He stared into space. "It's a damn lonely life."

"Is that why it's hard for you to get close to people?"

His eyes jerked back to hers. "Look who's talking," he answered brusquely.

Her chin came up. "How nice to discover we have something so wonderful in common."

"Yeah, great." He stabbed a bite of swordfish and jammed it into his mouth.

Angela sighed. She'd been walking on eggshells all day because of Jake's dark mood. Her attempts to cheer him up had been futile. He had refused to admit anything was wrong when she inquired so she'd been left with simply trying to keep the atmosphere neutral.

She nibbled on a fried shrimp while she scanned the restaurant. Anthony's Fish Grotto was situated on the Embarcadero with a fantastic view of San Diego Bay and Coronado. She and Jake were regulars and enjoyed the people-watching as well as the great food.

"I'm sorry," Jake said, laying his hand palm up on the table. "Forgive me?"

Her attention swung back to him. She laid her hand in his, and he gave it a firm squeeze.

"No need to apologize. There's some truth to what you said. I don't get close to people easily. I have a lot of acquaintances, but few friends."

"And I can count my friends on one hand," he said.

"What about all the cops and deputies you know?"

"Acquaintances. Professional contacts. They really know nothing about…Which reminds me. I owe them a barbecue. I do one every summer. Will you help me by playing hostess?"

"Sure, but…" Her gaze shifted to the windows.

"But what?"

"Nothing."

"Tell me," he said sternly.

Men. They were so dense sometimes. Angela contemplated the best response. There wasn't one.

"I don't want people to get the wrong impression," she said.

"About what?"

She rolled her eyes. "About us. Our relationship."

"Why do you care what they think of our relationship? This must be a chick thing."

"It probably is. So never mind." She took a long drink of her iced tea and pointed with her pinky. "Can you believe the purple shirt that man is wearing?"

"Oh, no you don't. You're not getting out of this that easy. Hell, what is our relationship?"

She carefully laid her fork on the table, folded her napkin, and tucked it under the edge of the plate. Eggshells crunched loudly all around her. She had tried so hard all day to avoid a confrontation, but now it seemed inevitable.

Drawing a fortifying breath, she plunged in. "We're friends, good friends. We're dating. We enjoy each other's company. No strings, no commitments, no promises—"

"No sex," he interrupted, his voice angry. "Is that the part of the 'impression' you're worried about? That they'll *think* we're having sex? If it'll make you feel better, I can make an announcement that we're not fucking each other."

Trying to hide the hurt, Angela pushed back her chair and stood up. "I need to stop in the ladies' room. I'll meet you outside." She heard him curse under his breath as she walked away.

In the restroom, she stared into the mirror. She would *not* cry. It wouldn't help or change a thing. She loved Jake, but he didn't love her. He never would. Did she want that to ruin their time together? No. She wanted every minute before he disappeared from her life to be special.

She managed to smile at her reflection. She was so much stronger now than when they'd first met. Not only was her sexuality slowly returning, she was emotionally stronger as well. Her relationship with Jake—however it was described, whatever it entailed—was a positive one she would look back on with gratitude and satisfaction.

Jake was waiting for her on the sidewalk in front of the Corvette's parking space when she came out of the restaurant. He turned and greeted her with a serious expression. He caught her arm as she walked by and pulled her against him. He embraced her with the side of his head leaning against hers.

"We're a couple, Angela," he whispered in her ear. "An exclusive, committed couple. Damn, I hope I got the terms right. And sex or no sex, I don't want to be with anyone but you."

* * *

A week later, fifty or so people were partying in Jake's backyard: eating, drinking, talking, laughing. The pool offered a welcome respite on the hot day, and many guests were taking advantage of the refreshing water. The delicious aroma of barbecued ribs, teriyaki chicken, and hamburgers permeated the air.

Angela had been happily mingling. She'd worked her way around the yard, back to the grill where Jake had been stationed, cooking for the last two hours. The rest of the food was catered, but he'd insisted on grilling the meat himself. A male thing, she assumed.

But the man standing at the grill now wasn't Jake.

"Hi, I'm Kent Smithson, detective, Coronado PD," the man said, extending his hand.

Everyone at the party included their department and rank as part of their introduction.

She smiled and shook the offered hand. "Angela Reardon, owner, Heavenly Interiors."

He chuckled. "Sorry about that. I'm afraid we don't shed our law enforcement persona easily," he said, waving the barbecue utensil at the surrounding group.

"I'm certainly getting a more up-close-and-personal insight into those who choose to serve and protect than I've ever had. All of you are so…so interesting."

"'Interesting'?" Kent laughed. "What a diplomatic word."

Her cheeks warmed. "I didn't mean it to be derogatory."

"I know. I just think 'crazy' might be a better description. You have to be a little crazy to be a cop."

She smiled, instinctively liking the man. "And what's a little insanity among friends?"

"True."

"I'm looking for Jake. Have you seen him recently?"

Kent's gaze dropped instantly to the grill. "Uh, Stone handed me the tongs a few minutes ago. Said he had something urgent he needed to do."

Angela glanced toward the house just as Jake led a tall, voluptuous redhead inside through the patio door. They were holding hands. She noticed several guests watching the couple, and when the pair disappeared from sight, those eyes refocused on her. A prickly sensation ran down her spine.

"Thanks. Nice to meet you, Kent."

"You, too, Angela," he said without looking at her.

She strolled closer to the house, to where she could see Jake and the woman talking to others in the kitchen. After a few minutes, still holding hands, they exited down the hallway toward the front of the house.

"Her name is Tanya Neal. An old, very hot, flame."

Angela spun around and bumped into the man behind her who had spoken. He caught her shoulders to steady her. Before releasing her, he massaged gently.

"You must be Angela. I'm Ryan Brown, detective, San Diego PD." He smiled insolently, returning his gaze from the house to her. His pale blue eyes were intimidating.

"Yes, I'm Angela. Glad to meet you, Ryan."

The icy eyes seemed to assault hers, and she looked away nervously.

"Do you want to know more about Stone and Tanya?"

"No. I don't like gossip."

He snorted. "You know, there's a lot of gossip today…about you."

"That's to be expected, I guess. I am the newcomer." She sighed. "It's just that gossip can be so unkind."

"Unkind, but often true. There's a pool running."

"A pool?"

"Yeah, you know, the one who guesses closest to the date wins."

Angela peered at him with apprehension. "The date for what?"

"You honestly don't know, sweetheart?"

She shook her head.

A sneer curled his lips. His gaze bounced off her cleavage, swept down her bikini-clad body, and returned with a leering gleam. He stepped beside her and draped an arm casually across her shoulders. Ryan chuckled when she stiffened.

"The date Stone breaks up with you, of course."

Angela jerked away and faced him, eyes blazing. "That's rude and cruel."

"Just a friendly warning, sweetheart. We've known Stone a lot longer than you have."

She turned on her heels and marched quickly toward the house. A sharp pain pinched her chest. She felt the burn of eyes on her back. Ignoring the questioning looks, she rushed in the patio door, hurried through the kitchen, and trotted down the hallway.

She wanted to be alone, to tamp down her anger, to compose herself. The powder room off the hallway was occupied. She tried the door to the study; it was locked. Crossing the foyer, she scurried through the other hallway to the office. Also locked.

Then she remembered Jake saying he would "lock down the house" during the party for security reasons. But the meaning hadn't been clear. Apparently, his customized security system had yet another special feature that allowed him to lock individual rooms. She groaned.

Leaning her forehead against the office door, she closed her eyes and breathed slowly. How could a complete stranger say such a hateful thing? It wasn't a "friendly warning" at all. It was full of scorn and contempt. She wasn't going to believe it. She grimaced and clenched her teeth.

Just a few days ago, Jake had described their relationship as an exclusive, committed couple. She loved Jake. She trusted him. Didn't she?

Pushing away from the door, she walked back to the foyer. She glanced up the stairs and saw no one. Space to be alone. With each step, the lump in her throat seemed to grow larger until she could hardly swallow at the top of the staircase. Without stopping, she headed right and found the doors to the master bedroom closed.

Please don't be locked. Please.

Two voices—male and female—drifted out from the bedroom. The talking stopped abruptly when Angela turned the doorknob. Locked.

"Who is it?" Jake called from inside.

She clamped a hand across her mouth.

"I'll be out in a little while. Catch me then," he added.

And she fled down the stairs.

* * *

"You're not at all what I expected. Definitely not Stone's standard MO."

Angela steadied her nerves before she looked up at the woman. She was tall, brunette, thirty-something. The lean, muscular body her bikini revealed showed the results of many hours of hard workouts. Her hazel eyes peered at Angela with no-nonsense intensity. Cop, for sure.

"You look like you could use this," the woman said, pushing a glass at her. "Hope you like Scotch."

"Not usually, but right now it sounds good." She accepted the glass and sipped gingerly. "Thanks. I'm Angela Reardon, but I guess you already know that."

"I wouldn't be much of a cop if I didn't. I'm Bonnie O'Grady, San Diego County Sheriff's deputy." Instead of extending her hand, Bonnie dropped onto the loveseat next to Angela and glanced around. They were the only people in the formal living room. "So, how did you and Stone hook up?" She took a long drag of her drink.

Angela sipped again. The liquor burned her throat, and she coughed. "Jake hired me to do some interior decorating." She kept her head down and her answer brief, hoping Bonnie would get the message and leave.

"And the rest is history," the deputy quipped.

She cringed and drank again. Yes, they might be *history*.

Bonnie lowered her head so she could look up into Angela's face. "You got it bad for him, don't you, honey?" Their eyes met, held. She shook her head. "I remember how it felt."

Angela's eyes widened. "You and Jake?"

"Yeah. Hey, don't look so surprised." Bonnie's eyes sparkled as she laughed. "He's a great guy and an even greater lover. But I don't have to tell you that." Angela averted her gaze. "Problem is, he's a rolling stone."

"As in 'gathers no moss'?"

"Yup. Ask any woman here."

"I'd rather not. I don't think I want to hear this." She started to stand, but the deputy caught her arm.

"Honey, wait. Forewarned is forearmed."

"You're just full of delightful sayings, aren't you? Look, my relationship with Jake is none of your or anyone else's business."

Bonnie held up her hands in surrender. "Hey, sister, I'm not a buttinsky. I just thought I could save you some pain since I've known Jake for years, and I've seen lots of women come and go."

"What's your invaluable advice?"

"My advice is worth what you pay for it, honey, which means it ain't worth shit." She smiled. "Hey, another great saying."

Angela groaned and drained her Scotch.

Bonnie stared into her glass as if contemplating what to say. She finished her drink and set the glass on an end table. "Jake was the best thing that ever happened to me. When we—no, he—broke it off, I thought I'd be crushed, but I wasn't. Even as he left, he made me feel special, and he accepted all the blame for the breakup. Called himself 'an unlovable monster.' That was a couple of years ago.

"Of course, I knew his reputation and that his relationships rarely lasted more than a month or two. Somehow, he pulls off the friend thing afterward. To this day, we can laugh and joke with no animosity. Do I wish it had lasted forever?" She paused, twisted her lips. "You know, I'm not sure. And I think just about every woman here would tell you the same thing."

"Oh God, you don't mean—"

"Well, not 'every' but..." Bonnie shrugged.

Angela slumped against the cushions. "So you're saying not to expect too much from him."

"Yeah, a little of that, but mostly I'm saying love Stone for who and what he is. If you can do that, you won't have any regrets."

Feeling the buzz of the Scotch, Angela rubbed her forehead. "That man, Ryan Brown, said some awful things."

Bonnie swore softly. "Brown's a bastard. He tries to pick up Stone's women on the rebound, but no one ever wants him after they've had the big guy."

The two were silent for several minutes, each lost in thought. Angela's thoughts included the voices in the bedroom. "Tell me about Tanya Neal."

Bonnie looked surprised, then cautious. She scratched her head. "Are you sure you want to know?"

"Yes."

"Like you, Tanya isn't Stone's standard MO. They first hooked up about four years ago, broke up a year later, and have gotten back together at least twice that I know of. She's with the DA's office. Smart. Ambitious. Some said Stone was pussy-whipped in the relationship. Don't know if it's true, but there's something there, some magnetism, that keeps pulling them back together."

Unshed tears stung Angela's eyes. "Damn it, Bonnie, I don't want to lose him. What can I do?"

The woman laid a hand on Angela's shoulder. "Honey, Stone's his own man. I don't know if there's anything *you* can do. Rolling stone, remember? Just love him while ya got him. It's worth it." She patted Angela's shoulder, stood up, and left to rejoin the party going strong outside.

Angela stared at the ceiling and swallowed hard. Then she smiled. Bonnie's advice reflected what she'd been telling herself for a long time now.

She stopped at the bar in the family room and poured another Scotch before heading outside. She wasn't surprised when Ryan Brown instantly appeared at her elbow. Drinking the Scotch, which tasted better and better, she tried to ignore him to no avail.

"Hey, sweetheart, I didn't mean to piss you off. Just thought someone should warn you."

"You seemed to derive a perverse pleasure in warning me."

"Perverse? I'm not the pervert here." He snaked an arm around her bare waist and sidled closer. "Unless you want me to be," he whispered against her ear. His breath reeked of liquor.

"Let go of me, Detective Brown."

"Now the little lady's going all formal on me. Listen, sweet cheeks, when Stone dumps you, I've got a warm spot for you in my bed. I gotta give Stone credit for that. He's always been generous with his hand-me-downs."

Angela's elbow rammed into his gut. He grunted and released her.

"Shit. I'm just being friendly, sweetheart. You're gonna want a friend to ease your pain when Tanya gets her claws into your man again."

A nasty look slid across his face, but she hardly noticed. Her attention shot to the patio door.

Jake stepped outside. Alone. He tugged at the front of his swim trunks as if they were binding his groin. He scanned the backyard until his gaze landed on Angela and Ryan. He frowned but tried to hide it with a quick jerk of his head in greeting.

"Hot damn, Stone must've fucked Tanya so hard she needs time to recuperate," Ryan slurred in Angela's ear.

Her slap caught the cop completely off guard. The crack of skin on skin seemed to echo off the hillsides. Heads turned. Eyes stared.

Jake crossed the patio with rapid strides. He pushed Ryan away from Angela and stepped between them, his back to the detective.

"You all right, babe?" Jake asked.

"Yes," she replied, avoiding his probing eyes.

"What's going on?" he said through clenched teeth, slanting a glare over his shoulder at Ryan.

"Nothing."

He scowled at her. "You just felt like slapping one of my guests for no reason."

"It was a simple misunderstanding—" Ryan began.

"Shut up, prick," Jake hissed under his breath.

"Shove it up your cheating ass—"

Jake whirled around and sent Ryan sprawling with a jaw-crunching punch.

Kent Smithson appeared out of nowhere. "I heard Detective Brown was just leaving. I'd be glad to show him to his car." He grabbed Ryan's arm, wrenched him off the ground, and escorted the red-faced man into the house.

An awkward silence hung over the crowd.

"Show's over, everybody. Last one drunk has to clean up after the party," Jake shouted.

Slowly, people turned away, conversations restarted. Undoubtedly, the new topic was speculation on what had just happened.

"C'mon." Jake clutched Angela's hand and led her into the house. She didn't resist, didn't speak. Her heart was pounding too hard.

He led her upstairs, but when he turned toward the master bedroom, Angela put on the brakes.

"No."

"What's wrong?" he asked, puzzled.

"I don't want to...go in there."

"Why not?"

"I don't want to...see *her*."

"Her?" He closed his eyes and pinched the bridge of his nose. "Aw, shit. It was you at the door."

Angela's knees threatened to buckle. She wobbled over to a recliner in the library alcove and collapsed onto it. She buried her face in her hands. Jake knelt in front of her.

"I'm sorry for embarrassing you. But I can't go in there and face that woman."

"You saw me with Tanya?"

"Yes."

"Did someone tell you who she is?"

"Two people. Ryan and Bonnie."

"I can imagine what filth Brown had to say, but not Bonnie."

"No, no. She didn't say anything negative. Bonnie was very nice."

"Yeah, she's good people. Look at me, Angela." He tenderly stroked her hair until she lowered her hands. "Ask me anything you want about Tanya."

"What were you two doing in the bedroom?"

Hurt and disappointment flooded his eyes.

"Damn it, I didn't fuck her. I can't believe you think I did. You still don't trust me." He shook his head and blew out his breath. "Tanya asked to talk to me. In private. She wanted us to get back together again. She was planning to spend the night."

Angela's eyes asked him what her lips couldn't.

"Shit. What do you think I said? Not no, but *hell* no. I told her I'm in the best relationship of my life. With you, Angela. You." He took both her hands and squeezed them tightly between his. "Tanya Neal doesn't take 'no' very well. She was mad as hell. She's not in the bedroom. Tanya left, and she won't be back."

Chapter 24

The present

Well, shit, someone just shot my theory full of holes. Jake awoke to the same thought that had been his last before finally dropping into a dead sleep. And since Leonard Waterton had been the embodiment of the theory, it seemed only right that he lay in the morgue full of bullet holes.

And one tiny puncture in the neck that no one would ever notice. Jake would always believe—because he needed it to be true—he had killed the man who raped Angela Reardon.

He yawned. He had forced himself to sleep in until 9:00 a.m. Unfortunately, he was unable to luxuriate in the laziness because his mind was already hard at work. But that didn't mean his body had to get up. He rolled onto his back, clasped his hands behind his head on the pillow, and stared at the ceiling.

God, he hurt all over. Before going to bed, he'd doctored the graze on his left arm with the first aid kit from the Corvette and allowed himself a Vicodin for the pain and to help him sleep. But the medication had worn off hours ago, and the pain had returned with a vengeance. His head felt like a coconut someone had split open with a machete. The rest of his body felt as if it had been run over by a Mack truck. None of it—except the arm—made any sense. Last night's events had not taken that much physical effort.

Realization dawned like the ray of sunshine blazing through the crack in the drapes and hitting him full in the face. He rolled onto his side to avoid the brilliance, but he could not as easily escape his epiphany.

Jake Stone was hurting, not from physical exertion, but from emotional excess. *Holy shit, where did that come from?* His emotions were dead, petrified since his years as a SEAL. Killing didn't trigger depression *or* exhilaration. It left him numb.

But the killing wasn't the log ramming into his gut, stealing his strength, taking his breath away. He was reacting to something else. Jake Stone had changed dramatically over the past three months. Angela Reardon had chipped, chipped, chipped away until she had exposed his granite heart again to the world. *Damn it, Angela.* Now his heart was suffering from emotional overload. Hate, love, anger, joy, regret, relief—and other feelings he couldn't even name.

His cell phone saved him.

"Morning, Burke," he said and yawned. "How deep is the shit?"

"Up to my ass and climbing. God, you left me with a mess, Stone."

"Hey, man, don't complain. No one invited you to the party."

"Yeah, well, I'll be lucky to get out of this with my badge."

Jake scooted up to sit against the headboard. He scrubbed a hand across his face and noticed small nicks there that must've come from the broken window glass.

"You didn't kill the councilman, Detective, so what's the problem?"

"For starters, why the hell was I there?"

"Hey, I asked you the same question. What lie did you tell your buddies?"

"That I'd tracked down Waterton because I'd heard a rumor he was a regular user of J.J.'s escort service, and I suspected he might've been involved in the pimp's murder. I suggested they check out the customer list. That shut them up fast."

Jake laughed. "You're not as dumb as you look."

"Thanks. Of course, all the kinky crap in the bedroom backed up my story." Burke paused. "You know we've got a problem."

"Yeah."

"Any ideas?"

"Not many."

Burke sighed. "I thought you said the goons in the Suburban were Waterton's bodyguards. I don't think he hired them to pump him full of lead. Which reminds me. Some of those bullets—"

"Kevlar. Under my shirt."

"Damn. You were expecting trouble?"

"I *always* expect trouble."

"You were lucky."

"Yeah."

A long silence followed.

"Where do we stand?" the detective asked.

"You've got a dead rapist."

"Thank God for that. I requested a DNA test. The homicide detective looked at me like I was crazy, but he agreed to it." Burke swallowed hard. "It'll be a relief to close Angela's case. Finally."

"One down, one to go."

Burke groaned. "All right. You're the genius. Any theories on who killed Waterton?"

"No. And we're running out of people. Bad Angel, Angela, J.J., Waterton." He hesitated and scowled. "Becky Smelter is the only one left who was around that night."

"Jesus. You don't think—"

* * *

Becky's phone continued to ring as Jake sat in the Corvette at the curb, staring at the front of her home. Finally giving up, he disconnected and exhaled loudly. He stroked his chin, enjoying the absence of the fake goatee.

Last Thursday, less than a week ago, he had met and talked to Becky over donuts and coffee. Had she said anything about her usual Wednesday activities? Not that he could recall. But the talkative woman had been so full of life. Becky probably had places to go and things to do every day of the week. So why was his gut in a knot just because she didn't answer her phone at 10:30 on a Wednesday morning?

While surveying the neighborhood, he adjusted his sunglasses and pulled the golf hat lower on his forehead. Nice. Normal. Quiet. No sign of the Land Rover that had tailed him there on his first visit. And no sign of the black Suburban that carried around some very deadly people.

He thought about calling one more time, but Becky hadn't answered any of his five calls since he'd talked to Burke forty minutes earlier so he discarded the idea. After another heavy sigh, he climbed from the car and strolled to the front door. Absently, he patted the small Glock in his pants pocket. Still scanning the area, he jabbed the doorbell.

Only when he turned his attention to the door and smiled at the peephole as he'd done on his previous visit did he notice them. Two small holes. One about an inch and a half above the peephole, the other about fourteen inches below. He stared, not wanting to believe what he saw. Precise placement. Calculated to kill instantly.

"Young man, young man!"

Jake's head jerked around at the sound of the woman's voice. His heart skipped lightly. But the elderly woman teetering across the street was not Becky. He instinctively positioned himself to shield the bullet holes from her view. Then he pasted on a pleasant smile.

"Good morning," he said as the woman stopped and gasped to catch her breath. "I'm Jake, a friend of Becky Smelter's. She doesn't seem to be home. Would you happen to know when she'll be back?"

The old lady eyed him suspiciously and then braced her hands on her broad hips. "Oh yes, I remember Becky mentioning you. She said you knew Angela. Such a nice girl. So sad what happened."

"Yeah, very sad. Um, about Becky?"

"I'm Rita Jackson, by the way," she said, shaking her head. "I don't know where she is. We were supposed to go play the slots at one of the casinos this morning. I've been calling her since eight."

Rita stepped to the side to reach for the doorbell. Jake moved smoothly to block her. He put his hand gently on her shoulder and guided her away.

"I've rung the bell so many times I'm afraid it's going to break." He screwed up his face as if concentrating. "Has Becky had any visitors lately that might've taken her out somewhere?"

"Well, there was a guy here last night." She squinted at Jake, who was trying hard to hide his anxiety. "That wasn't you, was it?"

"No. I haven't seen Becky since Thursday. What did this guy look like?"

"I couldn't see that great. It wasn't dark yet, but after eight. I remember because my show was on." Rita tapped her foot and frowned while she thought. "He was a young guy, like you. About your size, maybe a little shorter and smaller. Clean cut. Dress shirt and slacks. Oh, now I remember. He had short, wavy, red hair."

"Red hair? Anything else unusual?"

"He might've come in the big, black SUV I saw parked down the street. I know that car doesn't live here. I'm head of our Neighborhood Watch group so I know everybody's car. I keep a close eye on things. Not a busybody, mind you, just observant."

"I'm sure your neighbors appreciate your efforts. When did you see the SUV?"

"I first noticed it when I saw the red-haired man at Becky's door. And it was gone by ten when I turned on my front porch light."

"Would you recognize the guy if you saw him again?"

"I don't know. Maybe. He looked kinda familiar, like I'd met him some time ago, but not recently." Rita's eyes narrowed. "Why?"

Jake cleared his throat. "There have been some con men working this neighborhood lately, talking seniors into investing in fraudulent financial schemes. Nice people losing their life savings. Real bad."

"Oh my. I'm glad you told me. But this guy didn't look like a shyster. You know, no briefcase or business-looking stuff. He was only carrying a little white bag."

Jake's ears perked up. "What kind of bag?"

"Paper, like a fast-food bag."

"Or donuts?"

Rita smiled and nodded. "Yeah. Donuts. Becky loves donuts."

"Yeah, she does." He swallowed hard. He put his hand on Rita's back and pivoted her toward the street. "Well, I guess Becky just got a better offer than the slots, Rita."

She stopped abruptly, looked at him with deep concern. "You don't think she fell, and she's lying in there hurt? That happens to us old folks."

"No, I don't. You go on home and don't worry."

Jake watched her until she was safely inside her house while he trotted to the Corvette and yanked open the door. He called 911 on the burner phone he kept in the secret compartment and anonymously reported a shooting at Becky's address. Next he dialed Burke's cell phone.

"I can't talk," the detective whispered. Several loud voices filled the background. "I'm still at the Mayor's press conference about Waterton's murder."

"Sure, no problem. This is just a courtesy call."

"Courtesy call? Look, Stone, I don't have time for your games right now."

"Oh, okay. I just thought I'd extend you the courtesy of letting you explain what you were doing at Becky Smelter's house last night. Especially since someone left two bullet holes in her front door, and she's not answering."

"Christ." Burke choked on the single syllable.

"You got anything to tell me before I call the LAPD Homicide Division and have Becky's neighbor describe the red-haired man with the donut bag?"

"You better not be jerking me around."

"Do I sound like I'm joking?"

"Shit, you can't be serious."

"You've got thirty seconds. Starting now."

"I told you, I can't talk now," Burke hissed.

"Twenty-five seconds."

"Fuck you. Hold on." The detective's whisper could barely be heard over the background noise.

The muffled sounds of the cop speaking to someone else, of footsteps, of a door clicking shut, of more footsteps, of a door slamming, all reached Jake as he waited impatiently.

"Okay, I found a room without any eyes or ears," Burke growled. "Shit, Stone, my career is hanging by a thread right now, and sneaking out of a press conference is not winning me any brownie points."

"Quit whining and explain last night."

Burke exhaled. "I took Becky some donuts, and we talked about Angela. She'd called me twice since you saw her. She was very upset she might've forgotten something that would've helped catch Angela's rapist. I was worried about her. Seeing her pain drove my rage over the edge. I broke a cardinal rule and hinted that you and I had a suspect. She was thrilled. Made me promise to call her as soon as we knew for sure. Talking with Becky convinced me to track down Waterton last night."

"What time did you leave?"

"About nine. I went home, changed clothes, and tried to persuade myself that I'd be an idiot to go after Waterton alone. But I couldn't talk myself out of it. So, on a whim and a prayer, I drove to the Southeast LA house. Then all hell broke loose, as you know. I was going to call Becky this morning with the news, but it's been so crazy, I haven't had time."

"Why didn't you tell me about your visit on the phone this morning?"

"Hell, you didn't give me a chance. As soon as the idea Becky might be in danger came up, you were gone." Burke hesitated. "Are you sure?"

Jake stared out the car window at Becky Smelter's front door. He pictured her smiling face with donut glaze around the mouth.

"Yeah, I'm sure."

* * *

"What?" Jake barked into his cell phone. He was back in the hotel room, drinking and waiting for Burke to call with the police report about Becky.

"Well, if it isn't the elusive Mr. Stone." The contempt in Maleena Reardon's voice grated on his frayed nerves. "I was beginning to think you were no longer among the living."

He bristled at her choice of words. "Sorry to disappoint you, Ms. Reardon. I'm busy. What do you want?"

"I'm calling to see if you've given up your futile pursuit."

His jaw clenched. "How do you know it's been futile?"

"I'm sure you would have called if you'd had any success. Any at all. Are you ready to let my sister rest in peace?"

"I'm sure Angela is quite peaceful. It's you that's upset. Why is that, Maleena?"

"I've told you, damn it. My wedding. I don't want it ruined. Your actions are a great distress for me and my parents."

"I don't see why. You haven't been involved in my investigation."

"My mother becomes physically ill at the possibility some scandalous murder might be emblazoned across the front page of the *Post*."

"Are you people for real?" Jake erupted. "Doesn't anyone in your family care about finding out what really happened to Angela?"

"Go to Hell, Mr. Stone. We know what happened. We knew Angela far better than you did."

"I'm beginning to seriously doubt that." He snorted derisively. "But I am getting to know *you* better, Maleena."

"What the hell does that mean?"

"Your former neighbor, Becky Smelter, remembers you quite well. In fact, she told me to say hello the next time we spoke."

"She's—" Maleena's voice faltered. "She's still around? I figured she'd be in a nursing home by now. She was flirting with Alzheimer's four years ago."

"You must have Becky confused with someone else. She's sharp as a tack. She distinctly remembers your hard drug addiction and your conflicts with Angela when you lived next door."

Maleena's rage was palpable. "Back off, Stone. I don't know what your game is, but I don't want to play. Why don't you just go away?"

"Not happening."

"Would ten grand change your mind?"

* * *

The dimly lit bar was practically empty at 3:00 in the afternoon. In a small booth near the back, Jake drank alone. Not that he minded. He preferred it that way. It wouldn't last, though. He was expecting someone.

As he stared blindly into his glass, he couldn't remember ever feeling so totally defeated. Someone had outsmarted him. Someone was getting away with murder—several murders, in fact.

And for what reason had all of these people died? The obvious common denominator was the rape of Angela Reardon. His theory had been correct. Up to a point. But the theory had crumbled with the murder of Leonard Waterton. Now there was no one left in the cast of characters.

Jake drained the last of his drink and caught the eye of the bartender. He shelled a peanut and popped it into his mouth. The cocktail waitress delivered the fresh J.D., retrieved the empty glass, and hovered, smiling coyly and fluttering fake eyelashes. A forbidding scowl from Jake terminated her flirtation instantly. He sipped the whiskey, set the glass down with a sharp thud, and sighed heavily. For the hundredth time.

I'm sorry, Angela.

He had failed her. Despite finding the man who had raped her four years ago, he hadn't found the person who wanted her dead. Leonard Waterton had denied buying the contract. And for some strange reason—possibly the fact that he'd been gunned down moments later—Jake believed him. Now there were no suspects, only straws.

A man plopped down on the opposite seat in the booth. He silently shelled a peanut and ate it. "You said you needed to see me ASAP."

"Yeah, thanks for coming, Burke."

"Sure. I can't stay long. I gotta get back to the circus."

"Understood. Becky?" He met Burke's eyes. They confirmed Jake's earlier conclusion. "Shit." He rubbed his forehead. "When?"

"Estimated before midnight."

"Along with what Rita Jackson told me, that definitely explains where the Suburban disappeared to for a while last night."

Burke grunted. "I never even thought to look for it. They were supposed to be Waterton's bodyguards, remember? Damn it. They were probably out there waiting for me to leave."

The two lapsed into silence.

"Speaking of leaving, I'm getting out of this fucking town," Jake said.

"Going home?"

"Just for the night."

"Then where?"

"Virginia. I'm flying out of San Diego early tomorrow morning."

"The Reardons?"

"Maleena." The cop's puzzled expression prompted Jake to continue. "This afternoon she offered me money right after I mentioned Becky had told me about her drug addiction."

Burke's jaw dropped. "You're gonna take it?"

Jake's eyes flashed. "Of course I'm gonna take it."

"But…but—"

"Ten grand is a lot of money. Then I'll find out how much more it's worth to her, her fiancé, and her stinking rich family for me to keep my mouth shut about her little ole drug problem."

"Blackmail? Jesus Christ, Stone, why are you telling me this shit?"

"Straws. I'm grasping at straws."

"Ya lost me."

"Maleena was into the hard drug scene here in LA. Who knows how deep? Waterton and the hookers were snorting coke last night. There might be a connection. Unless Angela was a random victim—which I can't believe based on everything that's happened—Waterton and Bad Angel found out about her somehow. Maybe they and Maleena bought their Big C from the same dealer."

Burke shook his head. "That's one damn flimsy straw."

"You got any sturdier ones?" he snapped. "Besides, the Reardons, especially Maleena, have been just too weird about this whole thing. I guess I have a morbid need to meet the dysfunctional family Angela escaped from. Call me crazy, but Maleena Reardon is a bitch with a dark side. My theory is that the threat of blackmail will loosen her tongue about her drug connections in LA, which could open up some new leads."

"Sounds more like a wild goose chase than a theory."

"Yeah, well, it's all I've got."

Chapter 25

Four weeks earlier

Angela cried softly, "Bad dream, bad dream."

"Ssshhh, it's okay."

Still half asleep, eyes closed, Jake draped his arm over her. When his hand landed on a bare breast, his eyes popped open. Trailing his fingers down her torso, his pulse accelerated with each inch of skin he touched. His fingertips brushed the top edge of her pubic hair, and he gulped.

Damn.

Angela was totally naked.

Where were her nightgown and panties?

When they'd gone to bed, Jake had coaxed her to sleep raw like he did, but all his teasing and pleading had failed to convince her. She'd explained how being naked made her feel vulnerable. He figured she was also afraid of his inability to resist temptation. Apparently, during the night, she had changed her mind and shed her clothes.

Unfortunately Angela's fear was justified, because a part of his anatomy was definitely tempted. He cringed at the hardening going on down there. His hand slipped between their bodies to rearrange his problem, but when his fingers slid over the firm, smooth curve of her ass, the situation worsened. As if it had a mind of its own, his hand palmed her butt, climbed over her hip, and cupped the small mound below her belly.

She went rigid. "What are you doing?"

"You're naked," he mumbled as an answer.

"Please don't touch me there," she said tightly.

His erection, now hard and full, pressed against her butt. "Angela, I want you. Let me inside." His fingers defiantly stroked her tender folds.

"No, I can't," she said, her voice rising. "Let go. Please."

"Naked…" Additional words were lost to his ragged breathing. His body demanded what it had been denied for so long. Jake clenched his teeth against that burning desire.

"Move your hand," she snapped.

Several heartbeats passed.

"Shit. I can't take this much longer. I've told you how I feel about us. And I want to be inside you so bad, I hurt." He grabbed her hand and wrapped her fingers around his swollen dick. "Feel me? Feel how much I need you?"

"Stop it, right now." Angela wrenched her hand free, whirled on him, and pushed herself backward across the bed.

Jake flung away the covers and stood. His flagpole erection pointed at her accusingly. "I'm not your bad dream, Angela. And I'm not the bastard who raped you. When are you going to trust me? When are you going to *want* me?"

"I don't know."

He hung his head and shook it with frustration. "I need some air." He marched to the balcony door and yanked it open.

"Maybe I should leave."

Without turning, he paused in the doorway. "Maybe so."

He slammed the door behind him. Refusing to look back into the bedroom, he stepped to the balcony railing and leaned on it. Goddamn it, he wanted her. Did she appreciate how uncharacteristic it was for him to have such patience? Not that he'd ever needed it before; women normally threw themselves at him. But this was different. Angela was different.

He cursed softly. Why did he care about curing her frigidity? With a trembling hand, he rubbed his forehead. In the end, he was going to kill her. Why the hell did it matter whether she ever had another orgasm? Was it some pitiful, twisted way to mitigate his guilt? Or was he just a horny, immoral bastard?

The sound of Angela's BMW broke the night's stillness. Jake watched the headlights glance off the landscaping to the south of the house as the car exited the circular concourse and began its descent down the steep, winding driveway.

"Fuck!"

* * *

"I apologize for the other night," Jake said, swinging their clasped hands between them as they strolled on the sand near his Rosarito Beach house three nights later. "You were right to leave. I was way out of line. It won't happen again, I promise."

"Hmmm."

"You don't believe me?" He stopped her by pulling her hand up to his chest.

Perhaps the fog rolling in created her melancholy, but Angela doubted it. During the three days since the incident, she'd done a lot of soul-searching. She was sure Jake would resist talking about it, but she needed to discuss her demons—and his.

When she met his eyes, they reflected a level of concern she hadn't expected. Did he think she was that upset about the other night?

"I believe you mean what you say, but I don't believe you can keep that promise."

"Huh?"

She smiled and reached up to brush aside a wind-whipped lock of ebony hair from his forehead. "Don't worry. I'm not angry. If I was, I wouldn't have agreed to come down here with you. I love your beach house, by the way."

"I know. That's why I wanted to come here. I thought it might give me a bit of an advantage."

She pressed a firm kiss on his lips but pulled back before he could react. She started to walk again, and he matched her strides.

"You don't need any more advantages, mister. You've got me wrapped around your little finger."

"Well, hell. I wish I'd known." He chuckled. "I'm sure you've noticed me hanging on your pinkie, too."

"Hmmm."

"That 'hmmm' of yours is starting to worry me. Is something wrong?"

"Not really."

She dropped his hand and hugged her arms around herself. Her eyes fixed on the sun glowing rebelliously through the falling fog, defying the misty curtain to close early on its show.

Fog. Amnesia. They felt similar.

"Angela?"

"Hmmm?"

"There it is again," he joked but didn't get a laugh. "Are you cold?"

"A little."

"Want to go back?"

"No."

"Well, let's sit down. The sand is still warm."

She sat between his legs, reclining against his chest. They huddled together, taking warmth from the dry sand and each other. The sun sank lower and lower but never succumbed to the fog. They watched silently until the golden orb disappeared below the horizon.

"What's the matter?" Jake asked, concern in his voice.

"There's something wrong with me."

"You're sick?"

Her head rested on his shoulder, and he tightened his embrace.

"Not physically sick. Mentally."

He sighed. "I know. The amnesia."

"Of course, there's that. But something else is wrong."

"What?"

She drew a deep breath and lifted her face to his. "It's a horrible statistic, but hundreds of women get raped. But as awful as rape is for each and every victim, almost all of these women find the strength to survive, overcome, and heal. They return to normal lives. I haven't. I can't. I'm convinced there's something else wrong with me."

"I couldn't disagree more. I think you're a helluva strong woman. Look what you've accomplished in four years. You moved to Coronado, bought a condo, set up an interior decorating business from scratch, and started a whole new life for yourself. And *you* did it, with virtually no help from anyone." He stroked her hair as he continued. "Yes, you've had a problem with sex. Perfectly understandable, in my humble opinion. I know I get impatient sometimes. But look how far you've come with that problem in the short time we've been together."

"Thanks, Jake. I appreciate the vote of confidence. Really, I do. But I'm scared I won't be able to take the final step." She snuggled closer. "Even though my brain and my body tell me I'm ready, I can't do it. What's wrong with me?"

"The cops and doctors explained to you that your rape was…was particularly vicious. It makes sense your psychological scars would be worse."

"Hmmm."

"Stop that. Tell me what you're thinking."

"I agree with what you said. I think it goes even further, though. It's like there was something so devastating that it's haunting me, screaming to be remembered. And the closer we get to having sex, the more frightening it becomes."

Jake swiveled her so he could see her face. "Your nightmare with the two…two figures? I've noticed you've been having it more often."

"Yes, almost every night now."

"Jesus, Angela, why didn't you tell me?"

"Why? What could you do?"

"I could insist you talk about it instead of letting you brush me off."

"Hmmm. I understand you want to help, Jake, but I don't think you can. I hate complaining about it, but the nightmare is really scaring me. I know it's making it harder for me to take the last step. It may also mean I'm backsliding psychologically."

"We're not going to let that happen. You have me now." He leveraged them both up off the sand. "You're shivering. Let's go back."

Snuggling under his arm like it was a protective wing, she accepted his strength and warmth gratefully. *Yes, I have you now, but for how long? That's the particular demon of yours I want to talk about.*

* * *

After dinner and a DVD movie, Angela left to get ready for bed while Jake set up the coffeemaker. She was under the covers when he passed through on the way to the bathroom. A few minutes later, he crawled into bed wearing only his boxer briefs.

Lying on his side, he reached to slide Angela next to him, but she resisted.

"C'mon. I only want to cuddle. I'm wearing my underwear like a good boy," he said, grinning.

"I want to cuddle, too, but first I want to talk *about you.*"

"I don't like the sound of that."

"Chicken," she teased. She leaned in, kissed him hard and fast, and pulled back before he could catch her. "We talked about one of my demons earlier. Now we talk about one of yours."

"You know, we Martian males don't like to talk about our demons." His expression didn't match his jovial tone.

"Too bad. Your Venusian girlfriend does." Her tone turned serious. "Please, Jake. This has been bothering me since your party."

He flopped onto his back and exhaled in resignation. "Okay, shoot."

"Why do you and Tanya keep breaking up and getting back together?"

His head jerked around. His eyes narrowed. "What the hell kind of question is that? You know I don't believe in discussing previous relationships, and I've told you all you need to know about Tanya."

"Humor me. I'm not digging for dirt on you and Tanya. My question goes deeper. Your relationship with Tanya is simply a good example of the demon I want to discuss."

"What do you want from me, Angela?"

"An answer."

He pushed the back of his head into the pillow and sighed. "Tanya believes our relationship has potential. She tries so hard to make it into something more, but I don't feel it."

"And Bonnie?"

"Damn it. She told you—"

"Yes, but she didn't get into any detail, and she's not bitter. She had wonderful things to say about the time you two were together."

"Women. Guys get a bad rap for kissing and telling, but you women…"

"Good try, Jake, but you're not sneaking away from the topic. Why did you break up with Bonnie and all the others?"

"All the others? What is this, an inquisition?"

She leaned over him, her face inches from his. "Answer me, Mr. Stone."

Jake pushed her aside, swung his feet to the floor, and sat up with his back to her. "This sucks. But okay. Here's the ammunition you want. Yeah, I dated Tanya, Bonnie, and *all the others*. I screwed them. A lot. But if they're honest, they'll tell you they had a really good time. We had fun; we had sex. It never got any more serious than that."

"Why?"

"Why did I screw them?" He twisted around and shot her a lecherous smirk. "I like to fuck, that's why."

Angela's eyes blazed. "Stop it, Jake. I'm not going to let you hide behind your vulgar vocabulary. I know you use it to put me off balance. It's not going to work this time."

"Well, aren't you clever, Miss Shrink."

She inhaled slowly, held the breath a moment, and then blew it out through pursed lips. "I'm asking why you never have serious relationships with women."

Jake tunneled his fingers through his hair and scrubbed his scalp, obviously stalling. "It's simple, Angela. They were superficial relationships that didn't have anything meaningful to grow on. Why would a woman want a long-term, serious relationship with me anyway? Even you called me a playboy."

"Maybe you always escaped before they had a chance to grow."

"Sure. Whatever you say, Miss Shrink."

"Okay, this is what I say. I think you cut and run because you're afraid one of these 'superficial relationships' might get serious. Deep down inside, you want it, but you're afraid of it, too. So you hide. You've hidden the real Jake from Tanya, Bonnie, et al. And now, you're hiding from me."

Steel shutters closed behind his eyes. Cold, hard, emotionless gray stared back at her. "Believe me, you wouldn't like the 'real Jake.' I don't even like him."

Chapter 26

Four stately white columns stood like sentries before the two-story, brick mansion. Surrounded by a tall fence and immaculate grounds, the house appeared cold and austere. Even the exotic pineapple, the universally recognized symbol of hospitality, on the colorful nylon flag flapping in the breeze near the front door did not bring a sense of welcome to the place.

While Jake scrutinized the impressive Reardon home from inside his rental car, he recalled Angela's disdain for her parents' love of wealth and society. As a disenchanted young woman, she had left the lap of luxury in McLean, Virginia, to live in a duplex in LA and a condo in Coronado.

Already tired from the cross-country flight, he wasn't entirely sure why he was here, and he sure as hell didn't know what he was going to say. His business was with Maleena Reardon, not her parents. Perhaps he simply had a morbid need to meet Angela's unsympathetic family, especially the parents who had turned their backs on a very special daughter.

He drove up the circular driveway and parked in front of the stairs leading to the front door. As he climbed the steps, he listened for signs of life but heard none. When he rang the doorbell, a smiling, impeccably dressed, middle-aged woman promptly answered.

"Good afternoon. May I help you?" she asked in a soft, polite voice.

"Good afternoon. I'm here to see Mr. and Mrs. Reardon."

"Do you have an appointment, sir?"

"No. I just arrived from San Diego, and I was hoping to catch them at home."

The woman slanted her head slightly. "Your name?"

"Jake Stone."

Her smile faltered. "Have you found her?" She drew a deep breath and extended her hand. "Excuse my poor manners, Mr. Stone. I am Rosa Sanchez. We spoke on the phone several days ago."

"Yes, I remember. Glad to meet you, Ms. Sanchez," he said, shaking her hand. "I'm sorry, but Angela...hasn't been found."

Rosa nodded solemnly. She gestured for him to enter and shut the door behind him. Then she leaned close and spoke barely above a whisper, "Don't give up, Mr. Stone. Don't let them stop you. My angel would never commit suicide." She straightened, her eyes glistening, beseeching.

"I won't give up."

"Good." She sighed. "Mrs. Reardon is with Maleena at the wedding planner's office, but Mr. Reardon is in his study. He prefers to have guests announced, but why don't you just come with me, Mr. Stone." She smiled as if they were coconspirators.

Following Rosa across the marble foyer and down a long hallway, Jake stole glances into several lavishly furnished rooms. The mansion's interior reeked of gaudy affluence.

They stopped in front of double mahogany doors.

"Stay right behind me," Rosa said.

She knocked once, swung the doors wide open, and walked into the room. Jake was her shadow.

Randall Reardon glanced up from the papers on his desk. His startled expression conveyed undeniable displeasure at Rosa's violation of household protocol.

"Mr. Reardon, Jake Stone to see you." She stepped around Jake and left the study, closing the doors behind her.

The two men stared at each other for several moments before Randall Reardon spoke.

Looking down at the paperwork, he said, "I'm very busy, Mr. Stone. I can spare you a few minutes, but if you need more of my time, I suggest you make an appointment." His cool, aloof gaze returned to his uninvited, unwelcome guest.

"This won't take long." Without an invitation, Jake lowered himself into an armchair. He rested his forearms on his legs and clasped his hands in a pensive attitude.

Randall pushed his chair away from the desk, leaned back, and folded his hands on his chest. "I assume this is about Angela. We've heard nothing from Detective Smithson in several days, but I know Maleena has been monitoring the situation closely. Is there some news?"

Jake pasted on a rueful smile and began his charade. "I wish I had something positive to report, but I don't. I'm actually in town on another matter and just wanted to take the opportunity to introduce myself to Angela's family." Randall didn't respond so Jake continued. "I'm terribly sorry for your loss. Although I knew Angela for only a short time, I was extremely fond of her. And now I miss her terribly. I can't imagine how awful it must be for her parents and sister."

Randall's expression softened. "It's been hard on all of us."

"Maleena has indicated my investigation has caused your family a great deal of distress. Please understand that is not my intention. I only want to find the truth." Jake waited, watching for a reaction.

The father's gaze rose to the ceiling. He laced his fingers and bounced them softly against his lips. When his eyes returned to Jake's, they shone with unshed tears.

"I've lost Angela twice, Mr. Stone. You have no idea how devastating that is. Four years ago, part of me died because I didn't know how to reach out to my daughter after the…the rape. Other circumstances in my life made it impossible to drop everything and bring her under my wing. She never understood why I wasn't there for her, and I lost her. I had always hoped someday, somehow, we could reconnect, find each other."

Dumbfounded by the man's emotional response, Jake could only listen.

Randall cleared his throat. "But then this happened. My hope was destroyed. I lost Angela again. This time for…for…forever." He sighed heavily. "My marriage barely survived the first crisis. The jury's still out on whether it will survive this one. Maleena and her mother have always been very close. But Angela, you see, was my favorite, my perfect angel." He stared off into space. After a long, poignant moment, Randall coughed and returned to the present. "Regardless of what Maleena and my wife may say, Mr. Stone, I want to know the truth about Angela's death. I loved her deeply. I'm just doing a very poor job of dealing with losing my daughter a second time."

Jake judged the man's sincerity. Oddly, he believed Angela's father. Was it because they shared the burden of remorse-filled hearts?

The older man's unexpected, heartfelt reaction momentarily disconcerted Jake. Blackmailing Maleena would bring even more turmoil into the distraught father's life. Well, that was just too damn bad.

Jake stood. "Thank you for your candor, Mr. Reardon. I'm not giving up. I feel I owe it to Angela. Thank you for your time."

Randall came around the desk, shook his hand, and escorted him toward the doors. "I apologize for being so obnoxious when we spoke before. My defensive reaction as a father was that you had, perhaps, been involved with Angela for less than respectable reasons. Please forgive me."

"No problem."

Near the doors, they stopped at a large wooden table covered with framed pictures. Randall selected one of a smiling teenager. "This is my favorite picture of Angela. But, in all honesty, she only grew more beautiful, inside and out, as she got older."

Jake spotted a familiar photograph: Angela wearing a red dress. He treasured the miniature of that picture, which was in his wallet. He carefully lifted the frame from the table and brought it closer.

"I like this one," he said solemnly.

Randall cocked his head, a curious expression on his face. "But that's Maleena."

"What?"

"That's Maleena. The photograph was taken about five months ago, shortly after she got engaged. I don't believe she even knows Adrienne recently had a copy enlarged and framed."

Maleena? Jake's jaw dropped, and his eyes grew wide.

Randall chuckled. "You didn't know Angela and Maleena were identical twins, did you? I'm not surprised Angela never told you." He shook his head sadly.

Identical twins. A strange swirling sensation filled Jake's head. Puzzle pieces spun, twisted, and landed, forming a heinous manifestation of hatred and betrayal.

"It was the weirdest thing. From birth, their personalities were completely different. Identical on the outside, opposite on the inside. The girls never got along, never liked each other. After Maleena moved back from LA, I don't think they ever spoke to each another. And the fact that my wife preferred Maleena, and I favored Angela, practically destroyed our family."

As Randall spoke, the floor shifted beneath Jake. *Identical twins.* Sweat formed on his upper lip and under his arms. Nausea gurgled in his gut. He thought he might pass out for the first time in his life. He grabbed for the table to steady himself.

Randall caught the frame as it slipped from Jake's fingers and laid it on the table.

"Are you all right, Mr. Stone? You don't look at all well," he said, clutching Jake's arm.

Dazed, Jake stared incredulously at the image of the woman in red. *Maleena. Not Angela. Damn. Damn. Damn.*

He yanked his arm free of Randall's grasp. "I've got work to do."

* * *

Jake's phone call had struck like a bolt of lightning.

Detective Sean Burke sat stunned at his desk. Maleena and Angela weren't just sisters; they were fucking identical twins. Why the hell had no one ever told him?

Every other breath was a gasp, as if his normal, reflexive breathing had been so disrupted that his lungs needed extra oxygen intermittently. His shirt clung to his damp skin, and rivulets of sweat streamed down his sides while his pulse raced frantically.

He stared at the screen of his cell phone, reassuring himself that he had not imagined the call. For despite all his body's physical reactions, his brain seemed intent on viewing the past several minutes as an out-of-body experience.

He shook his head vigorously. His hand groped across the desk for the Styrofoam cup. He drained the potent dregs of afternoon coffee and gagged on the disgusting taste. After the choking subsided, he closed his eyes and drew deep breaths until he got a grip on his nerves.

Opening his eyes, he exhaled, long and hard. Time to move. He had a million things to do and so little time. His mind raced through a list of the first dozen tasks in a flash.

The Waterton homicide case. *Shit.* The Police Chief had been calling him all day with endless questions about the shooting. *Damn it.* He could lose his badge for disappearing in the middle of the investigation—especially considering his barely explicable presence at the crime scene. Well, that was just too fucking bad. Some things were more important than a job. Like his soul.

Bringing up his e-mail, he concocted a lie to tell his boss. He briefly considered giving Detective Olsen a precisely abridged version of the truth but quickly shelved the idea. The plot was almost unbelievable to him, and he'd been involved since the earliest chapters. A lie was better; it avoided the inevitable complications of reality.

Sean wrote a sickening description of the developing stomach flu that would probably keep him bedridden for a number of days. As always, he'd be available by cell phone and would field calls when and if his illness allowed. He sent the message, glad he'd decided to stick with the K-I-S-S principle.

In truth, he was nauseous. However, his malady was not caused by a microscopic virus, but by the recognition of the embodiment of evil.

After shutting down the computer, Sean jumped up from the chair and checked his gun before slipping on his shoulder holster. When he stopped by the equipment room for the other items he needed, he'd grab additional ammo. He snatched his sport coat from the hook on the wall and slung it over his shoulder.

His hand was on the doorknob when the desk phone rang. His first reaction was not to answer. He took a step into the hallway and then spun back. His stomach clenched. It was probably the Chief again. He could use this opportunity to complain about feeling ill. He reached across the desk and seized the phone on the fourth ring.

"Burke," he said hurriedly.

"Sean?"

Chapter 27

Three weeks earlier

"Take off your underwear."

"Huh?" Jake said, awkwardly stepping back from Angela's bed.

She smiled seductively. "You heard me, big guy." She flipped the sheet back, offering him her nakedness.

His eyes widened, and his jaw dropped. Speechless, he stared at her tempting body. Absently, he wiped his mouth as if he were drooling. His eyes finally found their way up to hers. Desire sparked in the gray depths.

"Uh, wh-what are you doing?" he stammered.

"Can't you guess?" she teased.

"I'm not taking any chances. Spell it out for me. My brain's a little addled right now."

She laughed softly and patted the mattress. "Come here, silly. I won't bite. Unless you want me to."

"Hey, that's my line. Jesus, Angela, what's gotten into you?"

"Lust, I hope." Her mouth formed a pout. "I thought it might help if I acted the part of a temptress."

Still he didn't move.

"Well?" she said, feigning impatience.

He ran a hand across his face. "I can't do this."

"What?" She sat up and pulled the sheet over her lap.

His eyes followed every motion. "I promised you that I wouldn't lose control again, remember? But I'm so horny, I'm about to explode. I probably should be in a straitjacket, not just underwear." She laughed; he didn't. "I'm serious." He glanced down at the erection already straining against his boxer briefs.

Angela snatched the sheet up to her neck, covering herself completely. "Oh God, what am I doing?" Her cheeks burned as she turned away. "I'm sorry, Jake. Close your eyes, and I'll put my gown back on."

"Wait a minute. Why are you apologizing?"

Her words tumbled out. "I thought you'd be excited—not aroused-excited, just plain excited—that I wanted to sleep naked with you. All day, I've been on pins and needles, anticipating how proud you'd be. I'm so stupid. I never considered how hard—no pun intended—it would be for you."

"I am proud of you. This is a huge step. It's like step eleven and a half." He grinned and coaxed a smile from her. He exhaled in a whistle. "You're sure about this?"

"I thought I was. Now I don't know."

"Shit. I screwed this up for you. I'm sorry."

She followed his gaze down the sheet draped across her breasts, her nipples prominent and obvious.

He gulped loudly. "Here's a compromise. You stay naked, but I'll keep my underwear on until I'm sure I can handle this. Then you can take them off me."

Her mood brightened. "I like that." She slid down under the sheet and waited.

Jake's movements were slow and jerky as he climbed into bed and pulled the sheet over himself. He took two fortifying breaths before he rolled onto his side toward her.

When she scooted closer, his protruding dick poked her thigh. She started, froze. *I want this. I want Jake. I'm going to be strong. I can do this. I can. I'm not going to chicken out.* To Jake's obvious amazement, she reached beneath the sheet and tenderly redirected his erection so it was sandwiched between them. He groaned.

Feeling strangely empowered, Angela pressed her bare breasts against his naked chest and leaned in for a kiss. Her lips parted, inviting him in. He needed no further encouragement. Her fingers feathered through his hair and clung to it as the passion of his kiss overwhelmed her. Hesitation and reservation vanished.

The sparks in Jake's eyes lit a fire in hers. His hot breath on her neck and breasts fanned those sparks into flames that raced through her, settling like hot coals between her thighs.

While he gently sucked a nipple, his hand traced her spine from nape to tush again and again. The tenderness of his touch sent shivers across her skin. Oh God, he felt wonderful. Her pulse pounded as muscles clenched low in her belly. Lust at last.

Jake palmed her bottom and angled his dick onto, but not into, the V at the top of her thighs. She moaned and pressed against the steel rod tormenting her. Pushing his hand aside, she swung her leg over his hip and ground her pelvis hard into his.

"Easy now, easy. Don't freak out. I'm going to…touch you," he whispered in her ear.

She whimpered with a need she hadn't felt in four years.

His hand wedged a space between them. She jerked but continued to cling to his neck and bury her face in his chest. Gingerly, he separated her swollen folds, and his thumb touched that most sensitive spot. Her strangled cry vibrated against his skin, but she didn't pull away. His thumb continued to caress her as he pushed two fingers ever so slowly inside. She gasped and stilled.

Jake's hand froze. Several heartbeats passed. Trembling, she tightened her muscles around his fingers.

"C'mon. Let me give you this. Come for me," he pleaded.

His fingers slid in and out, deeper and deeper. His thumb stroked softly but persistently.

"Jake, Jake," she cried between pants, "I can't."

"Yes, you can. Focus on the feeling."

The pace of his thrusts accelerated. His thumb drove her crazy.

Her fingers dug into his shoulders. Her back arched. Her head flung back.

A combination cry and scream heralded her orgasm. Violent waves ravaged her body as penance for her celibacy. Gasping and shuddering, she rode the spasms until she fell, drained and satisfied, against Jake's chest.

Then the tears came.

* * *

A few nights later, the passion of their kisses flared as their tongues intertwined. Jake rolled Angela onto her back. His mouth pulled away and began a slow, seductive journey down her naked body. While his hand parted her thighs, his eyes searched hers for any sign of fear or rejection. Her faint smile revealed neither. Tenderly, his fingertips separated the delicate folds and found her hot and wet. Eyes still locked on hers, his fingers stroked, probed, and after a slight hesitation, slid gently inside. His thumb caressed her, causing her breath to catch. She stiffened but then relaxed. Her body tightened around his fingers as they plunged rhythmically deeper and deeper.

After withdrawing his fingers, he rose and bent his head over her thighs. Hoping she was prepared for what he was about to do, he checked her face for reassurance. Her smile faded, but her eyes watched him without fear. He lowered his head, his tongue touching, tasting, tantalizing. She squirmed and he retreated, waited. No complaints. His lips opened and explored her soft warm wetness. He captured her, his tongue sending shivers through her.

Her body was ready for him physically. Was she ready for him mentally? His painful, throbbing erection insisted it was time to find out.

He moved between her legs as Angela's eyes studied him and then closed. Her lips pulled inward and pressed tightly together.

Jake waited. No rejection. He braced himself on both hands beside her shoulders. He hovered over her, watching her closely. His heart pounded, and his breathing quickened. His hips lowered, inching forward. The warm, wet tip of his swollen dick pressed tentatively against her opening, longing for admittance.

Angela's eyes flew open. She stared up at the naked body bearing down on her.

Her first scream paralyzed him. Before he could move, the sec-

ond scream split his consciousness like an ax. While her fingers clawed at his face, her knee attacked his strategically poised genitals.

He swore loudly as he rolled off her and over the side onto the floor. He lay on his back, his chest heaving, his mouth sucking air. Lust forgotten, his hands cradled his assaulted package.

After a few minutes, Angela's crying penetrated his painful daze. "Shit," he muttered, gathering his knees under him and crawling back to the bed. Cringing, he pulled himself up the side.

Angela was curled, fetuslike, against the headboard. Between sobs, she whimpered, "It was like my bad dream. Oh God, I'm so sorry."

Jake filled his lungs and then let the air out in a long, slow breath before leveraging himself up to sit on the bed. "You okay?"

"No."

He touched her arm. "C'mere."

She shook her head.

"I need you, Angela. I need to hold you."

Watery eyes peered at him warily.

"Just hold. Nothing else."

She hesitated but then crawled onto his lap. His arms encircled her and hugged her tightly. Her body shuddered with a tremulous sigh.

"I almost made it, didn't I?" she whispered against his chest.

"Yeah."

"I'm...I'm sorry about the knee."

He grimaced. "That wasn't fair, you know, using the self-defense techniques I taught you against me. Bad form."

She smiled up at him and snuggled closer. "But they worked just like you said they would. You're a good teacher."

"Yeah, lucky me."

* * *

Jake stood next to the pool, admiring the dwindling sunset. Angela was due any minute for a late supper and to spend the night. Cringing at the memory of last night's fiasco, he softly rubbed his still-tender groin.

God, they'd been so close. Their disappointment had been palpable, but they'd laughed it off and expressed their affection in other ways. Maybe tonight would be the night.

When his cell phone rang, Jake fished it from his pocket and put it to his ear without checking the screen. "Running late, babe?"

"Time's up, asshole. If you don't complete the contract immediately, I'll hire an assassin who will." The Contractor disconnected before he could respond.

"Jake?"

He spun around to find Angela strolling toward him. She stopped abruptly.

"My God, Jake. You look like you've just seen a ghost."

Chapter 28

The present

J ake paced in front of the hotel room windows. The angry sky in Reston, Virginia, mirrored the dark, foreboding mood gripping him. Voluminous black storm clouds promised lightning and thunder, a phenomenon likely to occur *inside* the hotel room as well.

He rolled his head to the right and then to the left. Tension had built relentlessly in the twenty-seven hours since he'd arrived in Virginia. He wasn't nervous, though. He was coiled, ready to strike. Holding his right hand splayed in front of him, he smiled. *Steady as stone.*

He glanced at his watch: 7:30 p.m. Still half an hour until showtime.

Had he thought of everything? Was he prepared to improvise? Was everything in place? Should he have taken more time, another day, before springing the trap?

He shook his head in answer to the last question. Already, it had been too long. Fifteen torturous days had passed since that last night with Angela.

Angela. She had mocked him in nightmares. She had seduced him in dreams.

She had *not* smiled at him from the photograph.

Last night, Jake had tossed and turned for hours, berating himself for his stupidity. He repeated his self-condemnation now as he waited. It didn't console him that, without the last vital piece of information, he would not have been able to solve the puzzle. *Identical twins.* When he thought of all the people he'd spoken to, he couldn't believe no one had ever mentioned it. But he was absolutely certain no one had. The impact of that one crucial fact was so overwhelming, there was no way he could've missed it.

And he found no comfort in knowing Burke had been just as shocked by the news. To convince himself that he and the detective hadn't overlooked the significant clue, Jake had again reviewed every single item in Burke's file on the rape. As he'd noticed before, Maleena was barely mentioned, and not once had anyone described her as Angela's twin, much less her identical twin.

A hard knock on the door shattered his thoughts.

Smart girl. Come early, try to catch me off guard.

Pulling back his sport coat, he checked the Glock riding in the waistband at his side. Its inaccessibility would cost him a few seconds. He hoped it didn't cost him his life.

He patted his chest and inhaled deeply. *Showtime.*

He peered through the peephole. A shiver raced down his spine.

Her hair was shorter and styled differently; otherwise, he would've sworn she was Angela. But then Maleena's gaze fixed on the peephole. Jake jerked backward. Her eyes were the same color and shape, but the emotions they conveyed could never have come from Angela's eyes.

With the pretense of a smile, Jake opened the door. They sized each other up for a long moment. Then he gestured for her to enter. After closing the door, he turned and raked her figure, sneering ever so slightly. "Good evening, Ms. Reardon. Or may I call you Maleena now that we're going to be business partners?"

"Maleena is fine, although I don't believe this simple transaction makes us business partners." She returned his critical gaze, lingering on his crotch. "Well, I'm glad to see Angela was *not* screwing around with a piece of shit. We never had the same taste in men—or anything else, for that matter." She laughed snidely.

"Angela also didn't have a potty mouth."

"I'm smart enough to control my language when necessary. A Senator's wife needs to be very polished." Her chin rose in an arrogant pose.

Jake detected underlying nervousness, but then he wasn't doing so well himself. Talking to Angela's twin was unnerving. His pulse was too fast, his focus dangerously distracted.

A door slammed, and they both jumped. At the sound of angry voices, two pairs of eyes darted to the door leading into an adjoining hotel room and then to the hallway door. When the voices quieted, he scolded himself. *Shit, Stone, get a grip.*

Earlier, he had rearranged the furniture to better suit his needs. He stepped around Maleena and offered her the armchair facing the two doors. After she gracefully settled herself, he sat down in the other chair a few feet in front but a little to her left.

"Let's get this over with. I don't want to be here any longer than necessary," Maleena said, reaching into the large, leather purse resting on her lap. "I was glad you called me back to accept my offer. Ten grand should more than compensate you for your investigation of Angela's suicide." She pulled out a cashier's check and extended it to him. "But it seems a waste of time and money for you to fly all the way to Virginia for this. I could easily have sent it overnight to you."

Jake glanced at the check, folded it, and stuffed it into his coat pocket.

"Actually, when I called you, I wanted to discuss a business proposition. But I realized the proposal needed to be presented in person."

Maleena scoffed. "I have no intention of doing business with you, Mr. Stone."

"Ah, Maleena, let's get cozier. Call me Jake." His gaze dropped to her breasts and bounced back. "Don't you even want to hear what I was going to propose?"

"No. I couldn't care less."

"I wonder if Senator Blackwell will feel the same way."

Her eyes narrowed. "What the hell are you talking about?"

He rubbed his chin thoughtfully. "Now you're interested?"

"Don't screw with me."

"You're probably right. You're far too dangerous for me."

Maleena silently glared at him.

"You see, originally I wanted to talk to you about your drug addiction—"

"Bullshit. I don't do drugs."

"Not now, maybe, but I have several witnesses who say you did the hard stuff in LA."

"Witnesses?" She fidgeted in the chair.

"Don't worry. I've changed my mind about your drug problem.

I discovered something that should be a lot more...profitable...to me." He grinned slyly. "I know what happened to Angela."

Maleena shook her head. "God, you're back to that. Look, Jake, we all know what happened. By accepting the ten grand, you agreed to stop investigating. Maybe I should have my attorney write up an agreement to that effect."

"Don't bother with some legal crap because I've already finished my investigation."

"Then what's the problem?"

He dropped the fake smile and leaned forward, putting his hand on her thigh.

"You see, Maleena, I mean it when I say I *know* what happened to Angela. Should I elaborate?"

"Please do." Angrily, she brushed off his hand.

Jake chuckled. "Someone was hired to kill Angela and make it look like a suicide."

"Why would anyone want little Miss Perfect Angel killed?"

"Angela posed a risk to the person's future because of a terrible incident that occurred four years ago."

Maleena's breath caught, and her eyes darkened.

"Yeah. I know all about *that,* too. Seems there was this crack-addict hooker, called herself Bad Angel. Seems she worked for a pimp by the name of J.J. Seems she had a regular john who was an LA city councilman. Seems Councilman Waterton had a fantasy about fucking identical twins. A sick fantasy he paid big bucks to make come true."

Jake paused to let his words sink in. Maleena's face blanched to a creamy white.

"Seems Bad Angel just happened to have an identical twin. One night, she and the councilman paid the sister a visit."

"You're full of shit. I don't believe any of that."

"Sure you do. You were there."

"Bullshit. You have no proof of anything," she snapped, her eyes growing wide.

"Really? I told you before that I'm a good PI. I don't make accusations unless I've got proof to back them up. You see, I have a recording of a very interesting conversation with J.J. Good thing I was smart enough to record it, because during our little meeting, J.J. ended up dead. And an even stranger coincidence, three days later, while I was recording a far more fascinating conversation with Councilman Waterton, he was killed in a drive-by shooting, too. Odd, huh?"

He paused, unblinking, hardening his gaze to drill into hers.

"Oh, yes, I almost forgot. Becky Smelter had some not-so-fond memories of you. And most importantly, she was the only remaining eyewitness who saw the *whore* and Waterton leaving Angela's place on the night of the rape. Guess what. She was shot last Tuesday also, but not before I'd taped a key conversation with her. Are you getting the picture, Maleena?"

"Even if any of that's true, what does it have to do with Angela's suicide?"

Jake rocketed out of the chair. He grabbed Maleena by the shoulders and shook her, hard.

"Let go of me," she squealed.

His hands flexed with an all-consuming desire to silence her. Permanently. A little voice inside his head stopped him. *This is the most important interrogation of your life. For Angela's sake, don't blow it.* He wanted to strangle the little voice.

Gradually, reluctantly, he released her. With his hands on the arms of the chair, his face within inches of hers, his chest heaved with hot, ragged breaths that blew into Maleena's face.

Stunned, Maleena blinked at him dazedly until he pushed off from the chair and straightened. Never taking his eyes off her, he backed away. God, he hated the woman. If anyone deserved to die, Maleena did.

Patience. Wait until the time is right. Get her confession first. That damn little voice again. Slowly, deliberately, he lowered himself into his chair.

"Don't push me, bitch. You don't know who you're dealing with. That was the last time you'll call Angela's death a suicide. Understand?"

Maleena gulped and avoided his eyes. "Sure. Whatever."

"I guess I should finish the story. Let's see. Where was I? Oh yeah. After that night, Bad Angel disappeared. Neither J.J. nor Waterton saw her again. At first, I thought Waterton had Bad Angel killed. But actually, she skipped town the next morning with the huge payoff and flew home to mommy and daddy. Then she cleverly admitted herself to an exclusive drug rehab where even the police couldn't question her without a lot of red tape."

Maleena's eyes, narrowed and focused, slowly slid back to his. Pure, unadulterated hate glowed in them. Her lips were pressed tightly into a thin line.

Jake's glare never wavered.

"Let's fast-forward a few years. That drug-addict whore cleans herself up—on the outside, at least—and is now engaged to a US Senator. I figure she's afraid her twin might derail her future if she goes public with what happened in LA. So the whore decides to have her sister killed." He paused to tamp down his rage. "I'm damn good, aren't I, Bad Angel?"

A full minute of silence passed. The adversaries scrutinized each other, calculating their next moves like chess masters.

Maleena spoke first, shaking her head in disbelief, her gaze fixed on the floor. "One mistake. One goddamn mistake that night caused all of this." She seemed to slip into the past. "I showed up at Angela's place with a bottle of wine and crushed sleeping pills. She only let me in because I told her I was going back to Virginia to straighten out my life. She was such a goddamn, bleeding heart that I knew she'd fall for my lie. Later, I slipped the sleeping pill powder into her wine. She was almost asleep when I left so I made a point of reminding her to lock the door. Of course, she didn't know I'd kept a duplicate key when she'd kicked me out a year earlier." Maleena smiled wickedly.

Jake gripped the arms of his chair.

"Leonard had been waiting in the car down the block. We sat there for another hour snorting coke. When I let us in, Angela was passed out on her bed. We blindfolded and gagged her. Put earplugs in her ears so she wouldn't recognize my voice. Leonard dressed both of us in stupid matching outfits. Then we tied Angela down on the bed."

She paused. Grimaced.

"Leonard did all his usual shit—to both of us. Angela woke up in the middle of it. She was struggling, trying to fight him off. Of course, it was useless. Then he went completely crazy and beat her up bad. I think he was pissed Angela wasn't enjoying his fantasy. God, he was an animal. Total sadist. Maybe finally fucking *real* identical twins put him over the edge."

Her hands clenched into fists.

"The bastard decided he wanted some lesbian action. He threatened Angela with the pistol he always carried. She didn't make a peep when he took off the gag. The things he made us do to each other were sick. That's when the mistake happened. When I was climbing off her, I accidentally pushed the blindfold away. Angela's eyes popped open and connected with mine for only a second before Leonard slapped her and repositioned the blindfold. But I knew she had recognized me." Maleena stopped and gulped. "Leonard insisted on carving 'J.J.' into her ass with his pocketknife. We left shortly afterward. You want any more titillating details?"

"No, I'm good. I can't believe you did that to your own sister, your own flesh and blood," he said incredulously.

Her hate-filled eyes glinted.

"And I would've gotten away with it if not for that one stupid mistake," she said proudly. "Well, what do you want? Sex? Money? Job?"

"We'll talk payment in a minute. First, I want to hear you explain why you wanted Angela dead." Maleena continued to glare at him, but her lips didn't move. "Or I could go to the police," he added.

Fear flickered in her eyes. "You're a bastard."

"Don't throw stones."

Maleena clutched her purse. "Okay, you're right. I needed her dead. The perfect angel would've screwed up my life to pay me back. She'd been holding onto this, waiting for just the right time when she could inflict the most pain and damage. Everything always went her way. I wasn't going to let her win this time."

Jake snickered at the irony. "God, what a waste. The trauma of the rape screwed up Angela's mind. Amnesia blocked out the entire event—even your visit earlier that night. The cops and doctors had to tell her what had happened. She had no memory of it. All

Angela had was a scarred butt and a ruined life. You didn't need to kill her."

"Well, shit. Mother and I thought she was lying about the amnesia. Of course, Mother thought Angela was protecting some loser guy."

"And the others. Why have them killed?"

"Sooner or later, J.J. or Leonard would've seen a picture on TV, in a newspaper, or on the Internet of Bad Angel with her Senator husband. Those assholes would've blackmailed me in a heartbeat."

"Why did Becky Smelter have to die? She was a sweet, harmless old lady who'd never consider blackmail."

"True. But when I got out of rehab, my parents had told me what the cops reported about that night, including the mysterious couple seen by the elderly neighbors. I couldn't take a chance Becky would eventually figure out it was *me* she saw leaving, not Angela. You're right. She wouldn't have blackmailed me. The old witch would've gone straight to the cops. Any more questions?"

"Nope. I think we're done."

Maleena opened her purse. "I'm going to pay you $15,000 now, to hold you over until you figure out how much you want to go away forever." While her hand rummaged in the purse, she abruptly looked up at him with a puzzled expression. "When you learned all the shit about the rape from J.J. and Leonard, why didn't you think maybe Angela had suddenly remembered that night and committed suicide because of it? How did you find out about the contract?"

"Because I'm a damn good PI—" His left hand firmly covered the microphone and transmitter taped under his shirt. He hoped it had caught every word up to that point, but what he said next was for Maleena's ears only. He pulled the red-dress photo from his shirt pocket and held it out for her to see. Then he leaned in close to her ear and whispered, "—and because I'm the hitman you hired to kill her." With barely controlled fury, he crushed the picture of Maleena into a tiny ball.

She gasped, and her eyes widened with fear, but she recovered quickly.

Jake's fingers dropped to her thigh. "Now, about that payment."

Maleena's hand emerged from the purse, clutching a pistol. "Get your fucking hand off me, asshole." She shoved Jake backward into his chair as she sprang up.

"Whoa, lady, that gun doesn't look like a checkbook," he shouted.

The adjoining-room door blasted open.

Maleena's eyes, but not her pistol, jerked in that direction.

"Police! Drop the gun!" Detective Sean Burke yelled, his gun aimed steadily at Maleena.

Her eyes flashed back to Jake. Her hand trembled.

"Checkmate," he said quietly.

"Please, Maleena, don't do it!" a female voice cried.

Shocked, Maleena whirled toward the door. A shriek burst from her lips. Her face contorted with hatred.

Her gun swiveled.

Three shots rang out.

Near the door, a scream pierced the air.

Maleena crumpled to the ground.

The next five seconds were dead silent.

A gut-wrenching sob yanked Jake's gaze around just in time to see Angela Reardon collapse.

Chapter 29

Fifteen days earlier

"For someone who said we were celebrating, you're awfully quiet and serious tonight," Angela said softly, snuggling closer to Jake under the sheet. She didn't care that her pink silk nightgown provided little protection from his nakedness, for it no longer frightened her.

"You didn't have a good time?" he asked, stroking her hair.

"Dinner and dancing at the Hotel del Coronado. Moonlit walk on the beach. It was okay."

"You're spoiled."

"Yes, and you get credit for that."

He squeezed her tight and kissed the top of her head.

"I still don't understand what we're celebrating." She tilted her head back so she could see his face.

He studied her for a long time before answering. "A couple of things. First of all...*you*. You're the most amazing woman I've ever met, Angela."

She started to make a sassy retort but reconsidered at the seriousness of his tone and expression. "Thank you. I'm flattered."

Jake's train of thought seemed to escape him as his gaze covered every inch of her face as though trying to memorize it.

"And second…," she prompted him.

"And," he whispered, "that I'm finally brave enough to say…" He cleared his throat. "I love you."

She gasped. A melting sensation began in her scalp and traveled to the tips of her toes. Her gaze welded to his. Her lips opened, but no words came out.

Jake's head lowered, and he captured her mouth with a passionate kiss. His tongue ignited a fire that superheated the melting sensation, creating a flow of lava through her body. She moaned against his lips.

Her hand slid between their bodies until her fingers found and fondled his dick. His entire body jerked in surprise, but before his ever-eager dick could respond, he loosened her grasp. He pressed the guilty hand to his lips and then tapped it against his chest.

"This isn't about sex. I love you in here, not down there." He grinned. "I know it's hard to believe, but this isn't a trick to get inside you."

"But I want you inside me. *Now*."

Jake blinked stupidly. "Huh?"

"I'm serious. I want to do it tonight."

He shook his head in disgust. "I'm a worse asshole than I thought. I can't even say something as special as 'I love you' without you concluding it's a tacky come-on. Honestly, Angela, I'm not interested in sex tonight." He rolled his eyes comically. "Ssshhh. I think I hear pigs flying and Hell freezing over."

"Very funny. But I'm not joking. I want to have sex with you. Right here, right now."

An emotion Angela couldn't identify drifted across Jake's face, darkening his eyes. His smile faded, his lips thinned, and his jaw set stubbornly.

"Why tonight?" he asked. His voice had lost its tenderness, now sounding flat and detached.

She rolled onto her back, nestling her head sideways against the pillow so she could still look at him.

"I'm not sure, Jake, but I know I'm ready. No false starts, no mind changes, no knees to the groin. I've been so close for the last week or two, but for some reason, I just couldn't take the final leap of faith. Maybe part of me didn't like the idea that having sex with you was simply the last step in your twelve-step program. I needed it to be more than that." She hesitated. "My mind was ready. My body was ready. But my heart wasn't. Maybe subconsciously, I needed it to be an act of love, not lust."

Touching his face with her fingertips, she traced his lips and the line of his jaw. "You see, Jake Stone, I love you, too."

Turning onto her side, she pulled up the gown and pressed her pelvis into his. She felt the reflexive jerk of his dick as she rubbed against it. Her mouth covered his, her tongue squeezing between his lips, teasing, enticing.

Jake yanked his head back, gaping. "Christ, Angela, are you sure?"

"Absolutely."

He needed no further encouragement.

Framing her face with both hands, he kissed her mouth with an intensity Angela had never experienced. When they were forced to come up for air, he flung off the sheet. She could tell he was watching her eyes for any sign of distress while he helped her wiggle out of the gown and tossed it aside. Then his gaze raked her naked body from head to toe, lingering appreciatively on all the critical spots. The desire inside her flared.

His warm hands seemed to touch her everywhere at once, perhaps because they left a trail of heat behind. Tantalizing first with his fingers and then with his tongue, he brought her nipples to attention. An involuntary moan sounded deep in her throat.

His fingers threaded through her hair and stroked her neck. Flitting as lightly as a butterfly, his tongue teased her earlobes, tasted her breasts, and tickled her navel. Strong hands massaged her shoulders, waist, and ass. Even her legs and toes received his admiring attention.

Only their pounding heartbeats measured the passing time as Jake lovingly caressed her, inch by delicious inch.

She clasped her hands around his neck and brought him back up. She panted with anticipation and struggled to speak.

"What are you waiting for? You've wanted to have sex with me for three months."

"I don't want to *have sex* with you, Angela." He chuckled softly at her bewildered expression. "I want to make love to you, and there's so much more to that than mere sex. I want to explore you, savor you, please you, satisfy you. There's only one first time between us. You deserve for it to be extra special. I don't want to rush it."

"I don't know…if I can wait."

"You don't have to."

He pulled free of her grasp and scooted down in the bed. His fingers traveled down her belly to the V at the top of her thighs. He kissed her soft, curly hair while his fingers separated her sensitive, swollen folds. Her body was ready for him. As he gently slid two fingers inside her, his tongue fondled her.

Her back arched, and she cried out with pleasure. Moments later, waves of orgasm washed through her. "I'm sorry," she sighed. "I was...too fast."

He lay down alongside her. "Don't be sorry. You have a lot of catching up to do. I'll let you rest a little, though. Roll over on your stomach."

Languidly, she complied.

Jake straddled her legs and leaned forward. His fingers firmly massaged her scalp and her nape. They squeezed the muscles of her shoulders and back into relaxed submission. He continued lower, kneading, stroking, tantalizing in an arousing caress. When he stopped suddenly, Angela glanced over her shoulder.

His head hung forward, eyes closed. He grimaced as if fighting the pressure to release. "Rest time's over," he whispered hoarsely.

He rose so she could twist around under him. Her hands stroked his chest, tweaked his hardened nipples, kneaded his taut stomach. A carnal groan rumbled in his chest. His eyes opened and locked on hers.

"You okay?" he asked.

"Oh, yes."

He grinned. His hands held her cheeks as his tongue penetrated deep. His knee separated her thighs. He climbed between them and lowered some of his weight onto her.

Angela grasped his hips, angling herself up for their bodies to meet at the crucial spot.

"Easy, babe, easy. It's been four years. I don't want to hurt you."

She whispered, "I'm ready."

"I know. Look at me."

The instant their eyes connected, he slid partially inside her and stopped. She kept her gaze glued to his while Jake rocked gently and then penetrated deeper, filling her. She stiffened and tightened around him.

"Hurts?"

"No. Don't stop."

"More?"

Her muscles relaxed. She exhaled and nodded jerkily.

He sheathed himself completely inside her. She moved beneath him, and he cursed softly. "Slow down. I'm too close."

"Then what are you waiting for?" She smiled and clenched her muscles around him.

"Oh Jesus. Hang on." He withdrew slightly and thrust forward.

Angela rose to meet him, wanting him, needing him. Again and again and again. She watched his eyes, saw the crescendo of his tension as hers spiked.

She screamed with the first explosion of her orgasm. His dick swelled even more as his release jetted into her. A blend of a growl and a groan burst from him, celebrating the end to three months of celibacy. He pumped until the last spasm of her climax faded.

Collapsing slowly, he wrapped his arms around her and rolled onto his side, pulling her with him and staying inside her. He kissed her tenderly.

"I love you, Angela."

* * *

Jake slouched on the edge of the bed, his fingers clutching the deadly syringe hidden in his jacket pocket. Despite the timpani drum pounding in his chest and echoing in his ears, he kept his face expressionless.

He stared at Angela. Asleep. Naked. Unsuspecting. She was seductive even in repose, her blond hair encircling her head like a halo on the pillow.

The guilt gnawing at his gut did not spring from having been inside her, making love to her, but from what he knew was in her heart and mind and soul. Killing her was wrong. And even though he'd known it was wrong for a long time, he had been powerless to change the course of events set in motion almost four months ago. If he didn't kill her, someone else would, and that person would use the most efficient method without any regard for her suffering.

His fingers tightened around the syringe. A heavy sigh escaped his lips, releasing an avalanche of regret, remorse, and resignation. Yet sorrow still crushed his chest.

What kind of monster am I? I can't do this. I can't. His chin dropped to his chest. *I can't, but I must. Dear God, help me.*

Angela stirred. Her eyes opened, and she smiled up at him with those pools of molten dark chocolate. He hated what his eyes told her.

"Why," she began, "are you looking at me like that?" She frowned. "What's wrong? My God, Jake, you look like death warmed over." She pushed up onto her elbows.

Her eyes pulled him deeper. He sucked air through his mouth to fight the feeling of drowning. *Close your eyes. I can't stand for you to look at me. I'm an unlovable monster. Forgive me. I have no choice. I have to do it.*

An oil slick of pain drifted across Angela's eyes. "You're dressed. Are you leaving? I don't understand."

I don't understand either. Why would anyone want to kill you? You don't deserve to die. It's not right.

"For God's sake, talk to me, Jake. What's happening?" She reached for him. "Please stay. I need you. I love you. I love you…so much."

Inside his chest, a boulder crumbled. Her words crushed the remaining granite of his emotions into rubble.

I am not a monster. I can love and be loved. I can't kill you. I need you, too. If I die trying to save you, I'll die happy because I can't stand the thought of living without you.

He caught her hand and pulled her upright into his arms. Angela clung to him. Burying his face in her hair, he closed his eyes and embraced her like a drowning man clings to his rescuer.

"I love you, too," he said around the lump in his throat.

Her heart pounding with his, she sniffled and shuddered.

"Ssshhh. It's okay. Everything's going to be all right."

While he comforted her, his mind raced. Ideas, shadowy and vague, swirled in his head. Suddenly they melded, and a risky plan took shape. There were a thousand variables and no way to control any of them. Would his instincts and skills be up to the challenge?

Time. It was their enemy. He—no, they—would have to move quickly.

They. Jake was used to working alone, so Angela's involvement immediately loomed as a major risk. Unfortunately, there was no way to pull off the illusion without her cooperation and trust.

Trust. Such a fragile thing. Would she trust him? Would she believe him? How would she react?

He nuzzled her cheek and whispered, "Angela, I do love you. And I'm sorry for scaring you, but this is scary shit even to me. God, I prayed that you'd never have to know about this."

She raised her head from his shoulder and gazed into his eyes, confused. "What are you talking about?"

He gently laid her back on the bed as he struggled for the right words. Could he describe the danger she was in without revealing his role?

"I know this is going to sound incredible, but you must believe me. I wish there was an easier way to tell you this."

"Tell me what? What?" she asked, anxiety building in her voice.

Trust. He scrubbed a hand across his brow and swallowed hard. "All right, all right. I've learned there's a contract out to kill you."

The flash in her eyes revealed a combination of shock, disbelief, and panic. Her mouth hung open. "Oh my God. There must be some mistake. That can't be true."

"Damn it, I wish it weren't. I'm going to protect you, Angela. I have a plan, but we'll have to move fast."

She rubbed her temples and exhaled. "Give me a minute. I can't believe...I have to understand...How do you know about this?"

He hesitated only a second upon hearing the question he dreaded. "In my line of work, I often use contacts in the underbelly of society. Informants. Street bums. Mafia and gang wannabes. People who hear things. Chuck Thompson—remember him?—has been hearing things also." Was that a spark of suspicion in her eyes? "You're going to have to trust me, Angela."

She wrung her hands. "This can't be happening. Who in the world would want to kill me? And why? Why?" she asked, voice cracking. Her eyes pleaded for a reason.

"I don't know. But I have a theory." He squeezed her cold, trembling hands between his warm, steady ones. Guilt gripped him as he lied to her again. "It might be connected with the Malibu party.

Both Marco Romano and Sergio Zurlini reportedly have ties to the Mafia. Maybe the studly star didn't like being told no and publicly embarrassed."

"That's absurd. They wouldn't kill me because of that."

"Shit. Then you tell me who wants you dead, because someone most definitely does."

"I don't know," she said, sitting up, swinging her legs off the opposite side of the bed, and standing. "I'm calling the police."

Jake leaped off the bed and blocked her path. "Don't do that. It's a bad idea. The cops won't do anything." He watched a cloud of what he hoped was only disbelief—and not distrust—darken her eyes.

"Why not?"

"Because we don't have any proof. I need time to nose around and get something concrete to give them. Then they might help you." A lead weight dropped in his stomach and inched toward his intestines.

She stared at him. "Okay, but I have to do something. This is just too surreal." She shook her head and cringed. "What's your plan?" she asked reluctantly.

"First, we're going to fake your suicide—"

"Oh my God. That's awful."

"—here, tonight. Then I'll drive you to my beach house in Rosarito, and you'll hide there until I figure this mess out."

"Hide? I don't want to hide. I want to work with you."

"No way. Whoever is behind this must believe you're dead so he'll back off, let his guard down. It's too dangerous if I have to be looking over my shoulder trying to protect you while I investigate. I have to know you're safe so I can focus on finding the asshole. And working solo will attract less attention."

"Do you have to do this alone?" She fisted her fingers in her hair. "Why not call one of your cop friends? Or Chuck and Curly?"

His icy glare would have unnerved a weaker woman. "Is it me or my expertise that you don't trust, Angela?"

Her eyes searched his face. "Tell me again, Jake."

He frowned. "Tell you what?"

Her face set, she waited.

Grasping her shoulders, he pulled her to him, enveloped her in his arms. "I love you, Angela."

"I love you, too, and I do trust you."

Chapter 30

The present

The angry black clouds delivered on their promise. Lightning and thunder created melodrama as torrents of rain crashed to earth.

It was a dark and stormy night...

Normally, the famous line would have brought a smile to Jake's face but not this time. His expression was grim. Absently, he sipped the bitter black coffee in the Styrofoam cup. His watch glowed 12:15 a.m. as he stood outside the emergency room entrance to Reston Hospital. Despite the roof covering the area, gusts of wind sprayed him with rain.

He barely noticed.

Pulling his cell phone from a pocket, he dialed and waited. Silence finally answered.

"This is Granite. The situation we discussed has been resolved on this end. Permanently."

"Good to know," Salami said. "I investigated the rumor you told me about."

Jake frowned. "Rumor?"

"Yeah. Turns out this Contractor guy was an urban legend. Story goes he ran quite a side business using independent hitmen. When a private contract was particularly sensitive or required a specialty, he would deceive one of the Agency's assassins into taking it. Crazy story, huh?"

"Yeah, crazy story. How'd it end?"

"Like I said, he was only an urban legend. The Contractor wasn't real."

Jake's night had been hell, and the information took a few moments to filter through his brain. Finally, he responded, "Urban legend, my ass. I bet the bastard just made the mistake of fucking with the wrong assassin."

"Maybe, Granite, but I prefer to believe the Contractor never existed."

"I know. Like you and me, my friend."

"Right." Salami hesitated. "You never consummated the Reardon contract, did you?"

"No."

"I didn't think so." Salami snorted. "Guess you're a bit of a rogue now, Granite. Good man."

Jake grinned. "Well, thanks for everything. And by the way, forget about Istanbul. That debt is paid."

"Never," Salami murmured, and then he was gone.

Jake stuffed the phone back in his pocket. He had expected more satisfaction and relief than he felt. Perhaps, after what had happened during the last five hours, the Contractor's demise was more perfunctory than emancipating.

* * *

Detective Sean Burke shook off the raindrops as he hustled through the automatic door into the Reston Hospital emergency room waiting area. He spotted his target entering the men's restroom. His jaw and hands clenched before he sprinted across the linoleum floor.

He burst through the swinging door as Jake was unzipping his fly. Sean grabbed Jake's arms, pinned them to the startled man's back, and slammed him against the tiled wall. With one forearm, he hammered Jake's neck into an immovable position.

"If this little chat…is going to take awhile…at least let me breathe." Jake grunted the words through his teeth. "That…or get it over with…and kill me."

"Shut the fuck up, Stone! I don't know whether to *kill* or *kiss* you."

"Can't say…I prefer…either one."

Sean's chest heaved hard, and hot breath spilled onto the back of Jake's neck. "Angela…how bad…?"

"The hospital won't…tell me shit."

"But she's not…"

"I don't think so…but they won't say. What the hell…was she doing there?"

Sean sneered. "The bigger question—for you—is what the hell is she doing *alive*? I just about shit in my pants when she called me."

"Called you?"

"At my office, as I was leaving. Now answer my damn question."

"Didn't she…tell you?" Jake tried to pull his cheek away from the wall, but Sean smacked his face back down. "Damn. Can't we talk…like civilized—"

"No way. And yeah, Angela told me what she *thought* had happened. I want to see if you tell same story."

Jake groaned. "We faked her suicide…so I could deal with the contract…that Romano or Zurlini…had out on her. Thought it was…an Italian macho…or Mafia thing. I'd tell you more…if I could breathe."

"Well, shit." Sean released Jake and immediately sucker punched him in the kidney. Jake collapsed to his knees. "That's for putting me through hell." Sean's glare burned into the man on the floor.

With a hand braced against the wall, Jake slowly leveraged himself upright. The moment he regained his balance, he buried his fist in the detective's gut. Bent in half, Sean hugged his ribs and moaned.

"That's for *not* letting me know Angela had called you," Jake said, twisting his neck to get the kinks out and massaging his lower back. "Even?"

"Yeah, sure."

A few minutes later, they trudged out to the waiting area and claimed two seats in a deserted corner where they could talk privately.

"How did you originally hear about the contract?" Sean asked.

"I have good ears."

He hung his head in exasperation. "Sometimes, Stone, I just want to bust your ass."

"Hey, I'm like a journalist. I have to protect my sources."

"Yeah, right. When you came to LAPD, why didn't you tell us you suspected Romano or Zurlini?"

"I'd already checked them out and eliminated that theory. The rape connection seemed the only other possibility."

Sean looked at him doubtfully. "Let's assume you're telling the truth. I'm a cop. Why couldn't you tell me Angela was in hiding?"

"I didn't trust anyone. I rarely do." Jake arched his back and stretched. "Why did Angela call you?"

"She was scared."

Jake's gaze shifted to the floor. "Of what?"

"Obviously, she was afraid the hitman would find her. She felt too vulnerable down in Rosarito all alone. And she was frantic to find you."

"So why didn't she call *me*?"

"Good question," Sean said, slanting him a suspicious glance.

"Here's another one. Why didn't *you* call me?" Jake's steely eyes nailed him to the chair.

Sean returned the favor. "Angela made me promise not to."

"Jesus Christ, I thought we were partners in this."

"Hey, I'd just found out my 'partner' had lied to me about this woman being dead. Hell, I was still in shock. Who do you think I was going to cooperate with? When I told her I was meeting you here in Virginia, she freaked out and insisted on coming. So she flew out of Tijuana last night about midnight."

"Helluva trip."

"Yeah. And my trip from LA just about screwed up your whole plan. Man, I was sweating it when I missed my flight out of Dallas because of the bad weather. When I didn't roll into the hotel until seven last night, I thought for sure the sting was dead. Thank God, all that was left to do was slap the wire on you. Not a minute to spare." Sean grinned. "That's why I didn't kick your ass right then."

"Well, thanks. Maleena might've gotten spooked if I'd been bruised and bleeding."

"Get this. Angela called me from the hotel lobby to get my room number right as Maleena knocked on your door."

Jake pinched the bridge of his nose. "Damn. They almost ran into each other."

"No shit, Sherlock. And since Maleena was already there, I couldn't warn you about Angela."

"The door slamming and the angry voices must've been Angela arriving. Had you told her about Maleena?"

"Good God, no. I'd told her earlier only that you were going to interrogate a suspect."

"What happened in the room?"

"She was pissed you weren't with me. Then she heard Maleena's voice coming over the wire. We both froze listening to that god-awful conversation."

"Angela heard all of it?"

"All but the first few minutes."

"Jesus Christ." Leaning forward, Jake squeezed his head between his hands.

The two sat silently for several minutes.

Then Jake glanced sideways at Sean. "Who tipped off the cops?"

"*I* sure as hell didn't. I suspect Angela did."

"Why would she do that?"

"Damned if I know. She was in a panic. It was hard to understand what she was saying. Insisted on getting the room number and coming up. Sounded like she thought *I* was in danger."

"What did the cops tell you later?"

"They got an anonymous call from the lobby payphone about a big drug deal going down. Go figure. Believe me, I was as shocked as you when they stormed in a second after the shooting stopped," Sean said.

"Yeah, they grabbed me and slammed me up against the wall before I could get to Angela. Got my Glock, of course."

"I thought they were going to trample her when they barged in. They shoved me into the adjoining room before I could see…" Sean stopped and gulped. "Took my piece, too. How many shots did you hear?"

Their eyes locked.

"Three."

"Yeah, me, too. The uniforms told me two hit Maleena. By then, Angela was gone, and they didn't know her condition."

"Shit. I was screaming at them to tell me if she was all right, but the assholes wouldn't say anything. I couldn't see…"

"Me neither. The paramedics were blocking my view. I never heard a sound out of her." Sean's gut felt ready to explode. "Did…did Maleena shoot her?"

"Damn it, I don't know, man. I just don't know. That's why I'm going crazy here."

Sean stood and paced, clenching and unclenching his fists. "How the hell did you disappear?"

Jake exhaled. "Trade secret. Is there an APB or BOLO out on me?"

"I don't think so, but the cops were damn pissed. Once I convinced them that I really was with the LAPD and vouched for you, they calmed down a bit. Thank God for our little recording. Otherwise, we would've been up Shit Creek without a paddle. They still want to wring your neck, though."

"No doubt. How much trouble are you in?"

Sean scratched his head. "Other than being a few thousand miles out of my jurisdiction, you mean? Oh, and the other minor issue of the dead woman in the room."

After a moment's delay, laughter burst from both men. Tension snapped like guitar strings. They laughed until their eyes watered and their sides ached.

"I gotta go. My new Fairfax County cop friends are waiting for me to play another round of Twenty Questions. I was pushing their patience to come check on Angela in person. I thought I might find you lurking around."

"I had to play hide and seek earlier when a couple of them came here looking for me. You gonna tell them…?"

"Hell no. I'm counting on you to call me the minute you hear something about Angela."

"Sure thing."

The men's eyes connected. Sean's searched and probed. Realization dawned. "You love her, don't ya, Stone?"

Jake nodded solemnly.

Sean chuckled, turned away, and walked out into the rain.

* * *

Turning the corner with his fourth cup of vending machine coffee, Jake spotted Randall Reardon speaking with a doctor in front of the double doors leading to the examining rooms. Silently, he slipped back into the shadowy corridor and peeked around the corner.

Randall was crying and gesturing helplessly. The doctor spoke quietly, placing a comforting hand on the disconsolate man's shoulder. After a ten-minute conversation, the men shook hands, and the doctor disappeared through the double doors.

Angela's father stumbled to the nearest group of chairs and dropped leadenly into one of them. He rested his elbows on his knees and held his head between his hands, his shoulders shaking with sobs.

Watching from a distance, Jake wondered what he could possibly say to the distraught father. Probably nothing. The man would most likely blame Stone for his misery. But Randall was the only source Jake had for information about Angela's condition. He tossed the half-full cup into a trashcan and steeled himself as he strolled through the waiting room.

Randall was oblivious to Jake's approach. When he stood about two feet away, he bent and touched the man's shoulder. He started and glanced around, looking slightly disoriented, but his gaze soon landed on Jake.

"Mr. Reardon, I really don't know what to say, but I'm sorry for your—"

Before Jake could finish, Randall sprang from the chair. He wrapped his arms around Jake and held on as though he feared his legs wouldn't support him. His sobbing intensified.

Agony gripped Jake. *Oh God, not Angela, too. Please, God, no.* He tried to speak, but the lump in his throat turned his words into a sob. Tears stung his eyes. His arms enveloped Angela's father, and the two men clung to each other.

Gradually, composure returned, and they sat down together. Neither spoke for several minutes as they regained self-control.

"Is Angela…?" He braced for the worst. "I'm not family. They won't tell me anything."

Randall rubbed his forehead and inhaled deeply. "She's alive. Thank God—" He blinked and then looked directly into Jake's eyes. "And thank you, Mr. Stone."

"I'm not sure I deserve your gratitude, but you're welcome." He swallowed hard. "How bad was she hit, I mean, shot?"

"Shot?" Confusion flitted across Randall's face for a moment, but then he refocused. "Angela wasn't shot. She's in severe shock."

Jake's breath released in a rush. His fingers pressed against his eyes to stem the tears that threatened to resume. *Thank you, God, thank you.*

Randall cleared his throat. "The doctor said it's the most severe case of acute stress reaction he's ever witnessed. They were unable to get any response from her for hours. But she's doing better now. I should be able to see her soon."

"I can't tell you how relieved I am. How's your wife?"

Randall sighed. "I took her home after we identified Maleena's body. She didn't want to come to the hospital…to see Angela." He glanced sideways at Jake. "The police haven't told us much, Mr. Stone. Only that it appeared you and the LAPD detective fired in self-defense. What in the world was going on in that hotel room?"

Jake met his questioning gaze. "It's an incredibly ugly story, Mr. Reardon. I don't think this is the right time or place. But if the final police report doesn't satisfy you, I'll tell you my version. Deal?"

Randall studied him. "Deal. Honestly, I just want to rejoice in having Angela back. How can I ever thank you?"

He thought a moment. "Let Angela live *her* life. Don't interfere in our relationship. I love your daughter, Mr. Reardon, and more than anything, I want to make her happy."

"I hope you succeed. You two have my blessing."

The doctor who had spoken to Randall earlier called his name from the doorway. Randall jumped up, took two steps, and turned back.

"Care to join me…Jake?"

* * *

"God, I've missed you, and I'm so relieved. I was going crazy not knowing your condition. And I'm damn thrilled you're in one piece. So don't take this wrong, babe," Jake said, peering hard through the windshield as the wipers struggled to clear it. "But maybe you should listen to the doctor. He was royally pissed that you refused to stay in the hospital. He said you needed to be under observation for at least another twenty-four hours."

"I'm fine," Angela insisted, staring out the side window.

"You don't look fine. You look terrible."

"Thanks, I needed that."

"Shit, Angela, you look like a woman who's suffered a tremendous shock."

She turned an intense glare in his direction. "More than one."

"Huh?"

"Forget it."

"Are you sure you don't want me to drive you to your parents' house? Your dad wanted you to come home." Stony silence was her only response. "He loves you, Angela. He wants to try to make things right."

"Not tonight. Okay?"

"Okay."

They fell silent.

Angela rested her head against the cool glass and closed her eyes.

"Seriously, babe, you're scaring me. You're white as a sheet, and the tremors aren't a good sign."

She opened her eyes and held both hands elevated in front of her. They shook noticeably. She clasped them together and rested them in her lap.

"I can't stop shaking. Maybe they put adrenaline in the IV. You'd think I'd feel exhausted, but I'm wired."

"I know how to relax you," he said with a suggestive smile.

She frowned. "Only you would think of sex at a time like this."

He shrugged. "You can't blame a red-blooded guy for—" His cell phone interrupted. "What's up, Burke?"

"How's Angela?"

"She's being stubborn already, so that's a sure sign she's even better than when I last called you. We're headed back to the hotel. She refused to stay in the hospital."

"Jesus Christ. She's a helluva woman. You sure you can handle her, Stone? Maybe I should—"

"I'm gonna hang up now," Jake teased.

Burke chuckled. "I've got some interesting news. You want to hear it or not?"

"Make it quick. We're almost to the hotel."

"The CSIs figured out the three shots."

Jake straightened and held the phone tighter against his ear. "Talk to me."

"They finally found the third bullet buried in the wall in back of the bed's headboard."

"But the bed was *behind* Maleena. Her shot should've hit in the opposite direction, near the doorway where you and Angela were standing."

"Yeah. That's where they'd been looking and finding nothing. Here's why. The last bullet was mine, not Maleena's. I missed, hit the wall behind her."

"I don't get it. She was hit *twice*. Right?" Jake glanced at Angela nervously and looked away.

"You're not going to believe this. They pulled the two slugs out of her. Yours hit center chest. *Hers* entered the right temple," Burke explained.

"Holy shit. Maleena shot herself."

"Crazy, huh? She must've snapped when she saw Angela was alive. Anyway, thought you'd want to know."

"Yeah. Thanks."

"By the way, they cleared me to go back to LA tomorrow."

"Do you still have a job at LAPD, or are they going to throw you to the lions?"

Burke laughed. "I've already called Olsen. He's pissed I snuck away with only a lying e-mail. But considering I solved—"

"*You* solved?"

"Damn straight, *I* solved a rape and three murders. They may slap my wrist for not following proper procedures, but they'll probably let me stick around."

"Will Homicide close the cases without nabbing the actual shooters?"

"My guess is the detectives will investigate quickly, work any information they find in Maleena's stuff. But since the assholes in the Suburban were professional hitmen, chances are they won't be caught." Burke's long pause sent a shiver of apprehension down Jake's spine. "You know, Stone, hitmen are damn shadowy bastards. Hard to pin down."

"Really? I wouldn't know."

Burke snorted. "Don't forget that the Fairfax cops still need to talk to you."

"I'll call them in the morning. They're not going to throw me in the slammer for ducking out on them, are they?"

"Hey, buddy, you're on your own. Give me a call if they let you come back to sunny California."

"Will do." Jake paused. "Thanks again, Burke…for everything."

* * *

Angela did *not* want to listen to the conversation. She never wanted to hear her identical twin's name again. Reflexively, her hands covered her ears, and her eyes pressed tightly shut. But it was too late. The harm was already done. Tears spilled from under her eyelashes and ran down her cheeks. She jumped when Jake patted her arm.

"I'm sorry you had to hear that," he said, turning into the hotel parking lot. "Are you okay?"

She opened her eyes and shook her head.

Swearing under his breath, he parked the car and then slouched in the seat. "Damn, Angela, I wish you hadn't witnessed what happened to Maleena. I've already apologized countless times. I don't know what else to say. I hope you believe I fired in self-defense. And honest to God, after what she did to you, I don't understand how you can be sad about…"

She peered at him in disbelief. How could he think she was mourning for Maleena? How could he not understand the pain she was feeling, the agony she had bottled up inside for so long? But then how could Jake possibly know how it felt to be hated, betrayed, and violated by your identical twin four years ago? And now, to relive it and learn that hatred had expanded to murder? Emotional devastation burned through her. Her composure crumbled, revealing her inner misery.

"Jesus Christ," he murmured. "You *remember*. The shock…Your amnesia…Gone?"

"Yes," she whispered. "When I heard Maleena talking about that night, I felt like someone was pulling open the curtains on a stage. First, I could see the rape like a play being acted. Then I could smell it: the sex, the sweat. Then I could feel it: the pain, the fear, the humiliation. I was there, on my bed, and Maleena and that man were raping me. Again and again and again." She choked back a sob. "When I came around the adjoining room door and our eyes met, it was like that same split second during the rape when I recognized her. I just lived it all over again." She covered her face with her hands.

"God, Angela, I'm sorry. You weren't supposed to hear or see anything tonight. You were supposed to be safe in Rosarito Beach." He reached for her, gently pulled her hands down.

She tried not to flinch when he touched her but failed. A puzzled look knitted Jake's brow.

She wiped the tears from her cheeks. "Right. Rosarito. I know. I'm not blaming you."

"That's a relief." He drew a deep breath and continued. "By the way, why did you call Burke instead of me?"

She stiffened and reached to open her car door. "You had told me not to call you, and I didn't know where you were."

Jake caught her arm and pulled her back around. "That doesn't make sense. You had my cell number. If you needed to know where I was and what I was doing, you should've called me." He paused. "We hadn't talked since I left you in Mexico, so you didn't even know I'd contacted Burke. And if you wanted to let the cops know you were alive, why call him and not the Coronado PD?"

"I remembered Sean and thought he would understand. I trust him."

"But not me?"

Angela held his gaze defiantly. "You wanted me…out of the way."

"For a damn good reason. Burke said you were scared. Why?"

"I was all by myself."

"I left you with a gun and plenty of ammo. You said you'd be fine until I got back."

"You were gone for two weeks without a word. The longer I thought about it, the more vulnerable I felt. If someone showed up at the beach house, I might not recognize him for what he was until it was too late. I realized that a *professional* killer...might be good at *pretending* to be a friend, not a foe."

They stared at each other silently.

Angela blinked and glanced down at the bandage on her arm. She rubbed the spot where the IV had been. When her gaze rose, she kept it cold, distant. "Alone in Rosarito, I was totally isolated. No one knew where I was."

His eyes narrowed. "I knew."

She yanked her arm free and opened the car door. "Honestly, Jake, I don't understand why you're angry. Can we argue about it later?" She slammed the door, reached into her purse, and pulled out a key. "Thank goodness, my purse didn't get lost in the mayhem last night. My suitcase is still in my rental car."

Pensive and watchful, she followed Jake's every move while they retrieved her suitcase and checked into a room. Her constant observation seemed to perplex him. Several times, he glanced at her questioningly but didn't complain.

She carried her nightgown and toiletry kit into the bathroom and locked the door. While the shower heated, she studied her face in the mirror. Strained. Pale. She did look terrible.

The hot spray of the shower relaxed the tense muscles in her neck and back but couldn't uncoil the anxiety inside her. Was she strong enough to deal with the imminent confrontation? Perhaps she'd been a fool to leave the safety of the hospital.

While she toweled dry, she strengthened her resolve. She needed to know the truth. Unfortunately, that truth could be devastating... and dangerous. Still, she had no choice.

Again she gazed into the mirror. Her eyes swam with a myriad of emotions: sadness, anxiety, disappointment, fear, hope. Hope? Yes. Unbelievably, deep inside, the dream of a happy ending still lived. Although her heart ached for the dream to come true, her brain remembered that reality was a nightmare.

Stepping out of the bathroom in her pink silk nightgown, she found Jake already lying in bed. She avoided his eyes and instead felt them undressing her.

He smiled and held out his hand, but she ignored it. She flipped back the sheet and discovered him naked beneath it. She froze and swallowed hard.

"It's okay, Angela. C'mere. Let me hold you."

"I'm not sure..."

Propping himself on an elbow, he watched her. Concern and caution were etched on his face. "Hey. I'm not going to force you to... I thought it might help if... Hell, forget it. I just want to take care of you."

Her eyes searched his, probing deep, until he blinked and looked away. Her heart pounding, she pressed her lips together tightly as she fought the urge to run. Although it would soon be dawn, her night of horrors was not yet over. The mystery of her rape had finally been solved, but the shock had left her incapacitated for hours. Now she faced another mystery, a dangerous, intimate one. Alone.

A surreal sense of déjà vu washed over her. Same pink silk nightgown. Jake, naked, in bed. The night they first made love. Their last night together. The night he was going to…She shook off the thought.

With a tremulous sigh, she lay down and pulled up the sheet. He scooted closer and wrapped his arms around her. At first, she stiffened but then relaxed slightly as his hand caressed her back. She nestled her head beneath his chin. Finally, she stroked his chest and then splayed her hand across his back. For a long time, they simply embraced.

"Angela, I…I can't believe how I feel. This is uncharted territory for Jake Stone." He nuzzled her hair and massaged the curve of her tush through the silk. "God, I've missed you."

"So much has happened."

"Yeah, everything is better now." His breathing quickened as well as his hands. "You're an amazing woman. You haven't just survived, you've overcome unspeakable traumas."

His lips found hers, and after an initial hesitation, she surrendered. His hardening dick pressed against her thigh, sending a jolt of desire—and alarm—through her. The taste and feel of him were part of the dream. *Dear God, why can't the dream come true and the nightmare just go away?*

* * *

Jake worked the thin straps of the gown off her shoulders and down her arms. His mouth lowered to kiss the swell of her breasts, and his tongue trailed into her cleavage.

"Every day since I left Rosarito, I've thought about being inside you again," he said, his voice husky. "Did you think about it, too?"

"Hmmm."

He pulled the hem of the gown up to her waist and slid his hand gently between her thighs. His fingers found heat, but no welcoming wetness.

More frantic now, his hands moved urgently over her body, searching for the touch, the caress that would arouse her. His kiss was deep, his tongue working hard to mate with hers. His lips lowered to a nipple: circling, teasing, sucking. He palmed her butt and squeezed. He rolled on top of her, spreading her thighs with his knee.

Feeling no response, he raised his head to search her face. "You're okay with this, aren't you? I know it's been a while since we…" With his hands braced on either side of her shoulders, he hung over her, his body—all of it—rigid, hard, needy. His head dipped. His breath, warm and panting, blew against her ear, down her neck. The tip of his tongue caressed the hollow of her throat as the tip of his dick prodded her opening.

Still no response. He drew a shuddering breath, let it out slowly as though trying to deflate the part of him that was inflated to the point of pain. His eyes locked on hers.

"I love you, Angela. You do remember I told you that when we made love the first time?"

She stared back with wary detachment. "I remember."

"And you said you loved me. So what's wrong?"

Several pounding heartbeats ticked by before she answered.

"I saw the *syringe*, Jake."

Above her, he blinked. "What?"

"I saw the syringe. In Rosarito. Remember when you were leaving? I ran back into the beach house to get your jacket. The syringe fell out of the pocket when I picked it up. I just stuffed the thing back inside. I was in such shock already, and you were in such a hurry to get back across the border that I didn't even think to ask you about it." She paused, gulped, shuddered. "A few days later, I figured it out. *You* were hired to kill me, weren't you? You were planning to do it that night. If you lie to me, Jake, I'll never be able to trust you."

His eyes closed. His thoughts clung hopelessly to the warm, sexy woman beneath him. Their bodies weren't connected, only touching, at that most intimate spot. One hard thrust and he would be inside. But now he might never make love to her again.

Jake opened his eyes and peered down at her, amazed at her strength despite her vulnerable position. He pushed himself over and onto his back. The heat of passion left him, and he shivered with an instant chill. He felt the warmth drain from his eyes until they turned dead, stone cold. A very familiar feeling.

"Don't close yourself off and hide. No more hiding. I need the truth. It was *you*, wasn't it?" she asked.

Staring at the ceiling, he answered quietly, "Yes."

"And I wouldn't have been your first…victim, right?"

He wondered at the odd sensation of life draining from him. Ignoring her question, he asked, "Do you hate me?"

"No."

"Are you afraid of me?"

"No," she whispered.

"Maybe you should be."

"I don't think so, but I have to know something. What changed your mind? Why didn't you…kill me?" Her voice cracked. "Why?"

He addressed the ceiling even though he felt her studying him.

"Yes, Angela, I've killed people as a SEAL and as a CIA assassin. I can't disclose the details, but I was told the contract on you was a CIA-sanctioned national security hit. After I became suspicious of the reasons given for the contract, I pleaded with my handler to get it canceled. When he wouldn't, I tried to find a way out but failed. If I simply refused to kill you, there was a very good chance both of us would end up dead. But what kind of monster kills someone he loves? I couldn't be that monster, Angela. Loving you saved me from being that monster."

He sighed heavily, sat up, and swung his legs off the side of the bed. "To ease my conscience, I always insisted on knowing the target's crime so I could convince myself the person deserved to die. That the world would be a better place without them. My 'victims' were always terrible people, serious threats to our national security. So I couldn't understand why the Agency wanted you dead. And I believed, beyond a shadow of a doubt, there was no way in hell that *you* deserved to die."

Jake looked back over his shoulder. "I love you, Angela. That's what changed my mind. That's what changed my whole life. *You* saved *me*. You're my redemption."

He waited, painful heartbeats measuring the time.

Angela tenderly touched his arm, and she smiled. "I love you, too, Jake. *You* saved *me*…from a life without love, from a life of fear and distrust." Her lips trembled. "You healed my emotional scars, restored my sexuality, and made me believe in love again. Now, please…make love to me."

Check out Marissa Garner's FBI Heat series!

Catching bad guys in San Diego's underworld isn't
just FBI Special Agent Ben Alfren's job, it's his life.
He doesn't have time for a serious relationship,
doesn't want one either.
Until he meets his sexy new neighbor,
nurse Amber Jollett.

Please see the next page for an excerpt from *Hunted*.

Chapter 1

Special Agent Ben Alfren entered the lobby of the San Diego FBI office with a determined smile and a resolute step. He didn't care that it was Friday morning and the weekend was coming, because he loved his job. Was there anything better than catching bad guys for a living? That sentiment was something his professors and classmates at Harvard hadn't understood when he graduated with an MBA and took a government job with average pay instead of a private-sector position with an astronomical salary. Of course, most of them hadn't known his bachelor's degree from George Washington University was in criminal justice. His grin broadened at the memory and at the thought that they probably hadn't loved the past five years of their careers as much as he had.

The phone rang just as he sat down at his desk with a cup of coffee.

"Ben, my office," his boss said and hung up.

The man of few words had been a terrific mentor since Ben transferred from Washington, DC, two years ago. When he strolled into the office, Supervisory Special Agent Rex Kelley was stroking his chin and staring out the window.

"What's up?" Ben asked.

"Just got the damnedest call from ICE."

"Immigration and Customs Enforcement needs our help?"

Rex turned to him. "Yeah." He shook his head, a puzzled expression on his face. "But it's not the usual."

"Okay, you've hooked me."

His boss gestured toward a chair and took his seat behind the desk. "Helluva story. Five illegal aliens walked into the San Ysidro border crossing facility and turned themselves in."

Ben frowned. "Are they political refugees seeking asylum or something?"

"They're Mexican, and it's not political. It's definitely 'or something.' They claim to have information on a coyote who works for the Hermosillo cartel."

"Great. We've been trying to nail Enrique Hermosillo for ages through his drug-money-laundering operation. This could be a break."

"Maybe. But I doubt if they know much about the cartel kingpin."

"If their info's only about the coyote, then why is ICE calling us? They deal with human trafficking as much as the FBI."

"The illegals demanded it," Rex stated flatly.

"Huh?"

"I gather they don't trust ICE and are afraid our cops might be as corrupt as the Mexican police. Based on what they've seen on TV about the FBI, they must think we're more likely to give them what they want in return."

"What's that?"

"To hunt for their kidnapped wives and girlfriends."

* * *

The man in the gray hoodie was watching her. Amber Jollett couldn't see his face, but he was the right height and build. Even from the opposite street corner, the intensity of his stare bored into her. She shivered despite the sunny morning.

Her focus never wavered as she slid behind two people. The man's head turned with her movement.

The traffic light changed, and the crowd surged forward. Amber's hand dug into her purse until it gripped reassuring metal. Weaving between bodies, she moved to the outside edge to put as much distance as possible between her and the man before the other pedestrians passed on the street. With each step, her heart beat faster.

Halfway across, the man reached up, pulled back the hood…and smiled. Straight black hair. Almond-shaped eyes. Asian features.

Not him.

Amber's knees went weak with relief.

Not him. Not this time.

A car horn blared. She jumped and spun around to find a taxi idling a few feet away, its driver gesturing impatiently for her to get out of the way. Waving an apology, she scurried across the street. She found a spot out of the pedestrian flow next to the corner of a building. She needed a moment to quiet her nerves.

She braced her hands on the knees of her pastel pink nurse's scrubs, inhaled deep breaths, and released them slowly. Fear began to fade as calm returned.

Damn you, Jeremy Nelson. I want my life back.

Amber grimaced and closed her eyes. It was starting all over again. Two years had passed since she'd broken up with her obsessed boyfriend, but he continued to stalk her. Restraining orders and calls to law enforcement had proved useless. Now she alone was responsible for her safety. She'd lived in Coronado, across the bay from San Diego, for only two months. But two or three months was the amount of time it normally took for Jeremy to find her. From now on, she would have to be on constant alert. The worst part was imagining him wearing every hoodie, hiding in every shadow, or following in every vehicle. Usually, she didn't wait for an actual sighting—that would be too late. No, she couldn't hesitate. Once her instincts told her he was closing in, she had to move on. She cringed. *How much longer will I be hunted?*

Amber straightened, squared her shoulders, and glanced at her watch. *Oh crap.* She was late for work.

Minutes later, she bolted out of the elevator on the eighth floor of the downtown building containing the offices of the San Diego Surrogate Agency. Instead of turning the corner and racing for the employee entrance off another hallway, she headed straight across the lobby toward the clinic's front door. In her peripheral vision, she noticed a couple huddled with a man in a corner. What caught her eye was the piece of blue paper he was gesturing with as he spoke. Her steps faltered as she took a closer look. *Not him.*

She sighed with frustration. Her specialty as a nurse in surrogate mother clinics was both a blessing and a curse. Unfortunately, Jeremy knew her skills, and he'd used that information before to track her down. Someday, she would probably have to give up the work she loved and accept a general RN position. The job would still be gratifying simply because she enjoyed helping people, but there was just something so special about the gift of babies to people who couldn't otherwise have them.

After grabbing a cup of coffee, she studied the assignment calendar posted on the wall in the employee lounge. Her first task of the day was an initial consultation with a Mr. and Mrs. Ranger. She smiled. In terms of satisfaction, initial consultations were second only to the meeting announcing the surrogate mother was pregnant with the potential parents' baby. As she reviewed the rest of her day's work, she noticed with surprise that Mrs. Swanson's egg retrieval procedure had been canceled. Her gaze traveled over all the staff assignments for next week, and she spotted five more appointments crossed off, everything from consults to surrogate mother interviews to sperm donations. Scanning over future weeks, she couldn't find when those services had been rescheduled, but she did see several more cancellations. *That's odd.* Now that she focused on it, there seemed to have been a lot of them lately.

With a shrug, she gulped down the rest of the coffee, popped a breath mint in her mouth, and hurried off to the small conference room for the meeting with the Rangers.

Her boss, Laura Eldridge, stopped her in the hallway just outside the door. "I need to speak with you for a minute after this consult."

"Sure. What's up?"

Laura pressed her lips into a straight line before answering. "We'll talk then. Right now, let's tell this couple all the marvelous things we can do for them."

Amber couldn't remember ever seeing such a serious expression on Laura's face. The petite, slightly graying, fifty-year-old woman was the office "mother." She loved everyone, and everyone reciprocated. Laura's strength was bringing out the best in people. Amber knew she'd grown as a person as well as a nurse under her boss's thoughtful guidance.

She followed Laura into the conference room and came face-to-face with the couple she'd seen in the elevator lobby earlier. After introductions, they all settled into the comfortable seating. Unlike most business conference rooms, this one didn't include a large table surrounded by stiff, uncomfortable chairs. To encourage a more informal, relaxed atmosphere, the décor resembled a casual living room with armchairs, love seats, and couches. As Joe Ranger plopped onto a love seat beside his wife, Amber caught a glimpse of blue paper sticking out of his pants pocket.

First, Laura gave a sales presentation about the San Diego Surrogate Agency's highly acclaimed services and its spotless reputation in the industry. She handed the couple a sheet of information on all the medical personnel and a list of previous clients as references. Then, she turned the meeting over to Amber, who as a specialized nurse could better describe the various medical procedures involved in surrogacy.

The couple fidgeted throughout both discussions and asked no questions. Only when Laura started to explain the financial aspects of the services did Mr. and Mrs. Ranger get involved.

"How can it possibly cost that much?" Joe Ranger asked. "We're using our own sperm and eggs. It's not like we're buying your inventory."

Laura blinked in surprise.

Amber knew clients were often unprepared for the fees, but their response was usually less accusatory.

"Mr. Ranger, I assure you that we never consider the precious life-creating eggs and sperm entrusted to us as 'inventory.' And using Mrs. Ranger's eggs does require the egg retrieval procedure. All services considered, our fees are in line with industry standards across the country. As we never want financial restrictions to prevent people from realizing their dreams of a child, we offer numerous flexible payment plans."

"How about discounts?" he pressed. His wife turned bright red.

"Discounts for what?"

"We're young, healthy specimens. Shouldn't take as much work."

"I've never heard of any discounts being offered. But as I explained, you only pay for the services necessary for your particular situation. Some services you may not need. For example, if the first viable embryo transplant is successful, you'll only be charged for one."

He grunted his displeasure. "How much do you make on each deal?"

"Not enough to stay in business, Mr. Ranger. If we didn't receive grants from various charitable foundations, we wouldn't be able to cover our expenses. The doctors who own this company also have their own separate medical practices. They view this agency more as a humanitarian venture than a for-profit business."

"Yeah, right. I bet they all drive Mercedes."

Mrs. Ranger looked like she wanted to fall through the floor.

Amber admired Laura's restraint. She would've told the guy to take a hike five minutes ago.

Her boss glanced at her watch before offering the couple a stilted smile. "If you don't have any further questions, I'm due in another meeting shortly."

Joe Ranger stood up. "No problem. We're outta here."

Without shaking hands or any parting pleasantries, he stomped out of the room, his wife following meekly behind.

"That went well," Amber said.

Laura sighed. "I think he's the rudest potential father I've ever met." She shrugged. "Maybe he thinks we should do this for free."

"Don't let it get you down." She placed a comforting hand on the woman's shoulder. "Now what did you want to talk to me about?"

Laura's expression went from sad to sadder. "You know what I told Mr. Ranger about the company's financial structure is true. What you don't know is that, due to recent cancellations, we're in a…a financial bind. We're looking at possible layoffs for the first time ever. The doctors hate the idea, but they've decided the only fair way to handle this is to use a last-in, first-out approach."

Amber's stomach knotted.

"Since you're our newest employee, I'm afraid you'd be the first to go."

* * *

Ben glanced around the table at the five Mexican men. Their forlorn expressions and haggard appearance spoke of a grueling ordeal. He couldn't wait to hear their story, but first, he needed to gain their trust.

"Let's take off the cuffs and get them some water," he suggested to one of the two ICE agents in the room.

"But—"

"Hell, they're not going anywhere. They asked for this meeting."

The agent reluctantly removed their restraints and then left the room to get the water.

"I'm FBI Special Agent Ben Alfren," he said, reaching across the table to shake hands with each of them. "I don't condone your coming into our country illegally, but I'm willing to listen to your story."

"My name is Pedro Casas," one said. "My English is not so good, but I speak the best."

The man appeared to be in his late teens. Despite his youth, he exuded confidence. But Ben also detected a hint of panic in his eyes. Pedro had lost someone very dear to him, and he was desperate to get her back. This would definitely be the person to deal with, and not just because of his language skills.

"That's great, Pedro." Ben made eye contact with the other four. "Do you all *understand* English? If not, I can get an interpreter."

Each man nodded. One mumbled, "We are good."

"All right. If you want to add anything to what Pedro tells us, just speak up, and he'll translate for me." He grinned and patted his chest. "*Comprendo muy poco de español.*"

The Mexicans chuckled.

He turned his attention back to Pedro. "Start at the beginning."

The young man told a harrowing tale of dealing with a ruthless coyote who used the nickname Loco and told everyone he worked for the vicious drug lord Enrique Hermosillo. Pedro described riding in a large truck, a semi, and a van. He explained how the armed guards had separated the men from the women, and how he'd been knocked out.

"What happened when you came to?" Ben asked.

"Came to what?"

"It means 'woke up.'"

"Ah, *sí.* I woke in the white van with the other men and the guards. They take us to a house to wait until night to go more north."

"Where was the house?"

Pedro shrugged. "It was with a few others but not in a town."

The ICE agent returned with five bottles of water and set them on the table. The Mexicans grabbed them immediately.

"Did you see a house number or a street name?" Ben asked.

Pedro frowned as he concentrated. "I do not remember."

The others shook their heads.

"No problem. We'll work on that later. Then what happened?"

"They tell us to sleep on the mattresses on the floor, but we are too angry." He glanced at his companions. "After they lock us in a room, we talk. We do not trust Loco." Pedro drew a deep breath. "When it is dark, they open the door, let us out of the room. The blue van comes. There are only three women. Five are missing. My Maria is gone."

ACKNOWLEDGMENTS

My dear husband has always been my rock. I am grateful every day for his support as I experience the ups and downs, the achievements and disappointments, of publishing. My heartfelt gratitude goes out to my family and friends for their continued support and encouragement. Thanks also to my talented editor, Alex Logan, and the Forever Romance team for publishing my story.

ABOUT THE AUTHOR

I'm a wife, writer, chocoholic, and animal lover, not necessarily in that order. As a little girl, I cut pictures of people out of my mother's magazines and turned them into characters in my simple stories. Now I write edgy romantic thrillers, steamy contemporary romance, and sexy paranormal romantic suspense. I live in sunny Southern California with my husband but enjoy traveling from Athens to Anchorage to Acapulco and many locations in between.

You can learn more at:

http://marissagarner.com

Facebook.com/MarissaGarnerAuthor